THE
GREAT
DESTROYERS

CAROLINE TUNG RICHMOND

THE
GREAT
DESTROYERS

Scholastic Press / New York

Library of Congress Cataloging-in-Publication Data

Names: Richmond, Caroline Tung, author.
Title: The great destroyers / Caroline Tung Richmond.
Description: First edition. | New York : Scholastic Press, 2021. | Audience: Ages 12 and up. | Audience: Grades 7–9. | Summary: Jo Linden lives in a world where there are no atomic weapons, and the Cold War between the United States and the Soviet Union is played out in the Pax Games, fought with powerful robotic mecha war machines operated by young pilots; Jo needs the prize money to save her father's mecha repair shop, and keep what is left of her family together, but when competing pilots start dying from poisoning, Jo finds herself caught up in Cold War politics and political conspiracy, and she discovers that it is not only her family's survival at stake—she may have to prevent World War III.
Identifiers: LCCN 2020046833 (print) | LCCN 2020046834 (ebook) | ISBN 9781338266740 (hardcover) | ISBN 9781338266757 (ebook)
Subjects: LCSH: Mecha (Vehicles)—Juvenile fiction. | Robots—Juvenile fiction. | World politics—Juvenile fiction. | Conspiracies—Juvenile fiction. | Fathers and daughters—Juvenile fiction. | Brothers and sisters—Juvenile fiction. | Alternative histories (Fiction) | Adventure stories. | CYAC: Mecha (Vehicles)— Fiction. | Robots—Fiction. | Conspiracies—Fiction. | Fathers and daughters—Fiction. | Brothers and sisters—Fiction. | Adventure and adventurers—Fiction. | LCGFT: Alternative histories (Fiction) | Action and adventure fiction.
Classification: LCC PZ7.R39867 Gr 2021 (print) | LCC PZ7.R39867 (ebook) | DDC 813.6 [Fic]—dc23

2 2021

Printed in the U.S.A.   23
First edition, August 2021

Book design by Stephanie Yang

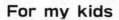

For my kids

1

By the time I reach the doorstep of the Jade Lily Lounge, I'm sweating and panting yet still running late. I even sprinted all the way up Stockton Street, but it's already 4:44 in the afternoon, meaning I've got sixteen measly minutes to prep for the match ahead. I usually like to give myself at least an hour to stretch and warm up and run a ten-point diagnostic on my Goliath before a fight, but I'll be lucky to suit up in time for this one.

But I won't forfeit the match. I need to win it, no matter how late I am or how illegal it might be. How does the old saying go? *Desperate times call for desperate measures*? Well, right about now, I'm neck-high in the desperation department. Cash is cash, and my fingers are positively twitching to get ahold of that prize money.

I barge through the front door of the Jade Lily even though the sign has been flipped over to read *Closed, Please Come Again*. A neon light greets me on the far wall, flickering on and off in a frightening shade of green. It's shaped like a daisy, not a lily, but I doubt the clientele notices the difference. As far as bars go, the Jade Lily is on the seedier side. The floors are always sticky and the glasses never quite clean, but the regulars don't seem to care. They keep returning to this little hovel in San Francisco's Chinatown, and it isn't because of the weak drinks or chatty staff. There's something else that lures them in.

Old Wen stands behind the bar in his usual spot, wiping down the counter with a cigarette balanced between his prune-like lips. A Philips radio plays behind him, offering an update about Kennedy and Khrushchev and that treaty they've been cooking up over Vietnam. The war has been simmering for years, but now they're going to shake hands and put a lid on it apparently.

"You're late," Old Wen says, not bothering to take the half-burnt Newport out of his mouth.

"I know, I know. Got caught up with something." That "something" happened to be a detention at school. During my seventh-period home ec class, my teacher Mrs. Davis was giving a lecture on our future wedding registries and which type of silverware to include. It was complete Dullsville if you ask me. So while the rest of the class scribbled down the various kinds of spoons that we should register for—a different one for soup, dessert, tea, and then grapefruit of all things—I decided to look over the strategy notes for my match this evening. I thought I was doing a decent job of sneaking a peek at them until I looked up to find Mrs. Davis standing over my desk with her nostrils huge and flaring.

"If you got here any later, I would've had to cancel," Old Wen says, tapping his cigarette against an ashtray. "Not very professional."

"Sorry, Mr. Wen," I say, but only half meaning it. *Professional* is a funny way to describe an illegal mecha fighting ring, which is exactly what he's talking about. It's a far cry from my varsity matches at school, where there are regulations and rulebooks.

"Your mother was never late, you know," Old Wen is quick to point out. He has mentioned this before, how my mom would arrive ten minutes early to every shift, the picture of the perfect employee. I only wish I could say the same about her parenting.

I glance at my watch. 4:45 already. "Key, please?"

Old Wen takes a drag of his smoke and says, "You sure about this?"

He didn't seem all that reluctant when he penciled me into the schedule last week, but I keep that to myself. It's taken me over a month to convince him to let me fight in the first place, and I think he only did it because he has a soft spot for my mom. Years ago, they worked together at the Jade Lily—him in the kitchen and her waiting tables. Back then the place was a friendly sort of establishment that served up a decent shrimp lo mein and garlicky green beans.

Over the years though, the ownership of the Jade Lily has transferred a couple times. Out went the lunch buffet and in came the bar with the dodgier clientele, not to mention the under-the-table fighting ring in the abandoned boxing gym down in the basement.

Yet one thing has stayed the same this whole time, and he's standing right in front of me. Old Wen hasn't changed much since my mother first met him eighteen years ago. He still has the same graying hair that barely covers his scalp and the same sun splotches that form a map on his cheeks. And his falcon-sharp eyes don't miss a thing, so think twice before you try to pilfer a dime out of the tip jar.

"I need to suit up if you want me to make it on time," I remind him.

With a sigh, he fishes a small silver key out of his pocket but still doesn't hand it over. "You'll be facing the Ravager in the pit."

"Fantastic," I say, but I cringe inside. The Ravager earned his nickname by smashing his opponents in the face even after the refs have declared him the winner. Despite that gruesome image, I take the key from his fingertips. My family needs this money.

Before I turn to go, Old Wen leans toward me to whisper, "Aim for the right ankle. I noticed him limping a little on the way in."

I slip that juicy bit of intel into my pocket. That's Old Wen for you. One minute, he's waxing poetic about my dear mother who died too young, and the next, it's all business, all money. I'm pretty sure he's put a bet on me today, even though he isn't sup-posed to, as the bookie. We either swim together or sink together, and a sly street cat like Old Wen has no plans on drowning any time soon.

"Go on and good luck," Old Wen says, but I'm already winding my way through the restaurant's kitchen and making a beeline to the locked door by the utility sink. That's where the key comes in. I open the thick metal door that leads down to the basement, which used to house Chan's Boxing School, now out of business. The owners of the Jade Lily bought the place for a steal, and they've drawn up plans to convert it into an underground bunker in case the negotiations between Kennedy and Khrushchev fall through and we end up with another Cuban Mecha Crisis on our hands.

I shudder thinking about it—how close we teetered toward a global disaster. Back in October the Soviets decided to secretly move a brigade of their mechas to Havana. We're talking four thousand of Khrushchev's finest Vostoks—twenty feet tall and armed to the teeth with machine guns in each hand and a belt of grenades around their titanium waists—and they were twiddling their deadly thumbs in America's backyard, just a hundred miles off the coast of Florida. As soon as Kennedy caught wind of it, he demanded that the Vostoks be removed or else.

For thirteen terrifying days, the whole world held its breath while the US and the USSR played one heck of a game of chess. Some of the rich white folks fled San Francisco, but the rest of us had to stay put. At school, we had duck-and-cover drills every day, where we would curl into little balls underneath our desks, as if that would save us from World War III. But eventually Khrushchev backed down, thank God. He does have some bark in him, but none of Stalin's bite.

In any case, the basement bunker is merely a cover story. The Jade Lily's owners have been hosting mecha matches down there for nearly five months, and they've been raking in more bread than their bar upstairs makes in a year.

At the bottom of the steps, I enter a narrow hallway. If I go right, I'll round a corner and walk into a large open space that has been converted into the fighting pit, with rows of folding chairs surrounding it. Voices echo from that direction.

"Last call on bets," I hear one of the bartenders say. "Better get 'em in before the match starts, you cheap drunks!"

Laughter rumbles into my ears, and I can tell that there is a decent crowd gathered for my fight. There'll be eight matches total and most of the spectators will stay for the whole night, with their wallets thinning after each round, but they'll remain glued to their seats for hours. It's blood-pumping entertainment, after all, and what's more entertaining than watching two people climb inside giant robots and try to knock each other out?

I take a left in the corridor, which leads me to the prep rooms. I hurry to the one reserved for me because I don't want anyone seeing my face. That's why I took the long way here instead of going through the main entrance on Waverly Place. If anybody recognized me, they could tip off the state's oversight board that I'm making money off illegal fighting, which would put an end to my athletic eligibility at school and quash any career prospects I might've had. Granted, female fighters have pretty skimpy options in the professional fighting world since there are so few of us and we never get to headline the big-time matches in Vegas or Atlantic City. But I'll take skimpy over zilch.

The prep room used to be a storage area, but it's been stripped bare aside from the basics that a fighter needs. A ladder. A sink for drinking water and rinsing out bloody cuts. A single esterium battery, the size of a paper towel roll. And there, right in the middle of the room, a Goliath.

It's a 301C model, a sports-grade version instead of the weaponized ones that the military has been using since World War I. Like all mechas, it's shaped like a human being—two arms and two legs, connected by a V-shaped torso. Its engine is tucked in between the hips, giving the Goliath the necessary oomph to punch, kick, jab, thrust, run, climb, and whatever else you need it to do when you're squaring off against another fighter in the pit.

Since my prep time is ticking away, I skip my usual warm-up and go straight into getting suited. First, I slide the battery into its slot on the Goliath's back. It glows the prettiest color of blue, rich and dark, like the ocean at sunset. The blue hue comes from the esterium itself, originally discovered in the Dakotan plains in 1932. It's a real wonder of a power source, clean and long-lasting, but there's a limited supply. There are only a few dozen esterium veins that have been discovered worldwide, and its price is further driven up by the fact that it requires a long refinery process to turn a lump of esterium into the glowing liquid that fills my battery.

That's why there's a five-dollar cover charge to watch the matches tonight. A good chunk of that goes to the Jade Lily's owners, but it's also to pay for the batteries.

The very first generation of mechas, however, weren't powered by esterium but by good old gasoline. This was back during World War I, when a German engineer named Wolfgang Althaus was tasked with a mission—to help the Kaiser's soldiers survive No Man's Land, that deadly stretch of battlefield full of barbed wire and mustard gas that could drown men in their own juices. Althaus's solution came in the form of a mobile suit of armor, which was controlled by a series of levers and buttons. His early mechas—dubbed Kriegsmaschines—were slow and clunky, but they got the job done by ferrying the Germans across No Man's Land without their men getting turned into Swiss cheese.

Not long after that, other countries scrambled to roll out their own mechas. There was the Soviet Vostok, the British Condor, the French Colosse, the American Goliath, and so on. By the end of WWI, over forty million people had died, but the mechas lived on, growing bigger and faster and stronger year after year, with each country trying to one-up one another, Germany in particular. A couple decades later when World War II broke out, Hitler used his massive mecha armies to conquer half of Europe while his pal Hirohito amassed a gigantic empire that stretched across the Pacific, from the Philippines to Thailand, and took a big bite out of China. And the Japanese didn't stop there. They tried to invade us too. In December '41, they sent a fleet of ships carrying thousands of their Kyojin mechas to attack Pearl Harbor, and we barely beat them off. There's a decent chance that we'd be speaking Japanese today if the war hadn't swung back in the Allies' favor—and that's because the US introduced a new mecha into the mix.

The esterium-powered Goliath.

It was three years in the making and required over a hundred scientists at a secret lab in New Mexico to create a working prototype, but the 9890A model changed the war. Tens of thousands of them were soon marching across North Africa and liberating France and pushing into Germany while more of them landed on Okinawa and steadily swarmed north, island-hopping toward Tokyo. Without the need for gasoline, these Goliaths were lighter and faster and didn't have to stop every few hours for refueling. They steamrolled over the Kyojin in a matter of months.

"Eh, you almost finished in there? Eight minutes," Old Wen says on the other side of the door.

"Sure thing, boss," I call out.

I climb up the ladder to reach the control panel between the Goliath's shoulders, switching on the buttons one by one until the whole machine hums to life. That's when I swing open the abdomen and clamber inside the cockpit. It looks like a giant cocoon from the outside—the lower half is constructed out of solid steel to protect me from incoming hits, but the upper half is made out of latticed metal so I can see and hear what's going on.

I settle into the cockpit and put on the sensory sleeves that control the Goliath's movements. They cover my arms from shoulder to wrist and the same goes for my legs, running from thigh to ankle. Then I tug on the gloves and boots. The material is stretchy and soft, but it has a thickness to it due to the dozens of tiny wires running inside it, which attach to each corresponding limb on the Goliath.

I wrinkle my nose because the previous fighter who used this mecha obviously didn't take the time to wipe down the equipment. It stinks of sweat. Otherwise, the Goliath seems to be in working order. It might be showing its age, but it's still an upgrade from the one I use at school, which is a post-WWII model that had its heyday almost twenty years ago. Richer schools can afford to buy new mechas every year, ordering them from swanky catalogs that tout "all steel frames!" and "deluxe models available!" Then they donate their old ones to teams like mine. If it wasn't for my dad, who's a mechanic, and my little brother, Peter, who's a human encyclopedia when it comes to gadgets, I doubt I'd have a functioning mecha week after week.

I really wish that Peter were here now. He's usually buzzing around me before each match, acting as my engineer because he knows Goliaths inside and out even though he's only thirteen. But there's no way I told him about my little after-school activity here at the Jade Lily today. Our dad has no idea either. His face would probably turn violet if he caught wind of what I'm doing, which is funny when you consider that he fought in his fair share of illegal matches when he was young. But he has made it clear that I'm never to step foot in an off-the-books game.

Those matches are no place for girls, he has told me more than once.

So you're saying that Peter could go if he wanted to? I'd retort.

Don't sass me and I meant what I said, Josephine.

Well, I've listened to him, haven't I? I've never fought in an illegal game before; I've never even watched one. The varsity season has kept me more than busy, and when I'm not training, I'm usually working at our shop, ringing up orders or fixing a vacuuming bot or whatever else that needs doing at Linden's Repair & Refurbishing. Trouble is, you can't run a store if you don't have customers, and our business has gotten real lean ever since Rocket Boys Services Co. opened a location down the road from us, siphoning our clients one by one with their flashy commercials and special corporate pricing. Last month, Dad had to pawn his watch to make sure we had running water, and now our rent is overdue. Again. If we don't cough up the money soon, our landlady said that we'll have to pack up and move out.

A glance at the clock tells me that I better hurry.

"Let's see what you can do, old girl," I murmur to the Goliath.

I open my gloved right hand, and the Goliath's hand opens up too.

When I squat, it squats.

When I jump, it jumps.

The mecha is an extension of me, a copycat made of steel and gears and wires and powered by beautiful blue esterium.

There's a tap at the door. Old Wen again. "You ready?"

To be honest, I could use another hour to run a proper diagnostic, but thanks to my detention that isn't an option.

Old Wen frowns up at me after I've opened the door and points straight at my face. "You want people to recognize you out there?"

I swear something fierce under my breath. I'm already wearing a helmet, but it doesn't cover the whole front of my face—but I did come prepared. I pull an old ski mask out of my back pocket that I picked up at the consignment shop a few days ago for this purpose, since I can't have anyone recognizing me. I slip the mask over my head, then pull on my helmet again and tighten the chin strap before I follow Old Wen into the hallway, which is barely wide enough to fit the Goliath's shoulders.

Once more, Old Wen looks up at me. "You're sure you're ready for this?"

A nervous jitter ripples through me, like it does before every game, but today it's stronger, more like a shock than a thrill due to what's at stake. Where will we go if we get evicted? Dad's family is all the way back in Nebraska, and he hasn't seen them since he hopped a bus out of there twenty years ago. I'm sure our neighbor Mrs. Watters would take us in if we asked, but we aren't on the lease, so she would get tossed out as well if we stayed too long.

Thinking about that reminds me why I'm here. Desperate times and all that.

But it's not like I have anything to lose.

Right before I make my entrance, I curl my hands into fists and keep my eyes forward. No looking back.

Under my breath, I say to myself, "Let's go pound some metal."

2

I've gotten used to hearing boos and jeers when I walk out for my varsity matches. It comes with the territory when you're the only female fighter in the school district.

You lost, sweetheart? the hecklers like to say. *The kitchen's out back.*

You're outta your league, little lady.

This ain't no place for a girl.

But as I enter the main floor today, some of the spectators whistle and clap at my arrival. I'm confused for a moment and glance over my shoulder because they must be cheering for someone else. Then I remember that, outside of Old Wen, none of them know that I'm a *little lady* underneath this helmet, and I better keep it that way. The type of people who flock to an underground fighting ring are the exact same kind that my father has warned me about. Gamblers. Alcoholics. Men with a little too much time on their hands and not enough sense in their brains. I can handle myself just fine in a match, but the ones through school are regulated and, well, *legal.*

"Welcome to another night inside the pit!" the announcer calls out. About forty men have gathered around the cage with a hazy cloud of cigarette smoke hovering above their heads. The crowd is a blend of ages and races, mostly white and Chinese, but they don't mix together. The white men have gathered on one side of the pit while the Chinese take the other, and I notice a few Black attendees on the far end of the room. Even in California, even in San Francisco, there's segregation wherever you look.

A few chairs remain empty, but it's still early in the evening. Give it another hour, and the place will be standing room only.

"First things first, drinks are half off until six o'clock, so get your orders in before then," says the announcer. "Second, as you all have heard, the Pax Games are starting up in a week. We'll be playing the matches live upstairs at the Jade Lily—on our new Zenith color TV, mind you—so mark your calendars, gentlemen."

None of us need the reminder. We've all been counting down the days because the Games only roll around once every four years. They're the pinnacle of the sport—think the Olympics but bigger, bloodier, and deadlier. It all started in 1919, back when a charity tournament was held in London to raise money for WWI veterans, pitting fighters from competing nations in a round-robin competition. The organizers called it the Pax Games to honor the end of the war, and the turnout was so big that more mecha matches were soon planned. They cropped up in Paris and Rome and hopped overseas to New York, and that was how the sport of mecha fighting was born.

I watched my very first match in '51, when I was only four years old and not too long after my mother died. Dad had coped with the death by smoking and drinking and plunking baby Peter and me in front of our tiny Teletone television set, letting us watch whatever I picked out, which happened to be the Pax Games in Brussels. When the USA versus Sweden match came on, I couldn't take my eyes off that seven-inch screen. I've been hooked ever since.

The announcer grins. "So come join us for the opening match and tell all your friends, but maybe skip out on telling your wives."

The audience chuckles until one of the men sitting up front says, "Get on with it already!"

"Yeah, yeah, I hear you, buddy," the announcer says. More laughs. "You all ready for a fight?"

A cheer rings out, and he eggs them on.

"I said, are you ready for a fight?"

The crowd gets louder as I start my way toward the pit.

"Making their debut at the Jade Lily, we have . . ." The announcer holds a dramatic pause while pointing at me. "The Rookie!"

I sigh at the stage name, which Old Wen picked out without consulting me. It doesn't sound intimidating at all, like the Ravager or the Bone Crusher, but he said it was fitting. Except it isn't true.

I'm no rookie. I've been fighting since I was eight years old, starting out with lessons that Dad gave me inside our workshop. When I turned nine, I joined our neighborhood's chapter of the Little Fighters League, where I lost so many matches that my own teammates called me "Lose 'Em All Jo," but I got better game after game, season after season, thanks to Dad's guidance as well as the karate lessons that Mrs. Watters's son Michael taught me, which gave my technique a unique edge. By the time I got to high school, I became the first freshman ever, boy *or* girl, to make it on the varsity team.

Old Wen shuffles ahead of me to raise the gate to the pit. The pit itself forms a perfect square, fifteen meters on each side. There are no bases or goal posts or painted lines, just a patch of packed dirt and a metal cage that encloses it. I step inside and take my place on the north wall, my back facing the solid steel bars that are placed wide enough for the onlookers to watch all the action.

"Next up, coming to the south end of the pit, with a 16–6 record, we have . . . the Ravager!"

The crowd starts stomping and hollering. It's obvious most of them have placed bets on my opponent, and why wouldn't they? With a record like his, I'd be tempted to put a dollar or two down myself, but then again my own record is better. 19–1 this past season, including schools across northern California and a tristate tournament up in Oregon. The varsity season might've ended two months ago, but that one loss still eats at me.

The Ravager strides toward the pit. He's controlling a 301C model too, and he's strutting with his chin tipped high like he's ready to take a victory lap. He's confident all right, and I consider how I might use that to my advantage. A cocky fighter might have the skills to back up his arrogance, but it's that same sort of pride that can make him overlook a weak spot—if I can suss it out. Luckily, Old Wen has already done that for me this time around. I zero in on the Ravager's right leg, and sure enough, he's limping. It's slight, but it's there.

"You two know the rules," the referee says to the Ravager and me. To be honest, I'm not sure why he's here since he isn't going to enforce any of the usual regulations, but I nod anyway. "You fight until knockout. A KO counts as five full seconds lying flat."

The ref scuttles out of the pit and counts down from ten. "Ten . . . nine . . . eight!"

At my school matches, we're expected to shake hands with our opponents before a fight, but etiquette isn't a priority here. Instead, the Ravager lifts his arms up and down, getting his fans worked up.

"Seven . . . six . . . five!"

I jump in the air, testing how high I can go and how well the shocks absorb the descent. The top half of the cockpit rattles when I land, which makes me frown and wonder if the screws joining the two halves need tightening.

"Four . . . three . . . two!"

I crouch down, knees bent, and glance at the Ravager's ankle. I need to aggravate the existing injury somehow. Get him to twist it more. Let it weaken him. Then go in for the KO.

"One!"

At the blow of the whistle, the Ravager hurtles toward me, fast as a rocket. He wants me to quake in my boots and make a mistake. And if I were a *real* rookie, I probably would do just that because it's natural human instinct to run away screaming when there's a twelve-foot-tall robot coming at you like a revved-up Jaguar E-type. But I know to breathe in slowly and wait, letting him get closer and closer, until I can see his face inside his cockpit. Our eyes lock, and his mouth twitches, like he can almost taste an easy win.

That's when I spin to my left and just in time. His Goliath rams its shoulder against the pit's bars, hard enough that they vibrate. The Ravager stumbles backward, and I use these precious seconds to strike. I sweep out a leg to trip him and stick an elbow into his gut to send him careening back. They're not sophisticated moves by any stretch, but I wouldn't describe my dad's fighting style as sophisticated and he's the one who taught me. Some people would call his fighting style crude and underhanded, but Dad would probably tell them to look at his record (122–31) and go eat a pile of rocks.

I grab the Ravager's right foot and yank it up to knock him off-kilter. He falls hard onto his back and tries to shake me off, jerking his leg side to side, but that only makes me hold on tighter. I want him to keep using that right foot. Maybe tear a few ligaments. Snap a tendon or two. He calls me some colorful names that would make even Old Wen raise an eyebrow, but I've heard worse from some of the high school boys I've beaten at matches.

When the Ravager cries out in pain, I figure that I've done my job. He's hurt and he's angry, two qualities that make him vulnerable. I readjust my grip to flip him onto his stomach so I can pin him and get this finished. But he's mad as a wet cat, snarling and swinging punches. The first few are easy enough to dodge, but then one of them clocks my cockpit, right along the seam that divides the shell in half. As far as hits go, it's nothing to write home about, but then something happens that makes the crowd go silent.

The top half of my cockpit comes straight off its hinges and rolls onto the floor like a decapitated head. My entire upper body is left exposed, out in the open air, and for a second, both the Ravager and I look at each other slack-jawed. Then I hear my father's voice in my head, his voice like gravel as usual.

Always inspect your mecha before a fight, he's told me more times than I can count. *That's rule number one, and if you can't even remember that little piece of advice, then you'll get what you deserve inside the pit.*

I might've rolled my eyes at him whenever he said that, but I'd stuck to the rule because it was plain common sense. I've always been diligent to follow it.

But not today of all days.

The crowd starts hooting and hollering again. They've come here for a fight, and now they're really getting a show, before they've even finished their first round of drinks. From the corner of my eye, I catch sight of Old Wen. His face has paled, and he's motioning for me to come out. To cut my losses and quit.

The Ravager smirks at me. "You gonna forfeit, Rookie? You've got three seconds to walk outta the gate." He smashes his fists together to make his point, and I can't help but wince at the sound since I don't have the protection of my cockpit anymore.

I glance at the gate. I know what the smart thing is to do. No match is worth losing your life over.

But who said anything about me losing? I've faced cocky scuzz buckets like the Ravager my entire career. I know their moves, and I know how to beat them. That sort of thinking might teeter on the line of arrogance, but I can't repeat enough how much we need this money.

I crouch down into a fighting stance, sending a clear message to the Ravager and everyone watching that I'm not going anywhere.

He grins at me, showing off a glinting gold incisor. The audience roars, ready for a fight they hadn't been expecting.

"Rip off that helmet!" someone yells from the crowd.

"Let's see his face!" somebody else adds.

Hmm, maybe now *I'm* being a cocky scuzz bucket, but the thought scatters as soon as the Ravager starts hurtling toward me, his Goliath's arms outstretched.

Don't you dare start panicking, I remind myself. The Ravager is halfway toward me. The good news is that I've clearly aggravated his ankle injury because he's visibly hobbling. The bad news? There are various ways that he can maim or kill me since my cockpit is lying on the ground instead of protecting me like it was built to do. I'm about to kick it aside because I don't want to trip over it, but then I get an idea.

Just before the Ravager reaches me, I grab the shell of the cockpit and hoist it in front of me like a shield. He slams into me hard, making me stumble back a couple paces, but I've definitely caught him by surprise. He's gone a little cross-eyed, and I swear he must be seeing cartoon birdies flying around his head.

As he shakes off the dizziness, I'm already on the attack, using the cockpit like a weapon and swinging it at his head, at his chest, at his wounded leg. It's not exactly fair since he doesn't have one in turn, but I don't let up. I play to win. I've got bills to pay.

When the Ravager is well and truly dazed, I flip him onto his stomach and pin him there, counting down the seconds until the ref blows the whistle to call the match.

"The game goes to the Rookie!" he cries.

I lift an arm into the air, panting hard, not quite believing that I won this game with half my cockpit sheared off. The audience is going nuts, and the announcer eggs them on.

"You sure don't see moves like that at the Pax Games, now do you? So stick around because the night is just getting started!"

The Ravager spits at me before stalking out of the cage, probably to go sulk. Honestly, it doesn't even bother me because the crowd is shouting so loudly. They're chanting my name now—"Roo-kie! Roo-kie! Roo-kie!"—and some of them might be slurring their words a little, but to my ears it sounds like the Hallelujah chorus. Maybe I'm letting myself get a little bit prideful, but I punch my fists into the air to the beat. This is why I can't quit fighting, despite the bruises and torn ligaments, despite all the jeers and *little ladys*. It's the rush of a win, the adrenaline pumping through my blood. Outside the pit, I'm just another city kid with a C-plus average at school, just another girl who's supposed to get hitched and get pregnant as soon as she gets her diploma.

But in here, I feel like the sun.

And that's the exact moment when it all comes tumbling down. There's a crash through one of the small boarded-up windows that look out to the street. Bits of plywood and glass go spraying all over, and a voice blares via a megaphone, "Under the laws of the state of California, you are under arrest—"

The bartender yells out, "It's the cops! It's the cops!"

I blink out of my haze and bug out of here fast.

3

Chaos breaks out. Through the broken window, the police toss in a small black box, which bounces twice on the floor before it lights up. It must be a bot. Within seconds, a set of wheels pop out from its bottom side while two pipes emerge from its top, spewing out a white steam.

Tear gas.

The crowd scatters away from the stuff, but a few unlucky ones are coughing and clutching at their sides. They crawl on all fours toward the exit, but there's already a pileup of people there, rushing to get out.

I race out of the cage, still inside the Goliath. Worst-case scenarios are flashing in my mind—getting arrested and waving goodbye to my athletic eligibility, not to mention the look on Dad's face when he has to bail me out of jail. Who am I kidding though? There's no extra cash to pay for my bond.

I start thinking up an escape plan when I glimpse Old Wen from the corner of my eye. He's grabbed the money box and is heading the way that we came in, through the hallway with the prep rooms. I take off after him.

As soon as we've scaled the steps, I climb out of the mecha and leave it behind. I wouldn't mind using its speed to get me far away from the Jade Lily, but I might as well wear a target on my chest for the police to spot me since a runaway Goliath doesn't exactly blend into a crowd.

Old Wen navigates the maze of alleyways like he has a road map in front of him. We zigzag over cracked concrete and puddles of who-knows-what muck until he stumbles and hits the ground. I yank him to his feet, but he's gasping for air and won't budge.

"We gotta keep going!" I say, impatient.

"Let an old man catch his breath," he wheezes.

I sweep my eyes around us for any sign of the pigs, but I don't see them for now. "How'd the cops find us?"

"Someone must've tipped them off," he says in between breaths. "Blame Appleby."

He's probably right. After the first Senator Appleby died of a stroke a few months ago, his widow was appointed to fill his vacancy. Most people figured that June Appleby would simply keep his political seat warm until a special election could be held this fall, but she's making herself real comfortable and using her late husband's clout to tackle her own initiatives, like pushing mayors across California to crack down on illegal fighting rings. And now I'm feeling the hit on my wallet because this lady senator has eliminated my income stream.

Which reminds me.

"How about my cut?" I say to Old Wen, looking straight at the money box. I know it's rude, but I stick out my hand toward him, palm facing up. "We agreed on seventy bucks."

Old Wen stares at my hand for a long second before he laughs. "You really aren't like your mother at all, are you?"

"She was no saint," I say sharply.

He tuts at me. "Don't be so hard on her. She was only a kid when she had you, and it wasn't easy when your dad shipped off to Korea."

I frown. I never said that my mom had it easy. She grew up in some no-name farm town in central California, the seventh of nine kids. As soon as she'd hoarded enough pennies from picking oranges, she booked it north to San Francisco and never looked back. Mom got a job waitressing at the Jade Lily and that was how my parents met. My dad came in for the fried dumplings and stuck around for the young, pretty waitress assigned to his table, who was saving up her money again but this time to take piloting classes. It didn't matter that he was white and she was Chinese; they were smitten. He'd even proposed after their third date, although it was illegal back then for them to get hitched. It all sounds rather romantic until you hear how it ended.

Old Wen might carry around a rosy picture of my mother, but I don't know this lady he keeps raving about. Sure, she was barely eighteen when I was born, but my dad was only a year older. Besides, what does Old Wen know? He wasn't there when Mom would let Peter cry and cry when he was only a baby. Dad had deployed by then, so it was up to me to climb into the crib and rub Peter's back until he fell asleep. And then even after Dad had returned home, Mom didn't seem that happy about it. One night their fighting got real bad and she had shouted, *You'd promised me that I could have this one thing, but I guess your promises mean nothing, huh?* Whatever that meant.

Granted, my father is no Andy Griffith. The words *I love you* aren't in his vocabulary, and I can't remember the last time he hugged Peter or me or anyone else for that matter, but he has always stuck by us.

Old Wen doesn't seem finished waxing poetic. "Have a little mercy on the dead. You should've seen your mom with you when you were a baby. She carried you around like a little doll."

The tear gas must've jumbled his memories because that doesn't sound like my mother at all. I motion for him to cough up the cash. "I'll take three twenties and a ten if you got them."

He scowls but starts searching for the right bills. "Have you ever heard of the saying 'A satisfied man is happy even if he is poor'?"

That's hilarious coming from him, considering that he grabbed the bet money and nothing else when he escaped from the Jade Lily. "Sounds like someone who has never missed a meal in his life."

"It's a Chinese proverb. You ought to read up. Learn about our history."

Now it's my turn to scowl. *Our* history? Any interest I might've had about that died along with Mom. After her big fight with Dad, she packed a suitcase and grabbed most of the cash out of the coffee tin they kept on the highest shelf in their closet and fled the city. Three months later, she was dead. Killed in a small plane crash outside Los Angeles. She'd used our family's savings to live the high life, I guess.

Old Wen is rooting around for a ten-dollar bill when we hear those police sirens again. Both of us swear under our breaths and he starts to close the box, but not before I dart my hand in and out of it like a viper. A couple bucks go tumbling to the ground, but I shove the rest of what I've taken into my pocket.

I take Old Wen by his skinny shoulders. "Where do we go from here?"

"You go left and I'll go right. We split up."

"I don't even know where I am!"

"Head southwest and you'll make it back to the Tenderloin eventually. Better hurry."

Just like that he's already running off, dragging his left leg a little but making decent time. For a split second, I nearly go after him, but on second thought, I decide that I'm better off alone. I've got a hunch that if we ran into the cops, Old Wen would shove the money box into my hands and somehow spin it that this was all *my* idea.

With my heart in my throat, I take off sprinting, but there's a chain-link fence blocking my way. I already have a running start, so I try to clear the fence in a single jump, but I'm no hurdler. I don't get enough height on the takeoff and the toe of my left shoe catches on the rail. I crash to the ground, hands first, scuffing my knees in the process, but I'm back on my feet again in seconds because those sirens are blaring a little too close for comfort.

After I've zigzagged over half a dozen blocks, I think I've shaken off the police, so I crouch underneath a billboard to give my lungs a rest. The sign spells out in big block letters: *BE ALERT! STAY ALERT!*—a message that went up all over the city following the Cuban Mecha Crisis, urging everyone to be on the lookout for Commie spies. But I don't spot any rogue Communists out to convert me today, thank God.

And thank God too for diplomacy. Ever since Khrushchev dragged the rest of us toward another world war, he's tried to play nice with Kennedy. He's agreed to install a special hotline that connects the Kremlin to the White House, and he also proposed a truce in Vietnam. The conflict there has been ratcheting up for years, with Khrushchev funneling money to the Communists in the north while Kennedy has sent thousands of military "advisers" to buoy up his allies in the south. But now the two of them have agreed to split Vietnam along the seventeenth parallel and recognize the halves as independent countries. The newspapers have been calling it the Khrushchev Thaw, and there has been chatter that this is the beginning of the end of the Cold War. All that's left to do is to sign the treaty to formally ratify the Washington-Moscow Accord.

My breathing soon returns to normal, so I reach into my pocket to count the bills I tucked in there, hoping there's a little left over to buy myself a Coke because I'm parched. But instead of finding a wad of cash, I feel a huge tear in my pants. The pocket is dangling half off, and it's miserably empty.

"God, no," I whisper.

My jeans must've gotten caught on that fence I tried to clear earlier. I backpedal the way I came, but I wasn't exactly paying attention to the street signs that I'd passed. I don't know how long I wander this way and that before I sink onto the curb in front of a soda fountain selling lime rickeys for a dime each, not that I can afford even that.

My money is gone. Poof. Goodbye. There's no way we're going to make rent now. It feels like the Ravager has punched me in the gut, in that soft place where it hurts the most.

I'm not sure how long I sit there on the sidewalk. Once or twice, a driver honks at me, telling me to get a move on it. Then a couple of beatniks hand me a flyer about a sit-in they're organizing over on Auto Row, but I stare at it blankly. Eventually a city bus stops across the street from me, and I blink at the advertisement on its side: *The Pax Games 1963. Twenty-Five Nations, One Victor. Who Will Take the Prize?*

I wish I could raise my hand and volunteer because that would fix our money problems in a snap. The winner of the Games gets a $500 prize. The amount is purposely kept low since it's an amateur tournament, not a splashy headliner at the Flamingo in Las Vegas, but it would easily cover a few months of rent. Besides, the real moneymaker is the sponsorships that the winner gets. Cereal boxes. Tennis shoes. Mouthwash. You name it.

But I won't be going to the Games. The American Mecha Fighting Association announced the two-person team over a month ago, and I obviously wasn't on the list. I doubt they even considered me despite my winning record, which was one of the best on the entire West Coast. Heck, west of the Mississippi. But I guess that doesn't mean much when you're a girl.

Before long, the manager of the soda fountain comes out to shoo me away, so I slog home to the Tenderloin district. I stop by our apartment first to wash up and change my clothes, which is tricky because we live in the little two-bedroom above the shop. I have to duck underneath the store window to make sure Peter doesn't see me before I slink up the stairs. With the curtains drawn tight, I change into my work uniform, a plain white button-down shirt paired with a navy skirt. I'd much prefer trousers, but Dad insists that I dress "feminine" because sometimes he can be frustratingly old-fashioned.

A bell jingles overhead as I push open the door to the shop. Here at Linden's we specialize in household repairs. Need the engine replaced on your lawn mower bot? We can help you out. Need a tune-up on your ironing bot? We can handle that too, and we'll even throw in a discount.

Household robots started becoming more common following WWII, but you have to be pretty well off to afford them since they run on expensive esterium. That's why Dad opened our shop on the northern tip of the Tenderloin, only a short walk from the ritzy Nob Hill neighborhood so we can cater to the rich clientele with their vacuuming bots that steam carpets and their dog-walking bots that'll take their poodles for a stroll on a preprogrammed route. Our monthly rent might be higher here, but it's been worth the expense—until Rocket Boys stole most of our regulars.

The store is small but bright, with sunlight spilling through the side windows and onto the limited inventory we have for sale, like a coffee maker bot that Dad bought for cheap at a junkyard and Peter fixed up.

"Say, would you take five bucks for this junk bucket over here?" I ask Peter, who's standing behind the front counter and looking worried, probably because I'm terribly late.

He looks relieved to see me. "Where've you been? You should've called."

"Didn't have a dime on me or else I would have. You all right?" Guilt gnaws at me for making him anxious. Dad thinks Peter is too much of a worrywart and ought to toughen up, but I've got a hunch that my brother has more than the usual run-of-the-mill fretting. Sometimes he gives himself a stomachache when he has a big test at school, and it gets even worse whenever he has to sit through a duck-and-cover drill. When he was younger, he would keep asking me about the possibility of a Soviet invasion and would barely eat for days after the alarms went off.

"I really am sorry, but my English project ran late, squirt," I say, using the nickname I've been calling him since as long as I can remember. But he's far from a squirt these days. He's taller than me now, and in a few years, he'll overtake our dad, who's six foot one. No doubt he'll have the height and build of the ideal American mecha fighter—strong and tall and with muscles to match. It would've been prime to have a built-in sparring partner, but Peter prefers fixing up mechas instead of piloting them.

"English project? You said that you were working on a history report about the Bay of Pigs," Peter says, his eyes skeptical behind his glasses. He needs a new prescription, but we haven't been able to buy him a pair, along with a hundred other things we can't afford.

"Did I? I meant to say history," I say quickly. We were supposed to run the shop together since Dad has a meeting at the bank this afternoon, but I fed Peter a cover story on why I'd be late. Trouble is, I need to be better at keeping my own lies consistent.

Peter sniffs the air. "Why do you smell funny?"

Oh, that could be due to a number of things, from the muck that I ran through to escape the cops to that awful stench of tear gas that they threw at me. And it all would've been worth it if I hadn't lost the prize money, but I can't think about that right now.

"You still working on Mr. Elton's crêpe-making bot?" I ask, changing the subject and pointing at what looks like a giant disk sliced in half, with little wires and metal parts glinting up at us. This is the very first crêpe-maker bot that we've gotten at the shop—at a hundred dollars a pop, only the most loaded customers can afford such a gadget—but I'm sure Peter will figure out how to fix it. I consider myself handy with a screwdriver and a bit drill, but my brother? He's positively brilliant, a real whiz kid, like he was born with blueprints in his brain.

I watch him for a minute as he removes the small esterium battery to access the bot's processing cube. That's the main difference between bots and mechas. Bots handle menial tasks and are generally self-running, but you have to give them very specific instructions, like *Clean the silverware with polish, not water,* or else you'll have ruined cutlery. Their cubes can only handle basic commands.

Mechas, on the other hand, don't have processing cubes at all. They're basically massive mechanical puppets that are controlled by a human pilot and that serve one main purpose. To fight, whether in the pit or on the battlefield.

Peter sets down his soldering iron. "Come on, why were you late today? You can tell me."

And make him worry more? No thank you. In reply, I take off his glasses and blow on the lenses to shine them up. "You had a smudge there."

He grabs them with a frown and pushes them back onto his face. "*Jo,*" he says, annoyed.

"*Peter,*" I reply in the same tone, trying to make him laugh.

But he doesn't. "I'm not a baby, okay?"

"Okay, okay," I say, maybe a little too sharply, but I was only joking around. Ever since he turned thirteen, it's like his hormones flipped a switch and turned him moodier. Or *surly,* as Dad says.

That isn't all that has changed either. He's looking a little more like Mom too. I see it in his cheekbones now that he has lost most of the baby fat on his face. Peter has always had shades of our mother in his features, like his brown eyes and dark hair that's as thick as a painter's brush. Me, on the other hand? I'm the reverse. I have our mother's slight build, but the rest of me is all Dad. Same noses. Same light brown hair. Same right hook in the fighting pit.

"Why won't you tell me what you were up to?" Peter says.

I pretend not to hear him. I want to put the Jade Lily behind me. Move on and figure out how to make rent some other way so Peter can worry more about fixing crêpe makers than where we'll crash every night. I'm about to tell him to go take a break already when there's a pounding on the shop door.

"We're open," I call out. I walk toward the entrance, but before I get there, the door swings on its hinges so hard that it shakes.

Standing at the threshold, I see a white man in a black suit, his eyes covered with sunglasses and his hair buzzed close to the scalp. My eyes trail down the lines of his suit jacket toward his waistline, which flares out a little right over the hip. It's a telltale sign that he's packing heat. A gun.

I freeze on the spot. He must be one of Hoover's FBI agents. That's their uniform. A few years back, one of our neighbors got busted for joining the Communist party and right before his arrest I'd seen men like this one hanging around our block. I'd thought that the police would've been the ones following my trail from the Jade Lily. Not this.

"Can we help you with something?" Peter says from behind me.

I block my brother from getting any closer and stare at the goon in front of us.

The man takes off his sunglasses and stares straight at me. "I'm looking for Josephine Linden."

Peter's eyes go round. "What do you need my sister for?" he asks, but I shush him.

"What's this all about, sir?" I ask, fighting to steady my voice. My eyes dart to the door. Should I make a break for it? I bet I could outrun him, but he already knows my name and where I live. Did Old Wen give me up? I swear I could strangle his wrinkled neck.

The man gives me a funny look. "I'm here to do a sweep of the premises on behalf of the senator's office."

"The senator?" Peter and I say at the same time.

My relief is short-lived though. The man proceeds to walk past us to survey our storage room and the adjacent workshop, switching the lights on and off as he goes.

"Is this some new state inspection?" I ask, wondering if Dad forgot to fill out our annual paperwork. Just like that, my heart is thundering again and I'm wondering what sort of fines we'll need to pay off.

"Nope, and I'm all done here," he replies.

"Done with what?" I ask. Does this mean that he isn't arresting me?

"Someone will be in shortly to explain," he says, which isn't any help at all. Then, with a curt nod, he exits the store as quickly as he entered it, striding outside to a car parked out front. It's a black sedan, a Cadillac, and I see an older white woman step out of the back seat and onto the curb. The first thing I notice is that she's very tall. I have to tip my chin up to get a decent glimpse of her face, which has a stern look to it, like a librarian getting ready to say, *Keep it down!* because you've turned a page too loudly. She's dressed like a librarian too, wearing a black dress with a white collar that has been ironed stiff.

Peter elbows my side. "That's Senator Appleby!" he whispers so loudly that the barber next door probably overhears him.

"How would you know?" I whisper back.

"You really ought to read the paper more."

I'm tempted to tell him that I've been a little busy trying to keep a roof over our heads, but Peter doesn't know how dire our situation has gotten. Dad and I have an unspoken agreement to shield him from that.

The woman approaches us, and I can only stare. There's a US senator coming toward me, and I have to question all over again if I'm in very big trouble, but then she juts out a hand for me to shake and her whole face changes with a smile. "You must be Josephine, although I've heard you prefer Jo."

Peter clears his throat loudly until I realize that I'm being a total ding-a-ling because I've yet to shake her hand, so I remedy that fast. Before I can cough out how does she know my name, she turns to Peter to shake his hand too.

"And you must be Peter," she says to him.

My brother, who has been slouching ever since a recent growth spurt catapulted him to become the tallest kid in his class, stands up straight as a stick. "Yes, ma'am."

"Well then, why don't we all step inside and have a little chat? I'm sure you're wondering why I'm here," she says, but doesn't elaborate. She simply walks into the shop like she's a regular customer, leading the way and expecting us to follow, which we do.

"Let me get you something to sit on," I say, spinning around in a circle as if a set of chairs will magically appear. The best I can do is the stepstool we have behind the counter, but Senator Appleby shakes her head when I pick it up.

"I'm fine standing. Despite my age, I'm far from fragile," she says, waving off my offer.

She's right about that. I'd never use *fragile* to describe her. It isn't only her height or her broad shoulders. It's the way she carries herself, like she isn't someone you want to tangle with, even if she's a few decades older than you.

"Can we help you with something, Senator?" I ask. Because I'm pretty sure she hasn't stopped by to buy a used vacuum cleaner.

"Indeed you can. I wanted to talk to you about the reel you mailed to the Association a few months back," she replies.

A second passes before I register what she's talking about. Every year, amateur fighters have the opportunity to mail in a demo reel of their season's highlights to the American Mecha Fighting Association, the national governing body of the sport. After going through thousands of reels and scoring them, the Association then publishes a list of the top amateurs in every region. But here's the catch. They hardly ever include female fighters on their lists. The last time that happened was back in 1943, when a decent chunk of the male population was overseas fighting in WWII. Despite those odds, I've sent in my reel season after season out of pure stubbornness, except I didn't do it this year. Money had gotten so tight that I didn't want to waste it on an envelope and postage that would probably get tossed away unopened.

"I think there must've been a mistake—" I start to tell her, but Peter digs an elbow into my ribs. When I glance at him, he gets a bashful look on his face and gives a little shrug. My mouth drops open. Did he put together my reel and mail it in? That precious little sneak.

"Sorry, please go on, Senator," Peter says, his cheeks flushed.

"Looks like Peter has some explaining to do," Senator Appleby says with a clap on his back, not missing a beat. "Back to the matter at hand though, the two of you might not be aware of this, but after my husband passed away, I not only took over his senatorial seat, I also replaced him on the Association's selection committee. And as their first female member to boot." She gives a little smile. "Some of my peers asked if I even know the rules of the sport, but I happened to coach an all-girls mecha fighting team back when I taught in Sacramento. There are rumors I even fought in a few matches myself when I was younger," she adds with a wink.

"I'm hoping that's evidence enough that I come by my expertise honestly," she continues, "and that's why I truly believe that you, young lady, are very impressive in the pit."

"You . . . well . . . thank you." I'm struggling for words. I still can't quite believe that she actually watched my reel.

"Frankly, you should be getting much more fanfare. A 19–1 record in the NorCal senior division? There should be reporters and recruiters knocking down your door at all hours of the day." Her smile turns wry. "But let me guess. That hasn't been the case, has it?"

I wish she was wrong, but she nailed it on the nose. If I were a boy, I'd bet good money that the *San Francisco Chronicle* would've sent a reporter to cover most of my matches. And once my record ticked up to 10–0 this past season I'm sure the Association would've taken notice and invited me to one of their training camps that they hold throughout the year to find new talent. If I'd passed their muster, I could've joined Team USA and represented them on the international circuit, traveling around the world throughout the summer to fight in elite tournaments like the Armistice Cup and the English Invitational. And if they *really* liked me, I might have gotten the nod to go to the World Championships in late August, which are held yearly unless there's the Pax Games.

The senator notes the look on my face and keeps talking. "We both know from personal experience how tough female fighters have it here in the States. The scene internationally might be marginally better but not by much. I counted three girls out of fifty fighters at the Games in '59."

She doesn't have to remind me of that, even though I'm happy to let her. Mecha fighting is one of those rare sports that isn't separated between the men's game and women's—we all compete together since our mechas are supposed to level the playing field. During the '23 Games, one of the American fighters was Jeanie Gibbons, a seventeen-year-old spitfire from Wisconsin who cleared her own pit in her backyard and flew single-engine biplanes in her free time. She was the first woman to represent the US, out of a grand total of two. The second was Louise Armstrong-Reed, who fought in the 1935 cycle in Rome, coming in at a respectable ninth-place finish. There were rumors during World War II that women might even come to dominate the sport since so many of them were working on the factory lines, making mechas and testing them out for the battlefield, but after our troops came home, all that chatter died out. Women were shuffled back into the kitchen, and for almost thirty years, Team USA has only featured boys.

"Now I'm a red-blooded American through and through, but the Communists are far ahead of us when it comes to this matter," Senator Appleby says. "Over in places like the USSR and Romania, the girls train alongside the boys, sometimes starting as young as five. And guess what? They're just as talented! Look at Trude Bürkner," she says, referencing the Austrian fighter who got third place at the '31 Games.

"Or the Federovas," I add. I'm talking about Lidiya and Zoya Federova, the two Soviet sisters who are currently ranked among the best in the world, with the older one, Lidiya, claiming the number one slot while the younger one, Zoya, has taken fourth and is moving up fast. It's heavily favored that one of them will win the Games this year.

"Meanwhile in the States we keep underestimating half our population and wondering why we haven't won the Games since Malcolm Maines did it in '47," Senator Appleby points out.

"Exactly!" The word charges out of my mouth at full speed, matching my pulse. I never thought I'd hear an American senator say something like that, and now I'm really curious why she has stopped by for a visit. Just to tell me, *Keep up the good work?*

"Here's what I believe. If we really want to beat the Soviets, we ought to try something new. After all, they've won the Games in '51, '55, and '59. So for these upcoming Games, we need to shake things up. Choose a pair of fighters who are fresh. Unexpected." She pauses and sighs. "So I made my case to the other committee members but was roundly ignored. Let's just say that they already knew who they wanted to bet on in the race. But two days ago, a wrench got thrown into the plans."

Peter and I exchange a look.

"What kind of a wrench?" he asks her.

"One about the size of a meteor." Her face pinches, like she's recalling a bad memory. "During a recent sparring session, Ted Rochester took a bad fall and broke his elbow."

"Ted is out of contention?" I say, gobsmacked.

This is big. Huge. I've never faced Ted in the pit before, but I know of him that's for sure. He's seventeen and rumored to be the best fighter in Texas, with a left hook as mean as his right. Last year, he got sent to the World Championships in Sydney, where he'd finished sixth, but he was getting over the measles, so he could've finished higher.

"He'll make a full recovery, but it'll take a couple of months and lots of recuperation," she explains. "However, this means that we must replace him immediately since Round One of the Games starts on Saturday."

It's already Tuesday.

My heart starts to thud fast.

She can't be— No, I won't let myself believe it.

"The committee went through our list of alternates, but none of them sat well with me. They were fine fighters, yes, but they were also like Ted. All power. Built like bricks. And utterly *expected*, which meant that the Soviets would know how to beat them. So why in the world would we play into that?" She chuckles to herself. "It took me a good portion of the night to convince my colleagues to go in a different direction—and I had to remind a few of them that they owed their careers to my late husband—but we're in agreement that it's time to make a little history. To choose a fighter who will shake things up."

Her eyes meet mine, and I have to say even the Ravager's gaze didn't have the intensity of a former coach turned senator. "We're tapping you to join Team USA."

She looks at me expectantly, like I'm supposed to squeal or scream or faint, but my fingers go numb and I don't think I can feel my face anymore. I start wondering if I'm dreaming this all up. Maybe I got a concussion back at the Jade Lily and I'm hallucinating.

Peter yanks at my arm. "Say yes, Jo! Or I'll have to do it for you."

"Heck yes!" I blurt so fast that I'm not sure that it counts. "I mean, *yes*, I'd be absolutely honored to join the team, Senator."

"I was getting a little worried there," she says, ribbing me. "Now then, I'll need your parents to sign off on a few forms, and we should tell them the good news too. When might they be around?"

"Our dad won't be back for another hour, and our mom—" Peter's voice catches, and we share another glance, like we always do whenever we meet someone new who doesn't know about our mother.

"She died when we were young," I finish for him.

"Goodness, my staff didn't brief me on that. I'll certainly have a word with them when I'm done here," she says, not looking very pleased. I get the sense that she runs a tight ship, and she isn't happy to have discovered a leak in the hull. "My sincerest condolences. How terrible that must have been."

I shrug, a knee-jerk reaction whenever someone finds out that Peter and I are motherless. That we ought to be pitied. I wait for the inevitable question at how our mom died, but much to Senator Appleby's credit, she doesn't ask.

Instead she says, "I'm sure your mother would be very proud of you. Look at the young woman you've become—an all-American fighter ready to represent our nation at the Games."

Her words are kind, but I can only blink at them. I know what *all-American* means to most people. Wholesome. Patriotic. *White.* Which makes me realize that Senator Appleby and her staff probably have no clue that I'm part Chinese.

My pulse taps a heavy beat in my throat. If the Association knew what my mother looked like, would Senator Appleby be standing here right now and extending this invitation to me? The answer pops into my head much too quickly.

No way.

The US has never sent a fighter of color to the Games before. Not even to an international exhibition, and those don't count toward rankings. In any case, our national laws aren't exactly friendly to people like me. If our landlady discovers that Peter and I aren't fully white, she could evict us just like that and it would be perfectly legal.

Should I tell the senator about my mom?

The question buzzes around in my head like a fly, but I smash it quickly. I might as well say to her *thanks but no thanks* and that I'd rather stay home than go to the Games. There's no way the Association would let me represent our country if they caught wind of this.

So I stay quiet and calm my nerves by telling myself that it's very unlikely that the senator will find out. Her staff would have to do some real digging since my mother died so long ago. She also had a white-sounding name. *Clara Lee*. Even if the senator's people came across my mom on some old records, they would probably think that she had light skin like they do.

"Well, will you look at the time?" the senator says, clapping her hands together. "I've got a late dinner meeting to get to, and you should get ready. You'll be taking a red-eye flight to Washington tonight."

"Wait, *tonight*? What about school?" I say. It's the middle of May, so the semester is almost over, but I've got an algebra test tomorrow and a social studies project due on Friday.

"My staff will speak with your principal and make sure that you receive an excused absence for the rest of the academic year. We need to fly you out as soon as possible since the other fighters have been getting acclimated and training for well over a week. That's why we've booked you on the next flight out of San Francisco. The ticket has been bought and paid for, and I've also arranged for a car to pick you up here at eight o'clock sharp and bring you to the airport. I hope that won't be a problem."

It's a statement, not a question, but the timeline makes me dizzy. My dad doesn't even know about this yet.

"I can help Jo get packed," Peter says.

"No need for that, young man. The Association will provide everything that your sister will need. Clothing. Shoes. Toothpaste. They'll have it covered, but you're sweet for offering. The only favor that I ask is to please keep this quiet until tomorrow. I'll be speaking with several reporters tonight, and the announcement will be in the papers come the morning. Until then, I trust that you won't share this with any of your friends?"

I almost laugh. This will be the easiest promise I ever make. I don't have time for friends since I'm either training or working or, during rarer moments, doing homework. I suppose she could mean my teammates—all of them male—but they've barely tolerated me for years, loathing the fact that I keep showing them up in the pit but begrudgingly grateful that I give us a winning record.

The senator turns to Peter. "I'll also be sure to reserve a ticket for you and your father at the Parade of Nations in our special VIP section. You can pick them up at will call."

Peter thanks her, but I get a sinking feeling in my stomach. Unless she throws in a couple plane tickets as well, there's no way we'll be able to afford to fly Peter and Dad out. Even a cross-country bus trip would be out of our reach, but I don't say that. No need to broadcast how bad our finances have become.

"Here's my office phone number. Be sure to give the operator the special extension so that they can patch you through directly," she says, handing me a business card. The extension is 1010. Easy enough to memorize. "I'll see you soon. I'll be attending the welcome banquet at the Manger Hay-Adams so we'll chat again then."

Banquet? Manger Hay-Adams? Is that a town or something? There's no time to find out the details because she's at the door and her car is already running outside. We shake hands again, and I make sure to really look her in the eye.

"I don't know how to thank you for this opportunity, ma'am."

"Oh, I can think of one way." She winks. "Bring that title back home where it belongs."

As soon as her car leaves, Peter and I close the shop for the day, the first time in years that Linden's Repair shuts its doors early. The two of us book it upstairs. We've got about forty minutes before my ride comes to take me to the airport, so I start throwing things into my gym bag since none of us owns a proper suitcase. The Association might provide clothes and toiletries for me, but I feel like I ought to bring *something*. I'm searching for an extra pair of matching socks when Dad walks through the front door.

He calls out to us, "Mind telling me why the store's closed and it's not even seven thirty?" His voice sounds like sandpaper, all rough and grit, and I'm betting that his meeting at the bank must've tanked.

"Don't worry. We've got one heck of an excuse," Peter says to me.

"Do you want to tell him the news, squirt?" I say, watching his eyes light up.

Both of us rush out of the room like excited puppies to meet our father in the cramped little space we call our living room. Dad has already loosened his tie, and his collared shirt looks worn and crumpled, matching his mood. He's digging through his pockets for a stick of gum when Peter blurts out everything that has happened in the last hour, from the senator's surprise visit to her even more shocking request. As he listens, Dad's face shifts from exhaustion into disbelief and finally into a blank look where he can only stare at us.

He stares at me with bewilderment in his eyes. "You mean to tell me that you're going to the Games?"

I break into a grin. "I'm supposed to leave in ten minutes."

"You have to sign some papers and Jo still has to finish packing," Peter says. He's ticking off a list of things I ought to bring, like floss and soap. "And books! You'll need something to read on the plane."

"You better find your sister something, then," Dad says, but Peter has already hurried back into our shared bedroom to dig through his little library of instruction manuals and technical magazines that he buys used over at the Author's Attic. When Peter is well out of earshot, Dad crosses his arms and asks softly, "You sure this ain't a mistake?"

I flinch. That hurts. After all this time, even with my nearly perfect record this past season, he still can't fathom that I could make Team USA?

"Senator Appleby sought me out actually," I retort. "She even hired a car to pick me up, so I better get ready." I try to shoulder past him, but he catches me by the arm.

"I didn't mean it like that. Don't get delicate," Dad says.

How many times have I heard him say that? *Don't complain, Jo. Don't get delicate. Grit your teeth and get back up again.* Those were his stipulations if I wanted him to teach me how to fight in the first place. If I saved up half the money to buy my own Goliath and the parts needed to fix it up, he would loan me the other half and the labor to get it running. I think he figured that I'd give up after a couple weeks, but I was determined, starting my own paper route and doing odd jobs for Mrs. Watters next door and anyone else on the block. Eventually I'd saved enough cash that Dad found me a beat-up Goliath—an ancient 21E model that had been sitting out in a junkyard since '46. It took another three months to get the thing up and running and fitted for my frame. By then I considered quitting my paper route to spend more time training, but Dad had cracked a rare smile and reminded me that I still needed to cover the cost of the esterium batteries, not to mention the loan I had to repay.

That's my father for you. He raised Peter and me the only way he knew how. Tough. It was all that he knew himself, growing up as one of five kids on a corn farm in Nebraska. That sort of life was hard, but then came the droughts and the locust swarms and the Dust Bowl that left Dad and his siblings half starving. When he turned fourteen, he hopped on a train and came out west where he nabbed a job working on an assembly line making military-grade Goliaths for the war effort. This was back in 1942, not long after the attack on Pearl Harbor. That was how Dad learned the ins and outs of mechas, which eventually led him to a lucrative side hustle—fighting in illegal matches around the city. He even earned the nickname of Tombstone because he won so many times, and the only reason he stopped was because of two broken vertebrae he got in Korea.

A car beeps outside, and Peter runs to tell us that the driver is here. Dad signs the paperwork while I make a quick circle around my room to gather up anything I might've forgotten before we all make a stop next door to tell Mrs. Watters the news. I know that Senator Appleby told us not to spread the word, but she's almost like family. She gives me a kiss on the cheek and tells me with a wag of her finger, "You flatten the competition, you hear me?"

After that, we head to the curb. The driver tells me that we better hit the road to beat traffic, meaning I have to rush through my goodbyes.

While Peter puts my bag in the trunk, I lower my voice to a whisper and say to Dad, "Tell the landlady that I'll get her the money."

He looks taken aback and flushes. "I've got that handled."

"Senator Appleby could put in a good word for us too."

"Absolutely not." He starts patting down his pockets, searching for his gum again, which he has taken to chewing because it's cheaper than smoking. "Don't trouble her with that."

His stubbornness can sure be a pain in the butt. Here we are, a month or two before we get evicted, and he can't own up that he needs help. I sigh. "I'll figure something out."

"What you need to do is focus on the Games, and be careful about the Reds. Watch your back both in and out of the pit," Dad says. His voice cracks a little when he adds, "You take care of yourself, Joey." And since he isn't the hugging type, we shake hands instead.

Peter tries to shake my hand too, but I won't let him off so easily. I wrap him tight in my arms like he's five years old all over again. He smells like soap and pencil shavings, and I don't want to let go.

He finally manages to wriggle free. "You'll call, won't you? After you land?"

"Sure, I will. I'll call every day if you want."

"You better," he says, grinning. "I want updates."

Despite my best efforts, my eyes prick with tears. I can't remember the last time I spent a night away from him, probably a few years ago when I got invited to Sue Baker's sleepover party, but aside from that we've rarely slept more than ten feet away from each other.

"Go and show those Commies what you're made of. You can beat them. You can win this," he tells me.

And I have to for him. It isn't just the title—as much as I've dreamed about it—but the money too. If we can't pay off our debts soon, we'll have nowhere to go except our father's old Crosley station wagon. I know that Dad and I could grit our teeth through it until we figured something out. Peter though? I really don't know. I'm sure he wouldn't complain about living out of a powder-blue box on wheels, but he would start worrying and giving himself headaches and who knows what else.

"I'm going to buy us a steak dinner with the prize money, and you can order all the root beer you want," I tell my baby brother before I give him another hug.

It's time to head to Washington.

It's time to bring that title home.

5

When my flight lands in Washington at half past seven in the morning, I have every reason to be a bleary-eyed grump. Before we took off from San Francisco, the plane had air-conditioning troubles, so we had to sweat it out on the tarmac while the repairmen took a look at it. Then, after we'd been flying for a while, we hit a patch of turbulence so bad over Salt Lake City that I honestly believed we might drop out of the sky like a giant boulder. I gripped on to the armrests and wondered if there'd be anything left of me for Dad and Peter to bury after the inevitable crash. With that heartwarming thought occupying my mind, let's say that I didn't get much sleep east of the Rockies.

As soon as we de-plane though, I'm wide-awake and the first one out the door, not only because I'm ready to get out of this tin can but because there's something I've gotta see. I race into the terminal only to plow into a white man in a black suit, who turns out to be my driver.

"Right this way, Miss Linden," he says after he has grabbed my bag. "This all you got?"

I nod, but I'm not really paying attention. "Where are the newspaper stands?"

"Out front, but I've got a copy of the *Washington Post* waiting in the car."

"Great. Where are you parked?" I say, resisting the urge to prod him along because he's moving a little too slowly for my liking.

While the driver places my bag into the trunk, I fling myself into the back seat and start thumbing to the real meat of the newspaper: the sports section. My heartbeat skyrockets, but I don't have to search long before I find what I'm looking for.

"Team USA Selects Unknown Female Fighter for the Pax Games," the headline reads.

My eyes skid to a stop there. "Unknown Female Fighter"? You'd think they could've used my name, but at least I find it in the first sentence.

The American Mecha Fighting Association has named San Franciscan fighter Josephine Linden to Team USA, replacing Edward Rochester who was injured during a training session. This marks the first time since 1935 that the US has sent a female fighter to the Games.

"Jo Linden will make an excellent addition to the team. She's one of the most talented fighters in the country, boy or girl," said US Senator June Appleby of California, who recently

replaced her deceased husband on the Association's selection
committee.

But the committee's decision was not unanimous. "The final
vote was 4–4, with the senator breaking the tie. Miss Linden
might be a successful athlete in her local division, but is she really
ready for the Games?" says a source close to the committee speak-
ing on background.

I realize that I'm gripping the sides of the paper so hard that I'm
starting to rip it. It's like waking up to a bucket of ice water poured
over my head. Senator Appleby had been so enthusiastic about having me join the team that I hadn't given much thought to what the
other committee members might've said about me. I don't even
know who they are, but I'm guessing they're a bunch of stuffy old
white men who've never stepped foot inside a mecha themselves.

As my feelings start to sour, I can hear Peter's voice in my head,
pointing out that I still got five votes and that's what counts, right?
Always the optimist. He could be dying of thirst but still see the
glass as half full. Classic Peter. But I'm not my brother.

I reread the quote again, especially the part that says: *Is she*
really ready for the Games?

I'll be more than happy to show them.

I keep my eyes on the sports section because we're still miles
away from the city. There's a piece about the French team and how
they might have a shot at winning this year. There's another
about the underdogs that could cause an upset, like Canada or

Yugoslavia. I shake my head at what these reporters are thinking. France should be out before Round 3, and Yugoslavia? Even sooner. But these articles are all appetizers leading up to the main course—a feature story about the Federova sisters.

There's a photo of them on page two. They look about six and seven years old respectively, with the baby fat still thick on their cheeks, and they're holding hands. Apparently they used to be quite fond of each other, training together and sharing a room at the Moscow fighting school where they lived year-round.

But then they started growing up and growing apart. Lidiya, the older sister by eleven months, saw her career trajectory take off as soon as she entered international competition at age ten. Three years later, she had won nearly every tournament in the junior division, more than any fighter before her. By age fifteen, there was talk that she would likely stand at the top podium at the next Pax Games, which was two years off at that point.

And that was when Zoya came knocking. She hit a growth spurt and swiftly scaled the rankings, jumping from number 133 to number 51 in her first year at the senior level, and then all the way up to number 9 after she turned sixteen. These days Zoya routinely ranks between number 5 and number 3, and it's clear she's knocking down her sister's door for that number 1 slot, which is likely why Lidiya asked to be coached separately.

But I don't think Lidiya should worry too much about her younger sister. Yes, Zoya is strong and fast and talented, but Lidiya has the edge.

She's sly.

Take what happened back at the World Championships in 1959, where Lidiya faced off against Johannes Lange of West Germany in the playoffs. Lange had a lot more experience than her going in, and twenty minutes into the match, it looked like he was going to win, especially since Lidiya's mecha had seemingly lost use of its left arm. So he kept focusing his hits on Lidiya's right side, figuring he only had to deal a couple more blows before he could pull her down for the KO. Turns out though that Lidiya had been bluffing. There was nothing wrong at all with her mecha's left arm. She'd merely let Lange believe that—and the rest of us watching too—to make him let his guard down. And as soon as he did, that's exactly when she clocked him on the side of his head with a mean cross and dragged him onto the pit floor for the victory.

She had just turned fourteen.

"Here we are," the driver says, pulling the car up to a sidewalk.

I step out of the vehicle and take a deep breath of fresh air, only to cough it right back out because it's thick as soup. The East Coast humidity will sure take some getting used to, but I certainly won't need any time adjusting to the views. Straight ahead of me I see the glowing white dome of the Capitol Building, and when I swing my head around, I spot the Washington Monument, like a great big pencil pointing up into the lightening sky. It's a postcard-worthy snapshot.

I'm not going to complain about getting my first real glimpse of our nation's capital, but I do have to wonder if we've taken a detour.

"Which way is the dormitory?" I ask.

The driver looks confused as he reads over his notes. "They told me to drop you off here since your flight was delayed," he says, plunking my bag next to me.

"Who's *they*?"

"The Association. Someone was supposed to meet you here." He glances around and then at his watch and mumbles to himself about needing to head to his next appointment. "You better come back with me to the office. They'll have to pick you up from there."

I balk at that. The last thing I want to do is to get shuttled off to some office building. "Look, there's a pay phone up the block. Give me the Association's number, and I'll call and work this all out."

"But, miss—"

"Didn't you say you were late for your next pickup?" I say as I grab my bag and get moving before he can stop me. "Don't worry. I'll tell the Association that this was my idea."

I walk about twenty yards toward the pay phone before slowing down. Up ahead I see a line of Goliaths, enclosed by a shoulder-high metal fence. It's an exhibition of some sort, probably set up by the Association for the tourists pouring into the city ahead of the Games.

It's like looking back in time. The mecha closest to me is one of the earliest developed, a dented old thing that dates back to World War I. Its neighbor, on the other hand, is a 1920s-era Goliath, taller yet more trim, like the ones used during the early Pax Games, complete with the heavy gasoline tanks strapped to its back. I walk alongside the fence and let my eyes roam over the next mecha, this one from World War II, which stormed across Germany to Hitler's own backyard and that finally forced Japan's surrender in '45.

As I walk, the Goliaths continue to advance technologically, from the exact 1947 model that Malcolm Maines used to win the Games to the 1959 rollout that swapped out the steel frame for titanium and then to a few specialized designs. There's a deep-dive model employed by the Navy SEALs and there's also a prototype developed by the US Air Force that may one day soar through the sky like a fighter jet. My eyes skip down the line until they come to a halt on the last two Goliaths, standing on pedestals.

I don't consider myself the religious sort, but it feels like I'm approaching something holy. They're beautiful. I search for their model number, but I don't see any in the usual location, a small grouping of numbers on the mecha's right calf. Instead I see letters running down each leg, alternating in red, white, and blue: Team USA. Even though there's a sign posted nearby that reads in a bolded font, *For Display Only—Do Not Touch*, I ignore the instruction and scale the fence.

I circle around the Goliath slowly, letting my eyes drink it in. I raise my hand and rest my palm on its knee, shivering at the smoothness of the metal that has been so carefully polished I can see my reflection. It must've cost at least a million bucks. Only the best for Team USA, and soon enough I'll get to take this out for a test drive.

"Trespassing is a crime, you know," someone says behind me.

My back goes straight. "I didn't mean—" But then I see who's addressing me, and the rest of my reply promptly dries up in my mouth. It isn't the park police standing there, ready to slap me with a fine. It's much worse.

"Kealey," I say flatly. I thought I was prepared to face him again. I'd told myself to let bygones be bygones, but soon enough all the bitter old feelings come rushing back.

Sam shines his easy grin on me. "Why so formal? I thought we'd be on a first-name basis by now. We've known each other for how long? A year?"

That's a year too long in my book, but he's right. We met for the first time last March at the tristate tournament in Oregon, right before the final match where we battled it out for the winner's trophy. As soon as the ref blew the whistle, we went at each other's throats.

Sam juts his hand at me through the fence to shake. "Aw, come on. No hard feelings. How about we clear the slate and start fresh?"

I glare at his palm for several seconds too long, but Sam doesn't let his arm drop. With a noisy sigh I give it a shake so that he'll stop bothering me about it.

"Want a boost to climb back over?" he says, motioning toward me. "How did you get in there anyway?"

In reply, I show him. I grab the top of the fence and hoist myself over it in one easy motion. "Thanks anyway," I say breezily.

He's shaking his head and laughing to himself. "Same old Jo. You never need anyone's help, huh?"

I frown because I've never said that to him and because I certainly don't need *his* help, especially none of his unsolicited advice that he loves to give out like candy. I pick up my bag and start walking down the pebbled path, before Sam calls out to me.

"You'll march yourself right into the Potomac River if you keep going that way," he says.

Gritting my teeth, I turn around. "Well?" I say, hand on hip and waiting for him to point me in the right direction.

"We're on the same team now, kiddo. All you had to do was ask," he said, gesturing the opposite way from where I was headed and smiling that smile of his again, exuding the type of charisma that only a handsome rich boy can possess because his whole life has been charmed. The private coaches. The new Goliaths every season. The wealthy father who bankrolls all of that and the adoring fan club that only strokes Sam's ego higher.

Sam and I might be teammates, but I won't count him as an ally and I'd never call him a friend.

Not when only one of us can win the Games, and not when he's standing in my way to get the title.

6

My reasons for disliking Sam Kealey are many and varied, starting with minor irritations like how he calls me kiddo even though we're only a year and a half apart in age and moving up to hair-pulling frustrations like how he has beaten me twice in a row at the aforementioned tristate tournament that caps off our varsity seasons. He's the best I've ever faced in the pit, although that's not why I consider him an arrogant dipstick. He's an arrogant dipstick because he knows precisely how good he is and he likes to show it off.

Sam offers to take my bag for me. "Let me help," he says, probably because he relishes the opportunity to flex his biceps. I remember how he peacocks around the stadium whenever his name is announced before a match, blowing kisses and urging the fans to scream louder. None of that is against the rules, but it cheapens the game. We're there to fight, not preen.

Sam ends up grabbing the bag out of my hand. "Come on. We're teammates."

I don't need to point out to him that we'll be teammates on paper only for the most part. The Games consist of five rounds and fifty competitors, and everything kicks off with a bang during the first round. That's when every single fighter gets tossed into a gigantic pit in a free-for-all brawl, a match of sheer mayhem until only sixteen remain. There's a reason why the fighters nicknamed it Purgatory, but the fans love it. After that, the Games return to a traditional-style bracket, pairing off fighter against fighter until sixteen shrinks into eight, then four, then two, and then one single winner. So there's not much teamwork involved at all, but I keep that to myself and decide to let Sam carry my things because why not? Let him put those muscles that he loves so much to use.

"We better pick up the pace," Sam says. "Everyone's been waiting for you to arrive so that we can get started."

"Started on what? And who's everyone?" I ask, trying to keep up with him because his legs must be nearly double the length of mine.

"The photographers. Hairdressers. Wardrobe folks," he fires off. "Not to mention the Association people with their pocket protectors. They were waiting for you over at Fourth and Independence, where you were supposed to get dropped off. Good thing I noticed your driver rounding the corner over here."

"My knight in shining armor," I say.

Despite my sarcasm, Sam laughs, looking very much like a dashing knight with his windswept brown hair and eyes to match, and not to mention his classic build that fits the perfect definition of what the Association looks for in a mecha fighter: tall, muscled, male, white. Sam ticks off all their boxes, and he has only one more to check—winner of the Games. Some people really are born lucky. Not that I'm complaining. Well, maybe a little.

Straight ahead of us, I spot a small tent that has been set up in the middle of the grassy lawn. I see more than a dozen people gathered there, buzzing around what looks like a photography shoot.

"Are we getting our pictures taken or something?" I ask.

"Didn't you read the itinerary on the way over from the airport? In your folder?"

"What folder?"

"The driver was supposed to give you a folder."

"This is the first time I've heard about that," I say grumpily because I thought I'd get a chance to shower after I landed. "What're they going to do with these photos anyway?"

"Make a calendar of the two of us. We could alternate months. I've got dibs on July." He must notice that I've stopped walking completely because he adds, "I'm joking. They're taking our official portraits for the Games. Now that the announcement is out, people are chomping at the bit to see Ted's replacement."

I let out a sigh. I already hate sitting for my yearbook pictures at school with all of those *Tilt your head this way* and *Why don't you smile more, honey?* suggestions. At least those sessions only take a few minutes, but I have a feeling this one will last much longer.

My face must give away my emotions because Sam is chuckling.

"It won't be *that* bad, and you might as well get used to it. Once those sponsors come knocking, you'll be holding up Cracker Jack boxes or wool socks at the next shoot."

"Sponsors?" I ask, brightening a few watts. While I don't like how commercialized the Games have gotten, I'll set those feelings aside to hawk some Sugar Stars cereal to cover the rent. That's how a lot of amateur athletes earn cash because most of our tournaments don't offer purse money. Sam doesn't have to worry about that since his family is dripping in wealth and they live on some exclusive island near Seattle, but that hasn't stopped him from shilling Birds Eye orange juice (*Savor each special sip!*) and Baron's multi-sport sneakers (*Choose from five vibrant colors!*). Makes me wonder what he plans to do with all that green. He must have a huge pile of it somewhere. "How do you get those anyway? Do you have to write letters to the companies or something?"

He shrugs. "Nah, they're the ones who'll be knocking on your door, not the other way around. You'll end up with so many offers that you'll have to turn most of them down."

That's easy for him to say considering he's Mr. Photogenic with the confidence to go with it. Plus, he's a boy. I wonder if any sponsors will be keen on hiring a female fighter like me. All I need is one or two though, and I'd let them curl my hair and even pluck off my arm hairs if that meant getting paid.

Sam waves his arm and shouts toward the tent. "I found her!"

I'm quickly surrounded by a team of very attractive people who plunk me onto a folding chair. One of them brushes my hair while another buffs my nails, and I'm almost ready to admit that this isn't so bad. It feels pretty nice to get pampered for once, but that's before someone attacks my eyebrows with a pair of tweezers and I take it all back.

"You have such unique features. The color of your eyes is much darker than your hair," says the lady smearing cream on my face offhandedly. "You must have some Mediterranean blood in you, hmm?"

I tense up and blurt out the first thing that lands on my tongue. "What's that lotion you're using? It smells great," I say, changing the topic fast.

My forehead beads with sweat. Are they going to start asking where my family came from originally? I could tell them that it's nobody business, but now that I'm an official member of Team USA, I doubt I can be that rude.

In the end, my nervous sweating works to my advantage. The makeup people begin digging around in their suitcase full of little bottles and brushes and compacts instead of prodding me about my family's heritage.

"Where's the heavy-duty powder? We can't have her face dripping like that for the shoot!" one of them says.

I release a slow breath. I should be safe for now.

Thirty minutes later, they push me in front of a full-length mirror in the new outfit that they've changed me into—a satin dress that's fitted through the waist but flares out at the skirt like a gumdrop. It's patterned in navy-blue gingham, reminding me of a picnic blanket. I'm handed a pair of red shoes, like I'm Dorothy from *The Wizard of Oz*. Only, I don't want to go home.

"She looks perfect," they say cheerily. "Like Patty Duke—the fresh-faced girl next door. Great job all around, everyone!"

Girl next door is the exact opposite of the fighting pit, but at least no one is talking about my complexion anymore.

Speaking of which, as I look at my reflection, I don't recognize myself at all. They've curled my flat hair into something out of the movies, shiny and springy, and they've powdered my face so white that no one will wonder if I have "Mediterranean blood." I should be relieved, but I get an itchy feeling to wipe it all off. This isn't me at all.

But me isn't what the Association wants.

I glower at what I see in the mirror. Why can't I be *fresh-faced* and *all-American* without the hair and the makeup? Without hiding what my mother looked like?

I'm just as American as everyone else here.

Aren't I?

I'm soon whisked off to meet the photographer, who's barking orders at everyone because he doesn't want to lose any more light, which doesn't make much sense. With the sun above the horizon, it looks like there's plenty of light to go around, but the photographer is telling us to beat our feet.

"Well, well," Sam says, wagging his brows when he sees me.

"Save it, Kealey." I flush, feeling self-conscious, especially standing next to him. The styling team has combed back his hair and has dressed him in a blue suit and striped tie. His getup might look tacky on anyone else, but Sam pulls off the look with irritating ease.

"Save what? I was only going to say that you look swell, kiddo," he says, even sounding like he means it. But then he has to ruin it by adding, "At least compared to the last time I saw you, when you were all sweaty and frowning at me."

That "last time" was when he beat me at the tournament. Since he has reminded me of that low point in my life, I swat him on the arm.

"My name isn't kiddo," I say.

"Aw, come on! You do look swell," he says, but I'm already walking to my mark.

Sam and I are positioned in front of the two Goliaths that I'd been drooling over earlier. Someone must've moved them from the exhibition to where we're standing now. The photographer starts off by shooting us side by side in front of the mechas, but little by little he asks Sam to inch forward until he's practically blocking me.

What am I? A background prop?

It gets even worse when the photographer tells Sam to climb into one of the Goliaths.

"Let's get a couple live-action shots," the photographer says.

I'm assuming he wants me to do the same thing, so I stride up to the other Goliath and kick off my shoes because there's no way that I can mount it in these heels, only for the photographer to yell at his assistants, "Get her down before she hurts herself!"

Hurt myself? I could do this blindfolded and half-asleep. But then the assistants swarm around me and pry me away from the Goliath like I'm some sort of porcelain doll.

"Don't you need a few live shots of me too?" I ask.

"You're all done for the day!" they chirp. "How about we get you a coffee? You like cream and sugar?"

I'm not thirsty at all. Shaking my head at them, I keep my gaze on Sam and his Goliath. One of the assistants has to help him access the thing because it requires a numerical password to turn it on—a safeguard against nosy tourists or fighters like myself, I guess. I watch Sam climb inside the cockpit and take the Goliath on a little stroll around the Mall, with the photographer clicking away. Jealousy flares through me. That's the type of picture that I want for my own official portrait.

"I really wouldn't mind taking a couple action shots myself," I tell the assistants, making sure to paint my voice syrupy sweet, but it doesn't help.

"Oh, we've got everything we need already. Don't you worry! You'll look perfect in them," they reply.

I doubt they would say that to Ted Rochester if he were here. I should have expected this sort of treatment since I've dealt with it my whole career, but it still stings. And if I dare to complain? I'll get called ungrateful and difficult—and that'll be to my face. Who knows what they'd say behind my back?

Maybe I ought to read that new book *The Feminine Mystique* that I keep hearing about.

Fortunately the photo session soon comes to an end when the park police arrive to tell us to wrap things up because our permit has timed out. Still dressed in our fancy clothes, Sam and I climb into a chauffeured car that takes us to our next destination. As we wind through the streets, I see that the city has woken up. Men in dark suits zip off to work, heading into enormous buildings with impressive-sounding names like the Department of Innovation and the National Archives. Some of the tourists are up early too. They're easy to spot in their bright T-shirts and their cameras hanging around their necks while they wait to board the shiny new monorail that was built for the Games. The tracks are elevated above the road, and the trains themselves resemble long silver snakes that glint in the sunlight as they curve around the blocks.

"How come we aren't riding on the monorail?" I ask Sam, pointing outside. We have the trolley back home, but nothing like this.

"They've been dealing with a bunch of delays. Besides, look at all the leg room we have in here," Sam says, stretching out and making himself comfy. "Anyhow, the monorail doesn't go where we're headed."

The car veers onto a bridge that spans the Potomac River, and I notice a sign that says, *East Potomac Park*. Except this place isn't only a park. It's an island.

I swivel my head toward the mainland. "Did we take a wrong turn?" This can't be right.

Sam, however, has rested his arms behind his head. "Nope, our stop is right ahead."

I look at him doubtfully because all I see are cherry trees and grassy lawns, but sure enough I spy a bunch of buildings in the distance.

The Pavilion.

Styled after the Olympic Village, the Pavilion houses all fifty of us fighters who have flown in for the Games, our home for the next two weeks. Sam takes it upon himself to become my tour guide and points out the various buildings in our eyeline, from the massive training center to the dining hall to the administrative office, where I can go in case I lose my key. The stadium itself, where all the matches will take place, is located in the city proper, but we'll be spending the bulk of our time here in the Pavilion.

"Home, sweet home," Sam says. "Between you and me though, the dorm rooms are nothing spectacular."

"No towel warmer for your morning bath? Or a butler bot to make you a cup of coffee?" I say with a lifted brow. His father is some big shot at Boeing—one of the richest companies in America that has made its money by manufacturing planes and missiles and mechas—so I wouldn't be surprised if his family's estate is filled with a fleet of bots to serve his every need.

"Tease all you want, but my Bertie Bot 2000 fixes an incredible omelet." He arches a brow right back at me, and I don't know if he's joking around or not.

Our car pulls up to the Pavilion's gated entrance. It's heavily guarded, as if we've arrived at Checkpoint Charlie at the Berlin Wall. The guards ask to see my official Games' badge, but I don't have one because I was never given one. As soon as they notice Sam sitting next to me though, they seem to relax. It isn't long before they're ribbing Sam for an autograph, and I may as well have vanished.

"Sorry about the hassle," one of the guards says to Sam, "but we've had to tighten security because of what's happening down in Birmingham."

I go stiff in my seat. He's talking about the Children's Crusade—the news was all over the papers a couple weeks ago. Peter has been following the developments and would sum up the articles for me over breakfast. Civil rights protests have been popping up all over the country; even in San Francisco where we've had sit-ins on Auto Row, but Birmingham has been the real focus of the movement. There've been loud calls for the city to desegregate, and the Children's Crusade was the latest development. Thousands of Black students marched out of their schools to apply pressure on the mayor, but what did they get for it? The police blasted them with high-powered firefighter hoses and hauled them off to jail. By the time my brother had finished reading the article, I was grinding my teeth.

"Some of those kids are younger than I am," Peter had said, his eyes wide.

"Those Birmingham pigs ought to be ashamed. Arresting schoolkids?"

Peter shushed me. "Maybe don't say *pigs* so loudly," he'd said, glancing across the street, where a cop car sometimes sits.

The window was shut tight, so we were in no danger of anyone hearing us, but I nodded anyway because I didn't want to upset him. I could tell that the article had shaken him.

"At least we don't live in the South." I'd gestured at the newspaper headline and tried to take it from him. "We don't have to worry about that happening here in California."

Without missing a beat he'd said, "That's only because we don't look like Mom."

Now that had really stumped me—because he was absolutely right. Both he and I know how the Chinese have been treated in this country. There's the Chinese Exclusion Act that forbade immigrants from entering the US for seventy years and wasn't repealed until 1943. Then, after the Cold War started, the FBI has kept close tabs on Chinese Americans, assuming that they must be secret spies for Chairman Mao. And let's not forget how the Chinese have been called dirty and diseased for generations. I think that's why our mother left her little backwater town in the first place. Plus, she'd wanted to fly airplanes, and most piloting schools wouldn't take on a girl like her.

The security guard leans against the car window and slides down his sunglasses. "We don't want a riot here in Washington. There were some SCLC protestors gathering by the stadium, but we told them to beat it," he says, referring to Dr. King's Southern Christian Leadership Conference. He waits for Sam and me to nod our heads in agreement.

I tell myself to keep quiet. Let his comment slide even though it makes my skin crawl. I'm only half white, after all. I shouldn't give him any extra reason to scrutinize me.

But then the guard goes on to say, "Some people just don't know their place anymore."

I narrow my eyes at him and the words shoot out of my mouth. "The police were jailing *children* down in Alabama. Maybe *you're* mixing up who doesn't know their place."

The guard startles, surprised at the challenge, and his gaze turns chilly. "You one of those beatniks?"

Sam clears his throat loudly. "Thanks for all your help. We sure do appreciate it," he says, using that smile of his to put the guard at ease and let our car through.

As our driver pulls forward, Sam gives me a look. "Didn't pin you as a beatnik."

"I'm not." Obviously. I don't recite poetry or listen to jazz or spend my weekends reading up on Eastern religions. "Do you see me wearing a beret?"

"Word of advice?"

I'm about to tell him no thanks, but Sam barrels on like usual.

"You don't have to say out loud everything that you're thinking," he says.

"You sound like my first-grade teacher."

"Haven't learned that lesson yet?"

"Oh, cool your chops, Kealey," I huff out. I know that he's teasing, but I'm not in the mood. He has no idea how much tongue biting I have to do all the time. Because I'm a girl. Because I'm not fully white. Because if I say everything that I think, we could lose customers at the shop or I could lose my place on varsity. Or worse. I've learned to bottle up all those feelings and take them out in the pit.

We finally enter the boundaries of the Pavilion, which resembles a spread from an architectural magazine. The buildings are all built in an ultra-modern style, like big boxes of concrete but balanced out with glossy windows. To soften the look, the landscapers have added plenty of lush grass and flower beds in between each building, popping in shades of purple and pink. We climb out of the car, and I shoulder my bag.

"Those are the dormitories ahead. Boys on the right; girls on the left." Sam gestures at two structures before us. The boys' dorm is about quadruple in size compared to the girls', like they ran out of poured concrete when they got around to making ours. "They'll give you your room assignment and badge at the registration desk. Remember to swipe your badge to access the elevators and stairwells. It took me a minute to figure that out."

I'm not really listening. My eyes sweep over the Pavilion and land on a grassy quad in front of the dormitories, about the size of a football field. There are a few mower bots making their way across the lawn, snipping at the grass as they go and flashing a red light whenever they approach a group of fighters lying in their path. I can tell where the fighters are from by the clothes that they're wearing—athletic jumpsuits broadcasted in their nation's colors and with their country's flags sewn onto the backs. I keep my eye out for a golden sickle and star—the Soviet's emblems—but come up empty.

"Hi there, Sam!" a girl calls out.

"Who's your friend?" another one asks in a flirty tone. From the looks of their uniforms, they're representing Austria and Switzerland respectively, and I can't help but roll my eyes. Everywhere he goes, Sam has fans.

"This here is Jo Linden of Team USA," Sam says back, flashing his stupid easy grin.

I poke him in the side before he drags me over to meet his pals. "What's the plan from here on out? Do we have a strategy in place for Purgatory or what?"

Sam stops waving at the girls and glances at a tall white guy walking toward us, who's wearing a tie and a suit jacket even in this swampy weather. "Why don't we ask the man himself?"

The fella in question halts in front of us, and I swear I do a double take. I know him. Or, rather, I *feel* like I know him, thanks to the number of hours I've watched the reels of his matches. But he's older now. There's a little bit of gray around his temples and there are crinkles around his eyes too, but there's no mistaking who he is.

"Been looking for you," the man says to Sam before he gives me a quick once-over.

"You're—" The name gets stuck in my throat. I can't wait to tell Peter about this. "You're Malcolm Maines."

He's a living legend. Peter has a poster of Malcolm hanging in our bedroom, a blown-up black-and-white picture of him at the '47 Games in Helsinki, emerging from his Goliath right after his win at the finals where he beat his Swiss opponent in under twenty minutes. He was the last American to win the Games and now he's my coach. I have to resist the temptation to ask him for an autograph.

Malcolm leans toward Sam. "You know the rules. Only fighters and coaching staff are allowed in the Pavilion, and we don't need any stories coming out that you've been breaking the rules." His eyes glide over toward the fence encircling the Pavilion, where I notice a few reporters filming television news segments. "So your friend here needs to scram."

I draw in a sharp breath when I realize what he's hinting at, and I immediately start shaking my head. "I'm not his friend," I say loudly.

"Ouch," Sam says, feigning a pained look.

Sam isn't helping this situation at all, so I take it into my own hands. "I'm Jo Linden, sir," I say to Malcolm, figuring that he'll start apologizing as soon as he hears my name.

But I've assumed incorrectly.

Something does seem to click in Malcolm's eyes, but the first words out of his mouth aren't *I'm sorry I assumed you were Sam's arm candy.* Instead he says, "You're Rochester's replacement. Didn't recognize you from the picture in your file."

I don't know what picture or file he's talking about, but he doesn't explain further. He merely nods at the building across the quad, a hulking thing made out of gray cement, like a giant piece of sidewalk but with windows. "That's the training center over there. Your new home for the next little while. So let's get you suited up, rookie."

7

I go stiff when I hear the word *rookie* come out of Malcolm's mouth, but I'm only being paranoid because he's already striding toward the training center and expecting us to follow.

Malcolm slows down a touch so that Sam and I can catch up. "I thought the two of you were supposed to get changed before you came back," he says, not too happy with our getups.

If it had been up to me, I would've tossed this gingham dress off as soon as we were finished with the pictures, but we didn't have time. "We came straight from the photo shoot, sir."

"You can drop the *sirs*. Just call him Coach like I do," Sam says to me with a wink before he slaps Malcolm on the shoulder. "Isn't that right, Coach?"

"You know full well that it should be Coach Maines," Malcolm grumbles, but I can tell that they have a rapport. After all, they've worked together for years. Amateur fighters typically spend the academic year representing our school teams, but if you're elite enough (and rich enough), the summer months are reserved for national and international tourneys—all of which are invite only and the Association dictates the guest list. As soon as Sam turned fourteen and became eligible for senior-level competition, Malcolm tapped him to represent the US at the North American Invitational, which Sam went on to win soundly. They've done dozens of matches together since then.

"There'll be uniforms in the locker rooms, but be quick about it. We're running behind schedule as it is," Malcolm says.

"Sure thing, Coach," I say, but I'm thinking to myself, *Gee, nice to meet you too.* I've heard that he demands a lot out of his fighters, but I didn't think he'd be so testy.

I sneak glances at him as we walk into the training center. Malcolm must be over thirty by now—I notice the crow's feet stamped at the corners of his eyes—but to me and the rest of America, he'll always be the youngest fighter in history to have won the Games, clocking in at fifteen years and fifteen days old. Even then he was already six-two and possessed that prized fighters' build, broad-shouldered and lean, a Greek god of the sport. Prior to the Games, he had won three World Championships, twice at the junior level and once as a senior, and the '47 Games was supposed to sky-rocket him to new levels of fame.

But it ended up being the highpoint of his fighting career.

After Helsinki, he blew out a knee and then broke a collarbone, a string of bad luck that kept him out of serious competition for the rest of his amateur eligibility. There was some hope that he'd mount a comeback when he went pro at age eighteen. He even headlined matches from Macau to Monte Carlo, but he never really got his fire back. A few years and a few more surgeries later, he was forced into an early retirement.

I doubt anyone would've blamed Malcolm if he'd bummed around a sandy beach with beach bunnies after that, but he immediately jumped into coaching. He nabbed an assistant's position on Team USA's junior division, which oversees fighters ages ten to fourteen, and rose up the ranks from there. In his short career, he has racked up three Junior World Championships titles and three Senior ones, the most any American coach has gotten. All he's missing is a victory at the Games, and he'll cement his name in the history books—the first to win as a fighter *and* as a coach.

But he has one last shot to accomplish that. Four years ago in Montreal, he led our team to a silver medal, losing to the USSR (who else?) in the final round. So the '63 Games will be Malcolm's swan song. Another second-place finish might as well be last when the Association—heck, the entire country—expects nothing but first.

We venture deeper into the training center, passing by weight rooms and dry saunas and an infirmary, and my eyes go wide as I take it all in. Small floor-waxing bots, no bigger than a shoebox, polish the linoleum to a shine. Another bot greets me inside the women's locker room, a boxy laundering machine the size of an oven that can wash, dry, and fold your used towel. It's top of the line too, judging by its shiny sleek frame. I'm betting the Association has spared no expense to make an impression on our international visitors—especially the Reds. As if to say, *Look at all this money we have, thanks to fabulous capitalism!*

I change into my training uniform—a snug white top and black pants. A patch of the American flag has been stitched onto my sleeve, but the corners are already lifting up, like it's been hastily sewn on. I frown, disappointed. I was hoping to wear something more polished and official-looking. Something with a little more red, white, and blue.

I sigh and start moving again, taking the exit that leads directly into the training room. Well, *room* isn't the right word for it. The space is massive, as big as a football stadium, and divided into twenty-five equal sections for each team. The size is so overwhelming that I have to consult a map to find where Team USA is located, which appears to be on the opposite corner of where I'm standing.

To get there I feel like I'm walking through the United Nations, striding past Canada and Mexico, Australia and Japan, Egypt and Brazil. Each section has been blocked off with portable partitions that soar over twenty feet high, which teams can later reconfigure to create a bigger space as others get eliminated. The partitions are thick enough that there's no way to see through them, but up ahead at Team China's section I notice a slight gap between two walls that haven't been lined up correctly. Out of curiosity, I slow down to take a little peek inside.

Last year in my World Events class, I had to write a report on modern China, and I try to remember what I had put in it. China hasn't appeared at the Games since 1927. That same year, a civil war broke out across their country, pitting the Communists against the Nationalists. The conflict stretched over two decades, and when the dust finally settled in '49, it was Chairman Mao and his Commies who were the victors. They had completely obliterated the Nationalists, rounding them all up before they could flee to Taiwan and putting them in "reeducation" camps that had little to do with learning, unless you count the lesson to never disagree with the Communist Party.

With Chairman Mao at the helm, the Chinese put up a big *KEEP OUT* sign to all Westerners and isolated themselves for a decade and a half, like a gigantic silkworm. But recently they've decided to poke their heads out again. They qualified for the Games a couple months back, and here they are now in Washington, DC, one more Communist country on American soil. That must be why I spot a pair of intimidating security guards strolling up and down this aisle in particular, keeping a close eye on them.

Through the gap in the partition, I spot a Chinese fighter maneuvering a cherry-red mecha. I don't see anything out of the ordinary. The fighter is warming up in a caged training pit, and I'm about to move on, when he suddenly breaks into a run, launches into a cartwheel, and curls into a perfect cannonball flip before landing neatly like an Olympic gymnast.

"Holy smokes," I whisper. I've never seen a fighter do that before. None of the newspaper polls have Team China making it out of Round 1, but maybe the Chinese will surprise us.

By the time I reach the training section for Team USA, I bet I've trekked over half a mile. There's a little confusion at the door since I don't have my badge yet, so the security guard posted there refuses me entry. I keep telling him that I'm Jo Linden, Ted's replacement, but he assumes that I'm one of Sam's rabid paper shakers and won't let me in. Eventually Malcolm has to intervene to get me inside, but not before I overpronounce my name to the guard so that he won't make the same mistake again.

I pause to get my bearings. I've stepped into a big square of a room, with a line of storage lockers along the back wall that hold tools and spare equipment and rows of esterium batteries that must've cost tens of thousands of dollars. There are two training pits side by side in front of me, each one the standard-size cube but made out of titanium versus the steel ones I'm used to. I'm itching to suit up and climb into the pit, but Malcolm stops me.

He frowns at my outfit. "You're not wearing a team uniform."

"But this is what I found in my locker, sir. I mean, Coach."

Malcolm calls over his assistants, three middle-aged white men whose names all coincidentally begin with J. There's a John and a Jimmy and a Joe, all of them around the same age and height too, and I decide to think of them as the Jays.

"We can't have her walking around like *this*," Malcolm says to them. "She looks like she walked out of some middle school tournament."

I feel my cheeks flame, even though this isn't my fault.

"Sorry about that, boss, but we had to special order her uniform and it won't arrive until tomorrow. We didn't have any in stock," one of the Jays replies.

"This is Team USA. Everywhere she goes she'll be representing the country," Malcolm says, and I find myself nodding along and thinking maybe he isn't as much of a grouch as I'd initially thought. Until he adds, "She's looking like some second-rate fighter out of Albania."

I look down at myself. What's that supposed to mean?

"Get this sorted out, all right? And where's that report on the Federovas I asked for?" Malcolm barks to the Jays. "And as for you, Linden, go get suited up."

"Yes, Coach," I say. My mood improves significantly as my eyes land on a brand-new Goliath that's calling my name, all polished up and top of the line. It's a mirror of the one used during the photo shoot, except this time I'll actually be able to try it out.

I approach the Goliath with my spine tingling. One of the Jays wheels a ladder toward me, but I won't need it. I've had more than enough practice climbing into cockpits—the trick is to slot your fingers in the hip joint and hoist yourself up. In under five seconds flat, I've already scaled the thing and slipped inside it.

"Do you need a hand in there?" a Jay calls up. "We weren't told what specific models you've used before so—"

"I'll be all right, but thanks!" I get to work strapping my arms and legs into place. As soon as the Goliath gets powered up, I lift the right leg to take a step, and I practically leap forward, forcing the assistants to careen out of the way.

"Whoa there. Easy, girl," I say to the Goliath, giddy with power. My mecha back home is so old that I have to exaggerate my movements to get it going, but this one? It mimics even the smallest of motions, like how its chest puffs in and out along with my breaths. It's that sensitive.

It's also very light due to its fancy titanium frame. This will take a little time to get used to since I've spent years training in steel Goliaths, but I'm already thinking about how much higher I'll be able to jump and how much faster I'll be able to run. A new rush of adrenaline pumps through me as I consider the possibilities.

I step into the empty training pit and figure Malcolm will join me soon enough. He's occupied with Sam at the moment, who's hanging from the top of his cage and swinging from bar to bar. One of the Jays comes over to lead me through a simple warm-up, and after we're finished, I run through a few exercises of my own to work out the kinks in my muscles after being stuck on a plane overnight. I focus on some martial art moves like the simple hiza geri, a Japanese-style knee strike, and the more complicated ushiro geri, a combination back kick that my karate teacher, Michael, particularly favored. If only he could see me now. Right after I'd worked my way up to a brown belt, he joined the Marines for the better pay, but he died during the '58 Lebanon Crisis. It wasn't from hostile fire or anything like that; he and his buddy had gone out for a swim and drowned. But I think of him every time I use one of the stances he taught me.

I've worked up a decent sweat by the time I'm done, but Malcolm still hasn't come over to my pit. Instead, he sends one of the Jays—I think it's John—to spar with me, which I do gladly because I want to give this mecha a proper go. John surprises me with his speed and strength, but his stamina is limited. I give him the run around inside the pit, using the strategy that Dad has instilled in me from day one, letting him try to catch me and burning up his energy.

When he starts struggling for breath, I strike. I employ the handy ushiro geri, nailing him square in the chest and sending him careening backward before I pounce. I press my Goliath over his, count to five, and that's the match. I couldn't have planned it better myself. It's excellent fighting. I doubt even my dad would have many notes to give me.

But when I get onto my feet and glance over at Malcolm, he isn't looking my way. I don't think he has caught my scrimmage at all because he's lecturing Sam and using a handheld chalkboard to map out strategies.

My jaw clenches. I'm used to getting heckled in the pit.

I'm not used to getting ignored.

I march myself across the room. I know that he's Malcolm Maines, an American legend. I also know that he's my new coach and that I should make a good impression. But if I can fly across the country and come to training on barely any asleep, can't he spare a little time to actually coach me?

"Just finished up the scrimmage," I say to Malcolm, trying hard to mask the irritation in my voice. "I won by the way."

"Good. Great. What time is it anyway?" Malcolm says, distracted.

His face shifts when one of the Jays alerts him that it's nearly eleven. "We better get going."

"Go where?" I ask, crossing my arms.

"To the luncheon. Didn't you read your folder?" Malcolm says with a frown. Behind him, I see Sam trying not to laugh, and I wish he were standing closer so I could drive an elbow into his gut.

"What luncheon?" I ask, throwing my hands up in the air. My Goliath mimics me, which makes the move even more dramatic.

Sam coughs to cover up his chuckle. "It's the welcome luncheon for the fighters, along with their coaches and ambassadors and other fancy-pants sort of people. The International Committee hosts it," he says, referring to the governing body of the Games that has over thirty members. The full name of the organization is the International Committee of the Pax Games, or the IC for short, and its main duties include choosing the host cities, overseeing the qualification tournaments, and evidently hosting unnecessary luncheons.

"We have to cut our session short to attend some stuffy banquet?" The question goes flying out of my mouth, which causes Malcolm's frown to deepen, and I wish I could snatch it back. My dad has always said that my mouth will get me in trouble, and here I am about to screw up the Games before I even get in the ring.

"Attendance is mandatory. Senator Appleby has made that clear," Malcolm says brusquely. He cuts a look at Sam. "Not a drop of alcohol today. I've heard that the CEO of Baron's will be there."

"I'll be a choir boy, Coach," Sam says before his eyes brighten, like he has remembered something. Turning to me he adds, "I could introduce you to Mr. Francis if you want. Weren't you asking me earlier about getting an endorsement? I bet Baron's would be interested since they're launching a ladies' line of sneakers."

My face turns red. Sam might think that he's helping me out, but now I look like some money-grubbing opportunist in front of Malcolm. It isn't like I *want* to shill toothpaste or boxes of fruit punch or ladies' sneakers in this case.

"Malcolm always has to vet potential deals," Sam explains to me. He doesn't seem to notice the sour look on our coach's face, like he's smelling curdled milk. "The sponsors have to go through him to comply with all those long and boring rules for amateur fighters."

"I do indeed. Why don't you let me take over from here?" Malcolm says dryly, then dismisses Sam to get showered and changed. He waits until I've climbed out of the Goliath before he continues. "Joining this team is an honor. Not some opportunity to rake in the cash."

My cheeks burn hotter than before. I could skewer Sam for putting me in this position, but since he isn't within strangling distance, I round my shoulders and nod. "You don't have to worry, Coach. I'm here to fight."

"So you asked Sam about sponsorships because . . ."

I know I don't have anything to be ashamed about, but that doesn't stop the blood from rushing into my face. Malcolm has barely met me, so how am I supposed to launch into my family's sob story about unpaid bills and eviction notices? I don't want him to see me as a charity case, especially compared to Sam, who probably slept in a solid gold cradle as a baby.

"Saving up for college," I tell him, which sounds like a decent excuse. But then I think about Sam and his endorsements with Baron's and who knows what else, and yet he doesn't seem to have gotten the third degree. "If Sam can have sponsors, why can't I too?"

"We aren't talking about Sam." Malcolm sighs through his nose. "Look, Senator Appleby might've thrown her husband's weight around to get you here to Washington, but this isn't her team. It's mine. You want an endorsement? Then you better prove yourself in the pit and listen to what I tell you to do. Show me that you're capable of that, and maybe I'll sign off on a deal or two when this is all over. Understood?"

"Crystal clear. I can do that."

He seems to take this as an open invitation to order me around. "You can start by studying the folder I'll send up to your room tonight. You'll find the team's code of conduct in there, and I expect you to abide by it during your time at the Games. You're representing our country, so you need to look the part." His eyes skim over me and apparently find me lacking. "Back straight. Hair combed. *Smile*. Or at least stop scowling all the time. You ought to speak the part too. In private you can rant and rave about the Vietnam War or King's letter from jail, but in public? Don't get political. Talk about how gosh darn excited you are to be here, not some deep dive into what's in the news, like that mailman who died down South."

"Who was *murdered*," I mutter. Malcolm is talking about William Moore, a white postal worker who was protesting segregation in Alabama last month when someone shot him twice in the head. When Peter read about the death in the paper, he asked me if I thought the killer would get arrested, and I said that we'd have to wait and see. But deep down, I think we both knew that no one would ever get charged. And no one has.

Malcolm shakes his head. "That's Exhibit A of what exactly you *shouldn't* do, rookie. So I'll repeat myself: Don't get political like you did with the entrance guards today."

My eyes fly toward his. How does he know that? He must have spies planted all over the city to tattle on his fighters.

"Okay, okay," I say with a sigh. I don't like the thought of being muzzled, but I'll put that muzzle on myself if it means saving the shop and our home. "I'll talk about the weather and my family."

"Actually, I'm glad you bring that up." Malcolm pauses like he's searching for how best to phrase what he wants to say. "If anyone asks about your family, stick to stories about your dad and brother. Don't mention your mom at all."

I blink fast at him. "What—why?"

"For one thing, your parents weren't married when they had you and your brother."

"How did you know that?" I blurt. He really does have a small ring of spies, doesn't he? Because it's true what he said. When my parents got together in '46, it was illegal for whites and Chinese to marry. The California Supreme Court ended up striking those laws two years later, but I guess my mom and dad never got around to getting hitched. Maybe they got too busy to head down to city hall or maybe they didn't care about making it official.

"I do my due diligence on my fighters," Malcolm explains, "which is how I also learned about your mother's *background*."

I flush. My heart feels strange and fluttery, and my palms feel hot. He doesn't spell out what he means by "background," but I know exactly what he's referring to. I'd thought that my race had slipped by unnoticed because Senator Appleby hadn't mentioned it, and I let my guard down because of it.

"Like I said I do my research, unlike the senator's staff apparently," he says as he scrutinizes my face. "Although if I'm being honest, I wouldn't have guessed from looking at you that your mother was Oriental."

I may not be my mom's number one fan, but he makes it sound like she was some sort of rug. "Gee, thank you," I reply, unable to hide my sarcasm.

"You should take that as a positive. Wilma Rudolph might be the fastest woman in the world, but how many commercials have you seen her in?"

As if I hadn't noticed. Rudolph won three gold medals and a bronze at the '56 and '60 Summer Olympics, and yet she has had precisely zero sponsors. You won't find her face on the front of a Wheaties box—because she's Black.

"I'm only telling you how it is," he continues like he understands my plight. "When my grandfather immigrated to the States, he knew he better change his name from Manikowski to Maines. He did what he had to do and so should you. Endorsement deals don't fall out of the sky, all tied up with a pretty bow. Companies are choosy about which athletes they work with."

In other words, sponsors don't want a half-Chinese fighter selling cornflakes and coffee beans. They want someone who looks all-American.

All white.

"Glad we're agreed on that," Malcolm says, even though I haven't said a thing. He starts heading toward the exit but pauses halfway there, only long enough to glance back at me.

"By the way," he says, "welcome to the Games, rookie."

"It's Jo," I reply, but he doesn't hear me.

8

After I take a scalding hot shower in the locker room, I wrap a towel around myself and wipe the fog from the bathroom mirror. I've got about five minutes before the hairdresser knocks down the door to primp me for this luncheon, but for now I'm blessedly alone. In the quiet, I breathe in the wet air and try to forget what Malcolm told me about my mom, but it's impossible.

Ever since she died I've trained myself not to think about her. It was too painful at first, and then it made me too angry. So ignoring my mother's memory was the next best option.

I stare at my reflection, relieved that I don't find a trace of her there. I've always felt a little bad for Peter because he takes more after her in appearance, even if it isn't by much. What's it like for him to look in the mirror every day and see pieces of her staring back?

But if that has bothered my brother, he has never mentioned it to me. If anything, it was the opposite. When he was younger, he'd ask all sorts of questions. What was Mom's favorite color? What did her voice sound like when she sang? Eventually he stopped pestering Dad and me about it because I didn't know the answers while Dad would clam up and say he'd forgotten something at the shop. We stopped talking about the fourth member of our family, and I preferred it that way. It felt like justice. Mom didn't want to be a part of us; why should we make room for her at the table?

So Malcolm's request should be an easy one for me to follow. It's not like I *want* to talk about my mother to the press or bring up her "background." Why should any of that matter since I hardly remember her anyway? She's practically a stranger to me—and one that I'd rather forget.

I sigh and glance away from the mirror. Dad has never asked Peter and me to flat-out hide that we're part Chinese, but we have this silent agreement that we don't bring it up with other people. Not at school. Not to our customers. Not even to Mrs. Watters. It's safer this way, I've told myself. Look at the Chinese Exclusion Act. Or simply turn on the nightly news to catch Governor Wallace chanting, *Segregation now, segregation tomorrow, segregation forever.* He might've been talking about Black people down in Alabama, but it's obvious that he wouldn't let my mother enter that schoolhouse he was standing in front of.

Or girls like me for that matter.

But Malcolm's advice pricks at me. I'm not sure why, considering I don't feel very Chinese, but it's probably because of the unfairness of it all. No one cares if Sam's family emigrated from Ireland or if Ted Rochester has roots in Germany. For some reason, that's all fine and something to be proud of. And yet if the press catches wind of where my mother's ancestors lived, that'll get written up in the headlines and I'll have to kiss any sponsorships goodbye. Thinking about that difference makes my stomach clench.

The mirror has fogged back up again, blurring my reflection until my face is only a haze. I don't wipe it away though this time.

An hour and a half later, I arrive at the historic Manger Hay-Adams Hotel, where the luncheon will be held. The elevator opens onto the hotel's rooftop terrace, and I make my grand entrance in a teal-blue dress, with a skirt so full of taffeta that I can barely fit through the doorframe. I feel like an ostrich considering the amount of plumage around my midsection.

As much as I don't want to be here, I do have to admit that the view is spectacular. The White House is only a couple blocks away and the Washington Monument is just a bit farther down. The hotel itself has also been decked out to the nines. The vases overflow with peonies and hydrangeas the size of my head while a string quartet plays classical music—probably Mozart or Vivaldi, though I couldn't tell the difference. The guests aren't looking too shabby either—the men in their dark suits and the ladies in their silk and satin gowns even though it's the middle of the day.

I can't help but feel like a sad old dandelion compared to the rest of them. None of the other women seem to be stumbling in their heels or tugging at their bodices. The dress I'm wearing has a sweetheart neckline, and the stylists told me that it was "modestly flirty," but it feels strange for me to expose any skin beneath my collarbone. And yet when I cross my arms, that only seems to draw more attention to my bustline.

"I give up," I mumble to myself before I search for something to eat since I'm starving.

Flat-topped service bots roll slowly up and down the hallway, carrying bubbling flutes of champagne and platters of hors d'oeuvres that make my mouth water sweet onion tarts small enough to eat in one bite, slices of baguette topped with pâté, and poached baby artichokes. I take one of each and start feasting.

"Don't they feed you back home?" Sam says, sauntering up to me as I've bitten into another onion tart.

"Speak for yourself," I say through crumbs, not caring if I'm being unladylike because it's only him I'm talking to. Besides, he's holding a plate piled high with cheese and olives and rolled-up cold cuts. "Careful with all that cheddar. It'll make you bloat up before the opening parade."

His eyes go wide because I don't think he's used to girls talking to him about bloating, but he laughs. "I appreciate the advice." There's a glint in his eye when he asks, "Does it come from first-hand experience?"

"No," I say flatly and humorlessly, which only seems to delight him more. I pivot away from Sam and sweep my gaze around the room to keep him at bay, but I soon realize that it's a mistake. People are looking at us. Or at me in particular. I'm the new kid, after all. The rookie.

"Eh, you'll get used to the gawking," Sam says, not taking my warning and eating a big bite of cheese. "Ignore it and they'll stop."

But they don't. Soon, more fighters start whispering and eyeing me up and down since I've crashed their little shindig. Most of them have spent a full year of qualifying to reach the Games. They first had to get through their own nationwide trials that whittled down their respective competitor pools. Then they had to survive a dozen international tournaments that determined the top twenty-five countries that would enter the '63 Games. It's a grueling process of elimination and hand-wringing, but even after you've been selected, there's more work to do. Drills. Scrimmages. Watching countless reels of other fighters to pick up their tics and sniff out their weaknesses.

I'm the unknown quantity though—the wild card coming in at the last second. They don't know what to expect out of me in the pit, whether I'm left-handed or right-handed, whether I favor punches or kicks, whether I come out of the gate swinging or if I prefer to hang back.

"Anyway, we should go make the rounds. Say hello to the guests," Sam says.

"You go on ahead," I say, busying myself with a bite of a potato croquette that I picked up from one of the service bots. It melts in my mouth, and I wish I had grabbed a few more.

"Come on, it might not be fun, but it'll be educational."

"Educational how?"

Sam doesn't answer that. Instead he starts pulling me toward a group of fighters on the balcony. "Look, Team Britain is standing by a tray of onion tarts. I can do the talking while you eat."

I sigh but follow him, mostly because I'm still hungry after our training session and these little bites of food are barely filling me up. At least I'll be able to eat all the tarts I want since Sam will keep the conversation going based on how much he likes to flap his lips.

We've walked about ten paces when my foot slips in my heel, and I go a little sideways and almost bump into Team Senegal.

"Pardon me," I say, and they wave it off like it's no problem.

I can't help but notice that the two of them are only a handful of nonwhite faces at this luncheon, along with teams like Iran and Egypt. And me. Although only Malcolm and I know that secret. I wonder how the Senegalese feel about coming to a city like Washington, which was only desegregated nine years ago. If my mom had visited back then, which bathroom would she have used? Thinking of that makes me want to grab a glass of wine from one of the bots and down it fast.

No alcohol, Malcolm would chide me.

And don't bring up your mother's background.

Just like that I'm in a prickly mood again, but I have to spread a smile across my face because I need to look like a pitch-perfect hostess—because Malcolm or one of his little birdies is keeping tabs on me.

Sam sidles up to a group of European fighters, four of them total, and all of them from fellow NATO nations. There are the two boys from Team Britain, both of them in smart-looking navy blazers, alongside a fighter from West Germany, who's probably the tallest person at this banquet, standing at six foot six. I don't catch his name though because I'm too busy scowling at him for using his height to peer down the necklines of every female in sight, me included.

"Flake off, buddy," I say to him, with enough oomph in my voice that he slinks toward the only other female in our little group.

The girl in question is Giselle Boucher of Team France, and she reminds me of a swan with her long pale neck and her formfitting dress draped in white feathers. She's the picture of cool elegance—I've heard that she's dating the French rocker Johnny Hallyday too—but when she catches the Ogler trying to peek down her cleavage, she jabs an elbow into his stomach, hard enough to make him choke on his bite of crudité. When he's done coughing, she thrusts her half-empty champagne glass at him and tells him to get her a refill.

Looks like the Ogler just learned that swans can have a pretty sharp bite.

Giselle greets Sam and kisses him on both cheeks. "You look very handsome tonight, Samuel."

"Oh, this old thing?" Sam says, tugging at the cuffs of his very new tuxedo, custom-made for him.

"You are Ted's replacement, no?" Giselle says, turning to me. "It's wonderful to have another girl at the Games."

Her words are kind, but I can tell that she's scrutinizing me too, trying to snuff out something useful for her advantage in the pit. The two Brits are doing the same, sizing me up. I guess I should be used to this type of treatment—it happens at most of my matches during the school year since I'm such a novelty. But I usually deal with the stares by climbing into my Goliath and getting down to business in the pit. There's nowhere to hide on the terrace though, not even behind my thousands of layers of taffeta. My only defense is to stand up straight and pretend to look bored.

"So has anyone spotted the Soviets out in the wild yet?" Sam asks.

One of the Brits, whose nose looks like it has been broken a couple times but not properly set, shakes his head. "I heard the Soviets are training early in the morning or late at night," he says, his accent threading through each word. He introduces himself to me as Albie and says that he's from a city called Essex, which I couldn't place on a map to save my life, but there's a familiarity to him, a roughness that I recognize from growing up in a big city.

"And when the Soviets aren't training, they're hiding away in their nest," Giselle adds with a laugh. When I look confused, she goes on to explain that the Eastern Bloc countries—the USSR, Romania, Bulgaria, Czechoslovakia, East Germany, and Yugoslavia—have insisted on having their own floors in the dormitories, away from the rest of us riffraff.

"Communist Row," I say, thinking that my comment is pretty clever, but the others don't seem to hear me. They're suddenly sneaking glances at the company that has joined us on the balcony.

It's a small group of Commie fighters. The Federovas are nowhere to be seen, but I recognize the others from last summer's World Championships, which Peter and I watched on our TV before Dad had to pawn it. I spot fourteen-year-old Mihaela Lazarescu of Romania, one of the youngest at the Games, and next to her I notice the Tilov twins of Bulgaria. The oldest and biggest of the bunch though is Lukas Sauer of East Germany, a real refrigerator of an eighteen-year-old, brawny and thick and currently ranked number three internationally, right behind Lidiya at number one and Sam at number two.

Sam tilts his head toward Lukas. "Anyone know if old Sauer Face has fully recovered from that knee injury he got at the Euro Cup?"

"I saw him running along the track yesterday. His knee wasn't even taped," says Albie.

Sam sips his drink and makes conversation about the other fighters that have arrived. Team Switzerland. Team Iran. Team Japan. He casually asks if anyone in our circle has faced off against the others, and I realize what Sam had meant earlier when he said that our conversation would be educational—because he's gathering intel about our competition.

I guess he isn't as meatheaded as I had thought.

But Sam can't dig up clues on all the fighters. Some remain complete mysteries.

"What have any of you heard about Team China?" I ask the group, remembering the fighter I glimpsed at training today, the one doing flips inside the pit.

Sam points out the Chinese team to me—a boy and a girl. The two of them look like they've been dropped into Disneyland for the first time, their eyes bright and their mouths open. The boy marvels at a service bot that's tasked with collecting empty glasses and used napkins while the girl can't stop gaping at all the food. She takes a nibble of shrimp cocktail, and I watch a smile creep onto her face as the spicy sauce hits her tongue. She finishes it off in one big bite before looking around a little embarrassed.

"You sure she's here for the Games?" I ask. The Chinese girl is tiny, barely five feet tall. And with her hair pulled back into a braid and not a speck of makeup on her face, she looks like she's about Peter's age. "She can't be fourteen, can she?"

"As a matter of fact, she just had her birthday a few weeks ago," the other Brit chimes in, in an accent so fancy that he ought to be holding a teacup with his pinkie sticking straight out. He introduces himself by his full name—all four parts of it. Fitz-Lloyd Foster Hughes III. I'm surprised that he isn't wearing a hat with a feather in it. "In any case, it shouldn't matter. Team China will likely get eliminated during the arena. They only squeaked into the Games because South Africa got the boot."

That's right. South Africa had initially qualified for the Games, but the IC declared that their team could only participate if they condemned apartheid. When the South African government refused, they were barred from the competition, meaning a slot opened up for the next qualifying nation, which happened to be China.

I peer at the Chinese team again. "Wonder why they're keeping to themselves," I say, noticing how the other Communists, like Lukas Sauer and the Bulgarians, haven't invited the Chinese into their little circle.

"Oh, they were like that at the World Championships last year too. China and the USSR had a—how do you say it?" Giselle asks Sam. "A falling-in?"

"A falling-out," Sam replies.

"Yes, a falling-out. The Chinese don't consider the Soviets to be *real* Communists," Giselle whispers to me, relishing the gossip.

"How do you mean?" I ask.

"Mao was a big admirer of Stalin." Giselle makes a fist. "Because Stalin was strong and firm." Then she slams her fist into her open palm. "And cruel. But Khrushchev is softer. He has overturned many of Stalin's laws and has tried to make friends with the West. With your President Kennedy."

"God forbid," Sam says, laughing softly. "Ol' Nikita has lost his way according to the Chinese."

I guess I don't see much of a difference—the Soviets and Chinese are both Communist, aren't they? But it looks like this dispute between Mao and Khrushchev has already trickled down to the fighting pit, and it will end up hurting the Chinese team much more than the Soviets. The Federovas will have plenty of allies in the Purgatory round to cushion them from attack, but the Chinese will be on their own, which usually means that you're doomed.

I'm thinking about the arena and what our own strategy should be when Giselle sidles up to me and gestures at Team China, in particular the female fighter who's still trying out the hors d'oeuvres. Her plate is full of onion tarts and cut fruit, and now she picks up a wheat cracker topped with pâté from another service bot.

"Poor thing. I bet she hasn't seen so much food in years." Giselle's voice drops to a whisper. "Because of the famine."

I don't understand. "Famine?"

"My uncle is a diplomat in Hong Kong, and he said that there has been a terrible famine in China. Millions dead."

My mouth suddenly feels dry, and I have to force down my bite of mozzarella, which soon feels like a brick in my stomach. Why haven't I heard of this famine before? Peter definitely would've mentioned it to me since he's such a bookbuster. Or maybe Giselle is getting her numbers mixed up. "You're sure? Millions?"

"My uncle would not lie," she sniffs. "Mao is trying to cover it up. He says that it's only a minor drought."

I know I should look away, but now I can't stop sneaking glances at Team China. Do they get enough to eat back home? Did they know anyone who died?

My thoughts are interrupted when the Ogler returns with Giselle's drink. He notices that we've been talking about Team China and says with a smirk, "They must be looking for some Oriental food—rice with roasted dog."

I go cold all over. Comments like his aren't new to me. I've heard it all before—how the Chinese are dirty, how they're taking jobs away, how San Francisco ought to send them back to where they came from, even though they've been in California for generations. Like my mom.

I'm tempted to grab his glass of club soda and pour it over his head.

Or wipe that grin off his face with a one-two punch.

But I have to tamp down that urge. Suppress it real deep. 'Cause I doubt I'll get an endorsement if I take a swing at another fighter.

"Looks like lunch is starting," I say, and march myself toward the tables before I do something I'll regret.

Turns out, Team USA is at table 10, near the very middle of the banquet space. As soon as I find my seat, there's a waiter scooting in my chair while a bot rolls over with a folded napkin. I've never eaten at a place so fancy before; growing up, we considered it a real treat whenever Dad took us to the Silver Diner and let us order the meat loaf special. I have to remind myself to keep my elbows off the table and to ask for the saltshaker instead of reaching across the table for it.

I'm sandwiched next to Sam to my right and to my left is Senator Appleby, who's wearing a simple black shift dress that has been fancied up with pearls. I'm relieved that Malcolm has been seated at table 7 with a few other coaches because now I won't have to play nice with him for the rest of the night.

Senator Appleby asks me about my flight and compliments Sam on his tux before she introduces us to the white-haired man sitting to her left.

"This is Minister Tran. He has recently been appointed by the

South Vietnamese government as their minister of trade," she explains. "He's here in Washington to attend the signing of the Washington-Moscow Accord, but he made sure to arrive early to catch a few matches."

"Wow, I didn't realize that South Vietnam had made it into the Games," I say.

Sam clears his throat and whispers to me, "They didn't actually," which makes my cheeks glow cherry red.

Minister Tran graciously takes my mistake in stride. "Perhaps one day. It's a dream of mine to see my country qualify for the Pax Games."

"I'm sure you'll get there very soon," Senator Appleby says, taking the basket of rolls and passing it on to him. "As I was telling you before, I would love to set up a few mecha fighting schools throughout South Vietnam. You have plenty of esterium, and I can search for funding to send a shipment of sports-grade Goliaths for your youth to use."

That's awfully generous of her, and I'm thinking I wouldn't mind one of those mechas for myself if she could spare one.

Minister Tran's eyes light up too. "That would be most welcome. My granddaughter is nine and learning how to fight, but she has been using an older Canadian model."

I'm about to tell him that I was about her age when I first started the sport, but then a young woman taps the minister on the shoulder. She has a charming smile with dimples to boot, and she introduces herself as Envoy Yu of China.

"May we speak for a minute, Minister? I bring word from Ambassador Fang, who sends his regards," she says.

Minister Tran, however, shifts uncomfortably. "Perhaps after lunch—"

"It would only take a minute, sir." Her words are polite and her smile widens, but there's a newfound iron in her voice, like she can't take no for an answer.

"Minister Tran and I are a little busy at the moment, but maybe you can circle back later, Envoy Yu," Senator Appleby cuts in, sensing the minister's apprehension. "I see that General Westmoreland has arrived with his wife. Shall we go say hello, Minister? I know that he would be delighted to meet you."

It's clear that Senator Appleby is trying to give Envoy Yu the slip, but Envoy Yu follows them for a few steps before finally giving up.

I toss a glance at Sam. "Who would've thought that Minister Tran would be the life of the party?"

Sam sips at his iced tea. "I'm not shocked. Everyone's trying to get chummy with him because they want to make a trade deal."

"For the esterium, I know."

"Apparently the veins discovered in South Vietnam are completely untouched. Virgin mines." He wags his brows at me when he says the word *virgin*, like he's in the fifth grade. I roll my eyes. "It's why Kennedy was so eager beaver to call for a truce to the war. Esterium makes the world go round, you know."

There he goes again acting like a know-it-all when this is common information. But he has a point. It's true that esterium veins are coveted worldwide. Here in the States, the federal government controls over half the mines in the Dakotas, but at some point, those are going to empty out. No wonder Senator Appleby was buttering up Minister Tran like a warm dinner roll. She wants those resources for the US, and she isn't afraid to dangle free Goliaths to sweeten the pot.

"So what does Khrushchev get out of the treaty? You'd think that he would want those mines for himself," I say.

"Hard to say. I've heard some of his advisers are urging him against the Accord for that very reason, but Khrushchev wants out of the war in Vietnam since he has funneled too much money into it already."

I think the world is breathing a sigh of relief that the war will come to an end before it gets the chance to intensify. Peter might only be thirteen, but in five short years he'd be eligible for the draft.

Lunch begins in earnest, and a line of waiter bots brings out each course on silver trays, like something out of an Elizabeth Taylor movie. We start off with a chilled beet soup topped with crumbles of goat cheese, followed by a bitter salad that I don't care for much, and then comes our choice of prime rib or New England lobster. I opt for the lobster because I've never had it before, and I make my dad proud by eating every single bite. I'm tempted to unzip my dress a little because it's feeling awfully tight just as Sam dares me to finish off another bread roll and says, if I do it, he'll go skinny dipping in the Lincoln Memorial

Reflecting Pool. He pouts when I tell him no thanks. I think he relishes the idea of scandalizing the tourists who might see him in his birthday suit.

The dessert course is soon served—a miniature white chocolate cake formed into the shape of the US Capitol, sitting in a pool of raspberry puree—and I've barely dug my spoon into my dome when the elevators pop open and a sudden hush spreads through the terrace.

Out step four men in stark black suits, followed closely behind by the Federova sisters, who split off in opposite directions. Zoya heads to the powder room while Lidiya strides up to the nearest service bot carrying champagne glasses. She promptly takes two, and I'm guessing that she must be saving one for somebody, but then she proceeds to down one and sips at the other.

Talk about making an entrance.

I set my napkin down on the table and get ready to stand up when Sam stops me.

"Don't tell me that you're going to talk to them," he says, glaring knives at Lidiya.

"Malcolm said we had to be good hosts," I reply. To be honest though, I want to satisfy my own curiosity and meet the most notorious fighters in the world. They're on our turf, after all.

Sam grumbles something unintelligible under his breath but comes along with me for the ride, threading around the tables. I manage to intercept Zoya after she has reappeared from the powder room, and I introduce myself through her interpreter. The

Federovas obviously know Sam already, but I'm an absolute stranger to them.

"I'm Jo Linden," I tell her, and I add a little extra oomph to my voice when I say, "Newest member of Team USA."

If Zoya is surprised by the news, she doesn't show it. Her face remains as placid as a frozen lake while we shake hands. She's uncharacteristically elegant for a mecha fighter, with her arms and legs as lithe as a dancer's. I've heard that some Soviet fighters are trained in classical ballet, which may sound silly, but take a look at what a ballerina can do with their body and you'll start to understand how it comes in handy. They're limber and balanced and have the stamina of a rhinoceros. I'll keep that in mind when I face her in the arena.

"Welcome to Washington," I say, and Zoya thanks me with an obligatory smile.

We don't even get that much effort from Lidiya.

"Hello, Lidiya," Sam says. His easygoing tone is nowhere to be seen, and I imagine that he's replaying their match at the World Championships last summer in his head.

He had fought beautifully for most of that game, all power and muscle, and he really seemed to have the upper hand because Lidiya was starting to look sluggish. About forty minutes in, she began to scale the bars of the cage and he had followed a step behind her, ready to yank her down for the kill, but then suddenly she reversed course. Dropping down a rung, she stomped on top of Sam's head and knocked him clean off the bars. Down he fell, thirty feet in total, and as soon as he hit the ground, she was right on top of him, pinning him before he knew what hit him. To add insult to injury, even after the ref had declared her the winner, she'd refused Sam's attempt at a friendly handshake. She had left him standing there in the pit, with his hand extended, while she strode away.

Lidiya doesn't deign Sam with a hello or a wave in return. She yawns instead—and I'm pretty sure that it's fake—which clearly gets under Sam's skin because I notice a large vein pulsing on his forehead.

"It's nice to meet you, Lidiya," I say a little too loudly to get her attention. Her gaze finally flickers toward me before it flits to the plated desserts and fixes on them. I guess a plate of cake is more interesting than I am.

Sam gives me a look that seems to say, *See what I told you?* But I'm not finished with Lidiya just yet.

I angle my body so that she has no choice but to look at me. With a syrupy smile pinned onto my lips, I say, "Let us know if you need anything."

Lidiya waits for the interpreter to translate before she thinks up a reply, which she delivers in English with her lips quirked on one side:

"You can polish the winner's trophy for me."

9

After my little exchange with Lidiya, I'm ready to make a beeline to the training center and punch some metal so hard that it flies into tomorrow, but my itinerary for the rest of the day is relentless. The luncheon stretches past three o'clock, and then I have to head to a short press conference, where Malcolm does most of the talking. I barely get to say that I'm looking forward to representing our country before I'm whisked off to a meet and greet with IC members, followed by a dinner with the coaching staff, and capped off with a moonlit bus tour of Washington with the other fighters.

By the time I've returned to the Pavilion, I'm about to fling myself in my dorm room and dive into bed before I remember that I'd promised Peter I'd call home.

Hauling myself onto my feet, I hurry down the hallway toward the common area on my floor, which has a single telephone. The dorm matron had given me a tour of the place earlier, in between the luncheon and the press conference, which didn't take very long because the girls' dormitory is small. There are three floors of bedrooms, with a total of twenty-four rooms, but the place is far from full because there are eleven female fighters in contention this year.

I'd hoped to make my call and slip into bed, but there's a line for the phone even at this late hour. A Brazilian fighter is using it now, and the girl from Team China is queued up behind her, standing alongside another East Asian woman who looks familiar to me, but I can't quite place her. They're both holding mugs of tea.

"You're Josephine, right? I'm Envoy Yu," the East Asian woman says, turning toward me.

A light switches on in my memory and I recognize her now; she was the lady at the luncheon who tried to speak to Minister Tran. She looks to be in her midtwenties, with black hair that has been bobbed at the chin. I remember her dimples too, which appear whenever she smiles, which is frequently.

She continues. "I'm a member of the Chinese delegation, and this is Zhu Rushi, one of our fighters on the team."

I shake both their hands, and I notice Rushi struggles to meet my eye, making me think that she might be shy.

"It is pleasing to meet you," Rushi says slowly, overenunciating each word.

"It is *a pleasure* to meet you," Envoy Yu gently corrects her. To me, she says, "I've been helping Rushi with her English. We've had lessons every day since the Chairman approved her selection to the Games." Her eyes positively glitter when she mentions the Chairman.

My guard goes up. After spending my life doing duck-and-cover drills at school and wondering when the Communists might attack, I'm on the defensive since there are two of them right in front of me. But Rushi is just a kid. And Envoy Yu seems more like an overexcited missionary who's about to slide me a brochure on communism with Mao's face on the cover. They seem pretty harmless.

Envoy Yu keeps making conversation while we wait for the phone. "I believe you're in the room by ours. I'm in two-two-zero and Rushi is in two-two-one."

"I'm in two-two-two," I say, surprised. I'd figured that the dormitory was only for fighters, not coaches or staff or envoys. I could've misheard her though. "Did you say that you're staying in two-two-zero?"

"Yes, our delegation thought this would be best due to Rushi's young age and that this is her first time abroad," Envoy Yu says, but I get the feeling there's another reason she's glued to Rushi's side. The Chinese government probably wants to keep a close eye on their fighters to make sure that they don't embarrass the Chairman. I wish I could ask Rushi what she thinks about having a nanny assigned to her, but her face is hard to read and partially obscured by the mug she's sipping from, which gives off a sweet flowery scent.

Envoy Yu must notice me eyeing the cup because she's quick to jump in again. "Would you like some tea? There's fresh water in the kettle." She nods at the little kitchenette in the room that features a sink, a two-burner stove, and a coffee-making bot that can mix in your preference of sugar and cream. "You can use some of our tea leaves."

"You brought your own tea? From China?"

"Your Western tea is . . ." Rushi seems to struggle for the right word. "Weak."

I laugh out loud, earning me a glare from the Brazilian fighter, who has been locked in a serious conversation with her boyfriend on the phone. Envoy Yu, however, looks horrified at Rushi's choice of adjective. Under her breath, she says something to Rushi in Mandarin, making Rushi cast her eyes downward.

"My apologies," Rushi says to me. "I didn't mean to offend."

"You weren't wrong exactly," I say, considering that the only tea that I ever drink is the iced variety, but she looks too chastened to reply.

Envoy Yu peppers me with polite questions until the telephone opens up, and the two of them put in a call to Beijing. When it's finally my turn, I dial the number for the shop, but the other end rings and rings and eventually I give up. And now I'm worried. Did Peter not hear me calling or is something more serious going on, like the phone company disconnecting our line because we're late on the bill?

I really need Malcolm to come through with an endorsement.

With a sigh, I head back to bed, and right before I fall asleep, it hits me that my room is right next to Rushi's and Envoy Yu's. A thought prickles at the back of my mind. What if my mom's family had never left China nearly a century ago? Would Peter and I have grown up singing Mao's praises like Envoy Yu? I blink away the questions. Me, a Communist? I'd as soon kiss Premier Khrushchev on the lips.

The next morning, I set out early for the training center, but when I reach Team USA's section, I find it already full. Sam's stretching inside one of the fighting pits, but he isn't the only one there. I recognize the others from the luncheon yesterday—Albie and Fitz-Lloyd from Team UK along with Giselle and her partner from Team France, a wiry boy named Auguste. Their coaches stand nearby as well, and I can feel their eyes on me when I walk in, assessing the new kid on the block. I might be allied with their fighters in the arena, but after that, we're back to fighting for ourselves.

Malcolm calls out when he sees me. "Nice of you to join us." I want to retort that I'm actually early when he adds, "We're training for Purgatory today. Get warmed up."

Adrenaline pumps through me. It'll be a real culling in Round 1, starting off with fifty fighters and whittling it down to sixteen. Peter and I always look forward to watching Purgatory at the Games because it's action-packed and unpredictable, but it'll be quite another thing to be fighting in it. My stomach churns at the thought, and I'm not sure if it's excitement or nerves. Probably both.

"You have fought in the arena before, yes?" Giselle asks me as we're jogging around the pits, her ponytail of blond hair bouncing as we go. Her tone is light, like she's trying to make small talk, but

I think she's trying to figure out my fighting background. Gathering intel for her coaches.

"Sure, I have. How many have you fought in?" I say, deflecting the attention back on her. She doesn't need to know that Saturday will mark only my third Purgatory. I've done it twice before at the tristate tournament where I faced off against Sam, and I survived both by taking Dad's advice and staying out of the fray, letting my opponents go to town knocking one another to a pulp while I waited them out. That strategy worked for me at the local level, but here in the big leagues, I doubt I'll be able to skitter around the cage like a spider.

"Internationally? Over twenty. I *adore* them." Giselle gets a gleam in her eye. "I get to beat the boys."

That might sound prideful if she was exaggerating, but she isn't. I've seen her fight and she's whip-fast. Her father was a 100-meter sprinter for the French Olympic team, and she's inherited that speed and applied it in the pit, outrunning her opponents and laying them flat after she has gone circles around them. I count it as a very good thing that we're allies in Purgatory.

"Is there any boy in particular that you're referring to?" I ask, figuring that I can pick up intel too.

"Not really. Perhaps Gunter."

Gunter? Oh yes. The Ogler of West Germany. "But he's our ally."

"For now." Her smile is back again before she kicks up her trademark speed. "Don't you want to hit him after how he acted at lunch?"

I chuckle at what she said, but she's already a meter ahead of me, leaving me in the dust to watch her ponytail swish back and forth. I realize I might not trust her, but I do have to admire the girl.

After we've stretched and cooled down, Malcolm gathers us around him. "We're going to run through our drills again like we did during Tuesday's session, but we've made several adjustments now that Rochester is out and Linden is here to replace him. Otherwise our main strategy stays the same. The Communists tend to favor speed and mobility—and they like to attack in pairs or trios. There's a good chance that they're going to try to separate you from one another from the get-go, so it's imperative that you remain in formation and listen to the orders from your captains." Malcolm nods at Giselle and Sam, who must be our "captains." The teacher's pets. "Strength in numbers."

It's technically against regulation to forge alliances inside the arena, but hardly anyone follows that stipulation, especially at the international level, where politics often rears its big old head. Since the 1947 Games, the fighters have usually split into three main groups in Purgatory—NATO countries, Warsaw Pact countries, and then the rest of the competitors, who try to stay out of the way and squeak into the next round of play.

For this year's NATO lineup, we'll also be allying with Australia, Canada, West Germany, and a few others in the arena, but for now, we've split up into smaller groups for this morning's training session. There'll be another one with everyone else following lunch.

"We've got two days until the Games begin, so we better make these hours count," Malcolm says after we've suited up.

We'll practice a defensive drill first, and Malcolm gives a rundown of what will happen. It'll be Sam and me against the others. Two against four. The odds might not sound fair, but there's nothing fair about this sport, especially in Purgatory. For all we know, we may find ourselves isolated from our allies with a troop of Warsaw Pact fighters at our necks. It could be four-to-one odds or five-to-one. Or maybe even more.

Sam and I stand back to back, adopting a traditional stance so we can protect ourselves on most sides. It's a simple formation, but sometimes simple is the way to go when absolute chaos surrounds you.

Malcolm goes over a few strategies outlined in our folders and tells us our objective—survive for ten minutes—before he exits. While he counts down to zero, I size up the other fighters. It's my first time seeing all their mechas. The Brits are wearing the classic Condor design, which looks similar to the American Goliath except they're taller and with longer limbs, like they've taken a Goliath and stretched it out a hair. Giselle and her teammate Auguste— whom I've nicknamed Napoleon in my head since he's short and slight—are tucked inside the slim and sleek French Colosse, both painted a crisp white. No doubt they'll be easy to spot inside the arena, which proves helpful when you're searching for your allies but not as much if you're trying to dodge the Commies.

"And go!" Malcolm calls out.

We might be doing a training exercise, but everyone inside the pit goes full throttle fast. Albie takes on Sam, while the other three gang up on me, probably thinking that I'm easy pickings.

Talk about a warm welcome.

I block the first dozen or so blows, but there are way too many of them, and before I know it I'm lying on my stomach, unable to budge while they've got me pinned.

A whistle blows. Malcolm comes over and doles out some advice. Get low and try a leg sweep. I nod. It's a decent tip, and I'm glad that it's a pretty standard move because I want to save some of my karate techniques for later if possible, after Purgatory is over. No need to reveal all my cards yet.

We go at it again, but it's the same as before, I'm up against three fighters while Sam is playing pat-a-cake for all I know. I don't even have time to glance over my shoulder to see what he's up to because I'm busy dodging and deflecting the attack. But Malcolm's advice does prove useful. With a swift kick, I manage to knock out Napoleon before I toss Fitzy to the other side of the pit, leaving me to contend with Giselle.

Finally I'm down to a one-against-one ratio, but Giselle keeps my hands full. She comes at me with a side kick, but as soon as I dodge it, she wraps me in a headlock. Her movements are fast and fluid, and it's obvious why she's ranked number seven worldwide, but I've gotten out of my share of headlocks before. Wriggling an arm free, I reach up to grab her mecha's head, crush my fingers around it, and yank backward. That's something that my father taught me—how our bodies have to follow our heads. This knocks Giselle off balance, and she loosens her grip, giving me the opportunity to shove her away and finally gain the upper hand. But as luck would have it, little Napoleon leaps on top of me out of nowhere and I'm KO'd yet again.

"Come on, guys," Sam says to the others after the fourth time I've been eliminated. "Take it easy on the new kid, eh?"

"I'm fine," I say crossly because I don't need Sam coming to my rescue. I know that my inexperience is showing, but having them coddle me won't do me any favors either. Will the Reds take it easy on me in Purgatory? No way.

Malcolm tells us to go for another round, and as I take my place, I glance at the other coaches. Judging by the pinched looks on their faces, I don't think that I've impressed them much. They clearly view me as the weak link on Team NATO, and I'm thinking they may want to invite Ted to return, one armed or not. I bite down on my mouth guard in frustration because I want to prove them wrong, but how?

I imagine my dad lecturing me and he's saying, *When you get stuck, change things up.*

It's clear that I can't take on three fighters at a time *and* remain in my defensive stance.

I have to get creative.

This time when the others launch themselves at me, I switch tactics. I rocket into the air, soaring in my mecha's light frame, so high that I can grab on to the bars overhead, which I do. I hang there, letting my legs dangle, and I figure if I wait around long enough, the others will come a-calling.

I hope this works.

Napoleon and Giselle leap up to drag me down while Fitzy waits below, ready to pin me as soon as the others have knocked me off. But before Team France can reach the top rung, I release my grip and zero in on Fitzy's location. I land on top of him before he can escape, and I KO him before the others can get to him.

The whistle blows again.

Aw, I was only getting started.

The French coach runs over, gesturing at Giselle and Napoleon to have a word, and the Brits do the same. I wait for Malcolm to approach Sam and me, but instead he tells us to climb out of our mechas.

"Take a water break," he says, tossing a bottle that Sam catches with ease. To me he says, "Shall we chat?"

I'm not sure what he wants to discuss, but it must be about that move I pulled off in the pit. I really wish that Malcolm hadn't blown the whistle so soon. I had managed to eliminate one fighter, and I could've taken on the others. I can't wait to tell Peter about it in detail, and that's when I see the look in Malcolm's eyes.

"Fancy moves. Senator Appleby was right. You do have talent," he says, except there's no bounce in his voice. Only stark seriousness. "But when you do something like that in Purgatory, you're leaving your teammate high and dry. In case you didn't notice, Albie KO'd Sam while you went off book in there."

Whoops. But Sam only had one fighter to fend off, which should've been easy pickings for him. Why isn't Malcolm chewing him out?

"We're going to run this again, and this time I want you to stick next to Sam no matter what. Back to back," Malcolm continues.

I almost laugh. "He's a little old to need a babysitter."

"He's your teammate. You need to protect him."

That's a strange choice of words. "Like a shield?" I say this off-hand because I don't think he really means it, but Malcolm doesn't correct me and I feel the blood drain out of my face. "Wait, are you asking me to be Sam's shield in the arena?"

Shielding is a tactic that's sometimes used in Purgatory. Since a team can field two fighters at the Games, one of them may get tasked to protect the other, basically turning into a shield to absorb any incoming blows and, if necessary, take the ax. This typically happens when one teammate is much higher ranked than the other, so the coaches want to maximize their chances to get at least one fighter on to the next round.

It can make sense strategically, but I'm already shaking my head at Malcolm. I've never in my life shielded another fighter before, and I have no plans to start.

"I'm dead in the water if I shield Sam," I say. No doubt the Warsaw Pact will try to knock him out quickly since he's their biggest threat, and they'd happily cut through me to get to him. This is a hard pass from me.

A nerve on Malcolm's face twitches. "What I need to hear from you is, 'Yes, Coach, I understand.'"

The anger starts simmering in my gut, but I manage to keep it in check. "I don't play to lose. I'm not built like that."

"This isn't a discussion." A sudden fire lights in his eyes, but his tone stays surprisingly cool. "My entire staff has spent four years creating a strategy that will get us onto that final podium. We're going to win that title, and Sam is how we're going to do it. Ted understood his role in this."

His words grip me by the throat, and now I can see his entire playbook laid out in front of me. He has all his eggs in one basket, and that basket goes by the name of Sam Kealey—American hero, our country's one big hope. My head starts spinning. Senator Appleby didn't mention a word to me about shielding anyone. Did she know about Malcolm's plans and conveniently not tell me?

"The senator said—" I start.

"As I've already stated, June Appleby isn't the coach here."

My jaw sets, and I spit out, "You never would've agreed to be someone else's shield."

"You're right, but I was ranked number six in the world when I was fourteen and number three a year later. Why would I get asked to shield anyone?" he says matter-of-factly not arrogantly, but the barb strikes the same. "Look, you've got pluck and creativity, but I've already tried reasoning with Appleby about this—you've never fought in an international match before, much less the Games. You're completely unproven."

Unproven? "I got an almost-perfect record last season in one of the toughest divisions in the country. If I'd been born a Joseph instead of Josephine, you can bet that I'd be ranked and I'd be ranked high."

Malcolm isn't swayed. "Sam still beat you. Twice."

I swear I could sock him in the stomach for that.

But I can't call him a liar.

Malcolm must regret speaking so boldly because his features soften, yet he doesn't take back what he said. "You've made your mark in your district. Take pride in that. And you'll get your moment in the spotlight here in Washington. How many fighters can say that?"

Not many at all, but it sure feels like a consolation prize. I've dreamed my whole life about coming to the Games, about suiting up in a spanking-new Goliath and entering the pit with my head held high, the audience roaring and stomping.

Little did I realize that I was being brought to Washington to help Sam take the title instead.

"Are we on the same page? It's time to get back to training." Malcolm juts his chin at the pit where the others await us. Sam is staring at me in particular, a smile on his lips, tapping a finger on his watch to tell me to wrap things up already.

I snap my head away from him. So that's why he's been so friendly since I arrived, acting like we're old pals. He must be happy to have another sacrificial lamb in the arena to help him win.

I taste bitterness on my tongue, and I can't hold back what I want to say next. "I won't be Sam's shield. If I have to go it alone in Purgatory, so be it."

For a moment, Malcolm and I simply stare at each other, him out of shock and me out of a rising panic. Could I really survive by myself in the arena? Sure, I've done it twice before, but not at the Games, which is on another level completely. But what's my alternative? At least this way I can fight on my own terms.

Malcolm looks like a volcano about to erupt. "Do you want me to sign off on a sponsorship or not?"

My mouth slides open. He wouldn't hold that over me . . . would he?

"Is that a threat?" I ask.

"Call it coaching. You want to go it alone? Fine, but there'll be consequences."

I'm this close to marching off and taking on those consequences, like it or not. But my feet don't budge. I can't let them.

Because I'm thinking about my brother and about the shop.

I have to get a sponsorship; I can't leave Washington empty-handed.

All I have to do is sell my pride for it.

A dark feeling slides into my stomach and settles there at the bottom. It isn't anger. It's resignation. Eight years I've given to this sport and this is what I get for my hard work and sacrifice—shielding a boy on what should be the biggest day of my life.

This is for Peter though, I remind myself.

This is to stave off the eviction notices and the past-due bills. This is to keep my family and our home and our livelihood.

"Okay, I'll do it," I say to Malcolm, forcing out each syllable.

He nods. "Smart girl. Keep in mind too that for the rest of your life you'll get to say that you were on Team USA at the 1963 Games. That's a real honor. Now go on."

I hold the tatters of my ego by my fingertips and walk toward the pit, his sentiment ringing in my ears and haunting me.

A real honor.

As if that's supposed to make me feel all gooey and grateful inside. As if that's supposed to keep a roof over my family's heads. What a true honor that'll be.

I pause midstride because a thought hits me like a jolt.

Malcolm wants me to shield Sam in the arena, but he didn't put any further stipulations on that command—just help Sam get to Round 2.

He never said that I couldn't make it through too.

10

The next day and a half pass by like a sped-up record. We have two more group training sessions, followed by hours of watching film reels to dissect the Federovas and Lukas Sauer and other major threats to Sam's safety.

"There's a decent likelihood that the Federovas will let Lukas lead the Communist attack out of the gate," Malcolm says as we rewatch last year's Purgatory round at the World Championships. He eyes me in particular, and it's clear what he's telling me: *Look out for Lukas and shield Sam as necessary.*

I nod back, saying, *Yes, Coach,* as he expects me to do, but what he doesn't know is that I've been racking my brain on how to survive the arena. So far, the only solution I've come up with is to fight like a maniac, somehow fending off the Reds while shielding Sam and getting both of us on to the next round. It'll be a gas of a time.

If it were up to me, I'd spend the lead-up to Purgatory in the training center to hone my strategy, but it appears that every single minute of my day has been planned out by Malcolm or the IC.

It's time for the Parade of Nations.

Just before noon, I wobble out of my dorm room and down to the grassy quad in a pair of royal-blue heels that pinch my toes. A heat wave has baked the city like a bubbling casserole. I'm already sweating in my short-sleeved white sweater and my red circle skirt that's so bright that you can spot it from outer space. With my blue shoes to complete the look, I'm basically a walking advertisement for the Fourth of July, but at least the other fighters are wearing similarly garish getups. Team Egypt, for instance, has been dressed to look like the ancient pharaohs, both of them in tunics and golden head-dresses. The Brits have taken a more subtle approach, but they also look like they're melting in their plaid three-piece suits. Albie has peeled off his blazer, but Fitzy seems intent on wearing his to the bitter end, making me wonder if he'll dehydrate before our eyes.

"Team Czechoslovakia! Please report to your float," one of the Games' staff members calls out over a loudspeaker that echoes over the Pavilion.

To one-up the Olympics, the IC started the Parade back in 1947. The basic premise is that every country designs a float that will wind slowly across the streets of the host city. The idea started off simple, but over the years, the floats have gotten more and more elaborate. For instance, during the '59 Games in Montreal, the West German float looked like a giant pretzel, with light bulbs acting as the flakes of salt and with their fighters sitting inside the bread loops, tossing out goody bags filled with—what else?—miniature pretzels, to the delight of the crowd.

For this year's parade, the fighters will board their floats here at the Pavilion before making their way toward the Tidal Basin and the Lincoln Memorial, then swinging north past the White House, and finally rolling down the length of Constitution Avenue to our last stop, in front of the Capitol Building. A stage has been built there, where special musical numbers will play and President Kennedy himself will give remarks.

If I don't spontaneously combust before then in this heat.

Since Team USA is the host nation, we'll go last in the lineup, meaning I've got a lot of time to kill. Most of the fighters have crowded around a buffet spread on the lawn, snacking on tea sandwiches cut into geometric shapes, while we wait to get called to our floats. Until then I'm supposed to play the part of the smiling hostess, but I put that off to watch the parade on a projector screen set up on the grass. Australia gets the honor of going first, and their float has a yellow-and-green color scheme, with a twenty-foot-tall kangaroo bot that blinks its eyes. Next up is Austria and then Brazil, but before I can catch a glimpse of their floats, Malcolm finds me in the throng.

"It's almost time for your turn with the reporters," he says, reminding me that I need to talk to the press who have descended upon the Pavilion too.

"Oh joy," I mumble. The last thing I want to do is talk to a bunch of journalists, but I tell myself that it'll be good for my visibility. If I smile enough and talk sweetly enough, maybe I can land an endorsement today.

We enter the dining hall, which has been transformed into a makeshift press conference area. Each fighter will answer questions at a wooden podium in front of the three dozen reporters in attendance, who are currently busy interviewing Lidiya.

I inch closer to hear what she has to say. She's dressed simply compared to the other fighters I've seen, wearing a basic shift dress in a Soviet red color. But the way she carries herself really does set her apart. With both of her hands gripping the sides of the podium, she looks like a general giving orders, ignoring the moderator and choosing reporters to her liking.

"Miss Federova, you've gained a reputation for your unconventional choices inside the pit," says a reporter from a British daily. "For example, when you faced Adolfo Agostino at the Junior Worlds a few years ago, you continued to strike him after he'd injured his back and had signaled to the referees to fetch the medics. What was the reasoning behind that?"

"My reasoning was to win," Lidiya answers through her translator.

The reporter frowns. "Some have called that unsportsmanlike conduct."

"What rule did I break? Show me in the handbook." She looks irritated by the accusation and tries to move on to the next journalist.

But the British reporter is insistent. "Just six weeks ago, you faced Duncan MacArthur at the Euro Cup, where you dragged him by the arm across the ground even though you had already dislocated his shoulder. There were calls for your suspension due to reckless endangerment. How do you respond?"

Peter and I had listened to that particular match on the radio. Even the announcer had sounded shocked when Lidiya pulled that move because it seemed so cold-blooded.

"MacArthur was known to fake injuries in the pit," she says, exasperated before her voice turns icy. "If I were male, you would have called me a master strategist. Next question."

I can't quite believe it, but I find myself agreeing with Lidiya Federova a bit. If Sam had done something like that, I bet everyone in this room would've called him brilliant. Ruthless too, but brilliant. Not that I agree with Lidiya's tactics exactly, but she does have a point at how female fighters are treated.

After Lidiya wraps up, Malcolm leans toward me and whispers, "Keep your answers short. No politics. And smile like you've just won the Games." Then he walks me over to the podium to take my place. I expect him to find an empty seat somewhere, but he stands a couple paces to the right of me. Looks like I've got a nanny, like Rushi.

Ignoring him, I try on my best smile and take the first few questions about the parade before the reporters get to what they really want to ask.

"What would you say to your naysayers that you've taken a male fighter's slot on Team USA?" says a reporter from the *Detroit Sun*.

My smile threatens to slip, but I keep it upright. If I could tell him the truth, I'd say that my naysayers can go eat rocks for all I care, but that won't endear me to any sponsors. Unless they want me to sell rocks, I guess.

"I'd tell them to give me a chance to prove them wrong," I reply, hoping that I sound sincere enough.

Another reporter goes next. "Miss Linden, you're the first unranked fighter since '47 to make it onto Team USA, which has puzzled many analysts and the public at large. Why do you think you were selected?"

"My record for one thing," I say with a good deal of pride, but before anyone can call me arrogant I add, "19–1 isn't too shabby, right? And for another thing, you should probably ask my coach that question." I glance at Malcolm, and I can't resist getting in a dig. "He may have mentioned that I've got a lot of *natural talent*."

What I don't reveal is how he ordered me to be Sam's shield right after he said that.

Malcolm looks a little surprised at the sudden attention, but he recovers fast, a skill I'm sure he has picked up after being in the spotlight over the years. "Linden here has talent in spades, as does her teammate Sam Kealey," he says, tossing his own dig my way. "They'll make an excellent pair in the arena."

Oh, I'll certainly show him how excellent I can be.

"Female fighters remain relatively rare in the sport," yet another reporter chimes in. "What drew you to fighting in the first place? Is it because you lacked a feminine presence at home after your mother died?"

I cough and glance at Malcolm, thinking, *What kind of ridiculous question is that?* But his eyes go wide, and he flicks his hand at me as if to say, *Just answer it, Linden, but don't bring up you-know-what.*

The reporters are awaiting a reply, so I tell them the truth.

"My dad was a mecha soldier in Korea, so you could say I'm just following in his footsteps. Like father, like daughter." I add what I hope is a charming smile.

After I've finished, Malcolm escorts me outside and toward the road where the floats await the fighters. He isn't actively frowning at me, so he must be somewhat satisfied with my performance.

"You did fine, especially on that last question," he says, which I'll take as a positive. "Although next time feel free to leave me out of it."

"Aw, I was trying to spread out the fun, Coach."

His face remains stony. "The real test is tomorrow."

As if I could forget.

Malcolm deposits me on the sidewalk and goes off to find Sam, leaving me to wait for Team USA's float that's slowly making its way toward the Pavilion. There are only three countries left in the queue, and I've arrived just in time to watch the Yugoslavian team hoist themselves onto their float that has been decorated to celebrate their president Josip Broz Tito, who was recently named "president for life." My gaze is already wandering elsewhere though.

I let my eyes roam over the Soviet's float. Since the USSR won the last Games, they get the honor of rolling out just before the host nation. Lidiya and Zoya have changed into matching golden dresses, and they now await the okay to climb on board. Standing alongside them, I notice a couple older men in suits, and I do a double take when I realize who they are—they're former victors of the Games. There's Vladimir Tereshkov, who won in '51, and Feodor Leonov, who won in '59. There's no rule restricting the number of people on a country's float—at the last Games, the Romanian head of state and his whole family crammed onto the ride along with their fighters—and it looks like the Soviets want to rub it in how they've come to dominate the sport. But there's a smear on that record. They also won in '55 with Mikhail Krikalev, but he defected to Canada a few years ago, which made Khrushchev none too happy. How is he supposed to keep up the pretense that all is well in the USSR when his athletes try to escape it?

The Soviet float finally arrives, and all four fighters, both current and previous, scale up the side. The Federovas stand on the top tier while the two men gather below them, right before their engineers turn on the lights to the float. I'm immediately blinded by the glow. Their float is decked out in what must be tens of thousands of tiny sparkling lights, so bright that it makes my eyes hurt, but I keep looking because it's that dazzling. The Association reps around me seem to think so too. They're oohing and aahing. Even a few diplomats, like Sweden's ambassador and Envoy Yu, venture forward to get a closer look and snap photos.

Curiosity gets the better of me, and I join them because I wonder how the float is getting powered and I'm sure Peter will want to discuss this later. Could it be esterium? I crouch down to see if I can get a glimpse of the batteries—I bet I'll find that familiar glow of blue—but someone starts shouting at me from above.

"What are you doing?" Lidiya says accusingly.

I frown because I hadn't even touched the float. "It isn't a crime to look."

She starts talking to me in Russian until a Pavilion staff member tells me that they're ready for me on Team USA's float, and Lidiya watches me the entire walk to the US float.

Soon I forget all about Lidiya and her narrowed eyes because of what I behold in front of me. I'm not sure if I can call it a float exactly—more like a moving island. It's *that* humongous and equally impressive. With a theme of America the Beautiful, it's essentially our country in miniature and built in tiers. The lower level represents the Atlantic Ocean, complete with a floating *Mayflower.* One level up, there's a field of wheat and a mechanical thresher bot that moves back and forth. Above that, I see the tier where I'll be seated, which represents our national landmarks, from the Statue of Liberty to the Hoover Dam and even the Golden Gate Bridge, a little piece of home.

It's impressive, all right, but I can't help but sigh after I've gotten a second look at it. This is the pretty version of America, the one that has been carefully sanitized. I'm no history buff, but I know enough to notice what they've left out. Slavery. The Trail of Tears. The Chinese Exclusion Act. Internment camps. There's certainly no hint of what's happening in Birmingham and other civil rights protests.

Sam is already waiting for me on the highest tier and extends a hand to help me up. I ignore his offer and get seated on my stool, frowning at the model of Mount Rushmore right next to me. Peter wrote a history report on the monument and told me the real story: how the US stole the Black Hills from the Lakota Sioux and carved them up. His teacher gave him a C- on it because she thought he was being disrespectful. It's a plum spot, and I'm grateful that the stool has been bolted into the float so it's extra sturdy. I've never been afraid of heights, but standing up this high, I do get a nervous flutter in my stomach, especially when we start moving. At least there's a handrail in front of us that should save us from falling to our untimely deaths in case we hit a hump.

Down below, two boys jump up and down and wave at Sam frantically, calling out his name. They look a lot like him too—the same open faces, the same floppy hair except blond instead of brown—and I realize that I've seen them before at our most recent tristate tournament. They're his little brothers.

"Don't forget to record it!" one of them calls out.

Sam starts fishing in his trouser pockets and pulls out a handheld video recorder. At the press of a button, a lens juts out of one side and a light pulses from inside the device, a rich and deep blue.

Holding the thing above our heads, Sam sidles up next to me. "Say hi, Linden."

"Is that a video camera that runs on *esterium*?" I can't even imagine the cost of something like that, and I've never seen one so small.

"It's my brother's. He asked me to make a little video while I'm up here," Sam explains. "You remember them, don't you? That's Sterling wearing the blue shirt and there's Stanford right next to him in the white."

Yikes, Sterling and Stanford? It sounds like the two of them were born at an exclusive country club, ready for an iced tea and a game of tennis. Behind them, I also notice Sam's mom. I'd seen her at the last tournament as well—she's very pretty and I can tell where Sam got his looks from—but I don't recognize the older man standing beside her, the one with a chrome dome and a pricey-looking blue suit.

"That must be your dad, huh?" I say. "I don't think I got a chance to meet him at the tristate tournament."

Sam doesn't look at me. He keeps panning the camera over the skyline, and when he finally gets around to answering my question, there's a newfound chilliness in his usually warm tone. "That's because he wasn't there. He only attends my international matches." He pauses and adds quietly, "He's my stepfather actually."

"I'm sorry, I didn't realize."

He shrugs and keeps filming, leaving me to stare at his back. For the first time since I've met him, I feel a little sorry for Sam. The tristate tournament is nothing to thumb your nose at. My dad made sure to be there, even though he had to put off paying our water bill to buy the bus tickets for him and Peter. But any sympathy I've mustered up for Sam dries up when I remember what he expects me to do in Purgatory tomorrow.

Sam twists around to get a shot of what's behind us, and his eyes open up wide. "Would you look at that? How much esterium do you think those monsters run on?"

When I crane my neck to get a glimpse of what he's looking at, I think my jaw actually drops an inch. We're staring at three Goliaths bringing up the rear of the parade, except these aren't ordinary mechas. They're enormous, like they've taken steroids. A lot of steroids. Squinting my eyes, I see that there are three pilots in the roomy cockpit, one of them controlling the legs, another the arms, and the third operating a switchboard that causes an array of fireworks to shoot out of the mecha's shoulders, much to the crowd's roaring approval.

"What *are* those things?" I ask.

"You're looking at the future, young lady," Sam says in an announcer's voice before I sigh at him. I don't know what it's like to have an annoying younger brother since Peter is mostly a saint, but I imagine he would act a lot like Sam. "What? It's true. Multipiloted mechas are supposed to be the next big thing on the battlefield. I heard they were supposed to get rolled out in Vietnam before the treaty talks ramped up."

But now with the war coming to a close, they're walking in the parade instead. And judging by the response from the crowd, they're a huge hit. The Soviets might have trotted out their previous victors, but we've one-upped them with these brand-new Goliaths. Makes me wonder what Khrushchev has to say about that. He and Kennedy might be shaking hands and posing for the cameras, but that hasn't quashed the rivalry between our two countries. The war in Vietnam might be ending, but not the Cold one. Where will the next hot spot pop up? Brazil? The Dominican Republic? We might've avoided one conflict, but another could be around the corner.

Sam keeps filming while I swivel around to face the front again. The float has passed through the Pavilion's gate when he asks me out of the blue, "Say, what happened between you and Malcolm?"

It's hard not to glare at him, like he has no idea.

"Come on, you've been dodging me since yesterday too," he goes on.

Well, that's true. Ever since Malcolm forced me into shielding Sam, I've been avoiding them both as much as I can. I might have had to deal with them during training, but I pretended not to hear Sam when he called out for me to join him and Team Britain in the dining hall or when he asked if I wanted to spar one-on-one during our free time. I could shake him off easily then. Now though? I'm stuck.

"Look, I don't know why you're so hacked off with Malcolm, but he's trying to win back the title—" Sam starts to say.

"Win *you* the title," I correct him, but he only stares at me.

He still has that blank look on his face as he sets down his camera. "What did he say to you?"

"Don't play dumb. I'm sure the two of you have been in cahoots, plotting out how I'm supposed to shield you."

"*Shield* me? Wait, is that what Malcolm told you to do?"

More like ordered me. I roll my eyes as our float makes its way onto the bridge that'll carry us over the river and into Washington proper. "You can drop the act; I'm not thick. You know the plan as well as I do—get you onto the winner's podium and get Malcolm a title as a coach."

He grips on to the railing, squeezing it tight. "This is the first time I heard of it."

"Oh, stop. Ted was in on this too. And when he got hurt, Malcolm simply slotted me in."

Sam releases the railing and jerks his head back at me. "He wanted Ted to shield me?"

"Obviously."

Now he's raking his fingers through his hair, ruining the perfect coif that the stylists have shaped it into. When he speaks next, I'm not sure if he's talking to me or himself. "Malcolm really thinks I need a shield?"

"No, but he's taking every precaution to make sure that you get through Purgatory."

Sam doesn't seem to be listening. With his jaw tight, he says, "I didn't ask you to be my shield, and I don't want you to do it either. We clear on that?"

I narrow my eyes. That hadn't been the reaction I'd been expecting. Did Sam really not know? Maybe, maybe not, but the outcome stays the same.

"It doesn't matter if we're *clear* on anything. Malcolm has already made up his mind," I say.

"Then I'll talk to him." He makes a face, like he can't even bring himself to say the words. "What does he think I am? Some thirteen-year-old newbie?"

"He won't care! You think I like this strategy?"

"Then why did you agree to it?"

Because of cold hard cash, I think, but I certainly don't say that. Sam has never had to worry about making rent or paying for esterium batteries. He was born with a silver spoon in his mouth, and he's about to trade it in for a golden trophy. So it doesn't matter if he doesn't want me as a shield—he's getting one anyway. I need those sponsorships.

"I'm going to take this up with Malcolm," Sam says.

"It won't change his mind."

We sit in silence, and I fix my gaze ahead. As we near the end of the bridge, I realize that it's almost showtime, and I have to put on the finishing touches of my look—a megawatt smile and a wave.

Since we're seated up so high, I get a bird's-eye view of the city. For blocks and blocks, I see the sidewalks filled with people, standing shoulder to shoulder on the blockaded streets. They're holding up banners and chanting, "U-S-A! U-S-A!" It's easy too to see Sam's fans in the mob. They're screaming his name and going bonkers, and I think one of the girls faints at the sight of him. Sam waves from his perch, but he's more subdued than before. I wonder if this shielding talk has gotten under his skin, which surprises me. I'd really thought that he was the sort of dipstick who would've known all along about Malcolm's plan.

My toes are starting to pinch in my stiff shoes and I can't wait to get off this ride, but we're not quite to the finish line yet. When we finally near the Capitol Building, an announcer shouts out the arrival of the Federovas by saying, "Next, please welcome the team from the Union of Soviet Socialist Republics!"

There's polite applause from the crowd, but it ratchets up as soon as Team USA rounds the last corner. I'm standing on my tiptoes by then and my arm is killing me from waving so much, but I keep it up and hope that Dad and Peter can see me on TV. I'm wondering if could try to mouth a message to them—Peter would get a real kick out of that—and that's when an explosion goes off.

11

Light fills my eyes, so bright that it can't be camera flashes. There's another boom that vibrates through our float, and I almost go toppling over the railing and onto the fake sheaths of wheat below, but Sam heaves me back onto the platform, shouting at me, "Jo! Are you hurt? Are you hurt?"

I shake my head, dazed, and stumble onto my feet, only to point a finger straight ahead. It's the Soviets' float, which was dazzling to begin with, but now it has lit up like a rocket.

"Fire!" I shout.

The fire flares up the back side of their float, licking up higher and shattering the glass light bulbs in its path. Some people in the crowd assume that this is all part of the festivities, and they're trying to take pictures. But when a thick smoke starts to appear, I start hearing screams. Policemen yell for everyone to stay calm— the blaze can't be bigger than my arm span at this point—but they might as well tell everyone to stop breathing.

"Did a circuit trip? What's going on?" I ask Sam.

Just then, two things happen at once. Our float careens to a halt, slamming Sam and me against the railing. And up ahead, the Soviet float loses all its power, like a giant plug has been pulled out of the socket. The only light on the float now comes from the fire itself, and through the haze I see the Federovas and the other victors on their hands and knees, trying to escape.

"We have to get off this thing!" I say, kicking off my heels because they're only slowing me down. Hand over hand, we make our descent. The wind is blowing the smoke toward us, which sticks in my throat. Coughing, I lose my footing. Slipping the last few feet, I land on my knees, scraping up the skin and tearing my panty hose completely, but I force myself up and stagger toward the Soviets' float until Sam pulls me back.

"There are still people in there!" I say, struggling against him. The Federovas weren't the only ones on the thing. There were the drivers underneath who'd been steering the whole production.

"How're you going to get inside without a mask?" he says, coughing out smoke. "Don't play hero."

"Why? Because I'm a girl?" I say, scowling.

He scowls right back. "Because you're not even wearing shoes."

I don't have a smart reply to throw back at him because I really am barefoot and there's broken glass on the ground. Then our whole argument is pointless because we're swarmed by police officers who force us onto the side of the road, where they tell us to stay put. A few other teams are waiting there as well, the ones who rode in the floats just ahead of the Soviets, like Yugoslavia and the

UK. Fitzy looks pale-faced as he stares at the fire, but Albie unabashedly snaps a half roll of film. When he notices me staring at him, he shrugs and says, "We're gonna tell our grandkids about this one day."

If we don't get stampeded on first.

The flames have now engulfed the entire back of the Soviet float, and I have to look away before my retinas get seared. The mecha fighters around me start to push against one another as the smoke creeps toward us.

"Everyone, move back!" the policemen call out, but where are we supposed to go?

Albie and one of the Yugoslav fighters are jostling for space, and I think they might brawl right here on the street when— hallelujah—I hear fire engines. The trucks are trying to reach the blaze, but they hit one of the road blocks set up for the parade. A policeman rushes over to move it, and without thinking, I follow him to help.

"Jo!" Sam says, but I'm already too far ahead.

I grab on to one end of the steel barricade while the officer takes hold of the other, and we shimmy it out of the way. We do this three more times until there's a gap wide enough to let the fire trucks through, and I'm panting by the time they gun their engines past me.

Within twenty minutes, the fire is put out, but the festivities are still on pause. A column of black smoke forms a tower in the sky while the paramedics tend to the wounded. Thankfully all the

Soviets on the float, crew members included, have escaped the blaze. The float's drivers have suffered a few burns that need treatment while Vladimir Tereshkov has smoke inhalation, but otherwise they got lucky. The Federovas appear unhurt aside from minor scrapes. Zoya sits on a stretcher while a medic shines a light up her nose, and Lidiya stands nearby with Lukas Sauer. He must've sprinted down from his own float when he saw the fire, and I'm betting they must be something of an item judging by how he has slung an arm around her shoulder. To his credit he keeps trying to comfort her, but Lidiya looks furious. I really can't blame her either since she and her sister almost got barbecued on international television.

But the show has to go on.

After the fire has been tamed and the crowd has settled—surprisingly, most of the bystanders have remained—the event proceeds as planned, although streamlined. The police lead us toward the Capitol Building for the ceremony, where we file into our seats on the grass, with Sam and me sitting toward the end of the first row. Sam subtly sniffs at his suit jacket, and I realize both of us must reek of eau de smoke. At least he's fully clothed, whereas I'm shoeless and wearing torn stockings. I'm about to ask him what he thinks might've caused the blaze, but we're back to an uneasy silence now that it's out in the open that I have to shield him in the arena. Just thinking about it makes my teeth clench—how it goes against everything I know, how all my hard work over the years is culminating into this one moment, when I might have to sacrifice myself for a boy. I shut my eyes at the thought.

"Rise and shine," I hear Sam whisper beside me. "The cameras are panning this way."

Sure enough, when I snap my eyes open, I notice a large television camera slowly moving over the audience. It hasn't arrived on me yet though. It's lingering over First Lady Jacqueline Kennedy, who's wearing an eye-catching red two-piece dress, a perfectly poised pillbox hat, and delicate pearl drop earrings, looking like a movie star who has wandered over to Washington for the afternoon. Then the camera skips over to the man sitting a few seats down from her. Premier Khrushchev.

If I'm being honest, his face doesn't look like it would belong to one of the most powerful men in the world. His predecessor Stalin had a dictatorial look with his enormous mustache and the military cap he wore everywhere. Khrushchev, on the other hand, looks like someone's great-uncle. There's the bald head with tufts of white hair on the sides and the gap between his front teeth, and don't forget the ears that stick out, giving him a slightly elfish look. He's not looking too happy either, but that's probably because his country's float literally went up in flames, but as the ceremony kicks off, he plays the part of the dutiful leader, clapping politely and straightening in his chair.

The Marine Corps Band plays a rousing march, followed by the Beach Boys crooning "Surfin' Safari" except they've rewritten the lyrics to include the names of all the participating nations.

After that, a ranking member of the IC gives a few remarks, but everyone is waiting to hear from the next speaker—President Kennedy himself.

As he takes the podium, I swear the entire city of Washington goes quiet. Compared to Khrushchev, he cuts a dashing figure in a blue suit and a bold red tie and with a beautifully coiffed full head of hair. He starts off by thanking the firefighters and paramedics for jumping into the fray, and he promises a thorough investigation to identify the cause of the fire, which earns a nod from Khrushchev. Then he launches into the meat of his speech, and I find myself sliding forward in my seat.

"To the audience here in Washington and to the many of you watching from all corners of the world, I extend a warm welcome to the 1963 Pax Games!" he says in that blue-blooded Bostonian accent of his. The crowd claps their approval, and Sam whistles beside me while Kennedy continues with his speech, remarking on how the Games was born out of the ashes of World War I, one of the worst conflicts in human history.

"Since the inaugural Games back in 1919, the nations of the world have come together every four years, setting aside their differences for ten days. We celebrate not only the talent and athletic prowess of our young fighters, we acknowledge the name of this event. These are the *Pax* Games, which represent mankind at our finest, demonstrating how we can heal after terrible suffering and shake the hands of former enemies. We did the same in 1947 following World War II, after the Axis Powers had spread so much havoc, leaving no country untouched. But as my predecessor President Eisenhower once said: 'The whole book of history reveals mankind's never-ending quest for peace, and mankind's God-given capacity to build.' And here we are at the eleventh Pax Games, standing upon the foundation that has been laid following the world wars," he says, motioning at the fighters seated in front of him.

Then his speech takes a slight turn.

"Further, we have taken a technology created for warfare—the mecha—and we have fashioned new purposes for it. The deep-sea mechas of the US Navy have allowed us to explore the Mariana Trench. Others have been fitted to allow scientists to enter active volcanoes. And one day, likely soon, we'll see mechas soaring into the sky and into the great beyond. Why space, you might ask?

"The great British explorer George Mallory, who died on Mount Everest, was once asked why he wanted to climb it. He replied, 'Because it's there.' Well, space is there, and we're going to climb it, and the moon and the planets are there, and new hopes for knowledge and peace are there. We shall soon set sail on this new sea, but who will lead us there? Perhaps the young fighters in the audience will fly us there. After all, there is new knowledge to be gained, and new rights to be won, and they must be won and used for the progress of all people."

Is it me or is he looking straight at Khrushchev when he says that? Murmurs rumble over the crowd. For years now, American engineers have been working to create a Goliath that can survive the last frontier of outer space, and their USSR counterparts have been doing the same. It has been a constant one-upmanship with the Soviets since the Cold War began, but no viable prototype has come out yet.

Is President Kennedy suggesting that he might send a Goliath into space sooner than anticipated? Or is he keeping the Communists on their toes?

I doubt we'll find out, not tonight anyway, because Kennedy doesn't elaborate. He ends his speech by repeating the words *freedom* and *democracy* a lot, earning him a standing ovation from several audience members but only tepid claps from Khrushchev and his pals. Following that, there are a couple more musical numbers and a grand fireworks show. The fireworks themselves are a little hard to see since it's not quite evening yet, but I get the feeling that the Association really wanted to close out the ceremony with a literal bang.

By the time Sam and I have finished shaking people's hands and answering a couple questions with the press, we're whisked back to the Pavilion for dinner and a shower and a quiet evening to rest up for the big day ahead. The whole dorm goes silent by eight o'clock, but there's a tension floating through the air that only seems to thicken as the minutes tick by.

Malcolm might've ordered me to bed early, but there's something I have to do before lights-out. I pad over to the telephone in the common area, and Peter answers on the third ring. Turns out that the phone company did indeed disconnect us, but Dad pawned an old jade bracelet of Mom's to get it back up and running. The two of them had watched the parade and the opening ceremony in Mrs. Watters's apartment, and Peter wants a complete rundown on what happened.

"Do you know what caused the fire?" he asks.

"The IC is still investigating it, but my guess is an overloaded circuit."

"Then you think it was an accident? Mrs. Watters was saying the whole thing looked fishy, like there was foul play."

I frown into the receiver. "The Soviets did decide to put thousands of little light bulbs on their float, which is kind of a fire hazard," I point out. "They got lucky that Lidiya and Zoya didn't get scorched in the process."

"You have to watch out for them tomorrow," he says, switching topics. I can hear the tension in his voice and can almost see him pacing inside the store, twining the phone cord in his fingers as he goes. "And Lukas Sauer."

"I know, squirt, I know," I say. It's rare for me to get irritated with him, but he isn't soothing my nerves exactly. "You can bet I'll have eyes on the back of my head tomorrow."

"Sorry, I'm not being much help, huh?"

I soften. "You're doing fine. Keeping me on my toes."

"I wish you could tell me what strategy you're going to use tomorrow. Can't you give me a hint?"

"You know I have to keep a tight lid on that." Which is true. I'm not supposed to divulge our game plan to anyone.

"I figured, but I bet Coach Maines has some interesting stuff up his sleeve."

"Oh, you could say that." Like how he's reducing me to a shield. My cheeks burn thinking about it, but that's why I'm going to figure out how to survive Purgatory and protect Sam and get Malcolm to sign off on a sponsorship or three. It's exhausting to think about. "Anyway, I should get to bed—"

I hear some noise on the line. It sounds like Peter is talking to a customer, so I tell him I better let him go.

"Nah, that wasn't a customer. It was a reporter, but I told him to call Dad later. That's the eighth one we've had at the shop! They're all doing stories about you."

My eyes shoot open. "What have they been asking?"

"They want to see your baby pictures and hear a couple of anecdotes. That sort of thing."

"Have they asked about Mom?"

"One of them did but—"

"What did they say?" I may have been tired a few seconds ago, but now I'm wide-awake, like I've downed a carafe of black coffee. "What did you and Dad say back?"

Peter sounds a little taken aback by my intensity. "They asked run-of-the-mill stuff, like how she died and how old we were when she passed."

"Did they ask though about her . . . you know . . ." I glance over both shoulders in case anyone can hear me, but the room is a tombstone.

"Her what?"

"You know what I mean."

He goes quiet. "I don't think you should be embarrassed by that."

"I'm not embarrassed! But the reporters can't find out," I say, flustered, and hating how I even have to ask this of him.

"Why though?"

"Can you trust me on this? It's important." Because we'll probably get evicted if the news spills, but I can't tell him that. "Please, Peter?"

I hear him sigh, but ultimately he gives in. "All right, although I wish you'd tell me what's going on. I'm not a baby, you know."

"I know," I say, even though I don't quite mean it because he'll always be my baby brother and I'll always want to protect him. "I better go and get some beauty sleep. Wish me luck?"

"Good luck, but you won't need it. I know you can beat all of them."

I crack a smile, relieved that he isn't too upset.

If only he could be my coach.

The next morning, I get changed and eat breakfast and take a chauffeured car to the stadium by ten o'clock. The stadium is located near the southernmost tip of the city in a neighborhood called the Southwest Waterfront, and the building itself is an enormous structure that resembles a gigantic bowl of concrete. Once inside, everything smells clean and new—from the ammonia on the floors to the drying paint on the walls to the buttery popcorn that you can buy for twenty cents a carton at the concession stand. I follow the signs down an elevator to the basement floor, where the prep areas are located.

It's hours before the match begins, but there's plenty to tick off before then. First up, I get in line to sign in for the Games, my badge and ID in hand. The IC implemented the measure a few years ago, when the Soviets tried to pull off a switcheroo at the annual Euro Cup, registering one fighter ahead of schedule but swapping her out for Lidiya last minute since she was only thirteen and not old enough for senior-level competition.

There are two lines for the registrar, and I slot myself into the shorter one. While I wait, I consider what I'll do if the Federovas decide to gang up on me, and that's when I feel someone get behind me in line, standing so close that I can feel their breath in my hair.

"You won't get away with what you did," Lukas Sauer practically growls into my ear.

I whip around to face him, my eyes narrowed. I have no idea what he's talking about, but then again a lot of male mecha fighters can be real dipsticks. "You know, I can smell what you had for breakfast. What did you eat, huh? Onions and garlic?" It's a line I've used before that always gets under people's skin.

Lukas only smirks. Maybe he has a tougher shell than my usual competition. "You don't even deny it?"

"Deny what? That you don't brush your teeth after a meal?"

"You think you're funny, don't you?" He leans forward until our noses are inches apart. He might be dim enough to actually take a swing at me in front of everyone. I'd welcome it if we were in the pit and properly suited in our mechas, but he has nearly a foot on me in height and over fifty pounds in weight, meaning I would have to get creative.

I'm considering if I should go in for a groin kick or a nihon ken—a two-fingered strike—to his left eye, but then Rushi of all people clears her throat behind us.

"You can go next, Lukas," she says, tilting her head toward the registrar, who is waiting for another fighter to step up to the desk. Rushi also hands him his water bottle, the fancy one gifted to us from the IC with our individual names printed down the side that he must've dropped on his way in.

Lukas grabs the bottle without muttering a thanks and takes a swig of it, staring me down the whole time, probably trying to intimidate me, but I pretend to look bored until he stalks away.

I can't resist getting in one last dig though. "Remember to brush those teeth!" I call after him. I still don't know what his gripe is against me, but it looks like I better be on my toes from the get-go in the pit.

"Thanks for that. You saved me from bruising up my knuckles," I tell Rushi. I'm not saying that I couldn't have taken Lukas on, but I don't like taking stupid chances, and he had the physical advantage by far. "Granted, it would've felt good to take him down a notch."

That draws out a little smile from her, but it vanishes quickly. Her face looks a little pale, and she keeps fidgeting as her eyes flit toward Lukas. I have a hunch what she might be thinking, how in a couple hours we'll be facing him and his Commie pals in the arena.

"Nervous?" I ask.

She shakes her head no, but I notice that she forces her hands behind her back.

"Where's Envoy Yu?"

"In the restroom." She sounds relieved to have a minute or two off leash.

"Well, good luck today," I say when it's my turn at the registrar. The official odds of her making it out of this first round aren't high, but mine aren't fantastic either.

After checking in, I head to the prep area to warm up and get suited. It's a huge expanse of a space, with every country crammed inside it, separated by steel barricades and not much else. It's a madhouse. Fighters are doing jumping jacks and push-ups in their sections to get their blood pumping while the staff finishes last-minute checks on their mechas. When I locate Team USA, the Jays have already run their standard fifteen-point diagnostic on my Goliath and just in time for the IC's inspectors to arrive to ensure that every mecha used in the Games meets compliance. I've finished my stretches and am about to move into lunges when Malcolm comes barreling toward us, a folder in hand, and he gathers the Jays around him. They're speaking in hushed voices, and I can see a vein pulsing on Malcolm's forehead. Whatever this is, it can't be good.

"Everything swell, Coach?" I call out.

His eyes narrow at me. "Come here, Linden. Now."

"What's this all about?" I ask warily. Does he want me to shield Sam *and* Team UK? Toss in the rest of NATO while we're at it? Perplexed, I walk over to meet him. "I hope you just want to wish me luck."

"More like watch your back." Malcolm gestures at a folder of paperwork that he has clutched in his hand. "Lidiya Federova has filed a report with the IC that she saw you acting suspiciously beside the Soviet float yesterday."

"She *what*?" That's the most ridiculous thing I've heard. "I didn't even touch the thing!"

"Well, there seems to be a difference of opinion. Lidiya is alleging that she spotted you lurking around the back of their float before they entered the parade. You can see how this sounds considering that the IC has yet to determine the cause of the fire."

I swear I could punch Lidiya in the throat. "I thought the fire was an accident."

"It's looking inconclusive at this point since the parts in question have been charred to a crisp. It could've been an accident—or maybe not."

"Whatever it was, I had nothing to do with it! Ask Sam. Ask anyone who was there." Suddenly a wave of anxiety jolts through my body. Can the IC bar me from fighting today?

"You're in luck. The IC plans on dismissing the case since they they've spoken to multiple witnesses who were there yesterday. They also recognize that Lidiya can be . . . dramatic at times."

Dramatic? I've got better suggestions for what to call her. No wonder Lukas was giving me a hard time earlier in line. Lidiya had already fed him some story about how I tried to turn her into barbecue at the parade, and now her boyfriend is out for blood.

"You know, you could've told me that to start," I say. I eye the folder in Malcolm's hand, wondering why he's so steamed if the IC isn't going to pursue the case. "You want me to look over that paperwork?"

"No, but because of this mess, I've heard from more than one source that the Warsaw Pact fighters will be coming for you in the arena."

"Great," I mutter, but it isn't too surprising. "But they were going to do that anyway."

"This is entirely different!" he says, jamming his fingers through his hair. "We'd assumed that the Communists would attack in pairs or trios, but if they focus their whole attention on *you*, then we've got a problem."

It takes me a few blinks to follow.

He isn't worried about me.

He's worried that I'll be positioned next to Sam as his trusty human shield. But what good is a shield when your enemies flock toward it? Neither of us will last long in that scenario.

Malcolm talks rapidly to the Jays and spits out possibilities. While they're yammering, a million little thoughts go zipping through my head. I think about what I've done in the arena in the past, how I used a jump-and-evade strategy to stay alive. Granted, I didn't have the Federovas and the rest of the Warsaw Pact chasing after me, but I've survived Purgatory before. And I'm fast.

"I'll draw the Reds away from Sam," I say.

Malcolm lifts his head toward me. "What?"

"When the match starts, I'll give the Federovas and Lukas Sauer and whoever else the run around. I'll steer them clear from Sam."

Malcolm is already nodding. "Yes, of course. I should've come up with that from the get-go. We'll do that."

He isn't smiling, but he does look relieved. He probably doesn't think I'll last a minute in the slaughterhouse, but at least it'll give his precious Sam some breathing room.

Well, it'll be fun to show Malcolm how much he's underestimated me. What was it that Senator Appleby said about why she picked me? I'm a question mark. Unpredictable. The Reds haven't had months to study the footage of my international matches because there isn't any. They probably think I'll be easy pickings too. Many of my prior opponents have done the same thing, so this is familiar territory for me. Realizing that, my mood brightens considerably.

"Stick to this new plan, and our deal stands," Malcolm says. "The PR team at Goody has expressed some interest in you selling their hair curlers."

Hair curlers? I've never worn those in my life, but I guess I could start.

Malcolm peels off to update Sam, leaving me to the Jays to get suited up. I'm already wearing my official gear to the Games. It's a stretchy white unitard that zips up in the front, with red and blue stripes racing down the sleeves and the sides of the pants. The Goliath is already powered up, so I nod at the Jays and climb into the cockpit, my fingers tingling as I strap myself into place. I should be extra giddy about a possible sponsorship, but I'm feeling a different sort of excitement. With this shift in tactics, I'll have some autonomy in the arena, which is more than I had hoped for. My chances for squeaking through to Round 2 are a lot more promising than they were ten minutes ago.

Now it's up to me to get the job done.

After the final diagnostic, the team and coaching staff wait for our turn to step onto the massive utility elevator that's wide enough and strong enough to hold all of us and our mechas.

As we move upward to the stadium level, I stand shoulder to shoulder with Sam while Malcolm goes over a few items with the Jays.

Sam turns his mecha to look at me. "So I heard about the change in plans."

"It shouldn't affect you and the others too much," I reply with a shrug. I was never a pivotal part of their strategizing anyway since my job was to cling to Sam like a barnacle.

"They'll be fine. Listen, if Lukas chases you right out of the gate—"

I finally meet his gaze. "He won't catch me. Not unless it's on my terms."

Sam stares right back, looking skeptical, and I realize he thinks that I'm dead in the water like Malcolm does. "Just keep moving out there, kiddo."

The elevator rumbles upward, and I start to hear the crowd. They're chanting the names of their favorite fighters; they're singing their national anthems; and when they see us step onto the floor, they go wild. No wonder Malcolm gave his last thoughts down below—I can barely hear myself think up here.

I gape at the enormity of the stadium. Tens of thousands of people have filled the space. And there in front of me, taking up most of the floor, I see a cage. A gigantic one, the length of a football field. It's shaped like an enormous box, built with thick titanium bars that are placed just wide enough that onlookers can see what's going on inside.

The arena.

One o'clock comes and goes, but the match doesn't start yet. We have to get through all the fanfare first. A band plays the official song of the Games, "To the Glory of the Cup," before the Chiffons join them to belt out "The Star Spangled Banner." Then the announcer calls out every fighter's name and the country they represent, starting off alphabetically. It takes a while to get through the list, so I gaze around the stadium. There in the VIP section I spot Vice President Johnson seated next to Premier Khrushchev, both of them with their arms crossed as they murmur to each other, who knows about what. The Washington-Moscow Accord? Bets on who will win? A row behind them I also spot Senator Appleby, who meets my gaze with a warm smile, and I notice that she's seated beside the South Vietnamese diplomat again. Minister Tran, I think. The senator must be gunning hard for a plum trade deal with his country; those box seats can't come cheap.

The fighters form a line at the mouth of the cage, where the official escorts show us on a map where we've been randomly positioned to start the game. One by one we file inside and take our marks. I end up in the southwest corner of the arena, which is pure luck because I want to stick to the outskirts if I can. While I wait for the others to find their places, a group of fifty referees position themselves around the outside perimeter of the cage, each one assigned to a particular fighter.

Because of the general anarchy of Purgatory, the referees are tasked with keeping a razor-sharp eye on their fighter as they run, punch, kick, and retreat inside the arena. As soon as their fighter gets eliminated—the five-second rule applies here as well—they press a button on a handheld console that powers down the fighter's mecha. Otherwise we'd have to rely on an honor system for eliminated fighters to stay down, and how many of them would actually do that? Not many. Especially not Lidiya. In any case, this is also why there were so many diagnostic checks ahead of this match; the IC had to make sure each console and mecha were in sync so that there aren't any mishaps once the game begins.

As soon as the fighters and the refs look ready, the announcer begins the countdown and the entire stadium joins in. I breathe in slowly, hold it briefly, and then release, like my dad taught me to do before a match. He might be three thousand miles away, and how I wish that he were here in the stadium, but I know that he's watching, glued to Mrs. Watters's television set. Peter will be crammed next to him, jockeying to get closer to the screen.

Now the countdown has reached ten.

Across the way, I glance at Giselle and Albie. They're both quality fighters and it's a bit of a shame I won't get to team up with them.

The announcer reaches five. Then three.

My gaze lands on Lidiya Federova, standing in the northeast corner in her red-and-yellow Valkyrie. Sure enough, her eyes are on me. My pulse starts slamming in my throat, but I stare right back. I won't let her cow me. Not if it's the last thing I do. I slap my hands together as the buzzer sounds.

And now the Games really begin.

12

All fifty fighters move at once. Machines soar into the air, scraping against the bars of the ceiling. Others clash and tumble onto the ground. It's absolute chaos, and in thirty seconds flat, I already count three mechas powerless on the floor, meaning the refs have already been pressing those buttons.

"Right out of the gate, we have our first eliminations!" the announcer cries, listing their names, but it's hard for me to make them out. "That's a fighter each from Egypt, Colombia, and China."

China? I wonder if it's Rushi, but I don't have time to check. I'm a little busy at the moment.

Just as Malcolm predicted, the Reds have set their sights on me. Three of their fighters zero in on my location, with Lukas leading the pack and the Tilov twins of Bulgaria flanking him. Panic turns my heart into a hummingbird, and I have to remind myself not to lose my cool because nothing good ever comes out of that.

Run, move, leave them in the dust, I think, forcing myself to focus on these steps.

I leap out of their way, just beyond the reach of their metal fingertips. Jeez, they're fast. The Purgatories I've fought in at the tristate level are no picnic, but the speed and athleticism of these fighters are on a completely different level. Malcolm's probably counting down the seconds until I become the next casualty, but I refuse to prove him right and push my Goliath to move faster and jump higher.

I keep waiting for more of the Warsaw Pact fighters to join the hunt, but a glance to my left shows that the Federovas and the remaining Reds are tousling with a coalition of Swiss, Swedish, and Danish fighters who've teamed up to take on the big fish. Lidiya has already downed one of them, and it looks like she's just getting started.

"Seven fighters total have been eliminated so far, and we haven't yet hit the five-minute mark!" the announcer says.

I'm determined not to become the eighth one out of here, but it's tricky when I have Lukas and the twins hot on my heels. Since it will be pointless to take them all at once, I employ a dodge-and-run tactic. As long as I'm on the move, they can't eliminate me, and maybe someone else might knock them down along the way.

I zigzag through the arena, jumping from the ground and up the side of the cage, then leaping to the other side before I hit the floor again, doing a quick roll to avoid crashing into Team Mexico, and then I'm soaring into the air again. I use my legs as much as possible to save the strength in my arms for later, but the trio of Communists chasing me is speedy so I have to get creative.

Pushing off the ground, I grab on to the cage's ceiling and swing across it like I'm eight years old again but with much higher stakes. When I was a kid, I spent hours on the monkey bars. I'd race across them as fast as I could; I'd practice skipping over every other rung; I'd hang on them, timing myself until my muscles burned and my palms calloused. I use all of that now. I reach the middle of the cage and wait. My arms start to ache, but I can handle it. One of the twins is the first to reach me, and I'm ready for him. I swing my legs in his direction, hooking them around his hips and yanking hard until he loses his grip. His limbs flail while he tumbles toward the floor, landing right by Sam and our allies, who've formed a classic defensive posture, standing shoulder to shoulder in a circle, facing out. I spot Team UK there along with Team Australia and Team Canada. Giselle's partner Auguste has been eliminated, but she's shouting orders to the rest of the group, asking them to cover for her while she slams her mecha on top of the Bulgarian twin who has fallen. As soon as he's finished off, her eyes flicker up to me, and she gives a thumbs-up.

"Team Bulgaria is down a fighter! The same goes for Team Sweden with Vilgot Karlsson eliminated by Zoya Federova of the USSR," the announcer says.

Lukas and the remaining Bulgarian twin come at me next, one on each side, but the twin doesn't last for long. I plant a kick on her shoulder, knocking one of her hands loose, and within seconds, she can't keep her grip. Lukas, however, proves harder to get rid of. He somehow dodges most of my kicks, and even when I do get in a hit, he doesn't flinch. By now, my arm muscles are tightening up, so I pick a landing spot and aim for it. When I hit the ground, I can feel the shock ringing in my teeth, but I hoist myself up again because I'm sure Lukas is on my tail.

"Looks like we've got a real chase happening at center court! There's Lukas Sauer of East Germany tracking down Josephine Linden of the US," the announcer says. Ugh. Didn't anyone send him the memo that I go by Jo? "Will he catch her? Not this time! She dodges his grab and there she goes again, but there's traffic up ahead."

Sure enough, I'm about to run smack dab into Rushi, who's fending off the Austrians. It's a two-on-one fight, but she's giving it her all, launching a high kick into one of their chins while spinning around to punch the other one in the chest. But when she ducks down and tries to somersault out of their grasp, they manage to catch her by the ankle.

I'm closing in on them, with Lukas only a few steps behind. Do I spin to my left and hope Lukas goes right? Or should I jump up and leap over the fray? I don't know if I have the momentum. Whatever I decide I better do it now because I'm about to plow into the others and then Lukas will have me trapped.

An idea hits me and I run with it—literally.

The Austrians are too distracted wrangling up Rushi to see me coming. I'm ten yards away. Now five. But I don't slow down; I speed up instead. With my velocity building, I hold my breath and launch into the air. The Goliath flies upward, but I get it even higher by using the Austrians as stepping stones, planting one of my feet on one of their backs and then the other on one of their heads, knocking them sideways in the process. Rushi scrambles free while Lukas gets tangled up in the pileup.

"What a move by Linden!" the announcer says to the screams of the crowd. "She survives that collision, but not Ludvig Milch of Austria. Now we're down to twenty-eight fighters, folks. No, make that twenty-six, and the action doesn't stop!"

I scuttle up the south wall of the cage to catch my breath for a few seconds. As our numbers have thinned out, the pit floor grows littered with broken-down mechas. The chaos that kicked off the match has faded, but now the battle lines have sharpened—and outliers like me are more vulnerable than ever.

I survey the arena and wipe the sweat off my forehead. I see that Lukas has found his way back to the other Communists. The Reds are hunting like a wolf pack now, picking off a Colombian and then a Turk. Then I spy Sam and the other NATO fighters on the other side of the cage, squaring off against the remnants of the Swiss-Swedish-Danish alliance that has already lost half their members. Sam and Giselle lead the charge, and I hate to admit it, but he's beautiful to watch. Every punch and swing perfectly textbook. Every grab perfectly executed. Irritatingly so. Malcolm must be pleased, but he has to be happy with my performance too, considering I've done what he has asked and led the Reds' charge away from Sam. And I've survived this far to boot. He better send at least three endorsements my way at the rate I'm going.

"Down goes Ambrogi of Italy, and that marks the halfway point! Twenty-five fighters have been eliminated and nine more have to go before we reach our final sixteen."

I try to save up as much strength as I can since I won't be able to lurk in the corners much longer. Across the way, Giselle chases after Rushi, but Rushi reaches the nearest wall and begins scaling it. She's about halfway up when she pushes herself off the rung like an Olympic diver, arching her back and executing a perfect midair flip before landing cleaning on her feet.

"Would you look at that! We've never seen these sort of moves in the arena before," the announcer marvels.

While the crowd oohs and aahs, a rush of movement catches my eye, and I tell myself it's time to scram. The Federovas have me in their sights.

Lidiya shouts an order to her comrades. There are more than ten of them, and it's Lukas who leads the charge at me, like he's Lidiya's loyal watchdog. He might as well be frothing at the mouth while I'm a slab of fresh meat.

Stay one step ahead of them, I tell myself.

I rely on my speed to shake them off. Despite the aching in my arms, I climb up the rungs once again, but the Soviets fan out like a real pack of wolves, nearly surrounding me. Before I can think, my vision flashes white. Lidiya has somehow launched herself into the air and clocked me in the head with the sole of her boot, sending me tumbling to the ground. I'm not sure how far I fall. Twenty feet? More? I land hard on my back, and the Reds really have me now.

Dread fills my stomach. This could be it. My mind goes to Dad and Peter back home. I can see Dad pacing, murmuring to himself, while Peter is pressed to the screen.

Come on, Jo, he's saying. *Get up.*

Get up.

Right. I'm not down for the count yet.

Clenching my teeth, I shake off the dizziness in my head and lurch up before the Reds can descend upon me. I'm sprinting again, which buys me a few seconds to figure out what to do, but my thoughts are blank. How am I supposed to get ten of the best fighters in the world off my tail? Now's the time when a shield could come in mighty handy.

A thought clicks together in my mind. A *shield*.

I spot Sam, Giselle, and the rest of the NATO fighters on the arena floor, and I point myself in a new direction—straight toward them. They're finishing off the last Dane standing when I slot myself right next to Sam.

He barely has time to look up at me when I yell to him, "Incoming!"

"You led them straight to us!" Giselle shouts to me on my left. It's obvious that she isn't pleased at all by this development, but it isn't like there are that many fighters left standing. The two factions— NATO versus Warsaw Pact—were bound to clash. I only sped the process along a little.

Sam calls out a defensive stance to the others, forming another circle to absorb the Commie attack.

"Nice of you to finally join us," Sam yells.

"You're welcome," I yell back. I crouch low in between him and Giselle, watching as Lidiya takes the charge and commands her fighters to fan out again.

The entire stadium is on its feet, and the announcer sounds like he's losing his mind. "Here it comes, the finale! We've got nineteen fighters left. Only three need to be eliminated . . . no, make that two! There goes Fitz-Lloyd Foster Hughes of the UK."

"Tighten the circle!" Sam says, stepping over Fitz's mecha to close the empty gap that he has left.

There are seven of us NATO allies still standing: Sam and me, Giselle and Albie, the Ogler from West Germany, and a fighter each from Canada and Australia. We're up against nine from the Warsaw Pact. Both Federovas, both the Romanians and the Czechs, along with Lukas and a couple others. Lidiya screams a new command, and they all sweep forward at once.

"Giselle Boucher of Team France has eliminated Dieter Albrecht of East Germany!" the announcer says. "Only one more fighter to go!"

Almost there.

Suddenly Zoya lunges at me, and we grapple for a moment, standing so close that I can see the blue of her eyes. Sweat runs down her face, and she's breathing heavily. She lacks her sister's stamina, but she still has some juice in the tank and she uses it to butt me in the head, sending a shock through my mecha's frame and down to my toes. I butt her right back and add in an elbow jab, and Sam is there on cleanup duty to fling her off me. Both of us move to hold her down, but Zoya rolls away. Lukas jumps in to spar with Sam while someone grabs me from behind, probably Lidiya or one of her goons.

I use a judo move to throw them off, something called a kani basami, which is forbidden in formal competition because you could break your opponent's leg with it. But there are no rules against that in the pit, and I wouldn't be snapping their calf bone apart, just their mecha's.

I hear a grunt, and when I spin around, I expect to find a Communist on the floor, but it isn't. I honestly gasp I'm so surprised.

It's Giselle.

She pushes herself up and comes at me in a blur of jabs.

"What are you doing?" I shout because we're supposed to work together in Purgatory, but she doesn't answer me. She keeps attacking, and it quickly dawns on me that we're not allies in her eyes. Not anymore. Maybe not ever.

So much for Franco-American relations.

Giselle puts in everything to eliminate me. More punches. A roundhouse kick. I dodge one, only to parry another. Even now, she's breathtakingly fast.

When she starts to slow, when her punches don't come as sharply as before, I go all in. I sweep out my right leg and knock her off balance, but she twists away before I can pounce.

The final buzzer sounds.

"Ladies and gentlemen, we have our final sixteen competitors!"

I look around in a daze while Giselle does the same.

The match is over.

I made it through.

The crowd is cheering and clapping and waving thousands of little flags. Giselle shrugs me off with a glare, but I don't care. I lift my arms up, hoping that Peter can see me back home. Here I am, one of the darkest horses in the race and yet I'm on my way to Round 2.

Sam is grinning, and his fans—there have to be hundreds of them in the stands—are going wild. So he must've made it through too, which floods me with relief that I kept my side of the deal with Malcolm. I hold out hope that Sam might've KO'd one of the Federovas while he was at it, but they're both standing as well.

Suddenly I'm nearly knocked over. Lukas Sauer has careened into the side of my Goliath, and I almost go tumbling down, but I manage to keep upright.

"Watch it!" I shout, and I'm about to push him right back.

But Lukas doesn't seem to be joking around. He collapses onto the pit floor, and I think his eyes flutter to a close. Did he faint or something? Too much excitement? None of the other fighters seems to notice; they're too busy celebrating.

I bend over to look closer when Lukas starts convulsing inside his mecha, causing its limbs to jerk haphazardly. An alarm bell goes off in my head. Something is wrong.

Very wrong.

"Medic!" I scream. "We need a medic!"

13

Nobody hears me. As soon as my words leave my lips, they get lost in my own mecha. I have to get out of this thing.

I wrestle my arms and legs free from their straps and scramble out of the Goliath to kneel next to Lukas. He's still inside his Kriegsmaschine, and he's still convulsing but worse than before. A seizure, by the looks of it. I yank open his cockpit door and try to unstrap him.

"Medic!" I cry out again. Where are they?

Lukas's face is turning purple, and it sounds like he's choking. I know some basic first aid due to my years in mecha fighting—how to treat a sprain or how to staunch a cut—but nothing like this. Should I turn him onto his side? Or pull his tongue out?

I'm about to jam my fingers into his mouth, when somebody pushes me aside. It must be the paramedic team, but when I jerk my head back, I realize that it's Lidiya Federova, fresh out of her Vostok with her face covered in sweat. She doesn't bother wiping her forehead though; she's focused on one thing and one thing only.

"Lukas!" she shouts, pressing her hands against his face. She's slapping his cheeks, which I doubt will help very much, but she looks desperate.

"I think we need to lay him on one side. Here—" I start to reach over, and she elbows me away.

"Do not touch him," she warns me in accented English.

I know that her boyfriend is in bad shape, but she's being ridiculous. Lukas's lips are starting to look blue. "I don't care if you do it yourself, but turn him over already!"

I don't think she understands me, and I doubt she wants to either. It doesn't matter because that's when the medics arrive. By then, the stadium has hushed. I can still hear some people singing loudly, probably drunk, but soon even they have quieted down. More fighters have gathered around Lukas, mostly his Warsaw Pact allies, but I spot a few others in the throng. Giselle is openly staring while Rushi looks more than a little green and has to look away.

The medics instruct everyone to move back, but Lidiya refuses until one of her coaches rushes in to intervene. Meanwhile the announcer tells the crowd to please find their exit and thanks them for coming, obviously trying to end the event.

A shadow crosses over me, and I look up to find Sam in his Goliath. "The refs are asking us to clear out of the cage." He crouches down and holds out the palm of his mecha. "Need a lift?"

I shake my head and walk back to my own Goliath because I can't leave it here on the arena floor. I glance at Lukas a couple of times, but the medics have surrounded him, blocking my view. I can't say that my opinion of Lukas has improved at all since he's still an idiot stick in my book, but no fighter wants to go down this way.

Sam waits for me at the gate to exit together, and as soon as we step out, the Americans in the crowd—of which there are thousands upon thousands—start clapping for us. Then they're tossing flowers by our feet and a few teddy bears too. As well as a pair of women's underwear that's undoubtedly for Sam.

Sam laughs and gives me a wink. "Why are you standing there all limp-armed? We just got through Purgatory at the Games!"

The corners of my mouth twitch up. The scoreboard reveals that the whole thing lasted barely forty-five minutes, but we've survived every single second. I beat the odds, even with the Reds breathing down my neck.

I start waving up to the stands like Sam, and I get so carried away that I might have blown a few kisses to some handsome boys who are whistling at me. It all comes to an abrupt stop though when Malcolm retrieves us and escorts us down the elevator, where we leave our Goliaths to the engineers. I finally get the chance to towel off my sweaty hair and gulp down a few cups of water while Malcolm gives his victory speech that consists of patting our backs and saying, "You did it. You got through Purgatory today."

I can hear the slight surprise in his voice that he's saying this to both of us and not Sam alone.

He goes on to say, "But keep in mind that there are four more rounds left and your individual matches can start as soon as Monday morning, less than forty-eight hours from now. We'll start training bright and early tomorrow at eight, but rest up this evening. And I mean that. No partying or staying up late. I'll come around to make sure that you're in bed by ten thirty."

"Aw, Coach," Sam starts to say. He even pouts out his lower lip like he's five years old.

"In bed at ten thirty *sharp*," Malcolm replies. It's all business and no play with him. No exceptions. "Now go get showered."

It's like he's dismissing us after an ordinary practice session instead of the Purgatory round at the Pax Games, but I guess there's no clocking out for him. He has one goal for the next week—win that title and clinch his legacy—and nothing will sideline him.

It makes me wonder if he's secretly a bot pretending to be human.

Only after I head inside the locker room do I realize he didn't really congratulate me.

By the time I return to the Pavilion, I'm ready to grab something to eat and take Malcolm's advice to rest for once, but the other fighters have a different idea in mind. Music booms from the quad; I hear the pounding drums from the Surfaris's new song "Wipe Out." Someone has dragged out a record-playing bot and hooked it up to a couple of speakers. Everyone is eager for a drink too—some to celebrate and some to drown the pain of losing. Albie of Team

UK cajoles the dining hall staff to give up a few crates of wine, and soon enough people aren't bothering to pour the stuff into cups anymore. They pass the bottles around.

Albie tries to get me to join in when he spots me heading up to my dorm, waving a bottle at me and saying that it has my name on it, but I beg off when I see that he's drinking with Giselle. She tried to eliminate me in Purgatory not even two hours ago, but she doesn't seem the least bit embarrassed by what she did. Nope, she's sipping chardonnay and lifts a single shoulder and says, "You should celebrate, Josephine."

"You mean, I should celebrate the fact that you tried to sink me in the arena?"

She chuckles and offers me her bottle. "It wasn't personal. Come now. Let's leave the game in the pit and have some wine."

I push the bottle back toward her. "Maybe that's how you do things over in Paris, but here in the States we don't have drinks with so-called allies who stab us in the back."

Giselle only looks amused and takes a long sip of wine. "We're all trying to win, aren't we?"

Like I need the reminder.

A car honks at us from the road. Glancing up I see Sam hanging out the window of a red Thunderbird, a stunner of a sports car. "Wanna bite to eat, kiddo?"

"Sure thing," I reply, not bothering to say goodbye to Giselle before I hustle over to the vehicle. It's a real beauty with a rounded hood and bright chrome running from the front to the razor-sharp tailfins, looking as sleek as a dolphin rising out of the water. "Where did you get these wheels, Kealey? It has Washington State plates."

He nods as I get in. "I drove it here from home."

"You *drove* this across the country?"

"Why not? Eisenhower paid for all those new interstate highways, so I was only trying to see where our tax dollars got spent." He steps on the gas, and the ride is as smooth as butter.

"It seems like an awfully long way to get to the Games though."

"I had the time. Besides, there were a few stops that I wanted to see along the way," he says vaguely. He nods at a paper bag near my feet. "You like crab cakes? They make them fresh over at this fish market by the wharf."

I wouldn't know if I like crab cakes or not since they're a whole lot pricier than our usual ground beef, which I can get for forty-three cents a pound on sale. "I guess I'll find out. Where are we going?"

"A little south of here. Ever been to Hains Point?"

I've never even heard of it, but it's within easy walking distance of the Pavilion if you head to the very tip of the island. Sam parks the car, and we sit down at a picnic table overlooking the Potomac, which surrounds us on three sides. It's quiet out here—if I shut my eyes, I would never guess that I was sitting in our nation's capital. The city feels miles away. It's a real switch from the pressure cooker of Purgatory, and suddenly I'm back at the stadium and inside my Goliath, sweating and running and jumping out of the Communists' grasp.

I shake my head to clear it of the memory. "Any word on Lukas yet?"

"Last I heard he was taken to the hospital for treatment." Sam begins to unpack the food, laying the spread out on the table. Crab cakes. Coleslaw. Piping hot french fries, slick with oil. Lemonade to wash it all down. I'm tempted to bury my face in it because I'm starved.

"What do you think happened to him?" I ask while I push a few fries into my mouth, not even bothering with the ketchup because I'm too impatient.

"No clue." Sam hands me a few napkins and a fork and motions for me to dig in. "I've never seen that in the pit before."

"Me neither." And I've seen my share of injuries. Dislocations. Concussions. Fractures. "Maybe it was the stadium lights."

"Or bad luck, I guess. We'll have to wait and see if he'll be able to fight in the next round."

"I wonder who he'll be up against. When does the Association announce the bracket?" I ask around a mouthful of crab cake.

"Take it easy there. You're gonna choke," Sam says, watching me eat in amazement. "The announcement is tomorrow morning."

I scowl and drag a fry through his dollop of ketchup. To ratchet up the tension in between rounds, the IC randomly selects the lineup for each match. Basically, they print our names onto slips of paper and toss them all into a glass cube, which gets swirled around. Then they pick out the papers two by two, and that'll be the bracket for the next round, meaning I could be facing Lidiya or

Lukas. Or even Sam. The whole thing is simultaneously broadcast on television and over the radio to drive up ratings.

I stare out at the water and swat at the gnats congregating around my face, considering who I want to face in the pit. The final sixteen includes the usual suspects. The Federovas and Lukas. Sam, Giselle, and Albie. Gunter from West Germany. A Czech and both Yugoslavians. A Canuck and an Aussie. Then there are the surprises. Me. Rushi. A fighter from Iran, another from Japan.

"Who would you want to go up against in Round Two?" he asks.

"Maybe Lazarescu of Romania," I say. My chances would be better against her since she squeaked through Purgatory on account of her more experienced allies. "Or maybe the tall guy from West Germany."

"Gunter? That's an interesting choice."

"He tried to look down my dress at the luncheon."

Sam gets that aha moment in his eyes. "I'd pay to see what you'd do to him in the pit. So what did your folks think about the arena? Did they come out to see it?"

"Nope, but my dad and brother watched it back in San Francisco."

"What about your mom? Is she in sunny California too?"

I take a sip of lemonade. "More like six feet under."

Sam gags on his bite of crab cake and starts coughing so badly that I give his back a couple smacks. "Jeez, Jo. You trying to kill me before the next match?"

"Sorry," I say, feeling a little guilty because his pretty face is all red now.

"I'll survive, but I can't say the same for my lungs." Sam clears his throat when his coughing finally subsides, regarding me differently. "Sorry about your mom though."

"Don't be."

His left brow arches. "Family feud?"

"Let's say she was no June Cleaver," I say. I don't really want to get into this, and not because of Malcolm's warning to avoid speaking about my mother, but because I've always hated the pity that people get in their eyes when they learn that she's dead.

"How old were you when she passed?" he asks.

"Four and a half." I swig some more lemonade and add, "Do me a favor and don't ask me how she died."

"And risk you clocking me in the nose? It's none of my business anyway." He chuckles to himself. "I don't mind it so much when people ask me how my old man died. That's better than having them think that my stepfather is my real dad."

I remember how tense Sam got when I made that mistake before the parade. It sure sounds like his stepdad is no Ward Cleaver either. "So how old were you when he died?"

"Zero. My mom was pregnant when his ship was attacked. It sank somewhere off Iwo Jima." His voice has gone flat, and he's staring out at the river, watching the waves bob along.

I wonder if his dad went down with the ship. That happened sometimes during the war, and the boats would sink so deep there was no way to retrieve the bodies. I'm about to tell him that he has my condolences, but he has already wiped his face clean of emotion and takes a big bite of food.

I glance at him with fresh eyes. Before I arrived in Washington I'd thought that I had a good read on Sam Kealey, with his money and his confidence and his irritatingly perfect record, but now I'm starting to question how much of the real Sam I actually know. For instance, why is he here with me instead of back at the Pavilion partying with the others? Or out with his family?

"Say, where are your brothers? I figured you'd all be out celebrating right about now," I ask.

"They wanted to, but their dad dragged them off to some fancy shindig downtown. Apparently Gunter's family is throwing it. They own a bot manufacturing plant in Dusseldorf that Boeing might try to buy out." His face sours. "My stepdad wanted me to make an appearance."

Wow. His own stepfather is milking the Games to further his business ventures? It sounds downright mercenary. I shake my head. *Rich people.*

Sam sighs and finishes off his last french fry. "What's the verdict, kiddo? Did you like the crab cakes or not?"

In reply, I show him my empty plate. "My name isn't kiddo, you know."

"I know, I know, but it's fitting," he says, reaching out to ruffle my hair, but I duck away. "When we first met a year ago, you really did look like a kid in your Goliath."

"Gee, thanks."

"I don't say it as a bad thing. Only that you're on the younger side. Want me to call you youngster instead?"

I screw up my face. "Only if I can call you geezer."

Sam lets out a bright laugh, and then we pack up and make our way back to the Pavilion, where he drops me off first since he has to find a parking spot. The quad is a different place than how we'd left it not even an hour ago. A few wine bottles lay on the grass, but the music has been shut off. Most of the fighters are gone too, and I figure that the staff must've told everyone to clear out. I'm not complaining though. After I call home and give Peter an update, I plan on taking a nice long nap.

Right then, I notice a few black cars entering through the Pavilion's gate and depositing their passengers onto the pebbled path. A couple of security guards step out first, followed by Lidiya, who's still wearing her uniform from the match. Truth be told, she looks like a wreck. Pieces of her hair have tumbled from her carefully pinned bun, and her face is streaked red. She's storming toward the dormitory, when something in her eyes shift, like a predator locking on prey.

She starts talking in rapid Russian, and she changes direction to march over to me. "What did you do?" she says in English, her breaths heavy, her throat raw.

I stare right back, wondering if this is one of her "dramatic" episodes that she's known for. "You're in my way," I say, trying to sidestep her.

She blocks me. "What did you do to Lukas?" Then she grabs me by the shoulders, shaking them, and tears are coming out of her eyes and I don't think this is an act, but then again this is Lidiya Federova we're talking about.

I manage to twist away and get ready to take a swing, but her security goons pull her back. They drag her into the girls' dormitory, and I'm left there on the sidewalk, panting and full of adrenaline that I don't know what to do with.

What the heck was that about?

"There you are." I hear a voice behind me, and I turn around to find Malcolm striding toward me. "I've been looking for you and Sam."

"Did you see what Lidiya did?" I ask, furious. I explain how she had turned into some shrieking banshee, but Malcolm doesn't frown or flinch.

"She's clearly upset" is all he says.

"Upset? She grabbed me! Isn't that against some rule?"

"Probably, but I doubt the IC would exact any punishment considering the circumstances."

I'm about to say that the IC can't be playing favorites, but then his voice goes strangely soft.

"There's no use sugarcoating the news so here it is," he says grimly. "Lukas Sauer is dead."

14

As soon as Sam returns from parking his Thunderbird, Malcolm sits us both down on a secluded bench on the far side of the quad to give us the details.

"The news isn't public yet, but it has already circulated among the coaches and fighters," he starts off. "It appears that Lukas had multiple seizures that eventually led to a heart attack. The East Germans are insisting on an autopsy, but it seems like he had epilepsy as a child, which may have something to do with the death."

I have about a hundred questions rushing through my head, but I stay quiet, too stunned to ask them. Fighters can die in the pit— we all know that going in. Back in the twenties and thirties, when the sport wasn't as regulated, it was common to lose a couple fighters per international tournament. But those numbers have plummeted after the Games picked up again in '47 because the organizers added more rigorous safety measures, like testing each mecha before every match. So Lukas's death is still quite the shock.

"His epilepsy came back somehow?" Sam asks, confused.

"We don't know that. I'm only telling you what I've been told," Malcolm replies. "As far as I know, this was a terrible accident."

Accident being the key word here.

"Can you relay that to Lidiya? Because she obviously thinks I had something to do with this," I say.

"She could've been looking to blow off steam and you were the first target she saw," Sam offers.

"But she blamed me for the fire too," I remind him. "That's twice now she has pointed fingers at me."

"The case about the possible arson was dropped," Malcolm cuts in. "Let's not get paranoid here."

"I'm not being—"

"I'll deal with Lidiya and her antics. You have to focus on what's ahead," says Malcolm, clearly eager to move on from this. "The Games are still on, and I meant it when I told you two earlier that you're supposed to rest for the remainder of the day. I want you giving those muscles a break and getting plenty of sleep. Is that understood?"

Sam and I nod before going our separate ways to our dormitories. I fall into bed without changing, keeping my eyes open because whenever I close them I'm back in Purgatory and I'm staring at Lukas's face. He was alive only a few hours ago. How old was he—seventeen, eighteen? I might not have been a fan of his, but all I can think about is how he's returning home in a coffin.

And that reminds me all over again how very dangerous this game can be.

I wake up sore and aching the following morning, but I bolt out of bed and propel myself back to the training center after I've gobbled down a bowl of plain oatmeal, a couple of boiled eggs, and a whole green apple, which is tart enough to make my lips pucker. The dining hall is also serving battercakes smothered in orange marmalade and crispy sausage links, but I force myself to forgo the heavy stuff for now. I've got a long day of training ahead to prepare for Round 2, but first I have to find out who I'll be fighting.

When I get to the training center at eight, there's an eerie feeling in the air. With thirty-four fighters eliminated yesterday, the place feels mostly empty now and our ranks will only continue to thin out. In our training section, the Jays are overseeing a work crew that's taking down the partition that used to divide us from Team Switzerland, whose fighters both got cut in Purgatory yesterday. Malcolm has already set up a television set in our new acquisition of space—a top-of-the-line Bush model with shiny silver knobs—along with a few folding chairs. A service bot rolls up to us to offer coffee and tea that's stored in its interior tanks, but I'm too anxious to risk holding a cup of hot liquid.

"The broadcast is about to start," Malcolm says, motioning at Sam and me to gather by the screen. He fiddles with the knobs and flips through the channels until he lands on the right one.

The broadcast kicks off with a message from the IC expressing condolences to Lukas's family and the whole East German delegation, followed by a three-minute recap of what happened in Purgatory before they get down to business. The setup is cheesy, mimicking the look of a game show. Various members of the IC gather around a big glass cube that sits on a pedestal, filled with exactly sixteen slips of paper. But they don't do the picking. No, they've hired a blond model to dip her hand into the glass and grab two slips at random.

"The first match pairing is . . ." The blond opens up the folded paper. "Zhu Rushi of China against . . ." She unfurls the second. "Archibald McDaniel of Canada!"

The IC folks claps politely although there's no reason for it before they move on to the next pairing.

"Next we have . . ." The model pauses to read the name. "Samuel Kealey of the US." She looks up at the camera, like she can see Sam watching her, and grins. "Up against . . . Mihaela Lazarescu of Romania!"

Sam's shoulders relax, looking relieved.

"You lucky dog," I tell him, trying not to sound too jealous. Lazarescu has the makings to become a formidable opponent, but she's still a couple years off from that point.

"Now we have Mirko Jankovic of Yugoslavia going up against . . ." The model opens the next slip of paper and her jaw tightens. "Lukas Sauer of East Germany." It looks like she's reading from a prompter now. "Due to the international rule book, Jankovic of Yugoslavia now has a bye to the next round."

There are no alternates as soon as Round 1 begins. There are no exceptions even if your mother dies back home. Even if *you* die. No fighter can take your place.

The blond titters, like she's unsure of what to do next, until someone prompts her off-screen to continue. She grabs the next piece of paper.

"Josephine Linden of the US will face . . ."

I tense up and I swear it takes the girl a full half hour to get my opponent's paper unfolded. "Giselle Boucher of France."

I bark out a laugh. I'll be facing Giselle? She's number seven in the world, nothing like fighting Mihaela Lazarescu.

I guess we might as well finish what we got started in Purgatory yesterday.

And it only gets worse from there.

After the pairings are firmed up, the IC assigns us our game times. Sam gets the plum slot of six p.m. on Tuesday, meaning he gets forty-eight hours of rest. Me, on the other hand? I'll be facing Giselle at the earliest game to kick off Round 2 at ten tomorrow morning.

In a little over twenty-four hours, I'll be back in the pit, so I can't count on the recovery time to get me back into tip-top shape. I'll have to grit through it though because it's the Games and there's a schedule to keep up. Round 2 will stretch over tomorrow and the day after, whittling our numbers from sixteen to eight. Round 3 will take place on Thursday, halving the group to four. Then Round 4 will take place on Saturday to select the top two fighters, and finally Round 5 will close out the Games on Sunday night. It's ten days from start to finish—a whirlwind of punches and KOs until we've crowned a new world victor.

"How're you feeling about your matchup?" Sam asks.

"All right," I say, hoping to sound nonchalant even though I'd trade to be in his position in a split second.

"Word of advice—"

"I'm fine, thanks," I cut him off, not in the mood for his nugget of wisdom.

But Sam is surprisingly persistent about this. "Giselle struggles to defend against aerial attacks. Remember that."

I squint at him, trying to decide if he's telling the truth or not, when Malcolm interrupts us.

"Sam, go stretch and we'll run through a couple ideas I had about your match, but we'll go light today because you need to rest up and drink fluids. You'll have more work to do later this week," Malcolm says, assuming that Sam will beat out Mihaela and survive to the finals. Then he turns his attention on me. He retrieves a cardboard box and removes the lid, revealing a dozen film reels, all carefully labeled by date. "Here's your homework. Happy birthday, rookie."

My birthday isn't until October. "What are these?"

"Giselle's greatest hits," he replies. "They're recordings of each one of her international matches from '61 and onward. I've watched three of them and wrote down notes, but you'll need to finish up the rest. Jot down anything that looks noteworthy, and we'll go over it together." He proceeds to plop the box into my arms and point me toward the viewing area that the Jays have set up in Team Switzerland's old training section. There's a projector, a screen, and a chair where I can sit and watch.

"Just like the movies," I say to myself, and pop the first reel out of its case.

Over the next few hours, I watch and rewatch the reels until I've made my way through half the box. I use Malcolm's notes as a starting point of what to look out for. He didn't write much, but what he has done so far is insightful, paying attention to any particular moves that Giselle favors, pointing out that she's left-handed, keeping a tally of every punch versus every kick to predict how she might attack me. She's very good, I have to say. *Very* quick and light on her feet, but she also packs quite the punch. As soon as the whistle blows to kick off a match, she becomes a blur of movement, jabbing and kicking and grabbing until the other fighter gets overwhelmed and makes a mistake.

But I do have to admit that Sam was correct. Giselle is only middling to average when it comes to deflecting aerial attacks. There's something about the mechanics of it that trips her up and makes her more sluggish than usual. Still, I'm going to have my work cut out for me tomorrow. While Giselle is ranked seventh in the world, when it comes to speed she's only second behind Lidiya in the time it takes to eliminate their opponents.

A crick is forming in my neck when Malcolm makes his grand return and tells me I ought to get some food before the dining hall closes for lunch.

"Let me finish this reel and I'll come right over," I say as I scribble a few sentences. "I've got a list of questions to talk through with you later—"

But when I glance up, Malcolm is gone.

"Coach?" I say, but it's useless. He and Sam have already turned the corner, probably hashing out more strategy. I consider following them, but pride holds me back. Well, fine. Just like I've done for years, I'll have to take over my own coaching.

I stride toward the restroom to splash some cold water onto my face because I need a good jolt to get me through the next couple hours of film watching. The training center really has become a ghost town, especially one particular hallway that housed the teams from Italy, Senegal, and Colombia, which have all been eliminated. Most of their equipment has been packed up and now awaits shipment, and I'm navigating my way through a few boxes left in the corridor, when a noise makes my head jerk to my left.

My gaze collides into Rushi, who's stepping out of Team Italy's section with her arms carrying two esterium batteries. She freezes as soon as she spots me.

"J-Jo!" she stammers. Her cheeks immediately flush. "What are you doing?"

"On my way to the bathroom." I could ask the same of her, but it's pretty easy to figure out what's going on. She's pilfering those batteries—although I'm not sure why.

"You see . . ." she says, fishing for an excuse. "Our battery shipment never arrived! Team Senegal said that we could have theirs."

My eyes flick upward toward a banner above her head that proudly displays the Italian flag. Rushi must notice it too because her face flushes redder than before.

"Please don't tell the IC," she whispers. She turns around, probably to put the batteries back.

"Wait," I hear myself say. Could Team China be so bad off that they don't have enough batteries for their fighters? I'd assumed that their government would've supplied Rushi and her partner with plenty, not only with batteries, but with mechas and equipment and spare parts as well. Like the Association has done for Sam and me.

But China isn't the US, now is it? I remember what Giselle told me about the famine over there. If the Chinese can hardly feed their own people, it would make sense that esterium batteries would be a real luxury.

"Don't worry. I won't tell anyone," I say to her. I guess I could get in trouble for this, but Rushi needs those batteries a whole lot more than Team Italy. Heck, I could've given her a few if she had asked. We've got storage lockers full of them, and I figured that every team had the same. But I should've known better. Maybe the countries at the Games are a bit like the schools back at home, split between the haves and have-nots.

Rushi's face fills with relief, and she grips those batteries tight. "Thank you! If you need anything, please tell me."

I nod and am about to let her hurry off until I decide to take her up on the offer. "Actually, I do have a favor to ask. I could use a little advice."

Now she looks a little surprised, but she says, "Of course. What about?"

"About Giselle. I'm facing her next in the pit, and I've noticed that she has a hard time defending against aerial attacks. Since you've got a knack for that, maybe you have a technique or some tips you could tell me."

Rushi hesitates as I expected her to do. Sharing intel with your competitors is almost unheard of, but it helps my case that I'm keeping her secret *and* that I bailed her out in the arena when she was tied up with Team Austria.

My good deeds swing back in my favor because Rushi, although looking a little unsure, gives me a nod. "Can you do a flip?"

I laugh. "Not like you can."

"I can show you."

I'm pretty doubtful that she can teach me something like that in a few minutes, but I'm a little desperate, so I follow her into Team Italy's unused training pit. Once inside, she climbs up four of the rungs and launches herself off, executing a perfect flip in the air where her feet fly over her head and yet she manages to land in one piece on the ground. And she's not even inside a mecha.

"I think that's a little advanced for me," I say. "Got anything else?"

"Try it with your mecha," she insists. "It will do the work for you, but you must arch your back and you must keep your eyes aimed at the ground. Your feet will follow."

I'm still pretty doubtful, but I'll take anything at this point. "Can you do that again?"

I watch her more closely this time, noting the positioning of her hands and feet before she takes off and scrutinizing how she moves through the air, memorizing as much as I can. Sam's video camera bot would sure come in handy right about now. I'm both eager and anxious to try this out myself—in the safety of my Goliath—but our lesson soon gets interrupted when we hear someone calling for Rushi. Her back goes straight as steel.

"That's Envoy Yu," she says. "I need to go."

So soon? But there's an urgency in her voice that tells me she can't stick around. "Thanks for the tip."

She's already walking away and grabbing those batteries before she stops and turns around. "Zhù nǐ hǎo yùn. That means *good luck* in Chinese."

I try to repeat the words back to her, but I fail spectacularly so I opt for a simple "Same to you."

She scurries off, her last words echoing in my head. But maybe I won't need to depend on luck tomorrow now that I'm armed with Rushi's advice.

I'm up by five thirty the following day to prepare for the match, jerking awake as soon as my alarm bot starts blaring. I run a brush through my hair and give my teeth a good scrubbing, but before I head down to breakfast, I make sure to call Peter again, even though it's basically the middle of the night in San Francisco. I expect him to pepper me with advice about my Goliath to pass along to the engineers or discuss my strategy against Giselle, but he only gives one-word answers.

"You ought to get back up to bed. I won't fight for another four hours," I say. "You must be tired, huh?"

"A little. It's just—" He stops himself. I can hear him breathing hard on the line, which sometimes happens when he's feeling nervous. "Never mind."

"What? Tell me." It takes a couple more tries before he spits it out.

"I overheard Dad talking to the landlady. She said that she'd give us another month in the apartment, but if she doesn't get the full payment by then, we'll have to go," Peter says.

I swear my heart splits clean in half because I can't hug him and I bet that he's standing in the dark of our store, trying to save a dime or two on electricity.

His voice twists sharp. "Why didn't you tell me?"

I curse under my breath. Of all times, why does this have to happen right now? "Look, I will figure this out. I promise."

"But you should've let me know. I could've helped; I could've done more repairs at the shop."

I sigh into the receiver. Fixing more vacuuming bots wouldn't have made much of a difference. "Don't worry, okay?"

"Will you stop treating me like I'm two years old?"

I pull the phone away from my ear for a second and blink at it. I can't remember the last time Peter lost his cool.

"I'm sorry, squirt—"

"My name isn't squirt," he replies in a huff.

I try again. "I'm sorry, *Peter*. I really am. Dad and I didn't want you to worry."

"You mean you didn't think I could handle it."

"No, that wasn't it at all," I say, but I stop myself. Wasn't that our exact reasoning though? "Listen, didn't I tell you that I've got this handled? I'll be signing an endorsement deal with Goody soon. We'll have plenty of cash for rent and more leftover."

He goes quiet. "Really?"

I shouldn't lie to him. I haven't even spoken to anyone at Goody, but at this point, I'll sell whatever they want. Hair curlers. Green face masks. They can take my pride too as long as I'm paid. "Don't say anything to Dad yet, not until I've signed on the dotted line. But just you wait. Soon we'll be saying arrivederci to the landlady, like I'm going to do to Giselle after our match."

Peter coughs out a laugh. "Arrivederci is Italian. I think you mean au revoir."

"Yeah, yeah, poindexter."

"I'm sorry I got mad at you. You need to focus on your match."

"I will, and I meant what I said. I'll take care of the landlady, I promise."

Peter might be feeling better after we hang up, but there's a weight sitting on my chest now. I've never broken a promise to my brother, and that's one record that I'd like to keep perfect.

I arrive at the training center on the early side to practice my back flip again. I spent a couple of hours last night trying out the move, nearly breaking my Goliath's neck in the process, but I managed to pull it off. It's pretty sloppy and my landing is all wobbly, but I plan on practicing a few more times this morning before going to the stadium.

I slip into a Goliath and duck into one of our training pits. I don't have Rushi to advise me, but I remember well enough what she told me yesterday. Bend the knees low. Arch my back until it hurts. Keep my eyes on the ground for the landing. I keep doing it over and over because this is my last dress rehearsal before the big show, and while I can't say I execute the flip smoothly, I do feel confident enough to file it into my arsenal.

When I arrive at the stadium, I try to keep my nerves at bay and focus on my usual routine. Stretches. A light jog. A warm shower, not too hot. I dry my hair and pull it into a ponytail before changing into my official uniform, freshly laundered and smelling clean.

Malcolm awaits me outside the locker room, nursing a big mug of coffee. "How're you feeling?"

"As good as I can hope."

"Giselle will come at you fast so stay on your toes. If you can, position yourself so that she swings at you with her right hand since that's her weaker one." He looks me over slowly, his gaze unreadable. "Here's your chance to prove yourself one-on-one against the seventh-ranked fighter in the world, so don't hold anything back."

I plant a hand on my hip. "Is that how you say *good luck* in Malcolm-ese?"

"Luck doesn't have much to do with it. It's all strategy and skill."

"Good thing I have those in spades, huh?"

"You can do anything you set your mind to, Linden," he says, which seems like a nice thing to say, but Malcolm delivers it like he's reading from a textbook.

With that vote of confidence ringing in my ears, we walk over to the prep area, and I approach my Goliath. The IC has already weighed and inspected it, so it's a matter of suiting up before I can go up to the main floor. I strap myself in and shove in my mouth guard, followed by clicking on my helmet. I run through a few moves to make sure the mecha is in sync with me before the Jays signal that it's time to go.

I take a deep breath as a whole flock of butterflies swarm around in my stomach.

Malcolm and I step onto the elevator, and when we pop into the stadium, I see that it's already packed. It might be a home game for me, but the French fans have turned out in droves, and I swear they fill at least a third of the seats. They're singing and chanting at the top of their lungs since Giselle has already stepped onto the floor ahead of me and is waving at the stands.

Compared to the Round 1 arena, there's a lot less fanfare to kick off our match. We gather by our team benches first to listen to the recordings of our national anthems. As the French fans sing along to "La Marseillaise," I look down at Sam, who has been trying to get my attention.

"Remember what I said about Giselle," he says just loudly enough for me to hear.

I nod back. "I've got a little something up my sleeve for that."

"Oh, really?"

I don't get a chance to reply because now "The Star Spangled Banner" has queued up, and we have to face our flag and place our hands over our hearts. I keep my eyes on the stars and stripes while I focus on my breathing, filling my lungs deeply before releasing them.

After the last note of the song rings out, the head referee tells Giselle and me to enter the pit, with Giselle on the north end and me on the south. The enormous cage from the arena has been removed and replaced with a standard-size one that we walk into. We shake hands as is customary, but I make it quick and drop her fingers fast. What she did to me in the arena still pricks at me and I'm itching for payback.

The announcer starts the countdown. I breathe out. Clench my teeth over my mouth guard. Crouch down.

Knowing Giselle, she's going to crash out of the gate at full speed, just like the Ravager did at the Jade Lily. I get ready to wait and dodge her attack.

The countdown hits zero and the announcer shouts, "And here we go—Linden of the US against Boucher of France!"

I stand on my toes, gearing up to sprint left or right, but Giselle catches me off guard.

She doesn't move. She stays rooted where she stands, not moving a muscle.

I start to sweat. What's she doing?

"Now, this is an interesting change of pace. Both fighters remain at their sides, waiting for the other to make a move," the announcer observes. He sounds as baffled as I am.

The crowd is going restless. They've come to see a fight, not watch the two of us stare at each other from across the pit. Giselle remains in the same position, flexing her mecha's fingers, and I wonder how long she'll wait me out.

It dawns on me that she must be switching up tactics to be less predictable, and I'll admit that it's working. She has to know I'm not a playmaker and that I like to go on the defense until the opportunity strikes.

A few people in the crowd start to boo, and the sound soon grows into a loud chorus.

Giselle glances up at them with her body growing rigid. I can tell that she isn't used to this kind of reception from her fans since she's the golden girl of France, but I tune out the jeers. I've gotten so used to them that it feels like I'm fighting in a match back at home, although it's much louder in a stadium of this size.

Don't get delicate, my dad would say.

I channel his voice as I consider what I should do right now.

The answer is simple.

I feign to my left, and Giselle rushes to her right, thinking that I'm finally ready to get moving. Then I feign to my right, and she mirrors me again. I do it a couple more times before she gives up, realizing that I'm toying with her. I might not be able to see her face behind her helmet, but I'm pretty sure she's scowling.

Good, let her get angry.

Even better, let her get furious.

I can hear my dad clear as a bell in my head now and it's ringing louder by the second. *Let her fight angry. Soon enough she'll make a mistake.*

So I do my part by doing a set of jumping jacks, followed by a round of sit-ups. Then I really pile it on thick when I gesture for her to join me. From the corner of my eye, I can see Malcolm pinch the bridge of his nose, obviously embarrassed by my antics, but Sam is slapping his knee.

"I don't think I've seen anything like this in all my years," I hear the announcer say.

I doubt anyone has, and my cheeks flush furiously because I really am making a fool of myself, but I do have a strategy in mind. Hopefully Peter is getting a good laugh out of this too, although I'm sure Dad might be thinking I've gone a little loopy, and on international television of all places. I can see him grinding his molars, murmuring that I better have a reason for monkeying around.

But it's working.

Giselle looks like an angry bull at a bullfight, and she's ready to charge at the matador. Or me in this case. Suddenly she takes off sprinting, straight down the middle of the pit, clearly giving up on her strategy to make me take the first move.

I'm ready for her. Springing off my toes, I leap up before she can catch me, reaching for the bars and swinging across them before dropping down back onto the floor. I plan on deploying my trusty dodge-and-run tactic for a while to tire her out, but Giselle is incredibly fast. In another life, she would've made an excellent sprinter like her dad.

I jump from one side of the pit to the opposite, then change it up by scaling the cage, but not swiftly enough. Giselle's fingertips close around my left heel, and that's all she needs to yank me back down to the ground. While she lands neatly on her feet, I careen onto my side so hard that for a second my vision blurs, but I have enough brain cells firing that I roll out of the way before Giselle can pin me.

"We really got a brawl on our hands now!" the announcer shouts.

As soon as I get to my feet, she juts out a leg to knock me over. I dodge it and scuttle back, right before she rushes forward to clock me in the cheek. I shake off the blow and clip her under the chin, but I don't get the momentum I need to really do some damage. I follow up by grabbing her mecha's shoulders and adding in a hiza geri to the gut, which hits home. I hear a satisfying crunch, but Giselle is ranked in the top ten worldwide for a reason. Even dazed, she has the reflexes of a street cat, clever and quick. Recovering fast, she makes a grab for me and almost slams me to the floor, but I twist away. I make her chase me again, and when she's nearly on me, I figure it's now or never. I still have enough energy to pull this off.

I race toward the side of the cage, making sure I've got enough velocity to make this work, and I run up the metal bars—one rung, two, three, then four—to get into proper position like I've practiced. I may not have Rushi's grace, but I remember what she showed me, making sure to bend my knees low to give myself the momentum I need before pushing off and soaring into the air, arching my back and keeping my eyes on the ground.

"Wow, would you look at that, folks!" the announcer cries. "Jo Linden is showing off some of her acrobatic chops!"

When my feet touch down again, I'm now facing Giselle's back. The crowd collectively gasps at my move, and my adrenaline is surging as I lunge forward and wrap my arms around her middle, wrestling her to the floor while I have the advantage of surprise.

I'm panting by the time the head ref reaches the count of five and blows his whistle, and I'm breathing hard when Giselle shoves me off and stalks out of the pit without the standard handshake.

The American fans have erupted onto their feet. I'm hit with a wave of the noise from the crowd, almost like it has grown into a living and breathing thing with a roar and a heartbeat. Over on Team USA's bench I see Sam whooping and jumping up and down while Malcolm merely looks stunned.

The announcer says, "The winner of the match is Josephine Linden of Team USA!"

I can feel the cameras on me, zeroing in on my face, and all I can think about is Peter, three thousand miles away, but he's here in my heart.

I pull off my helmet and pump my fist in the air as a huge grin breaks over my face.

Two matches down, squirt, I think. *Three more to go.*

15

Round 2 finishes up and our competitor pool of sixteen gets halved to eight. Sam wins his match against Romania in record time—under four minutes and with hardly a scratch on his Goliath. I watched the whole thing from Team USA's bench, and the crowd went absolutely wild, crying and yelling and tossing gifts onto the stadium floor like the standard roses and stuffed bears and more than enough women's underwear to keep the girls' dormitory stocked for the year. As soon as Sam lifted up his arms to wave to the stands, everyone started chanting, "Champ-ion! Cham-pi-on! Cham-pi-on!" so loudly that my ears rang for almost an hour.

After his victory, Sam and I get some time off to rest and recuperate—meaning we only have one training session each day versus two or three—but we can't get out of a dinner to honor the final eight fighters. I won't complain too much about this one though since it'll be hosted at the most exclusive spot in all of Washington. The White House.

At six o'clock in the evening, I step out of my dormitory and head toward a black limousine that awaits me. Both Sam and Malcolm are already inside the car, and I climb in carefully to join them since I don't want to wrinkle my outfit. The wardrobe team had brought in a whole rack of dresses for me to pick from, most of them pastel colors with too much frill, but I insisted on a navy sheath dress with a boat-neck neckline, something that Jackie O might be spotted in. No Patty Duke for me tonight.

"You look spiffy," I say to Sam, who's sporting a black tux and combed-back hair.

"Looking spiffy yourself, kiddo. Hardly recognized you with your hair down," he replies, but his usual charm can't be found. He has been acting subdued ever since we got news of the Round 3 bracket earlier this morning, and I can't blame him.

I'll be pitted against Zoya Federova, ranked third in the world.

But Sam has it worse.

He'll have to fight Lidiya.

It'll be Team USA versus Team USSR, not once but twice in the span of twelve hours. I have the morning slot for my match while Sam has the evening.

"I've already told the First Lady's staff that we'll stay for ninety minutes, tops," Malcolm says, sounding tired and frazzled. He's wearing a black tux as well, but it looks more rumpled than Sam's. "We'll go in, shake hands, eat some food, and scram. The two of you have big matches tomorrow. The biggest of the Games yet."

Sam and I nod and spend the rest of the ride over in silence until we pull up to the White House gate. A couple soldiers ask for our identification before they let us into the private driveway.

"Wow," I whisper as we pull up to the building and step outside.

A butler bot greets us upon our arrival, standing about the height of my shoulder and rolling on wheels, and I wonder how much it must've cost. It plays a short recorded message that welcomes us to the White House and to please follow it to the festivities. But I can't help but linger outside for a moment, staring up at the white marble columns, so tall that I feel like a mouse standing next to them. Just a week ago, I'd never left the West Coast before, and now I'm about to step inside the president's personal residence.

I stiffen as I enter the building, keeping my arms tight at my sides because I don't want to knock over a vase or a candlestick because everything looks like a precious antique that Martha Washington herself might've purchased. The bot guides us into the grand-looking Blue Room, which was recently renovated under the direction of the First Lady herself. The walls are covered in cream silk and gold paneling while a massive chandelier hangs down from the center of the ceiling, each of its crystals the size of my thumb. There's also plenty of blue decor too—a not-so-subtle nod to the room's formal name—from the blue silk draperies to the gold-and-blue chairs.

I grab a seltzer water from a nearby service bot and let my gaze roam around the room that's filled with dignitaries and IC members and, of course, the fighters. I spot Albie talking to the Ogler from West Germany. Rushi and Envoy Yu are admiring a painting of John Quincy Adams. But we're missing the Soviets, who must be running fashionably late as always.

Senator Appleby spots us from the crowd and walks up to Sam and me. "There's the dynamic duo!" she says, greeting us both.

I offer her a hand to shake, but she pulls me into a quick hug and murmurs into my ear, "You're making this Californian real proud. Keep up the good work, Jo."

I smile genuinely at that. Sam might have his fan club trailing him wherever he goes, but I have a US senator personally rooting for me, so I think I might win out in the end.

"And you remember Minister Tran of South Vietnam, don't you?" she continues, motioning behind her, but the minister isn't there. It looks like he tried to leave his empty plate on one of the trash-collecting bots and got waylaid by Envoy Yu, who's smiling and asking if he has a moment to talk.

Senator Appleby frowns slightly but adjusts her attention toward the center of the room. "Why don't you two come with me? There are a couple people who want to welcome you personally."

I realize that she's referring to the president and First Lady.

It's a blur what happens next. Senator Appleby makes the introductions, and as I shake their hands all I can think about is how the president has lovely teeth and that Jackie Kennedy is the most glamorous person I've ever laid eyes on. Tonight she's wearing a strapless gown that glides over her curves, paired with matching silk gloves and a bouffant hairdo that would look absolutely ridiculous on me and yet somehow perfect on her. The black-and-white newspaper pictures I've seen of the First Lady don't do her any justice. You really have to see her in Technicolor to get the full effect.

"I'll admit that when I first heard that Senator Appleby tapped you to replace Ted on the team, I wasn't sure what to think," President Kennedy tells me in his clipped New England accent. "But as soon as I saw you in the arena, I knew why she picked you."

Mrs. Kennedy chimes in next. "You'll have to sign an autograph for our daughter, Caroline."

While I stand there in a state of utter shock, Senator Appleby calls Sam's mother and stepfather over to join the throng. It's quickly apparent that Sam's stepdad and the president have met before since Boeing must have some pretty big government contracts. The two get talking about the first Goliath prototype that will one day fly in space, developed by NASA and contracted out to Boeing to make a few parts like the battery packs.

"In thirty years, if we scale this correctly, we could have a colony in space. A whole new territory for the US," says Mr. Kealey, a smile in his voice. "I've been trying to talk Sammy here into entering the pilot training for the program. We're going to need the best and the boldest, not to mention plenty of esterium. These new mines opening up in South Vietnam will be a big help."

"The treaty hasn't been signed yet, but we're very close," Senator Appleby says, looking a tad uncomfortable that they're speaking about this so openly. "And before that happens, we have the Games to keep us busy. Fortunately we've got two excellent fighters still in the running this year." She's beaming at Sam and me like a proud mother hen.

"That's right. Sam will be up against Lidiya," Mr. Kealey says, sounding not too pleased. "We were all hoping that he wouldn't have to face her until the finals. It would've been a real showdown."

"They don't have any control over that, dear," Sam's mother says, touching her husband's arm, but I can tell that he's still bothered. Beside her, Sam grips his glass of orange juice.

"Sammy will just have to bring his best tomorrow. Isn't that right, son?" Mr. Kealey says, patting Sam's arm like he's some faithful beagle. "Maybe your teammate here can give you a few pointers on how to beat another girl in the pit. What do you say, Miss Linden?" He chuckles. "How can he fight off those shifty feminine wiles?"

The First Lady covers her grimace with a strained smile, but I've pretty much run out of the ability to hold in my sarcasm.

"Maybe Sam could ask her to make a sandwich for him. Let those feminine instincts kick right in," I say.

I think Mr. Kealey is actually considering the idea while the First Lady stifles a laugh, but the president and the senator don't seem to hear me, which is both a relief and a shame because I think my retort was pretty clever. But the two of them are eyeing the door and nodding at the people approaching.

"If you'll excuse us for a moment," the First Lady says graciously before she and her husband head off to greet the Soviet delegation.

Premier Khrushchev has arrived with First Lady Khrushcheva on his arm, who's nowhere near as dazzling as Jacqueline Kennedy but has a cheerful smile for everyone she sees, which makes me warm to her. I've also heard that she's a big proponent of world peace, even going so far as to make a speech about dumping all military mechas into the ocean, so maybe the Reds aren't all warmongers like I've been taught.

Zoya trails behind the Khrushchevs, and I hold my breath and wait for Lidiya to come barreling in as well, but she doesn't show. Soon we get word that she has a headache, and her team doctor has advised that she take an early night. Sam visibly relaxes when he hears this because now he doesn't have to pretend to make nice with her. I can't complain either since I'm sure Lidiya would've used tonight to blame me for something else.

I keep my eyes on the Soviets. Speaking through his translator, Khrushchev compliments Mrs. Kennedy on the furnishings, remarking on the drapes that she'd picked out herself. Over in the corner, Zoya grabs a champagne flute from a service bot while Rushi claims one for herself. My mind flicks to tomorrow, when I'll have to face Zoya in the pit, but I get momentarily distracted when I notice Sam has taken out his video camera to film the festivities.

"Documenting the night for your brothers?" I ask.

"Just for a minute. Stan wanted to come and play hide-and-seek in the White House, so he's sulking. I told him this would be boring anyway." He pans over the guests before landing on his mother and stepfather, who's talking to Senator Appleby and First Lady Khrushcheva about the March on Washington that Dr. King is planning for August and how it won't be great for the economy and maybe there's something that she can do about it.

"That's dear old dad for you," Sam says dryly. "I think he sometimes wishes that my mom had given birth to bags of money rather than my brothers."

I choke a little on my drink. All this time I had been hoping to find a couple sponsors, but it sounds like I should've just asked Sam's stepfather for a check.

"How long have he and your mom been married?"

"Since I was five." His voice is uncharacteristically flat when he adds, "She'd been his secretary."

I whistle low. "Scandalous. But it can't be *all* bad, right? Don't you get a new Goliath at the start of every season?"

Sam scowls. "You kidding? My stepdad is a tightwad. I paid for my mechas with my sponsorship cash."

"But he's so rich! I bet he could buy a thousand Goliaths without losing any sleep."

"Then he wouldn't be as rich as he was before," he replies with a smirk. "And even with this whole space pilot thing, he only wants me to sign on so that Boeing will get more NASA contracts. He thinks my face will boost business, which is exactly why I would never do it."

"But you'd get to go into *space*," I say.

"I don't want to go on his terms. I've got other plans anyway."

"Like what? Going pro? Building a swimming pool and diving into all the cash you'll make in endorsements after the Games?"

He laughs at the image. "I hadn't thought about that, but it sure sounds fun."

"Seriously, what sort of plans are you cooking up?"

I didn't think it was possible, but Sam actually looks shy. He's hesitating too.

"I didn't mean to pry," I say, and am about to comment on the scallop hors d'oeuvre to change the subject, but Sam shakes his head.

"You weren't. After this is all over, I'm going to drive back to my old man's hometown. Vincennes, Indiana."

"Can't say that I've heard of it."

He chuckles. "I would've been shocked if you did. I already spent some time there a few weeks ago. That's why I wanted to take the car cross-country. Visit the ol' Dawson homestead."

"Dawson?"

"My dad's last name." The corners of his mouth tighten and he adds softly, "My last name too. Before Mom got remarried and we both became Kealeys."

He didn't even get to keep his dad's own name. No wonder he wanted to see his roots.

"Anyhow, my grandma still lives in town," he goes on. "In the same house that my dad grew up in."

I imagine a white farmhouse in my head, surrounded by blue skies and acres of corn. Is that what they grow in Indiana? Maybe wheat? And then suddenly I'm not thinking about corn or wheat or Sam's father anymore.

I'm thinking about my mom.

She grew up in a town surrounded by orange groves, but that's all I really know about it. I don't even know the name or where it's located or if her family is still there.

I've spent my life trying not to think about my mom, but for some reason, here at the Games she won't stop pestering me.

"It must've been tough staying at that house," I say to Sam.

"That part wasn't too rough. It was harder to visit his headstone. My grandma put one up in the cemetery in town, but it's all ceremonial since Dad never came home officially." Now his eyes go hard. Determined. "But I'll make it out to Iwo Jima someday."

"You should go," I say. I mean it too, and I can't help but wish that my mom had died a hero's death like Sam's father did. I know I can't really pick and choose that, but it would've been easier to mourn her—Sam's dad didn't want to leave his family, but my mom obviously had different feelings.

We're soon led into the State Dining Room at the end of the hallway, and it's probably the fanciest place I've ever stepped inside. The tables are decked out in crisp tablecloths and towering vases full of white orchids. Gold curtains adorn the windows, letting in the fading glow of the setting sun that illuminates a large oil painting of Abraham Lincoln, who seems to oversee our festivities.

I wind my way around the circular tables until I locate my place card. It appears that I'll be seated next to Envoy Yu on my right and Zoya Federova on my left. My eyes go wide reading that, and I wonder who made up these seating assignments because the last thing I want to do is spend the next hour making polite conversation with the girl who will be going after my throat in less than twenty-four hours.

Fortunately though, Zoya and I spend the first two courses politely ignoring each other even though our elbows are mere inches apart. We have a bit of a tangle when we both reach for the butter at the same time, but I motion for her to take it first and she gives a little nod, which is about as riveting as our interaction gets.

I have a feeling that she's biding her time here like I'm doing. She pushes her food around her plate and dabs her napkin on her forehead every so often, probably because the room feels warm with so many bodies and bots crammed into the space. More than once she excuses herself from the table and disappears for a few minutes. I figure she's sneaking off to the restroom to get a break or splash a little water over her face, and I have to admit it's not a half-bad strategy when you're stuck at a dull dinner.

We're waiting for dessert to be served when Zoya pushes her chair back yet again. I don't think much of it because I'm relieved for the extra elbow space, but then I hear a thump behind me.

Snapping my head around, I find Zoya collapsed on the floor. She's curled on her side, clutching at her stomach, and I start hearing people gasp.

"Is she all right?" someone asks.

"Did she trip?" someone else says.

I have no idea what happened, but as soon as I get to my feet, Zoya starts retching, and I know that this can't be good for her. Could it be food poisoning?

I grab Zoya's napkin to offer it to her, but she doesn't seem to notice me. She's whimpering and her face is as white as our dinner plates, and soon she's clutching at her throat.

The First Lady has stood up and is motioning at one of the security guards. "Call for Dr. Young!"

I go very still.

We're miles from the stadium, but somehow this feels like the arena all over again.

16

A crowd soon takes shape around Zoya, American and Soviet alike, gathering closer and closer until she vomits again. Only then does everyone lurch back.

"She must've had too much to drink," I hear someone whisper loudly.

But I sincerely doubt that since Zoya barely touched her wine at dinner.

More murmurs ripple while Premier Khrushchev pushes through to reach Zoya's side, where he kneels down to hold her hand.

"I think it's best for everyone to return to the Blue Room. Let's give Miss Federova a little space to breathe," President Kennedy says calmly. When he turns to his aides, however, his tone grows more urgent. "Call the hospital."

Dr. Young soon arrives, medical bag in hand, while a crew of security bots comes onto the scene as well to escort the guests to the Blue Room at the president's orders. I get one last glimpse of

Zoya before I'm ushered away, and I swear I'll never forget the look on her face, so very pale and with her eyes rolled back.

We linger in the Blue Room for the next twenty minutes before Zoya gets carted off on a stretcher to an ambulance waiting outside. Most of the Soviet delegation decides to depart soon after, and I can't blame them for losing their appetites. Khrushchev and the First Lady, however, stay behind, and they're some of the first guests to return to the dining room when the Kennedys urge everyone to sit down for dessert. But I'm not hungry anymore, and I end up pushing my scoops of sorbet around with my spoon.

On our way back to the Pavilion, Sam slides into the seat next to me, and we drive off.

"What do you think happened to her? Food poisoning?" he asks.

"Maybe," I say, staring out my window at the shadows of the city. But would they have driven her to the hospital for that?

"Something must be in the water. First we had Lukas and now it's Zoya."

I can only nod. Injuries happen all the time at the Games, but they're usually of the broken-bones-and-concussion variety. Lukas's seizures and Zoya's collapse are totally out of the norm, and then you add on the fact that they're both top-ten fighters who came from Warsaw Pact countries.

But this must be a coincidence, right? A string of bad luck.

Yet the nervous feeling in my stomach doesn't go away. Will there even be a match tomorrow? Zoya would have to make a speedy recovery, but she *is* a Federova. And if this all turns out to be a bad case of food poisoning, the match will go on. I have to pre-pare for it like tonight never happened.

When I get up the next day, I'm ready for some answers. After get-ting dressed and shoveling down a bowl of oatmeal at the dining hall, I make a beeline for the training center, only for Malcolm to intercept me on the quad.

"There's been a change to our schedule this morning. The IC wants a word with you," he says, his eyes red like he hasn't slept all night.

"Is this about Zoya? Will she be able to fight today?"

"They wouldn't say," he replies, irritated. "Come on."

Malcolm leads the way toward a small administrative building, a little cement cube on the back side of the training center that I hadn't noticed before now. A wall of cold air hits me in the face as we walk in; the air-conditioning must be turned up full blast. I cross my arms to chase away the goose bumps, but they rise up again as we turn the corner and enter a conference room. At one end of the table, I see two people seated, accompanied by a couple of security officers behind them.

"Good morning, Jo," Senator Appleby says, her voice unusually tight. She gestures across the table from her. "Won't you join us?"

I take a seat. Malcolm reaches for the chair next to mine, but the senator stops him. "We'll take it from here."

Malcolm grows stiff. "What exactly is this about?"

"You'll be briefed shortly," she replies, and I wonder if this same tension played out when she nominated me to join the team.

"I imagine there are a few things you need to take care of. Give us twenty minutes."

Realizing that he has been dismissed, Malcolm nods curtly, but I can tell by the look on his face that he isn't happy with this development. He has a plan to follow, and the senator is tossing a wrench in it. But she's the one with the power in this situation, so he has no choice but to go.

After Malcolm departs in a cloud of frustration, I knit my fingers together under the table, wishing I knew what's going on. "You wanted to speak to me?"

"Yes, Jo. First things first though, let me introduce you to Leon Schmid, the head delegate of the IC. He has a few questions for you concerning what occurred last night at the White House."

The head delegate of the IC? This must be serious. "Does this have to do with Zoya? How is she?"

"We'll make an announcement during the broadcast shortly," Mr. Schmid says in a soft accent that sounds German. He leans forward in his chair, his eyes a steely blue. He looks about the senator's age, late sixties, with a crop of graying hair and a pair of gold-rimmed glasses, which glint from the sunlight peeking through the window. "Were you seated next to Zoya Federova last night at the White House dinner?"

I glance at the senator, who motions for me to answer. At least this is an easy one. "Yes, sir, I was."

"Did you notice anything out of the ordinary throughout the evening?"

Aside from the fact that I was a special guest at the White House? "No, not really."

"Tell me about Miss Federova. Was she acting unusually?"

I have to think back. "I don't know—I don't really know her. But she didn't eat much of her food, although that could've been nerves. And she excused herself from the table a few times. I figured she'd gone to the restroom."

He jots down a sentence on a little black notepad in front of him. "Who had access to Miss Federova's food and drink?"

Now that's a strange question. "The servers, I'm assuming, and a few service bots."

"Did anyone get her a drink from the bar?"

"No, not that I saw. Like I said, she didn't seem to have much of an appetite."

He peers at me from behind his glasses, and his tone takes an unexpected shift. "Miss Linden, did *you* put anything in Zoya Federova's food or drink?"

I stare at him. He must be kidding, right?

"Are you asking if I poisoned her?" I ask, incredulous.

"It's a yes or no question."

My gaze volleys over to Senator Appleby, wondering if she's as shocked as I am, but she doesn't look surprised at all. Only grim.

"Go on, Jo. You may answer," she says.

I let my eyes shift back to Mr. Schmid. "Of course not."

"Is that a no?"

"It's a no. Go ahead and ask anyone who was sitting near us."

I don't know how to be more direct. My heart is hammering in my chest because I've got a match in a few hours to prep for; I don't have time for these allegations. "Who's accusing me of doing this?"

"We're simply conducting procedural follow-ups," Mr. Schmid replies. "And we're not finished yet."

He asks me some more questions about Zoya and the dinner before tucking his notepad into his jacket and making a swift departure without shaking my hand or thanking me for my time. I begin to get up myself, feeling dazed at what has just happened, but Senator Appleby doesn't rise from her seat. Instead she pats my hand and tells me to sit back down.

"I'm sorry you had to experience that, but the IC was insistent. Or rather, certain members from the Soviet delegation were putting the pressure on them," she explains.

I still don't understand what's going on. "So Zoya was poisoned?"

"We're awaiting the test results, but some of the Soviets are convinced that somebody has been targeting Warsaw Pact fighters."

I let this wash over me. They must think what happened to Lukas and Zoya is more than mere coincidence. "They're blaming it on me?" My jaw tightens, and my mind goes straight to Lidiya. She must be mucking up trouble again. She was the one who alleged that I had "tampered" with the Soviet float and that Lukas's seizure was somehow my fault. I'm almost sure she's spreading lies about me.

Senator Appleby sighs. "We'll get this settled, Jo. Both

Khrushchev and the president himself are keen on clearing this up once those test results come back."

I breathe a little easier hearing that. It seems like Khrushchev and Kennedy have a grip on reality at least. "What's the latest on Zoya?"

"She's recovering at the hospital and very weak from whatever caused her to collapse last night. The Soviet team will make an announcement very soon, which is why I feel comfortable revealing this to you now." Her mouth twitches. "There's no way that the medical staff will clear her for your match. You'll be getting a bye to the next round."

It takes a few seconds for the realization to sink in.

I don't have to fight today.

I'm already on to Round 4.

I imagine Zoya must be devastated, but I'm tempted to jump up and whoop. I settle instead on a great big grin. "Really?"

"Really." Senator Appleby lets herself return my smile. "It must be a relief. Why don't we go share the news with that coach of yours?"

We locate Malcolm back at the training center and tell him the news, which makes his brows shoot up, but otherwise it's hard to read his reaction. After Senator Appleby departs, he calls Sam over to update him too.

"Well, well. Looks like you got yourself a lucky break, kiddo," Sam says, clapping me on the shoulder.

I let the nickname slide this time around since this *is* a lucky break for me, but a shadow of unease slides through me at the same time. I want to win on my own, not on some technicality, and especially because it's only going to reinforce the idea that I don't deserve to be here, that I'm a girl who didn't earn her spot.

But I'm not going to volunteer myself to trade places with Sam, even if I could. Too much is on the line—the title, the prize money, the splashy sponsorships. I've promised Peter that I wouldn't go home empty-handed, and I have to take care of whoever might stand in the way. That could mean Lidiya. It could even mean Sam. If he wins his match, there's a decent chance that I could face him next. Team USA versus Team USA. He would definitely have the upper hand since he has already beaten me twice, but there's no way I'd let him make that three.

Thank goodness we're not at that point though—yet.

"Wish we could say the same for you, but you've got a match to prep for," Malcolm tells Sam, his shoulders tensing up again. "So let's get started. You'll have to be ready for whatever Lidiya might throw at you tonight. Don't take your eyes off her, not even for a second. She's one scheming little—" He glances at me and doesn't finish the thought, although I have a pretty good idea of what he was about to say.

"And don't turn your back on her if you can help it," I add. "You know Lidiya's MO. She'd skewer you with a butter knife if she could get away with it."

Sam grimaces. "Thank you for the support, you two. I'm touched."

Hours later, we're all back at the stadium for his big match, and thankfully I get to be a bystander. The stadium is a real pressure cooker tonight. Both Albie and Rushi have won their respective matches, so now it's down to this last game to determine whether Lidiya or Sam will move on. It sure feels like we'll be watching the championship since it'll be a face-off against the top two fighters in the world.

I'm wearing a fresh Team USA uniform as I make my way toward the bench. Sam and Lidiya have yet to make their big entrance, but the crowd—mostly American—is already chanting "U-S-A" to a beat. They're grinning and eating popcorn, and Sam's fan club is out in full force, looking like they've multiplied. You can't miss them since they're holding up posters in neon colors. Neither can I miss Sam's family, who has gathered in a few fancy box seats, only a couple rows up and to my left. His stepfather is busy talking to the man next to him while his mother hands out bottles of soda pop to Sam's little brothers who have painted their faces red, white, and blue. One of them—I think it's Sterling—notices me and gives a hearty wave. I smile and wave back.

But there's a tension in the air too. I can't help but notice how empty the VIP section looks. When I was here for Sam's Round 2 match against Romania, the whole place was packed with IC members and diplomats and a few heads of state—Prime Minister Fanfani of Italy, Prime Minister Ikeda of Japan, President Tito of Yugoslavia—but this time around the area is noticeably sparser. Kennedy had to fly south this morning to meet with Dr. King and the SCLC, and yet there's a whole entire row that remains unoccupied.

In the seats right behind me, I hear two British envoys addressing the absence.

"Looks like most of the Soviet delegation refused to attend," one of them says.

"They want to pause the Games since the Federova girl is in the hospital," replies his neighbor.

"It's open revolt against Khrushchev."

I shiver at that. This sounds very serious.

"But he isn't budging a single millimeter," the other envoy says. "He doesn't want to jeopardize the Accord with Kennedy."

I can't hear them anymore because the announcer starts talking over the loudspeakers, so I direct my attention to Khrushchev himself. A glance over my shoulder lets me see that he's seated next to First Lady Khrushcheva. She's trying to make small talk, but Khrushchev has his arms crossed and is frowning. It's strange to see the two of them surrounded by empty chairs.

Khrushchev really must want to get the Accord signed, even if it means going it alone against his own delegation.

The noise ratchets up again when the fighters come into view. Sam pops out of the elevator first with Lidiya not far behind. The match proceeds like the others, with the anthems and the handshakes, before the two of them enter the pit. The countdown begins, and all thirty thousand of us in the stands get to our feet, some of us on our tiptoes to see the action.

"Come on, Sam," I whisper, crossing my fingers tightly. Beside me on the bench, Malcolm is quiet as a statue. His anxiety is palpable.

As soon as the whistle blows, I lose sight of Lidiya. She's that blazing fast. She charges at Sam at full velocity, her Vostok's legs moving so quickly that they look like a blur. Sam, however, was clearly expecting this. By the time Lidiya reaches the spot where he'd been standing a scant second earlier, he has already leapt over her head, out of harm's way, and whips back around with a punch as soon as he lands.

"We're off to the races with a bang!" the announcer says, giddy with the speed of the match.

Sam clips her shoulder, but it isn't a direct hit. Shaking off the blow, Lidiya jabs at his face, but Sam ducks it easily. His left hand shoots up in an uppercut, and the punch lands squarely against the Vostok's chin. The whole stadium cringes at the sound of metal slamming metal, and I know from experience that Lidiya is feeling the impact down to her toes. She might even be tasting blood in her mouth guard.

The American fans roar, thinking Sam has taken an early lead, but Lidiya manages to sidestep him when he tries to pin her. Just like that we're back to biting our nails and watching what happens next, doing our best not to blink because they're moving so quickly.

Like some sort of superhuman, Lidiya crouches down and soars toward the bars, readying an aerial attack. But once again

Sam predicts what's coming. He leaps up to meet her—full-out, no mercy, fight fire with fire—and he reaches up to take her by the feet to throw her down. But Lidiya pulls her knees against her chest to avoid him, and Sam's fingers grasp at air. The two of them barely miss each other midair before they crash onto the ground.

"A near miss! These two are clearly evenly matched," the announcer says.

The game drags on, and the announcer's words prove true. Sam is stronger and possesses more stamina while Lidiya is faster and more ruthless. Put them together, and it's a match for the ages.

"Save up that energy, Sam," I hear Malcolm murmur next to me.

Twenty minutes pass, then ten more, and they're still going full steam. But another ten minutes pass by, and I start to notice signs of them flagging. Sam is breathing heavily while Lidiya has lost her trademark zip. They're both moving slower and pausing longer between scraps, trying to find a few seconds here and there to rest. It's a war of attrition at this point, waiting for one of them to trip up out of exhaustion, but Sam does seem to have the advantage. That boy is an ox, and I can tell he has more gas left in the tank.

Now it's a matter of how he'll use it.

Sam decides to go on the offensive and gives chase. To escape him, Lidiya takes to the bars again. She swings across them one by one, and Sam has nearly caught up to her when she unexpectedly misses a rung and down she goes thirty feet. It's a fall that fighters like us make all the time, and our mechas are engineered to absorb the shock of the impact—if you land upright. But Lidiya falls awkwardly. I can tell she tries to correct her positioning in the air, but she doesn't do it fast enough, and I wince when she hits, shoulder first, followed by her head. Everyone around me gasps.

"Federova goes down! We'll see if she's hurt or if she shakes this off," the announcer says.

We watch and wait for her to get up—her mecha and helmet should've protected her skull—but she lays limp. From my line of sight I see Premier Khrushchev go white and start murmuring to the First Lady, but there's nothing they can do. Not even the leader of the gigantic USSR can call a match. Those are the rules. Either a fighter forfeits or they get eliminated.

Sam knows this, of course.

He also knows that Lidiya is darn sneaky, and this could be another one of her tricks.

He circles her carefully, but she doesn't twitch. The medics start to gather their supplies and move toward the entrance gate, but they have to wait there until the match is officially called.

"Careful there," I whisper as Sam considers his next steps.

Sam moves around Lidiya's Vostok, assessing what would be the best angle to pin her in case she decides to rejoin the land of the living. He seems to have decided on the smartest and safest angle, positioning his knees over her legs to restrict her movement while holding her arms down with his hands.

And suddenly Lidiya rears up.

The announcer yelps, and I do the same on the bench. Malcolm is shouting something to Sam, but I doubt Sam can hear him.

My heart is stuttering, and I think it might stop completely at what I witness next—Lidiya kicks a leg free and aims her foot square at Sam's face. His neck snaps back, and while he's dazed, she punches his mecha and punches it again, titanium against titanium, and I swear she must've dented Sam's cockpit. She flattens him on the ground, and even though Sam tries valiantly to shove her away, she holds on.

"Sam!" I scream. "Get her off!"

The referee counts down the time. Sam only has a few seconds to turn this around, but then the ref reaches five and it's all over.

Lidiya stands up, pumping her arms into the air. She'd been playing dead all along, probably smirking the whole time too. The Khrushchevs are on their feet, clapping and beaming, but every American in the stadium is stunned.

There goes their golden boy.

Eliminated in Round 3.

Lidiya isn't done yet with her victory lap though. As soon as she emerges from her Vostok, she strides out of the cage and grabs a microphone from one of the refs. Her gaze roams to find me.

"This was for Zoya!" she cries, acting like the rift between the two of them never existed.

I grit my teeth and start moving toward her, but Malcolm holds me back.

"Take a seat," he orders me.

"Did you see what she did?" I spit out.

"I said take a seat," he growls.

But I have the crowd behind me at least. They're booing Lidiya loudly, and some of them start throwing their popcorn and drinks at her until her coaches try to escort her out. But it's obvious that she doesn't want to leave. She's shouting up at the stands, which isn't the smartest idea when you're on the away team and you've played your match dirtier than a pig in a mud bath.

After the Soviets finally wrangle Lidiya onto the elevator, I notice Sam finally emerging from his cockpit. I figure he hadn't come out sooner because he didn't want to face the crowd after a loss like this, but he's holding his head and swaying a bit.

"I think he's hurt!" I say to Malcolm, pointing at Sam. Come to think of it, Lidiya really did hammer his Goliath hard. Maybe when she dented the cockpit, the blow affected Sam too.

Or maybe what happened to Lukas and Zoya is happening all over again.

"Stay here," Malcolm tells me again. "I'll take care of this."

I don't listen to him though. I'm following a step behind, trying to get to Sam as fast as I can, but then I trip and go down hard on my knee. By the time I find my footing there's a trio of reporters surrounding me, shoving little microphones into my face and tossing out questions.

"Your comments about the match, Jo?"

"What are your thoughts on Lidiya's tactics against Sam?"

"Now that you're the only American fighter left, what is your strategy moving forward?"

My breath hitches because that last question slams into me like a Federova punch. The thought didn't truly hit me until now, but with Sam eliminated, I'm what's left of Team USA.

I'm the last American standing.

17

I don't sleep well that night. The air-conditioning has turned my room into an icebox, but when I open the window to warm myself, it ends up feeling like a swamp. I alternate between sweating and shivering before I give up on sleeping altogether and stare at the ceiling for a while.

I think about Sam. I tried to see how he was doing after the match, but the security guards wouldn't let me into the boys' locker room, and shortly after, I watched the medics wheel him off on a stretcher to an awaiting ambulance. Malcolm told me that Sam needed to be further evaluated, although he should be fine, but his injuries were serious enough to bring him to the hospital.

Around six in the morning, I drag myself out of my bed because my alarm is about to go off anyway. And I have to get ready for my next training session. We're down to the final four now—Lidiya, Albie, Rushi, and me. Three dark horses and the reigning World Champion.

I'm only one match away from the finals, and for a moment, I imagine myself on the winner's podium, my head held high with the crowd going wild. I'll hoist up that trophy that's almost as tall as me, the first female fighter to ever claim it. All the work I've put in, all the naysayers I've had to ignore, it'll all be worth it.

Then there's that prize money and the endorsement deals. My family and I would be set. Not for life, but for a good while— enough to pay the rent without worrying and save up for Peter to go to college. Enough to banish the worry we've felt every time we've lost a customer to Rocket Boys down the street.

I change into my training kit and get ready for the long day ahead. The dormitory is as still as a powered-down Goliath as I exit my room and lock the door behind me. I'm about to pass the commons area when I hear muffled crying.

I pause to find Rushi on the phone, her back turned so she doesn't see me. She's speaking into the receiver in Mandarin, so I don't know what she's saying, except when she murmurs something that sounds like *mama*. She sounds upset.

No, that isn't right.

She sounds distressed.

I try to back away silently just as Rushi hangs up the phone. She swivels around, and I notice the puffiness around her eyes.

Both of us freeze. I start to apologize while Rushi stands up and accidentally knocks over her mug of tea. The contents form a little lake on the floor, and I'd be a real jerk to leave now, so I grab a hand towel from the kitchenette.

"No, I can do that," she insists.

"I don't mind," I say, sopping up the tea. "Everything okay?"

She sniffs and hiccups a little and focuses on picking up the small dried flowers that were in her mug, each one the size of a nickel. I grab one near my foot, and it smells light and fresh, like summertime.

Just like that, a memory floats up in my head. I've seen these flowers before, a long, long time ago.

I can see my mother sitting at our old kitchen table, stirring sugar into a mug of tea that looks and smells a lot like Rushi's. Mom's belly is round—she must've been pregnant with Peter at the time—but that doesn't stop me from trying to climb onto her lap and ask for some of the sugar. She doesn't push me off though. She lets me bounce on her leg and eat a pinch of the sweet stuff while she untangles the knots in my hair with her fingertips.

I blink at this ghost from my past. I don't recognize my mother in that memory. She wasn't yelling or crying or curled up in bed. She actually seemed to like me.

I hold the little flower in my palm. "What sort of tea is this?"

Rushi startles a bit. "I'm not sure how to say it in English. Chry—" She frowns. "Chrys—"

"Chrysanthemum?"

Rushi nods, and my mind wanders back to my mother and then—of all places—to Old Wen. The last time I saw him, he said that my mom used to tote me around like a doll when I was a baby.

I hadn't believed him, but now I'm starting to wonder. How could the mother that I remember and the one that Old Wen knew be the same person?

We've almost finished cleaning the spill when I pick up something that looks like a clear crystal. I have no idea where this thing came from when Rushi offers an explanation.

"Rock sugar," she says. She makes a stirring motion, like she's holding a spoon. "You melt it into the tea."

I wonder if my mom knew that trick. I'm guessing not since she used regular sugar in hers.

"This was my mother's favorite tea," Rushi goes on as she picks up the last chrysanthemum blossom off the floor.

"Is that who you were talking to on the phone? Your mom?"

"My meimei. My little sister." Her voice warms at that mention, and I'm guessing that they must be close. "Our mother is . . . She passed away years ago."

"Mine too," I mumble.

Our eyes meet again, and I can't help but look at her differently. We're both part of the same terrible club. The Dead Mothers Society or whatever you want to call it. It's not a group that anyone wants to join, but when you do come across another member, you know that you have the same scars that no one else can see. You can't help but feel this kinship.

Because of that, I think about telling Rushi that my mom was Chinese too. I don't know if she'd even believe me if I told her that, but Malcolm's warning replays in my head. I get the impulse to rebel against that though. I've never taken orders from anyone before, so why start now?

But then I think about the sponsorship money, and Malcolm gets his wish. I stay quiet.

"Rushi?"

Both of us turn to find Envoy Yu standing in the doorframe. Judging by her tousled hair, it looks like she has just woken up, but her eyes are unusually sharp for this early in the morning. She speaks to Rushi in Mandarin, and Rushi stammers a reply.

"It wasn't Rushi's fault," I say to Envoy Yu and hold up the mug. "I was walking by the commons room and I noticed her—" I'm about to say *talking on the phone*, but Rushi's eyes shoot wide like a rabbit in the crosshairs, and I get the feeling that she wasn't supposed to be calling home. I quickly search for something else to say. "Uh, I noticed her making tea, and when I asked her what kind it was, I must've startled her and she dropped the cup."

Envoy Yu eyes me quizzically, but she seems to accept the explanation. "I hope she wasn't disturbing you?"

"No, not at all," I say. My own gaze slinks toward Rushi, who's looking relieved, but then her shoulders slump as soon as Envoy Yu starts talking.

"Come on, you clumsy thing. We have a busy morning," Envoy Yu says to Rushi. Her tone switches back to her usual sweetness, but it seems a bit too syrupy to me.

The two of them retreat to Rushi's room while I head downstairs to the dining hall for breakfast, feeling grateful that I don't have a chaperone breathing down my neck every minute of the day.

But I do happen to have one inside the training pit.

Malcolm waits for me there, with a day's growth of stubble along his jaw. I've got a hunch he slept as badly as I did.

"How's Sam doing?" I ask before he can tell me that I'm a minute late.

"Concussed," Malcolm says, rubbing his tired eyes. "The doctors are keeping an eye on him today and will evaluate him again tomorrow. He should make a full recovery though."

But Sam's pride will take longer to heal. He put years of training and work to get to the Games. He was the top-ranked American and was called our next great hope—and he didn't even get a chance to fight for a medal. If I were him, I'd take some of his family's green and hide out in the Swiss Alps for the rest of the summer. At least he could nurse his wounds with a great view.

My heart pangs as I glance over at Sam's training pit. I've gotten so used to seeing him there, either sparring with one of the Jays or tossing a smart-alecky comment my way, but now it's strange to find it empty. As much as he could get on my nerves, at least he knew how to lighten the mood. Make me laugh, even if it was accompanied with an eye roll. Dare I admit that I miss him?

"Can I see Sam?" I ask Malcolm. I'm not sure what Sam and I are at this point. Teammates? Not anymore. Friends? Not quite, yet we aren't rivals either. And it doesn't feel right not to pay him a visit.

"Maybe later on. Now isn't the right time. You'll only remind him of what he's lost."

Malcolm sure has a way of giving me a one-two punch with his words alone, but for once, I appreciate the honesty. It's probably best for me to give Sam some time to deal with the bitter disappointment of losing. And not to mention the anger.

Nobody wants to go out like he did.

I'm reminded all over again of what happened last night at the stadium. "What Lidiya did yesterday was—"

"Legal," Malcolm says gruffly.

"In my book, I'd call it downright sleazy."

"Sleazy is how she operates, and it's how she's going to win this whole thing unless someone stops her."

"I'm up for the challenge."

"Let's hope so," he says, not sounding very certain. He walks over to the television set. "Now let's find out who'll you'll be facing next."

We watch the bracket broadcast. Just like the last time, the IC makes a big deal out of it, showing clips from the previous round of matches and playing short videos about the countries that the remaining fighters represent. Then they get to the finale, and Malcolm is already pacing.

Lidiya will take on Albie at 3 p.m. tomorrow.

Following that, for the seven o'clock slot, it'll be Rushi against me.

I draw in a long breath. That's the Round 4 lineup.

Relief hits me first. This means that I won't have to fight Lidiya yet, at least not this go-around. But then comes a sense of unease. It isn't that I'm scared of Rushi—I'm not. She might have a mean aerial attack, but on paper, I'll have the advantage. I'm older and more experienced. I also saved her neck in Purgatory.

But I like her.

It won't be fun trying to beat her.

"What are you waiting for? Go get warmed up already," Malcolm says, hands on hips and sounding testy.

I go through my stretches, followed by a jog around the training center, which has become a ghost town. There are only three nations left in the building—the US, the UK, and China—because the Soviets have packed up their gear and moved to another site. Lidiya should be grateful for that because we won't get to cross paths, and I have a real bone to pick with her. And it's the size of a femur. She humiliated Sam on American soil. *My* soil. And where I come from, we don't have to climb inside the pit to take care of that sort of thing.

I go and get situated in my Goliath, strapping myself in and buckling my helmet. That's all run-of-the-mill stuff. But what's completely out of the ordinary is that Malcolm suits up right next to me.

"You'll need a sparring partner," he says by way of explanation. "So let's go, rookie."

I can't believe he's serious. "You sure you want to do this, old man?"

There must be a full moon tonight because Malcolm actually

smiles at me. Well, scratch that. It's more like the corners of his mouth twitch for a second.

The Jays open the training pit gate, and Malcolm lets me head inside first. A thrill shivers down my back. Malcolm might be grouchy and sour most of the time, but he's still *Malcolm Maines*, the American legend. He might be over thirty now, but he still maneuvers his Goliath like it's a part of him, a second skin.

"Let's run drills first," Malcolm says, dampening my mood. I thought we'd be sparring right now, but he's intent on giving his lesson. "I've been watching reels most of the night. She's very quick on her feet and spontaneous too, like fighting a ball of lightning."

"So how do you propose that I beat her?"

"Keep her grounded. Don't let her start backflipping and cart-wheeling around you, and definitely stop her from launching one of her aerial strikes."

"Easy peasy," I mumble. I've only got a day and half to perfect this, but I'll make it work.

He ignores that. "First step? Tail her as much as possible. I'm betting she'll try to scale up the cage and get airborne as soon as possible—it's a seventy percent probability based on her prior matches—so you have to prevent that from happening. Try this."

Malcolm demonstrates what he wants me to do. Specifically, he shows me how to grip on to a mecha's ankle and twist it to gain control of the whole leg. They aren't complicated moves and I master them fast, but I get no praise out of him.

"Put it into action, and we'll see how you do. I'll be Rushi."

We take our positions on opposite ends of the pit while one of the Jays starts counting us down to the start. As soon as we hit zero, Malcolm becomes a blur. He might be double my age, but he still has that trademark speed. I've barely caught up with him by the time he has scaled the cage. I reach for his ankle like we practiced, but he shakes me off. Lips pursed, I try again, but once more he dodges me. He's getting away, so I scale the bars after him, but then he leaps all the way to the other side of the pit before landing cleanly. He motions at me to go back to the starting point.

"Take it from the top," he says, not even out of breath. Then he gives me a look that seems to say, *I'm not going to make this easy for you, rookie.*

He sure keeps that promise too. We repeat the process more times than I can count. Malcolm might not be able to recreate Rushi's spinning and tumbling, but he sure can mimic her speed. Every time I think I've got him, he somehow wriggles out of my grasp or shakes me off completely.

"You've got to pick an ankle and aim for that one. Don't waffle between the two," he says between drills.

And when I finally do manage to grab his foot, he has more advice to throw out. "Pull her down with your whole body, not only your arm because that won't give you enough force. But as soon as you've yanked her down, you better get out of Dodge. Keep your chin down and spin away before her mecha crashes on top of you."

We go again. I take his advice and yank him down with my full weight, and sure enough his Goliath comes down fast. I'm about to scram like he told me to, but then my old training kicks in, and I decide to tweak Malcolm's instructions.

Instead of keeping my chin down, I tilt my face up to watch Malcolm's trajectory. I watch his Goliath falling and adjust my own to stay out of its way, scurrying back one step at a time but never taking my eyes off it. I'm using a strategy I learned in my karate lessons. Tai sabaki. I shift my body to move in relation to my attacker, not only to avoid a hit, but to gain a better position.

It's a good thing I do this too because as soon as Malcolm lands, he leaps up again to attack me. If I'd had my back turned to him, then I wouldn't have seen him coming, but since I've been watching him this whole time, I'm ready for it. I slam into his chest with my shoulder, knocking him back down, and he doesn't spring up so quickly this time. Instead he signals that the drill is over.

As I lean down to help him up, I can't resist getting in a little dig. "Take it from the top, Coach?"

He grunts in reply, but I can tell things have shifted. I've surprised him.

"Smart evasive maneuver," he says. It's just about the nicest thing he has ever told me, but he brushes his hands off and that's that. "Let's move on."

We switch to a couple offensive moves to round out my arsenal, a combo throat punch and a sweeping kick, followed by a rear chokehold that maneuvers into a toss to stun the competition. We hit it hard for the next hour, stopping only for water breaks, and I realize that Malcolm is finally taking my training seriously. Because I'm the only fighter he has left.

When we've finished yet another drill, I grab a drink and mop the sweat off my face, figuring I've got a couple minutes to catch my breath until we head back into the pit, but Malcolm juts his chin at me.

"Hit the shower," he says.

"Why?" I glance at the clock. "I want to practice the chokehold again."

"We'll finish up tomorrow. You've got a press conference to go to."

"What—*now*?"

"Not now but soon. Look, answer a few of their questions, and we'll call it a day. We don't want the papers spinning up stories that you're a no-show."

"I don't care about the press."

"I think you've made that clear already, but don't you care about the sponsors? They'll be watching the conference too. I'm sure Goody will be one of them, and you can bet that there'll be more of them showing interest now that Sam is gone."

I grumble a curse under my breath, hating how he dangles that in front of me, but I only have myself to blame because I told him I wanted sponsorships. *This is good news*, I tell myself. The more contracts thrown my way, the more stability I can give to Peter.

With that thought in mind, I drag myself to the locker room. I give my hair a quick wash and scrub myself clean before I change into the outfit that has been left for me in my locker, a crisp white blouse paired with a navy skirt. I follow Malcolm to the dining hall, which houses the press conference again. All four fighters will get a turn with the reporters, and so far Rushi and Albie have already finished their interviews. I'm up next with Lidiya as the caboose.

As I wait for the techs to adjust the microphone, I grab a water from a service bot and whisper to Malcolm, "I'll answer three questions."

"You have to do a few more than that," he says with a sigh. "It won't kill you to smile, you know. Do you think Goody or Sears wants a spokesgirl who scowls at the cameras?"

In response, I paste a ridiculously wide grin onto my mouth, and he digs an elbow into my side.

"Jo," he warns.

Fine, fine. I dial back my smile, not to please Malcolm, but to butter up the bigwigs at Goody and Sears. And then it's my turn to walk the plank.

I squint at the bright overhead lights as I march to the podium. A camera bot rolls in a wide arc in front of me, clicking its shutter at predetermined intervals to catch my face at various angles. My mouth feels dry as I stare out at the sea of journalists, and I realize that I left my glass of water by Malcolm. It's too late to grab it now though. The first reporter is already standing up to ask his question.

"Miss Linden, this Round Four lineup is historic considering that three of the fighters are girls. How does that make you feel?"

I smile genuinely at that because it's both an easy question and one that I don't mind answering. "It makes me feel honored, and it's really nifty if you think about it. The chances are good that we'll have a female winner this year."

"And what do you think your chances are at doing just that?" the reporter asks as a follow-up.

I wonder what I should say to secure those sponsorships on the spot. Something patriotic. Something quotable.

"I don't like to get too ahead of myself, but I sure want to bring that title back to the US of A," I end up telling them, which is rather catchy if I do say so myself.

I know that I've totally dodged the question, but the journalists are scribbling away, and from the corner of my eye I notice Malcolm giving me a subtle thumbs-up, so I must've said something right.

The press conference moves on. I answer a question about Sam's elimination and then about my matchup against Rushi tomorrow. It's nothing too hard-hitting until I get a reporter sniffing for a comment about Lukas and Zoya.

"It has been reported that you were in close contact with both Lukas Sauer and Zoya Federova before they collapsed," the journalist asks in a clipped accent. I squint at his press credentials and notice that he's from a newspaper based in East Germany. Figures. "The IC has since cleared your name, but you have yet to make a public statement. Do you have plans to do so?"

I wish I could say *Next question* very loudly, but since that's kind of rude, I have to come up with something else. I notice Malcolm motioning at me from the sideline, reminding me to smile, which is his way of telling me to be nice because the sponsors are watching.

"I'd say that the IC clearing my name is good enough for me, and I send my sympathies to Zoya's and to Lukas's family," I say.

There. The reporter and Malcolm can't nitpick that too much.

We've got time for one more question, and it just so happens to come from my hometown paper, the *Chronicle*.

"Miss Linden, when you were tapped to Team USA, you were practically an unknown to most Americans, even to those in San Francisco," he starts off.

I stifle a snort because I'm sure the *Chronicle* had heard about me. They simply never found me worthy of a story before.

"But as we've been interviewing San Franciscans about you and your historic role as the very first fighter from our city, we came across a family friend of yours. Lawrence Wen?"

My fingers curl around the hard wood of the podium. What exactly did Old Wen say? He can't be thick enough to have mentioned I fought in an illegal match that he took bets for.

"Mr. Wen remarked on your achievement here, not only as the first American female to go the Games in thirty years, but also as the very first Oriental fighter from the States." The reporter pauses to study my face. "Is it true that your mother was Chinese?"

My whole body goes rigid. The rest of the reporters look confused, whispering to one another, but soon they're all staring at me again, awaiting an answer. Meanwhile the camera bot is clicking away, and I can feel my cheeks heating up like little furnaces.

It'll be in all the papers tomorrow—photographs of me with my eyes wide and my cheeks flushed—and I can almost see the headlines in big fat letters.

My secret is finally out.

18

"Are you all right, Miss Linden?" the reporter asks.

I'm still at the podium and still trying to come up with a response. All I can think about is Old Wen and how lucky he is that he's three thousand miles away. Because if he were here, I'd have a few choice words for him, none of them ladylike. What was he playing at, revealing my mom's race to the reporter? Maybe he got slipped some money to talk. Or maybe he was trying to redeem my mother somehow. Whatever his motives, he has gotten me into an absolute mess.

The cameras keep flashing and desperation settles in. I scramble to say something, anything. Am I supposed to lie?

Then Malcolm joins me and is leaning into the microphone to address the crowd. "The Association will put out a press release shortly. We won't be taking any further questions at this time," he says before he guides me toward the exit.

But the reporters have smelled blood in the water, and a few of them swim after us like piranhas.

"Will you make a personal statement, Jo?" one of them asks.

I shake my head no.

"Why have you hidden your heritage from the public?" another one says.

Oh, maybe because I'd never get invited to the Games in the first place, I think. They must know that.

"Do you refute Lawrence Wen's accusation?"

Accusation? Like being Chinese is some sort of crime?

But I guess it is in a way. We couldn't become citizens until '52, and we were barred from entering the US for nearly a century before that.

"What province in China did your mother come from?" asks yet another journalist.

Something inside me snaps. Malcolm still has a hold of my elbow, but I whip around to face the small crowd trailing us.

"She was born in California," I say. She never stepped foot in China, and her family had been in this country for generations. They were as American as Sam and Malcolm.

"But will you confirm that she was Chinese?" they press.

"Chinese *American*," I correct them. My face feels scalded at this point. Did they ever ask Sam what part of England or Ireland his ancestors came from?

Malcolm leans into my ear. "Cool your chops and keep walking."

I have one more thing to say though. One more thing to get out. "Judge me by what you see in the pit. That's all I ask."

Then I turn my back to the reporters and let Malcolm escort me into my dormitory. The lobby is fortunately empty, and I crumple onto one of the benches in the sitting area.

"You should've let me handle that out there," Malcolm says, vibrating with frustration. "I had it under control."

"Did you even *hear* what they were asking? Forget it. You wouldn't understand." I watch Malcolm's face contort, and I think he's really going to let me have it, but then he blows out a long sigh. I think he feels bad for me, which tells me that this situation must be really terrible.

"Perhaps I don't understand your exact situation, but I do understand the press. They'll be taking your words and twisting them into something you won't even recognize." He rakes his fingers through his hair. "And now I have to play cleanup and deal with this press release."

I look up at him miserably. "The Association is going to cut me from the team."

"No, they won't. You *are* the team at this point."

I let out a shaky breath, grasping onto this speck of hope.

"They can't replace you after Purgatory begins, remember?" he continues.

They're stuck with me then. They either have to deal with me or boot me out and forfeit Team USA's place at the Games, which I severely doubt they would do. Meaning I'm still in game.

Relief sweeps over me, but then I realize: "My sponsorship deals are going to dry up fast, aren't they?"

Without even pausing he says, "It's likely, yes."

I wince. For once, I wish he could've sugarcoated his answer for my benefit. "Because my mother was Chinese," I add. My voice hitches. "I was good enough for them an hour ago but not now?"

"Is that what you really care about? Some endorsement deal with Sears?" His face is reddening, and I can tell he isn't going to hold back his tongue lashing this time.

"You wouldn't understand," I repeat before he can start flapping his lips. "My family—" I stop myself because I still can't bring myself to reveal how much we need a sponsorship, any sponsorship. And now that the whole world will soon know about my mother's "background," there could be consequences. My dad might be white, but his kids aren't. Our landlady could have us evicted. Our remaining customers could abandon us.

I feel the tears come, and I really don't want to cry in front of Malcolm, so I tell him that I'm going up to my room before I make a break for the stairs.

As soon as I open my door, I let it all out. The tears. The hurt. The rage. I punch my pillows until some of the stuffing starts spilling out, but I keep hitting them hard. I could strangle Old Wen, I'm so mad. But my anger goes deeper than that. Much deeper.

Of having to hide who I am.

Of living in fear of being found out.

Of never being judged for what I can do in the pit but by my gender.

And now by my skin color.

Finally I collapse into bed, the fury depleted and replaced by exhaustion. I'm not sure how long I lie on my mattress, but I cocoon myself in my blanket and watch the sun dip lower and lower into the horizon. I will myself to go to sleep, but my mind refuses to settle. It's useless to keep trying, so I force my legs over the side of the mattress. I've got a phone call that I need to get over with.

My father picks up on the second ring with the standard, "Linden's Repair and Refurbishing."

"Dad, it's me," I say, already tearing up. "There's something I've got to tell you."

It all comes spilling out. The press conference. Old Wen. The inevitable headlines in the paper tomorrow morning—in the *Chronicle* that most of our customers will be reading.

"We'll probably lose business over this," I say, keeping a fresh bout of tears at bay.

A beat passes. "That might be so, but we don't need those people anyway. You think I want their money?"

"Cash is cash," I reply weakly.

"We don't need that sort of money. Besides, traffic into the shop has doubled since you went to the Games."

"Really? That's incredible—" I cut myself off. Will those new clients peel away after they read the papers? I press the heel of my hand against my eye, fighting off the hopelessness. Dad and I rarely talk about how Peter and I are part Chinese. We've just ignored it, as if it might go away. As if keeping silent would keep us hidden. But I still find myself saying, "I'm sorry."

"Josephine, don't you ever be sorry about this and don't let anybody shame you for it. What do I always say? Don't get delicate. I've told you that because you're a Linden, and we grit our teeth and get things done." He takes a long pause, and when he speaks again, his voice cracks. "You're a Lee too, and you've got your mother's stubborn streak. You don't give up, you hear?"

This is the most sentences that my dad has strung together in a long time. I'm a little shocked. Not to mention the fact that he actually talked about Mom.

"I won't give up," I tell him.

"That's right. You hold that chin up, and you show everyone what you can do in the pit."

The tears threaten again, but I swallow hard. "Okay." Then I ask, "Can you put Peter on?"

"Hold on a sec. He's out in the workshop."

Half a minute passes before my brother picks up the receiver. "Jo? Dad said you've got something to tell me. Everything all right?"

I breathe deep and launch into what happened at the press conference all over again although I try to soften the landing this time.

"We'll be fine, I promise," I say, even though I know it's a promise impossible to keep. "And if anyone gives you guff about this at school, you tell Dad and me, all right? We'll take care of them." I'll flatten them, in fact.

Seconds pass and then a few more, and yet Peter says nothing.

"You there?" I ask, anxious about what he's thinking. Then I get worried. "Listen, don't panic. This will all blow over soon enough."

"I'm not panicking," Peter says at last, sounding a lot calmer than I'd anticipated.

"You aren't?"

"I was only thinking. I guess I'm not shocked. I figured we couldn't keep Mom a secret forever."

"But everyone will know that we're not fully—you know—"

"White?"

"Well, yeah," I say, taken aback by his reaction. I really thought that I would have to comfort and assure him.

"Everyone has always thought that you were white, Jo. Not me though," he says softly. "I always get questions like 'Where are you really from?' because I don't look like you or Dad."

"You don't look like Mom either."

"I look like her *enough*."

Now I'm the one to go quiet. "You should've told me that people were giving you grief."

"I was fine though. I ignored them," he says, sounding so much older than thirteen in this moment. "We don't have to get into this if you don't want to. Would you rather talk about your match tomorrow?"

This is not how I thought our conversation would go at all, but Peter doesn't seem bothered much. In fact, he starts discussing strategy with me, and I let him talk because I'm still trying to figure out how to weather this press disaster.

"Jo, are you listening? I think you should go strong out of the gate. Trip her up and go in for the KO."

I snap out of my daze. "Sure thing," I say, noticing how grown-up he sounds.

Peter is right though. I have to focus on this next match. I can't control our customers or the reporters, but I can win this game tomorrow and the finals after it. Everything else—the headlines, the lack of sponsorships . . . I just have to ignore it all. Like Peter does.

After a quick dinner by myself, I finally drift off to sleep, and when I wake up in the morning, I realize that a solid night of rest has done me some good. My muscles are sore but not too badly, and a hot shower helps to work out the kinks. Inevitably, the memory of the press conference invades my mind, but I block it off the best I can and try to keep moving. I won't read the papers today or listen to the radio or watch any news reports. Let people talk all they want about my mother and my race.

I've got a match to win and a ticket to punch to the top of the podium.

I try to pretend that this is any other game day. I make sure to eat a good-size breakfast—my usual bowl of oatmeal but sprinkled with brown sugar and a sliced banana—before I head to a light training session. Time seems to speed up from there. Lunch. A phone call home. A strategy meeting with Malcolm to go over last-minute details. Then I ring the hospital to see how Sam's doing, but the nurse says she can't give me any details over the phone since I'm not family. And then it's time for the 3:00 p.m. matchup between Lidiya and Albie. Malcolm and I watch it together in our training section, both of us opting to stand in front of the screen instead of sitting down.

As we listen to the anthems play, Malcolm gives me an update. "We put out the press release this morning about your mother. I sent a copy up to your room."

I thank him even though I have no intention of reading it.

"I canceled your press conference for later today as well."

"Can't you cancel them for the rest of the Games?" I don't want to speak to another reporter ever again.

"We'll have to see."

I consider asking him about the blowback now that my secret is out in the open. Has anyone on the Association asked for me to be dismissed? How much outcry has been stirring up in the public? But I chicken out. I'd rather duck my head in the sand and not think about that. Besides, the match is set to start.

"My bets are on Lidiya," I murmur.

"Let's see what the Brit can do," Malcolm replies dryly, but there's not much hope in his tone.

In the end, Albie puts forth a good effort, but Lidiya is too much for him. Too fast. Too agile. She doesn't even have to employ her trademark sneakiness. She merely tosses Albie from one side of the pit to the other until he's dazed enough and she puts him out of his misery. The whole thing lasts under twenty minutes.

Malcolm shuts off the television and doesn't remark upon Lidiya. Instead he says, "You have to focus on the ten-meter target before you aim for the twenty."

Easy for him to say since he won't be the one facing Lidiya in the pit. Then again, I won't either if I don't make it through this next round.

"It's almost time to head over to the stadium," he says, dismissing me. "I'll meet you there."

After I've gathered up my things, I take a chauffeured car into the city proper, curving around the streets and hopping out by the VIP entrance. A few dozen fans have gathered by the doors, eager for a picture or an autograph. They stand behind a metal partition that's guarded by some security bots that emit a warning (*Take a step back, please*) if anyone gets too close.

I give everyone a wave before heading toward the door, but my eye catches on a poster that a young white girl is holding up, which says, *Go, Jo, Go!*

I can't help but grin. This is exactly the pick-me-up I needed this morning. I switch directions and walk toward her, watching her mouth open wider and wider as I draw closer.

"Hi there. Want me to sign that poster for you?" I ask.

She squeaks something incoherent in reply and digs a pen out of her pocket.

"So what's your name?" I ask as I grab a corner of the poster. I've barely finished writing *Jo* when I notice someone pushing through the crowd toward us. Probably someone else who wants an autograph. I glance up to say that I can't stay long when they start yelling.

"Go back to Beijing! We don't need your kind on our team!"

The words hit me like a slap and I drop the pen, but that's not the worst of it. Before I can blink, something cold and slippery smacks me in the cheek. It smears half my face and catches in my hair, and it smells something awful.

The security bots go berserk. "Alert! Alert!" they say in their mechanical voices while the human guards idling by the doors finally look up from the magazines that they were reading.

Some of the crowd scatters while others click away with their cameras. For a second, I lock eyes with the little girl, who's gripping on to the poster, and I realize that I haven't finished the autograph, but I don't know where her pen has fallen.

"I'm . . . I'm . . ." I stammer. I want to tell her sorry, but my mouth isn't working properly and now the stink is really getting into my nostrils and I think I might throw up.

I bolt toward the stadium, flashing my badge at the guards, and stumble inside. I use my sleeve to wipe my face and realize that it's covered in rotten rice.

We don't want your kind on our team, the sneer echoes.

I have to get this muck off me—and out of my head.

Picking up the pace, I sprint for the locker room and try to hold myself together, but as I round the final corner, I plow straight into Malcolm. He catches me by the shoulders but pulls away as soon as the stench hits his nose.

"What happened to you?" he asks, bewildered.

"I got rotten rice thrown at me. What else does it look like?" I spit out angrily. The shock of what occurred outside now turns into rage. I'm so angry that I'm trembling. "They told me to go back to China."

He blinks twice, finally understanding the reference, and his mouth tightens. "Who said that?"

"Some bigot outside the stadium! They're probably long gone by now." Tears fill my eyes, unbidden, as if this day couldn't get any worse. But Malcolm doesn't notice that I'm crying. For the first time since I met him, he seems at a loss for words.

"You hurt?" he says gruffly.

I shake my head. Not physically, I guess.

"Good," he says before flinching. "I mean, hit the showers and get yourself checked in. I'm going to talk to the Association about bulking up security outside."

I nod. At least he's taking this somewhat seriously, but that's only a small comfort when I reach the locker room and try to get this mess out of my hair. The rice has partially disintegrated into the strands, and I have to run a fine-tooth comb through them to wash it all out. Even though I have a schedule to keep, I let the water run over me and breathe in the steam, trying to hold back the tears again.

Why hadn't I run after that coward outside? I could've given them a pummeling, but I froze up and the only instinct I had was to get far, far away.

I rest my forehead against the cool tiles in the shower as two emotions duke it out inside me. Anger and shame. They take turns tugging on my heart, but then they get company. Despair. What if this happens again when I enter the stadium? Or whenever I head back to the Pavilion? Or the next time I'm walking down the sidewalk, trying to live my life?

"Get a grip on yourself, Linden," I whisper. I wish there was something to make this all go away because I have a match to prep for and I don't have time for this. And I really can't let this affect me in the pit. I have to block it out. Shove it away.

But I can still smell that rotten rice even though I've already washed it down the drain and shampooed my hair twice.

I towel off and get dressed in my game-day uniform and remind myself that I have to keep moving. There's too much at stake to curl up and cry right now. So I keep my chin high and my eyes straight as I walk over to register for the match, only to see that Rushi is heading there as well and she beats me to the desk by a couple paces. Just my luck.

"Your ID, miss?" the registrar asks her.

"Oh, yes. It's right here." Rushi tries to reach into her bag, but the zipper catches and she only has one hand free since the other is gripping on to a thermos.

I automatically take the metal cylinder from her so she can get on with registration and I can take my turn at the desk. She nods at me gratefully.

When she's finished checking in, I try to sidestep her, but

Rushi matches my movement, effectively blocking me.

"I saw the newspapers today. Your mother was Chinese?" she asks shyly.

"Yes, she was," I say, my tone flat as the Great Plains. I know it's rude, but I'm not feeling talkative and I really don't want to discuss this right now.

She must notice because she says, "Good luck today, Jo."

I soften a little on the inside. Unlike me, Rushi hasn't been able to hide the fact that she's Chinese, and I wonder if she's heard racist taunts since she arrived in America. Chances are, she has.

"Good luck to you too," I say, my eyes finally meeting hers. Only then do I notice that she's looking pale. Maybe even feverish, since I can see tiny beads of sweat on her upper lip. I'm about to ask if she's feeling well. But Envoy Yu is suddenly at her side, shuffling her away before I can say anything else.

I'm running ten minutes behind, but to his credit, Malcolm doesn't chew me out about it. He just motions for me to move into my warm-up and says nothing more about the rice incident. I'm not sure if I'm miffed by that or relieved. Likely both. But I don't want to bring it up either, so I throw myself into the match preparations. I stretch and run laps, then I suit up and get in one last diagnostic check from the Jays.

"Will Sam come tonight?" I ask Malcolm.

He shakes his head. "He's still under observation, but he sends his regards."

I admit that I deflate a bit at this news. I wouldn't mind having

Sam on the bench, with his giant grin and his unsolicited advice. I'd even let him call me kiddo.

"Time to go," Malcolm tells me.

We stride onto the elevator, and right as we pop up into the stadium, my gaze flies around the stands, darting this way and that in case another handful of putrid rice gets thrown at me. None of it comes, but I can't help noticing that there are more empty seats than the last match, which makes no sense because this is Round 4 and Team USA is still in. Every chair ought to be filled at this point in the Games.

I get a sinking feeling in my stomach.

It's because of the headlines, isn't it?

Some of those ticketholders didn't want to cheer for a fighter like me.

Bigots, the whole lot of them, I tell myself, but it doesn't make me feel any better.

After the announcer has called out our names and countries, he lets everyone know that the final four at the '63 Games marks a historic occasion—the first time we've had more than one female fighter this late in the competition and now that record has been smashed.

And all of us are here tonight. Even Lidiya is up in the stands, sitting in the VIP section next to Khrushchev. She's not even hiding the fact that she's glaring knives in my direction, probably trying to get under my skin. I give her a hearty wave and blow her a kiss for good measure.

There. Now I'm ready to go pound some metal.

I bounce on my toes while we run through the usual proceedings. The speech from an IC member. The anthems. The customary handshake. I make sure to glimpse into Rushi's cockpit as we shake. She's looking pale, and I think it will work in my favor because she's under the weather. I'll admit that this isn't my proudest moment. A bigger person would never think that way, but I guess I'll never be a saint. I need a win here.

"And here we go again, folks! Round Four!" the announcer says.

We take our places, and the countdown begins, with the crowd joining in as we tick down to zero.

I bite down on my mouth guard and race toward Rushi right out of the gate, like Peter recommended. I usually don't go on the offensive this early, but I don't want to be predictable. Plus, after the rice incident, I have enough pent-up energy to power ten Goliaths.

Rushi tries to evade me, but I change trajectories and launch myself into the air. I move my arms and legs to form a flying kick, timing it so that my foot strikes her on the back. She lands on the ground hard, and I move to pin her and deliver the KO. I can hear the crowd grasp. If I can pull it off, this match will be one of the shortest in the Games' history, but that gasp turns into a groan when Rushi twists out of my hold.

"Zhu escapes at the very last second!" the announcer says.

I hurtle my Goliath toward Rushi. This is a great start for me. I can't let that make me overly confident, but I'm already thinking that I have the upper hand in terms of positioning and dominance.

Now I have to put that to good use and catch up to Rushi.

We play some cat and mouse, but strangely enough her usual speed isn't on display. She's still faster than the majority of fighters I've faced at the Games, but I manage to get close enough to unleash a few swipes, only for her to spin away at the last second, and we start the process all over again.

Rushi scales up one side of the cage like a squirrel, and I can sense that she's about to launch her aerial attack, but Malcolm has trained me for this moment. Reaching up, I grab her left heel like I practiced yesterday, clamping my fingers tight before using both hands to yank her off balance. I can almost hear Malcolm in my ear, shouting *Throw your weight into it, rookie!* And with one big tug from me, Rushi loses her grip and falls onto the ground, hard.

This is my chance now. I remember to use tai sabaki and move my body in relation to hers, which gives me the ripe opportunity to pounce as soon as she tries to wobble to her feet. We grapple, our arms tangled, but she still has some life in her yet.

Somehow she manages to launch herself into the air, dragging me along for the ride before she shakes me off with a swift scissor kick. Now I'm the one falling, but the people in the stands are marveling at the move because she did this all in *midair*. Some home team crowd, they are.

Rushi has barely enough momentum to grasp on to the top of the cage with her fingertips just as I leap back onto my feet. She doesn't let go though. She simply hangs there, with her mecha's chest rising and falling rapidly, and I realize that she's trying to catch her breath in the safest spot she can find.

My eyes zero in on her. It's now or never.

I leap up to knock her down. The first attempt, she kicks me away. The second time, I don't manage to get a firm enough grip. Right before I go for round three, I glimpse Malcolm back at our team's bench, pacing like a lion, his eyes intent on me. He's yelling something and there's no way I can hear him, but it's clear what he wants. Eliminate her—now.

Third time really is the charm. I hook my arms around her waist, and it's only a matter of five or so seconds before she can't keep her grip any longer. We both go careening downward, but I'm ready for the impact. As soon as I hit the ground, I move fast to flip her over and pin myself on top of her mecha. I expect her to try to wriggle free, but she's practically deadweight. I can't remember the last time I eliminated anyone with such little resistance. Either she has given up completely or she really is sick.

The head ref calls the match, and I push myself off Rushi's mecha with one arm in the air. It's like a cork releases inside me, and all the emotions from the last twenty-four hours—from the press conference to the rice to this moment—shoot out of my mouth in a deafening shout. I let it all go with both of my arms in the air now because this victory is mine and none of those lowlifes can take it from me.

Cameras flash and even Malcolm is clapping, and I tell myself to remember this moment because I'm really going to the finals.

Almost as an afterthought, I look over to Rushi's mecha. She fought with a lot of heart and I ought to shake her hand again, but she hasn't gotten back up. Her mecha is still lying facedown on the ground.

"Hey, you need a hand there?" I ask, walking over.

I bend over to get a better glimpse into her cockpit, only to find her cheek covered with damp hair. Her eyes have rolled into the back of her head, and she's convulsing.

Just like Lukas. Just like Zoya.

"Rushi!" I shout at her while I roll her mecha over onto its side. "Wake up!"

This time, I don't have to wait long for help to arrive.

Two referees lift the gate to the pit, and the medical team comes rushing in fast. They push me away to circle around Rushi and get to work. Beyond the bars, the crowd has hushed, some of them pointing while others shield their children's eyes from the sight.

I scramble out of my Goliath and try to approach Rushi, but one of the medics blocks my path. So I stand there, feeling helpless and scared.

Malcolm reaches my side. Taking me by the shoulder he grunts, "Let's give them some space."

We head over to our team's bench, but neither of us sit while we watch the medics working on Rushi. Envoy Yu, who had been sitting in the stands, is obviously panicking. She tries to enter the stadium floor, but the security bots won't grant her access until one of the refs waves her through.

I focus back on Rushi. The medics have hooked her up to an IV, and it appears they might've stabilized her because they're strapping her onto a stretcher now. That's a good sign, isn't it? I find myself walking up to the cage to get a closer look, but then Envoy Yu steps right in front of me.

"You did this to her!" she shouts in my face.

I gape at her, not sure if she's talking to me or someone else. But then she's pointing straight at me. The cheery Envoy Yu that I first met is nowhere in sight now.

Malcolm tries to intervene, but she pushes him away. "Jo poisoned Rushi!"

People start booing her. Others urge her to sit down, but the damage is spreading. Murmurs ripple out through the stadium, and a strange numbness claims my body. I'm not angry; I'm completely and utterly shocked. I turn around in a slow circle, realizing that this is getting broadcasted live across the world.

Pure instinct tells me to run. Sweat beads on my face as my heart picks up speed again, like I'm about to enter another match.

Malcolm clamps a firm hand onto my arm and starts dragging me toward the elevator. "We have to get you out of here."

Not knowing what else to do, I follow.

19

I can feel thousands of pairs of eyes glued to Malcolm and me as we walk onto the elevator platform and disappear underground. I wish that this thing would move faster, but it seems to insist on rumbling along.

Finally the numbness starts to fade and is soon replaced with something that feels fiery hot.

The words rip right out of me. "I didn't poison anybody! Envoy Yu was lying out of her teeth."

"Look, take a deep breath and—"

"She isn't going to get away with this." I try to reach for the elevator button to take us back up, but Malcolm stops me.

"What are you doing?"

"Giving her a piece of my mind!" Envoy Yu's accusation echoes in my ears. Everyone heard her too. I should've said something right then and there, but I had stood frozen, like there was a clamp on my tongue. But it isn't there now.

"Absolutely not. You want to cause an international incident on top of all this?"

"She's throwing around allegations that aren't true!"

The elevator reaches the bottom floor, and Malcolm practically pushes me out of it before I can get a hold of those buttons.

"Get a grip, Linden! You'll only make things worse."

I don't know how I can sink any lower at this point. Why can't he see that?

"Someone is trying to pin these poisonings on me!" I cry. "Lidiya accused me of tampering with the Soviet float and poisoning Lukas and Zoya. And now Envoy Yu thinks I'm to blame for Rushi. Somebody has it out for me."

He paces a few steps, back and forth, thinking this over. "I wouldn't go straight into a conspiracy theory."

"You can't wave this off like it's a coincidence!"

He has no reply to that, so I know I've gotten him there, but neither does he look fully convinced.

I'm about to say that I want to talk to Senator Appleby because maybe she could do some digging, but we're interrupted. Leon Schmid, the IC head delegate who interrogated me after Zoya collapsed, is marching down the corridor with two security guards following behind.

"We need to speak with Miss Linden," he says to Malcolm.

Malcolm stiffens. "About what?"

"I think we all know that already," he says before he glances at his guards. "Search Miss Linden's locker here and then head to the dormitory. The matron can let you into her room."

"Hold on, you're going to search through my things?" I say, my pulse taking off.

"You can't barge through my fighter's personal effects. You're standing on American soil here," Malcolm cautions.

"And you two are here at the invitation of the Pax Games, an organization not bound by your nation's laws," Mr. Schmid counters, pushing his glasses up his nose. "I'll be escorting Miss Linden right now to the conference room in hall C. As I'm sure you can tell, the IC has some questions for her."

"You listen here, Schmid—" Malcolm points a finger in the older man's face, and I have to wedge myself between them.

"I'll answer his questions," I tell Malcolm before I turn to Mr. Schmid. "Just so you know, I haven't done anything wrong."

Mr. Schmid gets this look on his face that says, *We'll see about that*, but he gestures down the hallway. "If you'll follow me."

We zigzag through the underbelly of the stadium and step into a sterile-looking conference room with no windows. A ceiling fan circles lazily above our heads, making a clicking sound with every rotation, but the air still smells like cheap Viceroy cigarettes.

"How's Rushi doing?" I ask after I've claimed a chair.

"She's being taken to the hospital. The doctors there are excellent, so she will be in good hands."

Hopefully this means that Rushi should be all right, which eases the tightness in my chest a little but not by much.

Mr. Schmid places his black notebook on the table and roots for a pen in his pocket. "To start, Envoy Yu filed a complaint against you to the IC this morning. She alleges that you cornered Zhu Rushi in your dormitory commons room yesterday."

He must be joking. *Cornered?* "Rushi and I were talking about tea! Our whole conversation couldn't have lasted more than five minutes." My shock soon switches into fury. "And Envoy Yu is one to talk! She follows Rushi around like a shadow. It's creepy if you ask me."

Mr. Schmid doesn't even bat an eye. "On top of that, we have the reports filed on you by the Soviet delegation. Consider how this looks, Miss Linden. You also had close interactions with Lukas and Zoya before they fell ill."

I see what he's trying to do. "The arson case was dropped and there's no evidence that I had anything to do with Lukas's poisoning or Zoya's for that matter."

His jaw clenches, but he barrels on. "Let's get to the issue at hand. Did you have any contact with Rushi before the match today?"

I glance at the door, wondering what he'd do if I left right now. He isn't the police and can't arrest me. But could he pull me from the Games? Maybe. So I decide to stay put. "I bumped into her at the registrar, but that's it."

He scribbles this onto his paper. "Tell me what happened in detail."

"I got behind her in line and we made small talk."

"What kind of small talk?"

"She asked about my mother," I huff, my frustration multiplying. "Is this really necessary? I didn't poison anyone. I haven't hurt anybody. Hook me up to a polygraph if you have to. I'll do it."

"I will make a note of that, Miss Linden, but I'm not done with my questions."

We go back and forth like this for another forty-five minutes, until there's a knock on the door. One of Mr. Schmid's assistants pokes his head inside and slides him a folder, which Mr. Schmid looks over with a frown.

"We've finished searching your locker and your dorm. Everything there looks in order." He sounds disappointed to be honest.

"Because I'm innocent," I say tightly. "Are we done here?"

"For now, yes, but you should know that we're delaying the final match by twenty-four hours so that we can investigate further."

An alarm bell goes off in my head. "Could the Games get canceled?"

"That has yet to be decided. Now, I have another meeting to get to," he says before pocketing his notebook.

I push my chair back and take my exit. My head is spinning. What if the IC calls off the Games entirely? There'd be no winner. No prize money. And any sponsor who hasn't lost interest in me yet will tuck tail and run.

I've spent half my life training for this sport, only to see it disintegrate in front of my eyes. I could stomach that if I'd washed out and gotten eliminated early. At least I could blame my performance on it. But that's not what's happening now. Someone is poisoning fighters and trying to lay it at my feet, and no one believes me.

I tear through the hallway, ignoring the locker rooms because I don't want to spend another minute in the stadium. I can change back in the dorm, but how am I supposed to get there? Call a cab? I don't have a single dollar bill on me.

"You all finished with Schmid?" Malcolm says, popping out from seemingly nowhere. He looks slightly out of breath, and there's an intensity in his eyes that I only see when we're in active training.

"He's delaying the next match by twenty-hours for the investigation. There's a chance the entire Games might get scratched." I expect him to freeze in his tracks and demand to speak to Mr. Schmid right this minute, but Malcolm keeps walking toward the parking lot.

"Nothing we can do about that except wait it out," he says, sounding distracted.

"Did you even hear me?"

Now that makes his head snap toward me. "I heard you just fine. Pick up the pace. We have to talk."

"Talk about—"

"Not here. Get in the car first."

What exactly is this about?

My heart is pounding again as we head to a black sedan parked out front. I move to open the back seat like I usually do, but Malcolm shakes his head.

"Sit up front. I'm driving," he says.

This really doesn't make sense. We usually have a chauffeur whisking us to and from the stadium.

"What's going on?" I press, but he doesn't say a word until we've driven off into the night and he pulls over onto a darkened side street a few blocks away.

Malcolm reaches into his trouser pocket and takes out a small glass vial, holding it up for me to see. It's about the length and width of my pinky, and I can see a fine white powder inside it.

"I was able to get in your room right before Schmid's lackeys arrived. I did a quick sweep and found this at the back of one of your drawers," he says, anger spearing through every word. "Not a very clever hiding place, Jo."

I stare at the vial, then at him. "Wait, you think that's mine? I've never seen the thing in my life!"

"Then what was it doing in your room?"

"How am I supposed to know? I don't even know what's in it!" My breaths feel thick and labored. My hunch was right—someone is trying to frame me. "I didn't poison Ruchi or any of the others. You have to believe me."

He laughs. He honestly laughs. "You can drop the act. I'm holding the evidence right here."

"This isn't an act!" I'm shouting now, but I don't care. "I've never played dirty, and I would never stoop so low to poison an opponent. I know how this looks, but that vial isn't mine. Somebody planted it!"

"Who, then? Security is airtight at the Pavilion." He stares at me and waits, challenging me to come up with a response.

"I don't know!" I throw my arms up in frustration. "There are dozens of Commies who have access to the Pavilion. Fighters. Coaches. Officials."

"You're saying the Reds would poison their own? Because that's who is getting targeted. Lukas. Zoya. Rushi." Malcolm shakes his head at me. "Fortunately for you, I had the wherewithal to search your room before the investigators got in. If not, we wouldn't be having this pleasant conversation because you'd be in the feds' custody."

It's getting harder not to cry—the emotions are building up inside me and they want out. But I manage to fend off the tears. "I didn't do this. I'm innocent." My voice hushes to a whisper. "You've got to believe me."

Malcolm doesn't seem to care. He's looking at the vial. "I'll tell you what. It's almost admirable what you've done, sneaking around and picking off your opponents one by one. Anything to win, huh? You know, over the last few days, I was starting to think that I judged you too harshly, that you really are the diamond in the rough that Senator Appleby had promised." He smirks to himself. "Just goes to show how much you've fooled all of us."

Our gazes clash, and I wish he had sucker punched me instead of telling me that. Because it would've hurt less.

I make a grab for the vial, but Malcolm is too quick and encloses it in his fist. "What are you going to do with that? Turn it over to the IC?" I ask, desperate.

He hesitates, and I realize that he hasn't thought this whole thing through. "If I do that now, I'll get pulled in for confiscating evidence," he says quietly, realizing the gravity of what he has done.

"So why did you take the vial in the first place?" I bite out. "As a little memento?"

"I did what I had to do!" he explodes. "Do you think I want to see the team eliminated? Or watch my reputation get flushed down the drain?"

"None of that will happen if you help me figure out who's setting me up!"

He snorts at that. "Are we back to that again? Your conspiracy theory?"

It takes everything inside me to swallow my anger. He really thinks I'm capable of these crimes, doesn't he?

I manage to hold myself together to say, "I'm no murderer and I'm no cheat. And that's the truth."

Then I throw open the car door and start walking

"Linden!" Malcolm calls out after me, but I don't turn around.

20

I end up at the Pavilion because there's nowhere else for me to go. By the time I get back to my room, it's well after ten o'clock, and my feet are sore from all the walking. But I can't plop onto my bed and go to sleep yet, thanks to the damage that the IC has done to the place.

The investigators have left no corner unturned. My drawers are all gaping open, and my mattress has been flipped up onto the bed frame. They've taken all my pillows too, probably to get cut up and dissected. I can't even find my toothbrush.

I have to bite down the urge to scream. It's all too much. The pressure. The accusations. The vial that Malcolm discovered. I thought I'd hit rock bottom when the press discovered that my mother was Chinese and I got hit in the face with rotten rice.

I had no idea how much further I could fall.

Exhausted, I curl up on the floor. My cheek presses against the cold tiles, but I don't care. I shut my eyes and hope for a little peace, but my mind drifts to Peter instead. He and Dad must be waiting by the phone for my call. They must be worrying themselves sick, but I can't bring myself to get up.

I wish I could fall asleep right here, but my thoughts keep me awake. Whoever is framing me is still out there, probably rubbing their hands together, pleased, because their plan is all coming together. I wrack my mind for possible suspects. It must be someone with access to the VIP sections of the stadium, but that's a staggering number when you count up all the fighters, coaches, and staff members, not to mention the security details and Association reps and any other cronies who got handed a badge. Or managed to steal one. There are possibly hundreds if not a thousand people in that pool. How am I supposed to narrow that down?

I'm running through that list when I finally drift off. When I wake up again, I've got a mean crick in my neck, but I go through the motions of getting ready for the day: asking the dorm matron for a new toothbrush and forcing down a plate of scrambled eggs and walking over to the training center because I still have the final match to prep for. The routine calms me a little, but as soon as I spot Malcolm, I start feeling anxious and angry all over again. I don't want to rehash our conversation though, and fortunately he doesn't even bring it up.

"Start stretching," he says as he glugs down his standard black coffee.

I begin with lunges. The silence between Malcolm and me turns awkward, and I wish that Sam was here to lighten the mood. He'd crack a joke or challenge me to a duel in the pit, and even if he ended up beating me, it would be better than this.

"Any word on Sam?" I ask.

"He's improving," Malcolm says without elaborating. Then he has to step out for a minute to take a call, and I'm left to finish my warm-up on my own, which I don't mind at all.

As I move into some torso twists, I wonder if Sam and Rushi are at the same hospital. Washington isn't a big city, so there's a good chance that they are. It makes me wonder what Sam thinks about all of this. Did he even watch the matches yesterday? I wouldn't blame him if he didn't, but I get the feeling that he must have. He wouldn't have been able to keep his eyes from the action.

Malcolm approaches me upon his return, his face looking even more sour than before. "I got word about Rushi. She's awake and recovering," he says. "Envoy Yu is telling anyone who will listen that she thinks you're at fault."

I'd thought that I had gotten a good handle on my fury, but it comes roaring back. "That little piece of—"

"But Rushi's blood tests have come back inconclusive, and the IC has no evidence that you poisoned her. It's all she said, she said."

"Then the Games are a go? We'll have the final match tomorrow?"

He nods, and I'm hit with a punch of relief.

Thank God.

I still have to beat Lidiya and win, but at least I'm going to get that chance.

"Don't go celebrating just yet," Malcolm says, bursting my bubble of bright news. "You've got a cloud hanging over you. Three countries have withdrawn from the Games since yesterday. East Germany, Hungary, and Bulgaria. They're arguing that the IC has been too slow to respond to the poisonings and that the entire '63 Games should be forfeited."

I cross my arms. None of those countries have fighters left, so this decision must be mostly for show, but it feels like sour grapes to me.

"At least it's only three," I say, trying to make light of it.

Malcolm isn't amused. "China is heavily considering it too. They're urging the Soviets to withdraw as well."

"I thought Mao and Khrushchev weren't chummy anymore."

"They aren't, but it appears they have a common enemy in this case."

A common enemy—as in me.

"Could there be a chance that the Soviets pull out of the match last-minute?" I ask.

"I doubt it. Rumor has it that Khrushchev himself has overruled the possibility even though the USSR Mecha Fighting Federation had been considering it. You'll have your shot at the championship tomorrow."

I have to wrap my head around this—a world leader meddling in a sporting match? Usually they just come for the photo ops. "I didn't realize that ol' Nikita was such a fan."

"I'm sure it's all political. He doesn't want to jeopardize the

Vietnam treaty in any way." He takes a long sip of coffee, scrutinizing me over the mug. "Consider yourself lucky that Khrushchev seems so intent on getting this Accord signed."

His words knock the wind right out of me, but I have to clench my teeth and not let it show. There's no use changing his mind. Somehow Malcolm really believes that I could've offed Lukas Sauer without a speck of remorse.

I'm no killer, but I'm sure ready to murder some metal right now.

We run through two training sessions, the first one in the morning and another one after lunch. Following that, Malcolm dismisses me for the rest of the day, but I insist on watching reels of Lidiya's prior matches. Tomorrow will mark the biggest match of my career. Of my whole life, really. I'm not going to waste my time with napping.

I've gone through three of the reels when I stand up to stretch to get the blood moving through my legs. Malcolm and the Jays have departed for dinner, so I'm alone for now.

Until someone pokes his head in.

"Just the person I've been looking for." Sam walks toward me in that easy way of his, a backpack slung over one shoulder. He doesn't even look like he was recently in the hospital.

Before I know it, I'm running toward him and flinging my arms around his neck. "Sam! When did you get discharged?"

"This morning actually."

"And you stuck around," I say, surprised. Some of the eliminated fighters will remain for the duration of the Games to attend the closing ceremony, but it isn't a requirement. Plus, since Sam got beaten by Lidiya for a second time in a row, I doubt anyone would've blamed him for ducking out early to lick his wounds, least of all me.

"You really thought I'd leave and miss out on all the free dining hall food?" Sam's mouth kicks up in one corner, but it's far from his usual megawatt grin. And I'm pretty sure I know the reason why.

"I'm sorry about everything," I say, solemn. "About the match. About what Lidiya did to you."

He grimaces. "You win some, you lose some."

"Right. Any given match day," I reply, but both our sentiments ring hollow. You can use those excuses when you lose a regular high school game, but not here. Not at the Games. I wouldn't be surprised if Sam's Round 3 match has kept him awake every night, analyzing every move and mistake. I know that's what I'd be doing in his shoes.

I better change the subject. "How's your head feeling?"

He knocks a fist against his temple a couple times. "This old thing? I'm fine. Not the first concussion I've had. By the way, thanks for all the flowers and balloons you sent to my hospital room. Really sped up the recovery process."

I flush because we both know that I didn't send him a single thing. "I really wanted to visit you, but Malcolm said it wouldn't be a good idea."

"Oh, you're actually taking his advice now, hmm?"

I know he's making a joke, but he does have a point. We're team-mates and the very least I could do was pop in for a quick *Sorry about your concussion.* "I acted like a dipstick."

"At least you've finally admitted it." That makes him smile, a genuine one this time. "I won't rag on you too much though. You've had a busy forty-eight hours, judging by what I've seen on the news."

My guard immediately goes up and I start talking fast. "The accusations aren't true. I didn't poison Rushi. I didn't poison *anyone.*"

Sam arches a brow. "You think I'd come here if I thought you did?"

"You . . . believe me?"

"Aw, jeez. You might be stubborn and you might not listen to my advice, but you're not a cheat. You're too proud for that."

I don't realize how much I needed to hear him say that, and before I can stop myself, everything comes pouring out—about how I think I'm getting framed, about the vial discovered in my room, and about how Malcolm believes I'm 100 percent guilty. I know I'm talking way too fast, but Sam doesn't ask me to slow down. When I'm finally finished, he whistles low.

"You've got every right to be hacked off," he says.

"And I've got no clue who's setting me up."

Sam thinks this over but shakes his head in the end. "Your guess is as good as mine. My advice? Never be alone. Always have some-one with you who can back up an alibi. And it might be a tall order, but you have to ignore the allegations. You've got a match to concentrate on." He stops himself. "Has the IC made a decision on that yet? Will there be a game tomorrow?"

I nod. "They don't have any evidence against me, so they don't have a choice. Meaning I get to say hi to Lidiya in the pit."

"Now that's something I might be able to help with. Here." Zipping open his bag, he grabs a black binder that's nearly bursting with reams of paper, so thick that its binding looks ready to give up. He holds it out toward me, and I thumb through it curiously. Inside, I find sections for different countries, like Great Britain and Egypt and Brazil. There's one for every nation that participated at these Games.

"What's this?" I ask.

"Research. Since I don't need it anymore, I'm bestowing it upon you." He looks a little pained to be handing this over to me though, like he's giving up a childhood teddy bear. "Turn to the section on the USSR."

I flip the pages until I reach the section dedicated to our beloved Russian friends. It's further divided into two parts, one about Zoya and one about Lidiya, detailing their stats and their style of play and their past injuries. There's also a few paragraphs about their favored moves.

This is a handwritten treasure trove of insider info. "Where'd you get this? From Malcolm?"

"Nah, it's all mine. I always update my binders ahead of a tournament."

I gawk up at him. "*You* compiled all of this?"

"I can't take *all* the credit. I hired some translators who helped me too."

"What did you need translators for?" I say with a frown.

"For the foreign newspapers and magazine articles mostly. That's the best way to dig up dirt on international fighters—where they've gotten hurt, if there's a pattern in their movements, and so on."

I run a finger down the page and notice how some of the pen marks are more faded than the others. An image pops into my head of Sam hunched over a desk well into the night, poring over articles translated from Russian or Bulgarian, before jotting notes into his binder.

This must've been one of the keystones of his success. Sure, his strength and natural athleticism had a lot to do with it, but there are a lot of strong and athletic fighters out there. What helped set Sam apart was the dedication he put in outside the pit—by dissecting his opponents to the point of obsession.

I have to admit that I'm surprised—and far more impressed. Sam hadn't relied solely on his physical prowess or his fancy training to get ahead. He'd been doing his homework all along.

"How long have you been doing this?" I ask.

"A while." He lifts a shoulder like this isn't a big deal. "What can I say? I like to be prepared."

That reminds me of something he did at the welcome banquet that we attended right after I arrived in Washington, before the Games officially began, when he went around casually asking about the other fighters' injuries and whatnot. He'd called it educational.

"So that's how you knew Giselle gets sloppy in the pit when she loses her cool."

He grins, unable to hide his pride at that. "I picked up that tidbit from a French fighting magazine. Had to shell out fifty francs for the translation."

"Those costs must've added up. Too bad your stepfather didn't bankroll it."

"Not to worry." His grin slides ride off his face. "He chipped in some cash here and there. He really did want me to win the Games—it'd be good for business."

He tries to hide his sentiment behind a layer of sarcasm, but I hear the pain in Sam's voice. I recognize it myself. It's how I sound after Dad tells me yet again, *Don't get delicate on me.*

Sam and I—maybe we have more in common than I thought. I didn't realize it before because he masks his hurt with his grins and no-sweat attitude. While I ignore mine, I guess.

No, that isn't quite right. I release it in the pit.

"You look like you're about to cry or murder someone," Sam says.

I quickly wipe my face clean of emotion and get back to the matter at hand. "Does Lidiya have a weakness like Giselle's?"

He laughs to himself. "If she did, I would've won my match against her, but hey, go over my notes if you think they'll help." Then his whole face becomes dead serious. "Just beat her, all right?"

I realize then why he has given me his binder. Maybe it's

partially out of loyalty for our team, but it's more about Lidiya. He'll do anything to stop her from winning the Games.

Sam shoulders his backpack but doesn't leave yet. With narrowed eyes, he says, "You know, whoever planted that vial in your room would've needed a fighter's badge to access the dorm."

"I've thought about that, but badges can get lost. Or borrowed out."

"But your badge only accesses the girls' dormitory while mine only works on the boys'. That narrows your pool quite a bit." He crosses his arms to think this over. "Which female fighter would benefit the most if you got tossed out of the Games for cheating?"

My mouth slips open. "You think Lidiya set me up?"

"She has had it out for you since the Parade of Nations," Sam says, lifting a brow.

"But why would she poison her own boyfriend and sister too?"

Sam looks me directly in the eye. "To win the Games, why else?"

That is one serious accusation, but this is Lidiya we're talking about. "Why didn't she try to poison *you* though? You're ranked second in the world."

"Maybe it would've been too obvious if she did. Or maybe . . . maybe she had beaten me before so she figured she could do it again without any help."

I have to take this in, but this could certainly fit Lidiya's MO.

"I'd believe it, but try explaining this to anyone with no proof," I lament. "I need a security bot to catch her in the act."

Sam thinks on this a moment and asks, "I don't have a security bot to lend you, but how about a camera one?" He fishes around in his backpack and presents the device to me, the same one he was using during the parade.

"I thought this was your brother's."

"I'm not giving it to you, kiddo. Do you even know how much this thing cost?" he says, his teasing trickling back into his voice. "Here, I'll show you how to use it. If Lidiya or her henchmen try anything on you, you'll have some proof."

After about ten minutes of walking me through the bot's functions and how to change out the videotapes, I've gotten a decent hang of the thing, and Sam hands it over to me completely.

"I don't know how to thank you for this," I say.

"Like I said, just beat Lidiya tomorrow. It's only a small ask, right?"

"Minuscule."

We share a smile, but mine fades quickly.

"You bring that title home," Sam says.

"I will," I promise him.

21

The hours tick by ahead of the finals. The sun goes down and pops up again, bringing with it searing temperatures and a sticky humidity thick enough to swat at with your fingers. It's going to be a soupy mess of a day for the final matchup, but it'll be one for the history books that's for sure. For the first time ever, we'll have a female winner of the Games. Either Lidiya or me.

My nerves wake me up before my alarm gets the chance. Everything is on the line. The title. Dad's shop. Our apartment. No sponsor wants to touch me at this point so I can either go home with $500 or zilch.

Will we even have a place to go home to if I lose today?

I'm grateful that I'm kept on a tight schedule in the morning, giving me something to focus on. My matchup against Lidiya won't start until three, but there's plenty to do before then. One last warm-up. More reels to watch. A very short press conference where Malcolm has screened the questions beforehand so the press can't ask about my mother.

Before I know it, it's time for lunch, and I get a small pocket of time to rest before I have to go to the stadium, but it's impossible to nap or even sit still. I decide to call the shop to hear Peter's voice, but the phone rings and rings and rings. I hang up and try again, but no one answers.

Where in the world could they be? I'd have bet cash that Dad and Peter would be waiting by the receiver when I called, but now I'm wondering if our line got cut again on top of everything else.

I sigh and decide to thumb through Sam's binder again. I've already studied all his notes on Lidiya, but I might as well reread them. Anything can help. Before I sit down at my desk though, I make sure that my door is locked and I check on the camera bot that Sam loaned me. I'd set it on the corner of my desk yesterday, propping it up so that it faces the door in case Lidiya or one of her cronies pay me a pregame visit. It might seem like an unglued thing for me to do, but I figure it's better to be paranoid at this point than not paranoid enough.

There's a knock on the door, making me jump. Maybe it's housekeeping. "Who is it?"

A beat passes, and I wonder if I'd been hearing things. Then a small voice says, "It's Rushi."

I jerk the door open fast, and there she is. Her face looks thinner than before, even though it has only been a couple days since I saw her last. But it's definitely Rushi standing there.

"Rushi!" I exclaim, and reach out to hug her. I must startle her because she shrinks back, but soon I feel her birdlike arms clasp around my shoulders. "I've been so worried, but what are you doing here? When did you get discharged?"

"Not long ago. I came to get my things. Envoy Yu packed for me, but she forgot these." She motions at a box beside her feet, filled with a couple shirts and a kettle and a frame that shows a black-and-white photo of two girls. Rushi glances over her shoulder, looking worried. "I wasn't supposed to talk to anyone, but I wanted to say good luck."

"R-really?" Now this is completely unexpected. I didn't think I would see her again, considering she must be convinced that I poisoned her, and yet she came to wish me luck? "Whatever Envoy Yu said about me, I swear to you that it isn't true."

"It's all right. Envoy Yu—" She has to take a breath to force out this next part. "Can be wrong sometimes."

I could kiss her on the cheek. "It means a lot that you believe me."

Rushi flushes at my words, and I gather she's feeling bashful. "May I make you chrysanthemum tea? For luck?" She picks up the box, and I notice that she has a tin of tea leaves in there too.

I open my door wider. She's really full of surprises today, and I wouldn't mind some company before I head to the stadium. "Sure, come on in. I've got a little time."

Rushi gets to work, filling the kettle with water from the sink before plugging it in. As she waits for it to boil, she gives the mugs a rinse and pats them dry with a small hand towel before she asks me to grab the tin. I go to retrieve the tea, but I pause when I get a closer glimpse of the photo in Rushi's frame. It's Rushi standing next to a girl who looks a lot like her, only a couple years younger.

"This your sister?" I ask.

Rushi looks up, and her features soften. "Yes. Her name is Lisha."

The kettle starts to whistle and she turns to switch it off. "Oh, I don't have any sugar," she says. "I think there's some in the commons room."

"I'll go find it," I offer.

Over in the kitchenette, I have to root through a couple cupboards and drawers before I locate a few packets of the stuff. By the time I return, Rushi has already poured the tea although it needs to steep.

I blow at the steam while we wait. "When do you head back to Beijing?"

"We fly tomorrow."

"I bet Lisha can't wait to see you." I glance at the photo again. The two of them even wear their hair the same, in a neat braid down the back. I realize that I know which leg Rushi favors in the pit and how to best deflect one of her aerial strikes, but I don't know much else about her at all, not the personal stuff anyway. She'd mentioned before that her mom had passed, but what about her father? Grandparents?

This is probably my last chance to get to know her a bit. "Do you have other siblings?"

"It's only Lisha and me. Our parents—" She shakes her head and doesn't say anything more about them, and my mind goes straight to the famine that Giselle had mentioned. Is that how Rushi lost her parents? That isn't exactly something I can bring up though, and in any case, she lifts up her mug. "It's ready."

I frown at my cup because the liquid doesn't look quite dark enough yet. "Is it?"

She nods and urges me to take a sip like we're in a hurry.

"Hold on a sec, don't you want sugar?" I say.

"Oh." She seems to have forgotten all about it. "Yes, please."

Rushi pours a packet into her mug while I tip in two for the extra sweetness. She proceeds to take a sip, so I figure it should be cool enough to take one too, but the liquid burns the tip of my tongue.

"You should drink while it's hot!" she presses me. "Didn't you say your mother liked this tea too?"

"She made it when I was little." I blow on the liquid a few more times before giving the tea another go. This time it leaves behind a flowery taste instead of pure heat.

"What part of China was she from?"

"She wasn't really from China. She was born in California." I take a long sip because I'd rather burn my tongue again than admit that I don't know what province or city my own family came from. I was too young to ask my mother about it, and Dad doesn't know either. "Her ancestors were probably from Guangdong." That's my best guess since a lot of Chinese Americans in San Francisco have roots there.

Rushi's eyes light up. "My nainai was from there! She would tell Lisha and me stories about the islands on the Pearl River."

I don't understand most of the references in that sentence. What's a *nainai*? Is that a relative? I've never heard of the Pearl River either or the islands that dot it.

There's something else that's new to me too—Rushi seems excited that I'm half Chinese. Not embarrassed for me. Not pitying. But genuinely curious.

It's a reaction that I wouldn't mind getting used to and, with that thought in mind, I drink more of the tea, downing about a third of it.

A knock on the door startles us both, and Rushi spills a little tea on the floor. I never have any guests at the dorm, so two in one day is quite the surprise. When I check who it is, I find the dorm matron on the other side, asking me to come downstairs because a gift has arrived from Peter and Dad. I tell her that I'll be right down.

"This should only take a minute," I say to Rushi.

"But the tea—"

"Is great. I'll be right back."

I grab my badge to access the elevator and by the time I step onto the ground floor, I expect to turn the corner and see a bouquet of flowers or balloons waiting for me there. But what I actually find is so much better.

"Jo!" my brother says, hurtling himself into me.

"Peter?" I catch him in my arms, utterly shocked. It's been barely two weeks since I last saw him, but I swear he's sprouted an inch. I'm soon laughing and crying while I hug him. So that's why he didn't pick up the phone back at the store. He was already here in Washington. "You little sneak. Where's Dad?"

"Surprise, Joey." My father comes up behind me and claps me on the back. "We couldn't miss the big match, now could we?"

"Mrs. Watters rounded up the whole block to chip in for our flights and hotel," Peter explains. "Everyone is rooting for you. The whole city!"

I swipe at my tears and laugh again. Bless Mrs. Watters and our neighbors. This is the best present I could've asked for.

"Wait, who's minding the shop?" I ask, a streak of alarm shooting through me.

Peter looks up at Dad, whose smile falters. "Ah, don't you worry about it. We locked the doors tight, and everyone in the neighborhood will keep a close eye on it until we get back."

That must've been a hard decision for him to make. Dad only closes the store on Thanksgiving and Christmas, arguing that we can't make money if we don't keep the doors open. But he's here. He came.

Peter soon gets distracted by a mail-sorting bot that he spies in the dorm matron's office, and while he checks that out, I scoot a little closer to my dad.

"Any updates on the landlady?" I ask quietly.

Dad's forehead wrinkles at the question. "Let's focus on the here and now. We're at the finals of the Pax Games." Those creases on his forehead deepen. "In any case, it seems like you're dealing with a mess and a half out here."

To put it mildly. But I don't want to hash all that out again because it'll only make me tense up. "Hey, anyone want a quick tour of the place?" I say loudly, knowing that'll get Peter's attention.

Peter comes bounding back toward us like a golden retriever. All that's missing is the wagging tail. "Can you show us your room?"

"No, boys aren't allowed beyond the lobby—" I stop myself because I suddenly remember that I'd left Rushi upstairs.

I ask Dad and Peter to wait for me while I haul myself back to my room, taking the stairs two by two. As soon as I get there, I already have an apology on my lips, but I find the place empty.

"Rushi?" I say, spinning around in a circle. I even poke my head into the bathroom, but she's not there either. Her box is gone as well, although she has left my mug of tea behind since I'd only drank half of it.

I don't know why she skedaddled out of here so fast, but she was probably worried about Envoy Yu chewing her out. Will I ever see her again? But I'll have to save that wondering for later. In less than forty minutes, I have to report to the stadium.

Until then, however, I give Dad and Peter a whirlwind tour of the Pavilion, pointing out all the buildings and telling them we ought to check out the views at Hains Point whenever we get a minute. Peter can't get enough of the service bots all over the place, especially the window-washing ones that cling to the glass with their suction-cup feet, while Dad seems most impressed by the dining hall. I show them all the fixings at the make-your-own waffle bar even though it's well past breakfast time, but they both could use a bite to eat after their long flight.

"Do you have tickets to the game?" I ask.

"Senator Appleby got us box seats," Peter says with a grin. Then both of them get quiet when I say I need to head out. They won't be able to come with me to the stadium right now since it isn't open yet to the public, but they assure me they'll come as soon as they can.

"You'll have the home-field advantage by far," Dad tells me. "Never underestimate that."

As far as pep talks go, I'd have to give it a three, but he is right. A crowd at your back can certainly help, although I'm facing Lidiya Federova, who seems to thrive off the negative energy directed at her.

"Any parting words of advice, squirt?" I ask Peter, who has a massive waffle in front of him stacked with strawberries and whipped cream. "I'm all ears if you've got a tip on Lidiya's weaknesses."

I say that as a joke more than anything, but my brother takes the request seriously. "She doesn't really have any weak points."

Ouch. I'm not surprised by his observation, but that doesn't help lift my spirits much.

Peter isn't finished yet though. "But her mecha might."

"What do you mean?" I say, blinking.

"A fighter is only as good as their equipment, right? When you faced the Federovas in Purgatory, did you notice anything about their Vostoks? A glitch you could use to your advantage?"

Purgatory feels like it happened months ago by now, so that game is mostly a blur, but you know what? I've got Sam's binder and that might jog my memory.

"You're a genius," I tell him. "I better go, but I'll see you both soon, okay?" I'm already running back up to my room, where I grab the binder, and then I'm off again to catch a ride to the stadium, flipping through the pages the entire way.

I scour Sam's notes to see if he mentions anything about Lidiya's Vostok, but I don't find much outside the particular make number. I curse under my breath but keep up the search, reading through the list of her injuries again but this time paying more attention to the causes. A fractured pointer finger due to a fall at home. A badly bruised right shoulder from a training session. A strained posterior cruciate on her left leg from a match against Sam at the Euro Cup last summer. I only know what a posterior cruciate is because I injured my own a few years back—it's a ligament in the knee—and that's what my doctor kept calling it.

No details about the Vostok though.

I curse again, louder this time. I need more time along with a library bot or two, but all I've got is Sam's binder.

A thought hits me. Lidiya isn't the only fighter using a Vostok. There are plenty of others on the Soviets' roster, starting with her little sister. With that in mind, I flip to Zoya's binder section and give that a read, but nothing jumps out at me. I keep turning the pages though because the driver has run into some traffic, and I see that Sam has included his notes on Oleg Lebedev, another

Soviet he faced two years ago. I'm not expecting much at this point, but as I reach the end of Oleg's file one of Sam's scribblings catches my eye.

Injured anterior and posterior cruciates on the left knee. Mechanical error in pit.

Mechanical error?

Could Oleg's injury and Lidiya's be related?

My mind starts spinning, but I can't get my hopes up yet because this isn't much to go on. Still, I'll take what I can get.

I need to find Sam.

When I get to the stadium, I open the car door cautiously, remembering what happened before my match against Rushi when I got told to go back to China. But there are no fans here today. The whole sidewalk has been blocked off, probably due to the rotten rice incident, and I'm grateful that's one thing I won't have to worry about.

I race through registration and make a beeline for Team USA's prep area, where I find Malcolm and the Jays running a diagnostic on my Goliath. My face feels flushed as I walk up to them, and I wonder if the air-conditioning is acting up because it sure is warm in here.

Malcolm greets me with a frown. "Where's your match-day uniform?"

"Has Sam arrived yet?" I ask at the same time. "I have to talk to him."

"About what? And what's that?"

I'm still clutching on to Sam's binder. "Research," I say, lifting my chin an inch and using the same line that Sam said to me yesterday. Malcolm and I have only exchanged a few words since our dustup following Rushi's poisoning, and I haven't forgotten how he thinks that I'm guilty as a jailbird.

"When's Sam coming?" I ask again.

"He should be on his way," Malcolm replies, crossing his arms.

"I have to talk to him about the match."

"If this is about the match, then you can tell me instead. I'm your coach."

Some coach you've been. "You sure about that? I didn't think you wanted anything to do with a cheat and a murderer."

His face darkens, and in reply, he snatches the binder right out of my hands and starts to thumb through it. Soon his frustration shifts into confusion. "What is this exactly?"

"Sam put it together." I make a grab for the thing, but Malcolm pivots away too quickly, his reflexes razor sharp. Frustration simmers in me. "I need that back."

"There's some decent stuff in here," Malcolm murmurs as he skims the pages.

"Yeah, and it might help me beat Lidiya, so give it here."

His head snaps up. "Beat her how?"

"That's what I need Sam for. I have some questions for him."

"Out with it," Malcolm says, nostrils flaring. "We don't have time to wait around on Sam when he might not show up until twenty minutes before the whistle blows." He must notice how I'm eyeing him skeptically, so he sighs and adds, "I'm offering you a hand here, Linden. We've got to beat Lidiya. Everything else comes second to that."

That isn't the apology I'm looking for, but we do have a common goal right now and ultimately my desperation wins out. I explain Peter's theory that I should try to find a weakness in the Vostok itself and how I came across Lidiya's and Oleg's similar injury in Sam's notes.

"They both strained the same ligament in their left knees," I say, summing it all up. "And Oleg hurt his due to a mechanical error."

Malcolm goes quiet as he thinks back in time. He even closes his eyes, squeezing them tight, like he's watching old match reels in his head. "That's right. I remember that game. Sam managed to trip up Oleg, and Oleg landed funny on his knee. His Vostok's leg kept dragging behind him after that."

"Do you know if the same thing happened to Lidiya?" I press him.

This time he recalls the match more quickly since it was only last summer. "Similar scenario. Sam managed to trip up Lidiya, and she landed hard on her knee. Come to think of it, she did seem to have trouble controlling that leg when she'd gotten up, but there wasn't much time to observe it. She KO'd Sam about a minute later."

I suck in a sharp breath. "So she could've had a mechanical error too?"

"Emphasis on *could've*, but yes. It's a possibility." His lips start moving silently like he's working out a long equation in his head.

"But there are two roadblocks. First, this could all be a coincidence. And second, even if you're onto something, the Soviets might have patched up that error months ago."

He's right. But my heart is thudding faster and faster.

What if he's wrong?

"I have to go after her and trip her like Sam did. I don't have anything to lose." I wait for him to contradict me and tell me that he's the one who calls the shots.

But he tilts his head toward the pit. "Then you better practice that before we head upstairs."

"You're actually on board with this?" Not that I was waiting for his permission; I was going to do this with or without his approval. I'm just surprised he didn't bat away my idea.

"I'm on board with beating the Soviets, and the more tricks up your sleeve, the better," he says before pushing me toward a Goliath. "Go get ready."

We speed through a warm-up before we conduct one last training session, albeit brief. I show Malcolm my leg sweep and he provides a few pointers to sharpen my movements, but in between drills, I have to mop the sweat beading on my forehead.

"Is it me or is it hot in here?" I ask.

"The humidity getting to you?" He barks at the Jays to get me some water. "With ice! Plenty of it."

In record time, I'm presented with a glass of ice water, which does help cool me down a notch, before Malcolm goes back to talking business.

"Remember the strategy," he says, standing atop a ladder so that we can talk face-to-face since I'm in my Goliath. "When that buzzer goes off—"

"Charge at her fast, aim for the knee," I say, a little distracted. My armpits are feeling damp now too. I'm always anxious before a match, but this is a new level that I haven't experienced.

He nods. "Don't stop until you take that knee out and remember to keep calm in there. Keep cool."

Soon it's time for us to enter the elevator that'll bring us up to the stadium. *Keep calm. Keep cool.* It's simple enough advice, but it's hard to do—literally. Sweat clings to the top of my lip and I wish I had some more of that ice water, not to drink but to dunk my face in. Someone really needs to get that air-conditioning checked.

Malcolm punches the button, and the elevator platform begins its chug upward. The air in the stadium vibrates like a living thing, and it's *loud*. Cheering. Chanting. Clapping. A sea of red, white, and blue. I let it all soak in for a few seconds before I point my eyes straight ahead. I can't get swept up in the fervor; I have to concentrate.

Lidiya emerges from the elevator on the opposing side. We don't acknowledge each other at all. No tilt of the head. No nod. But I do roam my gaze over her Vostok's left knee, my bull's-eye.

We take our places at our team benches. Sam is waiting there already, dressed in a spiffy suit. He winks at me, but I notice the strain around his smile. He's nervous too. I kneel down to shake his hand.

"Looks like Lidiya didn't pay you a late-night visit," he says. "I guess you didn't need my camera, after all."

"Thanks for loaning it to me anyway, and it's about time you showed up. I wanted to talk to you about something I found in your binder notes."

His brows shoot right up. "Like what?"

The announcer starts speaking overhead to welcome everyone to the final match of the Games, and I have to cut our conversation short.

"Malcolm and I talked it through and came up with a plan. We'll see if this works," I say before getting back to my feet.

The usual fanfare rolls out from there. A welcome speech from the IC and the Association. The playing of the anthems. My gaze seeks out Team USA's box, where I find Dad and Peter seated next to Senator Appleby. I hardly recognize them since Dad is wearing a tie and Peter has slicked back his hair, like they're going to church. Well, in the Linden family, I suppose the fighting pit is our religion, so it does make sense. Peter starts waving at me, and I immediately wave back. God, I'm so glad that they're here.

And I'm not about to let them watch me lose.

It's finally time to get to the pit. Lidiya and I walk into the cage, and we shake hands, as is customary, although she clutches my Goliath's hand longer than necessary, drawing me in toward her.

Her gaze locks onto mine. "I will destroy you. For Lukas and Zoya."

I roll my eyes because her words are ridiculously dramatic, like something out of a bad B movie, but from the look on her face, I know that she's dead serious.

"I'd like to see you try, Bolshie," I reply, just to get under her skin.

The head ref is shouting for us to take our places, so I turn on my heel and go to my mark before she can respond. Once in place, I roll my shoulders a couple times, but they stay tight enough to string a bow. The whole world will be watching this game, and I think Lidiya might try to murder me on live TV. No pressure or anything.

The countdown begins. I wipe the sweat off my forehead again, wishing that I had a built-in fan inside this piece of metal. I start to wonder if I might be coming down with something, which would be just about the worst timing to get sick. But I've fought in a match before while recovering from the flu, so I can grit my teeth through this one too.

My eyes lock on Lidiya. Her gaze is intense, like a hungry animal's.

Here we go.

At the sound of the buzzer, I bolt forward, carrying out the strategy that Malcolm and I planned, but Lidiya is already onto me. She soars up to avoid my trajectory and uses the momentum from her landing to launch right back in my direction, turning a defensive move into an offensive one.

"Buckle up, ladies and gentlemen, because it looks like this match will be a quick one!" the announcer says.

I jerk my Goliath around to face Lidiya head-on. She comes at me like a hurricane, first with a swing of the elbow that I dodge and then with a kick that I spin away from. Jeez, she's quick—faster than Giselle, faster than anyone I've ever faced—but I'm no slouch. I plant my palms onto the ground and sweep my leg out, aiming my foot at her Vostok's knee, and it's a perfect shot. I've timed it just right and Lidiya stumbles backward, but I must not have hit her hard enough because she recovers fast. But when she comes at me again, she lets out a pained grunt as soon as she puts weight on her left leg.

I've drawn first blood.

Adrenaline zips through me as we grapple at the center of the pit. It's a battle of strength, both of us trying to overpower the other, and I try to kick at her left knee again, but I miss this time around and Lidiya swoops in. She lands a blow on my cockpit, making the whole frame shudder, but I lurch out of harm's way.

"So far, Linden and Federova looked pretty evenly matched!" the announcer says. "Hold on though. Federova may have gained the upper hand!"

Lidiya pounces onto my back. I don't even know where she came from because she was in my sight line not even two seconds ago, but that's all the time she needed to latch on to me like a parasite. I try to throw her off, but we both take a tumble in the process. Repositioning herself, she locks me in an expert hold, pinning my chest down while hoisting my mecha's left leg upward so that I can't get any leverage to buck her off. I wriggle against her, but it's useless.

The crowd gasps. The announcer's voice turns frantic. "We're not even five minutes in, but could this be the end of the line for Team USA?"

The ref holds up one hand, ticking the seconds, and he's already on three. The title is almost Lidiya's.

Running on nothing but willpower, I let out a scream and jerk my leg out of her grasp before I roll over. She cries out because she had the win within her fingertips, but I'm not going to hand her the trophy *that* easily. Besides, I've already imagined how my name will look engraved on it.

I somersault out of her grasp and aim for her left knee one more time, and my strike hits true—my heel colliding into the Vostok's joint.

Lidiya's face screws up in pain. I think I must have the advantage now, but she only gets more furious and she uses that anger to fuel her next onslaught. But she does seem to be limping.

"Federova looks to have injured her leg, but let's not forget that she has feigned this before. Could she be trying that tactic again?" the announcer says. "Linden isn't in tip-top shape either from the looks of it. She appears very fatigued."

I wish that I were faking it. The sweat now drips into my eyes and down my face. I manage to wrench away from Lidiya, and that buys me a couple seconds to launch my Goliath into the air. My plan is to give myself a moment to think, but my arms feel like deadweights and I can't even grasp on to the nearest bar. I fall back onto the ground and barely roll away from Lidiya's snatches, but it's harder to get up this time.

My stomach cramps, and I think I might vomit, which has never happened to me before in the pit. Lidiya grabs a hold of my arm just as my last meal comes up, coating the inside of my face shield. Out of instinct and pure disgust, she stumbles backward, and I have enough wherewithal to get out of Dodge.

I use my draining energy to jump up again and my hands manage to clamp on to the bars. I gather the last tatters of my strength, but already my grip is slipping and I have no idea what's wrong with me. The match can't have lasted over fifteen minutes, but I feel like I've been at this for hours.

I don't feel well.

I don't feel *right*.

But if I don't get myself together, I'm going to lose because here comes Lidiya again

She joins me at the top of the cage and attempts to knock me down. I tangle my ankle around her Vostok's left leg and give it a sharp jerk to aggravate it—and it works. She starts to fall, but on the way down, she catches my foot and I don't have the strength to hold on any longer.

Both of us crash toward the ground and upon impact I retch again, but Lidiya comes out worse. Every time she moves that left knee, her face scrunches up in agony, and I'm screaming at my body to take her out now. But I'm dizzy and can only crawl on all fours. Soon even that's too much, and I keel over.

Lidiya throws herself on top of me, but I have a little fight left in me yet. I smash a fist against her injured knee, at least I think I do.

Cameras flash all around us in the stands, like little bursts of fireworks, but they're dimming fast. Black spots cloud my vision, and no matter how hard I try, I can't blink them away.

Those same black spots are growing bigger and bigger, when I hear the announcer say, "We have a winner of the '63 Pax Games!"

Before I can hear the rest, the darkness reaches up and drags me down with it.

22

My eyes crack open.

I cough and blink the blurriness away, but I'm not sure where I am. The room is dark and unfamiliar; the thick curtains have blocked out all but a sliver of light. My head is pounding, and my body hurts and my mouth tastes like . . . well, nothing pleasant. I reach out to grab the glass of water that I usually keep on my nightstand, but a sharp pain makes me groan.

There's a needle in the crook of my arm. An IV drip.

My dad sits up in a chair next to my bed, rubbing his eyes like he has just woken up too. As soon as he notices me, he scrambles out of his seat. "Jo! I ought to tell the nurses—"

I grab his hand to stop him. "What happened?"

"You collapsed and—" His features darken. "You don't remember the match?"

Of course I remember that part. But not what came after. "Did I win?"

Dad sighs through his nose. He isn't looking at me anymore.

I lurch up. "I lost?"

"Why don't you—"

"Tell me." I try to swing my legs over the side of the bed, but he takes me by the shoulders.

"I'm sorry," he says softly.

His words slam into my chest, knocking the breath right out of me. "I lost?" I choke out.

He doesn't need to answer. I see it on his face.

I lost the title.

"Oh, Joey."

I shrink away from him, pulling my knees against my chest and dropping my head down as the tears come. Dad presses his hand on my back, but his attempt at comforting me only makes me cry harder.

"Lie back, all right? You've got to take it easy. You've been unconscious for eighteen hours, and the docs are concerned you could have another seizure."

My gaze jerks up. "What do you mean *another seizure*?"

"You had one on the way to the hospital last night." His voice goes shaky. "Scared me half to death."

If I had a seizure that could mean . . . "Was I poisoned?"

"Just like the others," he says grimly.

"It was Lidiya, wasn't it?" I say, the accusation flying out from my lips. "She has had it out for me as soon as I got to Washington, and you know that she plays dirty. I have to talk to the police."

"No need because they already believe you. After you were taken to the hospital, the IC's security team searched through the stadium, and they found a glass tube in Lidiya's gym bag. They tested it and guess what? They found trace amounts of a poison in it, the same one that they found in your blood."

My head sinks against the pillows. They'd found a glass vial, like the one Malcolm discovered in my room, I bet.

"I knew it," I whisper.

"The doctors told me what the poison is called. Tetra or tetranort something. It comes from the berries of a white cedar tree," Dad explains. "They said that it isn't a toxin that their tests usually cover, which is why it didn't show up in the other fighters."

I take this all in. "How did Lidiya get that tetra stuff into me? Did she inject it?"

"That we don't know. Maybe she put it in your food."

I rack my mind for what I ate the day before, but my memory feels fuzzy like my head.

"What happens next? Will Lidiya go to jail? Will they strip her of the title?" I'm sure my blood pressure is rising and the docs won't like that, but I had the championship match stolen from under me. "I could've taken her out. I was *this* close."

"I know, Jo, I know."

"What's the IC going to do about it then?" I ask, but my question gets swallowed up by sirens. I figure they must belong to an ambulance on its way to the emergency room, but the alarms veer off somewhere else in the city.

"We'll see. They're working with the FBI on next steps," Dad says vaguely.

"'Next steps'? How about they arrest Lidiya and nix her win? They found the evidence in her bag!"

Dad rubs his temples. "It's complicated. The FBI is trying to connect her to the other poisonings, but they need proof. The Soviets are also refusing to turn Lidiya over to the authorities, even for questioning. They say that she has been framed and want to fly her back to Moscow, but her passport has been confiscated."

"They ought to do a lot more than take away a few pieces of paper." I've got some suggestions in mind. Here I am in the hospital after what she has done to me while she hasn't even got a slap on the wrist. *And* she has that trophy. "They need to break into wherever she's hiding and handcuff her."

"Let's wait and see. President Kennedy is supposed to meet with Khrushchev tonight to talk this through."

A chill snakes down my spine, and I don't think it's from the IV. I can't see Khrushchev abandoning Lidiya in the States, but neither can I see Kennedy letting her leave American soil. It's going to be a real showdown, and all that hangs in the balance is the fate of the world.

Outside, the sirens are blaring again, jumbling my concentration. "What's going on out there?" I ask, irritated. "Did the Soviets invade?"

Dad doesn't answer. He focuses instead on the cafeteria menu lying on the side table. "You hungry?"

There's something in his tone that makes me swallow. It's the same one he uses whenever he's trying to cover up the fact that our electric bill is in default again.

"Dad. What is it?"

"They've got tapioca pudding. You used to love that," he says, sounding nothing like himself.

I snatch the menu from him. "What's going on?"

"Can't you listen to me and rest for once?" he says, tossing up his hands.

"If you don't tell me what's happening out there, then I'm going to climb out of this bed and start looking for someone who will. In a hospital gown."

"You can be an awful pain sometimes, you know that?" He grips the armrests defeated. "Fine, fine. When the FBI tried to take Lidiya into custody and the Soviets refused, they hid her away in the Manger Hay-Adams and posted their Vostoks outside the hotel entrance."

"You mean the sports-grade Vostoks that the Federovas fought in?" I ask, trying to picture that in my head. Those models would be almost useless against a militarized mecha.

"No, it turns out the Soviet delegation brought a few weaponized ones over from Moscow. They were real clever about it too and kept them packed away in their plane and didn't declare them at customs. There are six of them, and they're standing guard at the hotel in case anyone tries to arrest Lidiya."

I swear loudly, and Dad lets it slide, which tells me that this situation really must be bad.

Before I can ask anything else, we hear shouts coming from down the hallway, followed by rapid footfalls.

"Young man!" a nurse yells. "Young man, visiting hours won't start for another hour!"

Dad rises to check out the ruckus just as a shadow appears in the doorway.

I jolt up. "Sam?" His hair is tousled, and his dress shirt is wrinkled, looking like it has been slept in. He has his backpack over one shoulder too.

Sam stares at me, confused, before saying to my dad, "She's awake?"

"Awake and alert," Dad says, motioning at me. "I just broke the news."

There's a familiarity between them that I hadn't expected. I didn't get a chance to introduce them back at the stadium, but apparently they handled things on their own while I was unconscious.

Dad turns to me. "Sam has been good enough to spend time with Peter whenever I've had to talk to the doctors, but he had to run a couple errands and get changed."

"I ended up skipping that last part. I got a little sidetracked," Sam says, which explains the crumpled button-down shirt and slacks. He unzips his backpack to reveal the camera bot he loaned me a couple days ago. "I stopped by your room first to grab this."

"How did you get inside?" I ask.

"I sweet-talked the dorm matron into letting me up," Sam says with a sheepish shrug. Of course he did. "I knew it was a long shot, but I wondered if we had caught anything on tape."

"Did you find anything?" I'd forgotten all about Sam's camera until now, but the look on his face tells me that we need to see this footage.

"Can't this wait?" Dad interjects. "Jo hasn't had time to get checked over by the doctors yet."

"No, I don't think this can wait, Dad." I'm ready to wrestle that camera out of Sam's hands. "What's on that tape? Lidiya?"

"It's probably better if you saw it for yourselves," Sam says, getting to work. He flips on the bot and makes a few adjustments to switch it into projection mode. Propping it up on the foot of my bed, he points the lens against a blank wall and gets the tape queued up.

"Hold on a minute. Care to fill me in on what's going on?" says Dad.

Sam gives him a swift rundown about his camera bot and how I had set it up in my room in case someone tried to sneak in ahead of the final match. "Most of the video is pretty boring until I got to this part."

The three of us turn our attention to the footage. The film shows a shot of my dorm room, with the lens pointed at my door and with a set of drawers next to it. Soon, my past self appears in the frame to let Rushi inside. The two of us talk before she starts to make the tea, placing the mugs on the dresser along with the steaming kettle. While she puts the ingredients together, I step out to grab the sugar from the commons area.

"This is it," Sam says urgently. "Watch her hands."

There on the screen, I watch Rushi digging her fingers into her skirt pocket where she takes out a clear tube that's small enough to fit snugly in her palm. She unscrews it and tips the powdery contents into one of the mugs, giving it a rapid stir with a spoon. The whole time she keeps glancing over her shoulder, her eyes nervous like a rabbit's.

My stomach feels queasy when I see my prior self come back into the frame and take the cup—the cup with the mysterious powder in it.

"You caught that, right?" Sam says, pausing the film.

I stare at the wall until it really sinks in.

Rushi was the one who poisoned me.

23

I feel punched in the stomach all over again.

"You're pale as a sheet," Dad says, urging me to take a drink of water, but I push his hand away.

"Why would Rushi do that?" I ask, my throat tight.

None of this makes sense. A minute ago, I would've sworn that Lidiya was to blame for everything, but I can't deny the proof in front of me. But . . . *why*? Rushi wasn't even in the competition anymore, so what did she have to gain? It wasn't like she and Lidiya were allies either.

My confusion mixes with a throbbing ache, right in the center of my chest. Weren't Rushi and I friends? Maybe that's too strong a word to describe the two of us—we didn't have the time to build that sort of connection—but I thought we were on the path to something like that.

She made me trust her.

She drew me in.

And she could've killed me.

"Who knows why she did it, but this means that Lidiya is innocent," Sam points out.

"What about the tube that the IC found in her gym bag though? At the stadium?" I ask.

"Rushi must've planted it to frame Lidiya. Or someone else on the Chinese team," Sam replies.

Like someone did to me with the vial that Malcolm found in my dorm. Could it have been Rushi too?

My dad walks over to the wall and gets a closer look at the footage that's still paused. He points at my mug. "Good thing you didn't drink all that tea she poured for you."

I hadn't thought of that, but he has a point. I'd only gotten about halfway through my cup before I got interrupted by my dad's and brother's visit. I shudder, thinking what might've happened if I had finished the entire thing.

"Could the Chinese have poisoned the other fighters too?" Dad says, hands on hips.

My head hurts to consider that. It sounds absolutely nuts—shy little Rushi poisoning Lukas and Zoya? But as I sort through my memories, I see snippets of possible evidence. Before Purgatory, I was standing right there when Rushi handed Lukas his water bottle—could she have slipped the poison into it before that? And during the dinner at the White House, I remember seeing Rushi and Zoya standing beside a service bot that was offering drinks. What if Rushi had added a little something to Zoya's champagne then?

Yet there's one thing I can't wrap my head around.

"Why would she drink her own poison?" I ask. More questions crowd my mind, one after the other, but no answers come.

Sam suddenly starts moving toward the TV. "Are you two seeing this?" He hustles over to the Philco black-and-white that occupies one corner of the room, working the knob to turn up the volume. The channel has switched from a game show to a live news broadcast.

"That's the Manger Hay-Adams!" I exclaim. There on the screen, I see the hotel Sam and I had visited only a week ago during the Games' welcome luncheon. Now it looks like something out of a Hollywood movie. A half dozen Vostoks block the entrance, standing tall and glinting in the hot sun.

It looks like a real nail-biter. The nearby streets have been barricaded by the National Guard, which has sent in at least twenty Goliaths by the looks of it. At least no fighting has broken out yet. Both the American and the Soviet mechas are merely standing there for now, awaiting orders, but I can't look away. One false move and this could mean war.

"Wait, who's that?" I ask, pointing at the corner of the screen.

A slim figure has sprinted out of the hotel's side entrance. I can't see their face in detail, but judging by their height and build, I have a good hunch who it might be.

"Lidiya," I whisper.

She's running up to the nearest Vostok, just as her KGB-looking bodyguards barrel out of the hotel to find her. They're already too late. Lidiya's muscling her way up to the cockpit, shouting something at the soldier inside, and before I can take another breath, she has somehow pulled him out and slotted herself into the thing.

"She's making a break for it!" Sam exclaims.

Leaping over a row of hedges, Lidiya catapults herself onto the street and away from the American forces. The broadcast starts to shake as the cameramen give chase, struggling to keep up with the action. The Goliaths have already sprinted after Lidiya, but the Vostoks move to block them even though they're heavily outnumbered. The two sides clash on-screen, metal smacking metal, but three Goliaths manage to break free from the tangle. Moving fast, they catch up to Lidiya, and one of them grabs her by the ankle, but she has dealt with moves like this her whole career. She kicks out with her free leg before pushing one of the Goliaths into the others, sending them toppling over like dominos. With a great big leap, she soars so high that even the cameras struggle to follow her, but more Goliaths bolt after her.

"We have to call down those troops!" I say, gesturing at the TV as if that'll do anything. "They're chasing after the wrong suspect!"

Dad and Sam are still staring at the television until I step in between them.

"Did you hear what I said?" I say, waving a hand in their faces. "We have to tell Kennedy to stop those Goliaths before they hurt Lidiya." Or worse, kill her. Khrushchev will have no choice then but to retaliate. "Because we'll have a real fight on our hands if they do."

My father finally snaps out of his daze. "There's a phone at the nurses' desk. I can use that." He looks at Sam and says, "Do me a favor and check on Peter, will you? He's napping next door."

"Right-o, Mr. Linden," Sam replies.

"Did I become invisible or something?" I call after them, but they're already in motion

"You stay where you are," Dad cautions as he and Sam disappear out of sight.

The door has barely swung back shut before I start moving. Who knows how long it'll take for my dad to get through to the White House? Probably too long.

We need an in-person confrontation.

I stare at the IV in my arm and grit my teeth. Well, here goes nothing. I peel up the bandage and remove the needle, fighting back nausea because I've never done this before and because it's disgusting. Once that's over with and the dizzy spell passes, I search for my clothes, which I find balled up in a bag in the closet. It's the same uniform I was wearing during the final match—was it really only yesterday?—but I put it back on because it sure beats my hospital gown that gapes open in the back.

I stuff Sam's camera into his bag and sling it over my shoulder since I'll need the proof to back up my allegations. Peeking out the door, I make sure that Dad and Sam are out of eyeshot before I slip into the hallway and locate the stairwell. Down I go, one floor, then two. I grab on to hold the railing because my legs are a little wobbly and the last thing I need is to take a tumble down these steps.

"Jo!"

I lurch to a stop and look up to see Peter standing there, his hair messy from sleep. "What're you doing out of bed? You should be resting!" he says as soon as he reaches me. "Sam and I have been looking for you. The nurses too."

"I need to stop the Goliaths."

Peter looks at me funny. "What Goliaths?"

"They're— Oh, never mind. All you need to know is that Khrushchev and Kennedy are about to duke it out, and we have to stop it!"

He gapes at me like I might need to go to the psych ward, but I don't have a minute to spare to explain what has happened. "Let me go, Peter," I say again.

"The doctors said—"

"I'm feeling fine, see? Besides, it won't matter what I feel like if an international crisis breaks out in an hour." I have to show the White House that Rushi was behind all of this, not Lidiya. "But I can stop it."

I try to move down a step, but my little brother is tall enough and strong enough to block me now. "Peter—"

"I'm coming with you," he says.

"What? No, you can't."

But he holds firm. "What if you collapse on the road, huh? Come on, you can explain what's happening on the way there. Where are we headed?"

I can't seem to make my mouth work. Where has this side of my brother come from?

"Aren't we supposed to be in a hurry?" he prods.

I realize I better get a move on, and we descend the rest of the way together. At the bottom of the staircase, there's a door that leads into the street, and I turn around in a slow circle as soon as we step outside to get my bearings.

We're in luck. A few blocks ahead, I spot the Smithsonian Castle, and beyond that, I glimpse the green strip of lawn of the National Mall. We're not far from the White House.

"So what exactly is the plan?" Peter asks as we start walking.

"We have to tell the president to draw down the National Guard before they kill Lidiya. She's innocent."

"Wait, she *poisoned* you, remember?"

"No, she was framed by Rushi. I got it all on videotape too." I pat the backpack. "We have to show the evidence to Kennedy or whoever else will listen."

Peter looks at me like I'm speaking Russian. "Why would Rushi poison you?"

"Your guess is as good as mine. Right now though, we've got a huge fish to fry."

I try to pick up the pace, but my body protests. I might not have drunk the full dose of Rushi's poison, but my legs feel like I'm dragging around tree trunks. Or maybe they feel wooden because I've been laid up in the hospital for almost a whole day. Either way, I have to push forward. That is, until I hear footsteps. I barely have time to glance over my shoulder before Sam catches up to us.

"You haven't even been discharged!" Sam shouts at me before he points at Peter. "And you! How'd she rope you into this?"

"Hey, leave him out of it!" I say. I try to sidestep him, but Sam is a wall of muscle.

"And where are you going with my backpack?"

"The White House!" I say, frustrated. And I probably would be there by now if these boys didn't keep interrupting me. "Look, I'm not going to twiddle my thumbs in the hospital when I could be doing something to stop an international war."

Sam's mouth tightens. He blinks at me, then at Peter. "Your sister's bent, you know that?"

Peter coughs out a laugh.

Meanwhile, I plant a hand on my hip. "Are you going to help us or not, Sam? Someone has to show Kennedy this video."

Sam pauses a little too long for my liking but finally replies with "I guess so, although you're going to give your dad a heart attack."

"We can ask for forgiveness later. We have to hurry."

Washington might not be a large city, but in this humidity and heat, every step feels like walking through soup. But we make decent time since most of the tourists have cleared out. They're probably racing to the airport to escape Washington after they learned about the showdown at the Manger Hay-Adams. We're halfway across the Mall now, and I'm trying to think about how I will convince the White House guards to let me in, when we hear a loud commotion behind us.

"What in the—" Sam says.

The three of us freeze as we watch Lidiya bolting down 14th Street, veering straight toward us until she makes a sharp right that leads to the Washington Monument. A group of Goliaths come sprinting after her in hot pursuit. They're using their built-in megaphones to shout at her to stop, and one of them fires off a few rounds into the sky, probably to scare her, and then one of his friends joins in.

Except he shoots directly at Lidiya.

He must be a poor shot because the bullet flies wide, but I could strangle him. If he keeps this up, sooner or later he'll find his target and Lidiya will go down. Wars have started over far less.

"We better get to the White House fast," Peter says, a newfound urgency in his tone.

Those Goliaths are gaining on Lidiya, and I've got a bad feeling that everything will blow up soon because she isn't the type to put up her hands and surrender. I'm about to start sprinting, when something catches my eye on the left—a piece of metal shining in the sunlight.

It's the Goliath exhibit on the National Mall, the same one that I gawked at when I first arrived in Washington. The mechas are all there, including the two that Sam and I posed in front of for the photo shoot.

I change course and head toward the mechas with an idea cooking in my head. "We can catch up to Lidiya if we suit up quick!"

"Hold on, aren't we going to the White House?" Sam says, confused.

"Change of plans!" I reply.

We reach the mecha exhibition and Sam gives me a boost over the fence, but I hit a snag when I try to turn on the Goliaths. I can't access the power switch without punching in the correct passcode.

"Can you please explain what you're planning in that brain of yours?" Sam huffs.

"We have to stop the National Guard ourselves! We don't have time for anything else. Didn't you see those soldiers shooting at Lidiya?" I motion at him to help me. "You used this Goliath before. What's the passcode?"

Sam taps a few sequences of numbers into the pad, but none of them work.

"A little faster, Kealey?" I say to him.

"I did this a week ago! Give me some room. You're practically breathing down my neck," he snips back.

I'm starting to regret this detour of mine until I notice Peter hovering next to me.

"Let me give it a try," my brother says.

He sounds so sure that I move aside and tell Sam to do the same. Peter approaches the Goliath, but he doesn't bother trying out different passcodes. He works to jigger open the control panel.

"Any of you got something sharp I could borrow?" Peter says.

Sam digs through his trousers. "How about a pocketknife?"

"That's perfect." Peter grabs the thing and flips open the blade, using it to pry open the keypad like a clamshell and expose the tangle of wires inside. With nimble fingers, he isolates a yellow wire from the rest and starts sawing away at it with the knife.

Sam observes all of this with a mixture of apprehension and amazement, especially when the control panel gives a happy chirp and its lights flash green, sliding open to reveal the power switch that it had been protecting.

"You're a gem, have I told you that?" I say to Peter before I motion at Sam. "You take this Goliath. Peter and I will work on the other."

While Sam gets suited up, Peter hot-wires the next mecha and I clamber up its frame to get settled into the cockpit. I stow Sam's backpack by my feet and strap myself in before I call out to my brother that he ought to stay put right here and we'll come back for him soon. But Peter is nowhere in sight.

"Peter?" I shout, turning my Goliath in a circle. Where did that kid go?

A third mecha steps in front of me. It's one of the 1959 models that's shorter than my own, but in perfect working order. And right there in the cockpit is Peter.

I have to blink a couple times. "What are you doing in there?"

"Coming with you guys," Peter says. His face has paled a shade. He might've spent hours fixing up my Goliath back home, but I can't remember the last time he actually suited up inside one. He's nervous, I can tell, but there's grit in his eyes too.

But I can't let him do this. "Out of the question."

"Give the kid a chance," Sam says, but I shush him. This is Linden family business.

"You stay here, Peter," I tell my brother.

"I'm coming," he replies, lifting his chin like I do whenever I'm feeling stubborn.

"I said no! Look, it's real swell that you want to help out and all, but you have to let Sam and me handle this, squirt."

Peter's face shifts. The nervousness there a second ago has already faded and replaced with something else. Something steely. "Don't call me squirt."

Then he pulls a real sneaky move on me.

He starts running after Lidiya.

"Peter!" I cry out, but good God, he is fast. I give chase over the soft grass with Sam a step behind me, leaving enormous footprints in our wake. I yell at Peter to stop, but he doesn't even glance back once.

"What's the plan now?" Sam shouts as we sprint side by side.

"Catch up to my brother, what else? And grab Lidiya before those Goliaths accidentally kill her!"

We must be quite the sight—a bunch of mechas running loose on the National Mall. A few bystanders scurry out of our way while others snap photos as we cross through the shadow of the Washington Monument and run parallel to the Reflecting Pool.

"There they are!" I say when I spot the Lincoln Memorial ahead.

Lidiya has taken a stand on the front steps. She's fending off four of the National Guards' Goliaths, taking them all at once. Our forces might have strength in numbers, but she isn't afraid to show them why she's ranked number one in the world.

She grabs one Goliath by the shoulders and tosses him away like she's flicking a housefly. Then she spins around and trips up another before throwing out an elbow to catch a third in the throat.

And that's when the fourth Goliath starts firing live rounds. The rat-tat-tat of bullets pops in my ears, and I'm screaming for Peter to get down. Mecha armor is tough, but it isn't invincible and I'd never forgive myself if he got hurt. We're thirty meters away from the action now and closing in fast, and all I can think about is that I have to reach my brother.

At least no one seems hurt—yet. Lidiya has rammed her fist into the last Goliath, steaming mad that he dared to fire at her. The two of them tousle and start rolling down the white steps of the memorial until Peter jumps into the fray. He manages to pull the Goliath away from Lidiya, right as Sam and I arrive, but by then she's already on the run.

Three of the downed National Guard Goliaths pop up to chase her again, but Sam grapples with two of them while Peter takes on the other. The fourth soldier is writhing on the ground and out of commission by the looks of it.

"Go, go! Peter and I will hold these guys off," Sam tells me, and that's all I need to take off running.

I follow Lidiya around the Lincoln Memorial and toward the Arlington Bridge, which spans the Potomac River and leads into Virginia. Traffic slams to a stop when people see us coming, forcing me to weave through their Pontiacs and Cadillacs. Between my weakened state and Lidiya's head start, I begin to doubt that I'm ever going to catch up, but I hit a lucky break when she trips while jumping over a Ford F100 truck and takes a tumble onto the road.

"Stop!" I yell at her.

In reply, she fires a round behind her, putting her newfound arsenal to use. The bullet flies wide because she has awful aim, but a piping-hot streak of anger sears through me. Why am I helping her again? I have to remind myself that I'm trying to avoid another war.

Although that doesn't mean I can't rough her up in the process.

Lidiya is starting to tire out after her marathon sprint across the city, and I use her exhaustion to my advantage by grabbing on to her left foot. She goes belly first onto the bridge and skids into a blue Buick Electra, crumpling the front bumper.

As soon as she's down, I hurl myself on top of her like we're back in the pit. She tries to twist free, but I headbutt to daze her. Then I do it again for kicks. But Lidiya doesn't give in. No way. I have to stop her from escaping once and for all, but there's no cage to box her inside and there's no ref counting down the time and calling the match.

But this time I'm going to win.

Lidiya manages to get to her feet, but she'll have to take me with her because I've wrapped my arms around her neck. Both of us are panting and sluggish, but I guess we're going to make this a bareknuckle brawl until the very end.

With a snarl, Lidiya bucks me off and swings around to clip me in the chin, but I absorb the blow and send a yoko geri—a side kick—into her hip. When she stumbles over, I employ a shoulder throw to hurl her onto the road, and I go in for the kill. I flip her mecha over so that I can access her power supply. Her Vostok's battery sits nestled between the shoulder blades, and I yank hard at its base until it tears away from the main frame.

The Vostok powers down immediately, its limbs falling slack like a puppet without a master. Lidiya yells at me in Russian, but there's nothing she can do because she's lying on the cockpit door. I've trapped her.

"You're welcome," I say in between breaths. "I just saved your pitiful life."

Lidiya spits at me in reply, and well, let's say that she should be grateful that she's stuck in that cockpit instead of standing in front of me because I could launch her into the sky with a one-way ticket to the clouds.

I straighten to the full stature of my mecha and notice a fleet of police cars and militarized Goliaths arriving at the mouth of the bridge. I put my hands up so they won't shoot me, and I wait for them to approach. As soon as they do, the words come out of me in a rush.

"I'm Jo Linden, and I need to speak with President Kennedy right away," I say, breathing heavily. "Lidiya Federova didn't poison me, but I know who did."

24

It takes a lot of back and forth with the National Guard before they take my request seriously. First, they try to take Sam, Peter, and me into custody for stealing federal property and attacking their sol diers. Then they consider dropping me off at the hospital because I was never formally discharged and they don't want to risk me falling into another coma while in their custody. Finally, after a lot of convincing, they let me place a single call, and I decide to ring up the one person who actually has some clout in this arena.

Senator June Appleby.

I dial for the operator to patch me through to the senator's office, using the special extension she gave me back at the repair shop the night this first started. The receptionist pauses when I give her my name, but after she has recovered somewhat, I get a direct line to the senator. I proceed to spill everything to her—about Lidiya's innocence, about Sam's video camera to prove it, about why we had to stop the attack before Lidiya got hurt or worse.

Within twenty minutes, Appleby sends a car to pick us up. We make a quick pit stop at the hospital, where I assure my dad that I'm fine. We drop Peter off while we're there before Sam and I are brought to speak to the senator herself. I figure that we'll head to her office, but the driver must get mixed up on the way over.

"Isn't the Capitol Building in the other direction?" I ask him.

"Just following orders here," he replies.

Sam and I frown at each other as we roll up to the gate that encircles the White House. The last time we were here, the two of us were dressed to the nines for a fancy dinner, but now we're covered in sweat and have a bad case of nerves.

"Maybe Senator Appleby is in a meeting with the president," I think aloud.

"Guess we'll find out," Sam says, drumming his fingers on his knee.

"Let me do the talking in there." I can tell that he's anxious. Heck I am too, but I'm the one who dragged him into this. "I'll explain that this whole thing was my idea."

"Last time I checked, we were both throwing ourselves at the National Guard," he says, his trademark humor nowhere in sight.

We enter through the West Wing, and we're seated in a windowless lobby and told to wait. A beverage bot wheels up to us with a logo of the White House printed on its sides. It offers hot coffee and water from two different taps, along with mugs and glasses stacked on its flat top. I pour myself some water, but I don't take a sip. I just grip the cup in my hands while I stare around the place.

There's a grandfather clock ticking away in the corner, next to a marble bust of FDR sitting atop a pedestal. All the furnishings look like they could belong in a museum, and then there's Sam and me in our dirty clothes.

My pulse is finally starting to slow after the nonstop action of the last couple of hours, but it picks right back up when an older woman in her forties, smartly dressed with a string of pearls around her neck, comes to fetch us.

"Right this way, please. They're ready for you," the president's secretary, Mrs. Lincoln, says.

They?

Sam and I step inside the Cabinet Room, a sun-filled space with butter-yellow curtains and a portrait of James Madison hanging over the fireplace, which seems to watch over the proceedings. A huge oval table takes up most of the room, with twenty leather chairs in its orbit. About half the seats are occupied, and every pair of eyes is trained on Sam and me. The two of us take the open chairs at the end of the table while I glance over our audience. The participants are overwhelmingly male aside from Senator Appleby. She gives me a nod.

Seated across from her, I see two more faces that I recognize—President Kennedy and Vice President Johnson. My back goes straight at the sight of them, and I really wish that I were wearing something more formal than my sweaty uniform. Or had a shower at least.

President Kennedy sits in the middle of the table, directly

opposite from me, with his hands knitted together in front of him. Vice President Johnson is beside him, leaning back in his chair with his cheek cradled in one hand. I get the sense that they've both had a long night and wouldn't mind catching up on sleep.

Senator Appleby makes the introductions, rattling off names and titles that I don't really recognize, but I get the point that everyone here is an adviser to the White House.

"If time allowed, I would've spoken to both of you in private before bringing you in here," Senator Appleby addresses Sam and me directly, "but since you're claiming to have evidence that proves Lidiya Federova's innocence, then we are ready to see it."

"Yes, ma'am." My voice comes out high-pitched, and I have to tell myself to relax. I'm not the one on trial here and yet my fingers tremble while I reach for Sam's backpack and pull out the camera bot. I hand the device to Sam and ask him to get it up and running.

"Right away," Sam whispers before nudging me back. "Looks like they're waiting on you."

I notice the vice president staring at me, which makes me gulp.

"Seems like the two of you caused some ruckus down at the Mall. Care to fill us in on what happened?" Johnson says in his slow Texan drawl.

"Well, sir . . ." I fumble for what to say next. Where do I even start? The National Mall? No, I need to backpedal further than that. "As you all probably know, I got hurt at the final match of the Games and was taken to the hospital, where I've been laid up until a few hours ago. When I woke up, I was told that Lidiya Federova had poisoned me, but the Soviets were refusing to turn her over. Then Sam showed up with proof that Lidiya wasn't the one behind this. She'd been framed." I swallow at the dryness in my throat, but I barrel onward. "By Zhu Rushi of Team China."

Murmurs flood the room. Heads snap from me to Kennedy and Johnson, who exchange a few words before the vice president speaks up again.

"That's a big claim to make, Miss Linden," he says, sitting forward now. "What exactly is this proof?"

"I have it right here, sir," Sam chimes in. "We caught the footage all on my video bot. It's my brother's actually." He stumbles over his words for the first time since I've known him, but he definitely has a good excuse. I silently send him encouragement. "I loaned it to Jo because she thought that someone was setting her up for poisoning the Reds. We figured it would be a long shot to capture anything, but—" He gestures at the bot, which he has set on the table and pointed toward the wall. "It worked."

"Now, let's back up a minute here," the vice president says. "Zhu Rushi was also poisoned at a match. So you're implying that she ingested her own toxin?"

"We don't know that, sir. That's something I hope will be investigated further," I say. "But I do know from this video that Rushi *did* slip something into my drink ahead of the final match."

"Where did this happen? At the dining hall?" asks Senator Appleby.

"No, in my dorm room." They're all looking at me again, and I feel myself flush. "Rushi and I were neighbors, and she showed up at my door before the final match. She said that she didn't believe the rumors that I had poisoned her and wanted to wish me good luck. Then she offered me tea."

"And you drank it?" one of the advisers quizzes me.

"I did," I say, fighting to steady my voice. I know how all of it sounds, how naive I must have been, how idiotic I was to even socialize with a Communist. I'm guessing a few of these advisers are silently considering if I'm a Commie myself since they all know that my mom was Chinese.

Senator Appleby looks at Sam. "Is that video ready, young man?"

Sam dims the lights before he switches on the bot's projector setting. The room falls silent as everyone watches the clip play out. There's Rushi preparing the mugs. There I go to fetch the sugar. And there she is pouring the powder into my cup.

The men start pointing and talking to one another fast, and before long, the room swells with their heated voices. Senator Appleby has to stand up to quiet them.

"It's clear from what we've seen that Zhu Rushi poisoned Jo—not Lidiya as we'd suspected," she starts out. "But let's not forget that we discovered a tube in Lidiya's personal affects with trace amounts of the toxin. Could it be possible that the two of them were working together?"

"Or maybe Rushi planted that tube in Lidiya's bag," I offer. Like what she must've done to me with the vial that Malcolm discovered in my drawer. "She's an official fighter of the Games, so her badge gets her special access everywhere—at the Pavilion and in the stadium."

Senator Appleby considers this a moment. "Quite true, but even if Rushi wasn't in cahoots with Lidiya, I'm inclined to believe that she must've been working with someone else. A crime like this requires finesse. For instance, how did she get the poison in the first place? It wasn't something that she could've bought at the corner store. And her age is something to consider as well. She's fourteen years old. Could someone have ordered her to carry out these crimes?"

President Kennedy grasps ahold of this last thought and finally offers a couple of his own. "I think it's safe to say that we must treat the Chinese with caution. They can't be trusted, not even a fourteen-year-old like Rusee."

I flinch and look down at my fingernails, not only because he butchered her name but because of what he said before that. That he can't trust the Chinese. Does that mean that he lumps me in with all the Maoists? I study his profile, wondering what he really thinks about me, but then I look away. Maybe I don't want to know the answer.

Senator Appleby turns to me again. "Jo, you know Rushi better than anyone else here. Could she have had an accomplice? Perhaps her teammate?"

Honestly, I can't remember the name of Rushi's teammate or the last time I even saw him since he got eliminated. But I can certainly think of someone else who might be of interest.

"You should look into a woman named Envoy Yu. She's a member of the Chinese delegation, and she has really stuck to Rushi like glue. She even stayed in the room next to Rushi's at the dormitory."

Senator Appleby jots all this down onto her notepad. "Mr. President, I would recommend that we look into this immediately. We've had four fighters total poisoned at these Games, and we must find out if Team China is behind all of them."

But before Kennedy can reply, the vice president brings up more questions.

"Here's what's bothering me," Johnson says. "Why would this Rushi girl target other Communists? And why in the world would she poison herself?"

That seems to be the question of the day, but once again no one has an answer for it. I only have more questions to toss onto the pile, like why would Rushi try to frame me for poisoning Lukas, Lidiya, and herself—but then blame my own poisoning on Lidiya?

No one seems to know, which makes me want to scream. Aren't these men supposed to be the best and brightest in the country?

"Is this Zhu Rushi stable?" one of the advisers brings up. "*Mentally* stable, I mean. You know how girls her age can get. Unbalanced. Unhinged. Then add in all the Commie propaganda that she has been fed back in China."

The people around him—the *men*—start to nod.

"Rushi wasn't unhinged," I say, the words tumbling out of my mouth because I can't believe that they're agreeing with this idea. They can't put the blame on Rushi's age or that she's a girl or that she's Chinese. That explanation is far too simple and, if I'm being honest, *really* lazy. Most teenage girls don't poison their enemies. The same goes with Chinese people.

Everyone is looking at me again, but Senator Appleby stands up to diffuse the tension.

"Now, gentlemen, I don't think we ought to blame this on a simple case of teenage hormones," she says, for which I'm incredibly grateful. "We all may have done a few things in our youth that we've come to regret, but how many of us were poisoning our peers? Lukas Sauer is dead because of that."

Kennedy and Johnson dip their heads toward each other again, exchanging a back-and-forth, until the president looks up. "Where is Team China now? They haven't left for the airport yet, have they?"

"They were supposed to fly out this evening," Senator Appleby says.

"Bring them back for questioning. Now," the president replies urgently.

More nods go around the room, and a couple of the advisers make a quick exit, most likely to carry out the new orders.

Following that, the vice president gestures at Sam and me. "That's all we need from you two for now. We'll be in touch if we have any more questions."

Sam releases a sigh now that our interrogation is over, but I'm not done with them yet.

"What's going to happen to Rushi? To Lidiya?" I ask, remaining seated.

"That'll get ironed out in due time," says the vice president, which doesn't answer my question at all.

"What about the Games' title? Shouldn't the results be nullified?" I press. I know this is likely a long shot considering the IC didn't toss out the other matches, but I have to ask it.

Sam clears his throat awkwardly while Senator Appleby pipes up again. "I'll be speaking to the IC about that. Now, thank you again for your time, Jo. I'm sure you want to rest after everything you've been through."

I hear the dismissal in her tone and not long after that Mrs. Lincoln returns to lead us outside, where a military truck will drive us to the hospital. Sam and I climb into the back, and the vehicle rumbles through the gate to exit onto the public street. Only then do I think over everything that has happened today, from waking up in the hospital to stealing a Goliath to fighting Lidiya Federova and then to meeting with the most powerful people in the country at the White House of all places.

And I haven't even had dinner yet.

"At least that's over with," Sam says. He slouches in his seat, looking exhausted, but his mouth twitches up as he spots the Capitol in the distance. "And we stopped World War III from kicking off today."

I trail a finger against the window glass, staring out at the government buildings that we pass but not really seeing them. My mind is elsewhere. "What do you think will happen next?"

"My best guess? They're going to throw the book at Rushi. Conspiracy. Espionage. Attempted murder. Anything else you want to add?"

I think about that question the rest of the way to the hospital.

Anything else you want to add?

The thought comes faster than a heartbeat.

I want answers.

25

When we get back to the hospital this time, I'm taken up to my room in a wheelchair even though I'm feeling fine enough to walk. The doctors scold me for overexerting myself and putting my body under so much strain, which means that they'll have to keep me longer for further observation.

"You're welcome by the way," I mutter after the docs depart my room. If I hadn't "overexerted" myself today, we might be heading for underground bunkers right about now because Washington would've turned into a hot zone.

As soon as everyone has cleared out, my dad starts pushing his armchair across the floor and toward the door, leaving Peter and me to stare at him.

"What're you doing?" I ask. "Trying to steal the furniture?"

"I'm blocking the way so that the two of you will have to stay put. No more of that sneaking out and causing a commotion all over the city," Dad says dryly before he plunks himself into the chair, arms crossed.

I hold my breath and wait for his lecture to come. He has never been much of a shouter, but he can sure lay it on thick when he thinks I've botched something up big-time. But to my surprise, Dad doesn't say much of anything. His eyes skip right over Peter and me, and they zero in on the television set behind us. It's still playing the news, and it just so happens that Sam, Peter, and I are the stars of it.

"Look at that!" Peter gasps. The TV channel has somehow gotten footage of the three of us bolting down the National Mall in our stolen Goliaths and chasing after Lidiya. I guess the whole country now knows what we were up to.

"So which one of you bozos took down the Federova girl?" Dad asks.

"That was Jo," Peter says, pointing at me.

I bite the inside of my cheek because this time I'm sure that the lecture will come. Dad is going to tell me how irresponsible I've been and how I put Peter's life in danger on top of everything else, but strangely enough he looks pensive, which isn't a word I'd ever use to describe him.

Dad chuckles out of the blue. "You really got Lidiya in the end, didn't you?"

"Maybe," I say, trying to smile, but my mouth doesn't quite cooperate. "Although what I really want is that championship trophy."

"The IC better reschedule the match. You would've won it," Peter says, frustrated.

"Guess we'll see—" I'm about to add *squirt*, but I stop myself because I remember how he feels about it. This is going to take some time to get used to. "But they haven't disqualified the results yet so who knows what they're thinking?"

"Turn up the volume. I want to hear this," Dad says suddenly.

I look at the screen again to see a live shot of National Airport, a few miles down the road from here. The camera zooms in on Rushi. She's stepping out of an airplane, followed by a small troop of FBI agents. Envoy Yu pops up behind them, flanked by her own set of agents, and she won't stop talking. I can't hear a thing of what she's saying, but I can only imagine that she's pleading to make a phone call to her beloved Chairman. Rushi, however, stays quiet. She keeps her head down, but she can't hide how pale her face has gotten. It's easy to see that she's scared.

Well, good.

She *should* be scared after what she has done. Lukas is dead because of her actions. Like Sam mentioned before, I hope the IC throws the book at her.

But the question nags at me.

Why did she do it?

"You're talking to yourself," Peter tells me with a nudge.

"Was I?"

"Everything okay? Should we get the nurse?"

"Nope, I'm fine," I say, but that isn't totally true.

I tell myself that I shouldn't care about what happens to Rushi. What matters is that she got caught and now she'll have to pay for it, but there's a stubborn part of me that wants to know why she'd go to the trouble to set me up and then poison me. She cost me the title and I want an explanation, and I'm not settling for the excuse that teenage-girls-can-be-unhinged nonsense.

We watch the rest of the broadcast in silence. Kennedy has called off the National Guard, and Khrushchev has done the same with his Vostoks. Lidiya is released from the hospital after a thorough examination. A crew of reporters swarm around her as soon as she steps out of the front entrance, but she replies with nothing but a glare. Figures. Some things will never change.

I spend a restless night on my stiff hospital bed, but the silver lining is that I get discharged the following morning—and just in time because I barely have a chance to grab a shower and change into fresh clothes before Dad, Peter, and I are whisked off to the Capitol Building. Senator Appleby has decided to host a special brunch to honor Sam and me. Truth be told, the last thing I want to do is squeeze myself into another dress and heels again, but I'm not really given a choice.

We arrive at the Senate Dining Room to find the entire place packed. I'd assumed that the brunch would be a small gathering, maybe a table for the senator and my family—a consolation meal since I got second place instead of first—but the room is stuffed full with important-looking folks. There are senators and congressmen along with Association members and a few fighters who haven't headed home yet, like Albie and Fitzy. It seems like a farewell send-off to Team USA.

"There's the young lady I've been looking for," Senator Appleby says by way of greeting me and shaking my hand. "I'm glad you could make it. After everything you have been through, I wanted to wrap up your stay in Washington with a celebration of what you and Sam achieved. That deserves a toast and much more."

I'm touched by her thoughtfulness. "Is Sam here yet?"

"I'm afraid he said he'd be running late. He had a family commitment to attend to first. Malcolm is also finishing up some business," she says before she gets distracted by the newest guest who has stepped into the dining room.

"There's Minister Tran," she says, with a broad smile spreading over her face. "We'll have to say hello to him and thank him."

"Thank him?" I ask curiously.

Her smile brightens. "For lowering the cost of esterium batteries here in the US. The news won't be public for a few days, but our governments have agreed upon an exclusive trade deal to access their mines. It'll be the very first of its kind for South Vietnam."

"Congratulations," I tell her. This is huge indeed, not only for the South Vietnamese but for Americans too. Cheaper esterium means cheaper bots and that could open up a new slice of business at the shop. All that time the senator spent wining and dining the minister has paid off. "I bet Minister Tran is excited too."

"I do believe so, although I hope he won't be too sore that he'll no longer be the center of attention. West Germany and China were both trying to buy up that esterium. The Soviets too. Khrushchev isn't making out too poorly though since he's signing a deal with the North Vietnamese. They have several gold mines that he has been eyeing as well as a couple of uranium veins."

I can see the appeal of gold but not the other stuff. "What's uranium good for?"

"Artillery, I believe. We'll have to keep a close eye on our Soviet friends to see what they'll be cooking up, but enough of this trade talk." She takes two flutes of champagne from a nearby service bot and hands one to me before tapping her glass against mine. "I have some good news," she says although she doesn't sound very joyful about it. "As you may have heard, Zhu Rushi is being held in the city jail for now. Envoy Yu as well."

I draw in a breath. "She was arrested too?"

"The FBI discovered a small jar of the toxin in her personal effects. It appears that she and Rushi were working together."

I'm not shocked, really, but it does take a couple seconds for this to sink in. "Did they say why?"

"They aren't saying much, but you can rest assured that they won't lay a finger on you ever again."

That's a relief, but my fingers tighten around the stem of the glass. "What will happen to them?"

"There'll be a hearing first, followed by a trial. There's a strong possibility that they'll spend time in prison for their crimes. For the most part, the Chinese government has been cooperative. They've denounced Rushi and Envoy Yu, but they've also requested that the two of them are extradited to Beijing to serve their sentences. We've turned down that request, of course."

Her eyes search over mine. "I imagine this is welcome news."

It *is* good news that both of them will be punished. "When and where will that hearing take place?"

"I'd have to ask my staff about that," she says distractedly. A waiter arrives to tell us that the food is ready, but I can't let her go yet.

"Has there been any news from the IC about the Games? Will the final result stand?" I ask.

She heaves a sigh. "The Association has filed numerous complaints, but the IC is a bureaucratic behemoth. If they decide to reschedule your match against Lidiya, then they'll have to reschedule all the games since Rushi and Envoy Yu affected the outcomes from the start of Round One. That would be a logistical nightmare for them, not to mention humiliating. So my guess is that the IC will stand with Lidiya as the victor."

"There's solid proof that the Games were rigged and they still won't do a thing about it?" I say a little too loudly.

"I'll keep doing whatever I can," she says, sounding sincere. "At the very least, I want them to nullify the results."

That's only a start though. Let's say they strip Lidiya of the title, but where does that leave the rest of us fighters? Many of us will be too old to qualify for the '67 Games.

We're called to be seated a minute later, and everyone at my table gets ready to gorge themselves on slices of cheese quiche, fruit salad, and crispy strips of bacon that we pick up with tongs from the service bots wheeling around the tables. Despite the delicious-looking spread, I've got no appetite. My conversation with Senator Appleby has completely stamped it out. I'm tempted to make an early exit because I'm in no mood to celebrate, but Dad and Peter are having such a grand time that I tell myself to clench my jaw through this. Dad proceeds to eat so many sausage links that he might have to loosen his belt. While he waits for the food to settle, Peter drags me toward the bartender bot set up in one corner of the room. The bot itself is an enormous metal box with a drink dispenser at its center. You have to press a button to order what you want, which is a little disappointing because it only has four selections. I tell Peter to get the Shirley Temple since it's the only nonalcoholic choice.

Peter watches curiously as the bot fixes his drink, and I feel a tap on my shoulder. I turn around to find Minister Tran standing there, wearing a black suit and a polite smile.

"May I have an autograph?" he asks, holding out a ballpoint pen and a program from the opening match. I see that he has already collected signatures from over a dozen fighters already. "It's for my granddaughter."

"Oh, that's right. She's the mecha fighter." I start searching through the program for my photo to sign when I reach Team China's. It looks like Rushi has already autographed her name under her own picture, writing it out in three neat Chinese characters.

Minister Tran, who usually seems so mild-mannered, looks a bit flustered. "My apologies. Zhu Rushi signed this a week ago. I didn't know—"

"You had no idea. None of us did," I say.

He nods, relieved. "I was very surprised at the news. I never thought she was capable of such a thing."

There's something in his tone that makes me pause. "Did you know her?"

"Before my current assignment, I was a diplomat in China," he admits. "Our countries have had a long history as neighbors, especially in trade—their coal and iron for our oil. A couple years ago the Chinese wished to strengthen our ties, so they invited some South Vietnamese fighters to Beijing to train with their national team. Rushi gave my granddaughter a few lessons."

It's easy to put two and two together from there. "That's how you met her."

"And her younger sister. They were both very talented—and very sweet girls. That's why when I learned about what she had done . . ." He shakes his head slowly. "I was shocked."

"Do you have any idea why she did it?" I ask, leaning forward.

But he looks as perplexed as I do. "I wish I had an answer. It's all very sad, and I can only hope her sister can remain at her training school. She's a promising young fighter."

I frown. "Why wouldn't she stay at her school?"

"The government in China—" He chooses his words with care. "It's very different from what you have here in America. Oftentimes, even if only one member of a family commits a crime, everyone else faces the same punishment as well."

I shouldn't be surprised by this given what I've heard about the Reds, but it's still unsettling how they keep their people in line.

And yet, this only confuses me more when it comes to Rushi. She must've known that her sister would face blowback at home if she even looked at someone the wrong way, and yet she still poisoned the fighters.

Only someone incredibly cruel and calloused would've done that.

Or someone very desperate.

A voice comes over the loudspeaker to ask us to take our seats because Senator Appleby will soon give her remarks. I realize I haven't signed the minister's program yet, so I give it a quick squiggle of the pen and hand it back to him.

Minister Tran thanks me, but before he heads off, he adds quietly, "Did you know that there'll be a hearing tomorrow for Rushi and Envoy Yu?"

"Tomorrow? That soon?" I'd figured it would be weeks away.

"The IC decided on the schedule. If you want to attend—"

"I'll be there." The words zip out of my mouth before I've had a chance to think it over, but I don't need to give it a second thought. If I want some answers, this will be the best shot I'll probably get.

I look the minister in the eye and say, "Where do I need to go?"

26

Bright and early the following day, I arrive at the International Tribunal Building on K Street and get whisked up to the fourth floor for the hearing. I expect to step inside a courtroom, like the ones I've seen on *Perry Mason*, where the judge sits behind the bench in a long black robe. Instead, I'm brought into an office space that resembles a big conference room, with rows of chairs on one side. Most of them have already been claimed by reporters and Association members.

"Jo!" says Minister Tran, who's seated near the front. He motions toward the three chairs beside him, which will perfectly accommodate Dad, Peter, and me.

My brother and father insisted on coming when I told them about this hearing. I wouldn't have minded attending it on my own, but they wouldn't hear of it. I think Peter wanted to tag along to see justice served while Dad simply didn't want me out of his sight again.

I introduce Minister Tran to my family, and he shakes their

hands before turning his attention back to me. "I wasn't sure if you would come."

"I wouldn't miss it," I reply.

Before the hearing starts, I let myself survey the rest of the attendees and realize that I recognize a handful of them. They're fighters. I spot Team France and Great Britain, my pal Giselle among them. There are representatives from Canada, Sweden, Australia, and others as well. A mini United Nations has packed into this one single room, but we're still waiting on our guests of honor.

The judge enters and takes a seat behind a table, followed soon by the bailiff who has two defendants in tow: Envoy Yu and Rushi. They're both wearing matching gray jumpsuits along with their hair tied back, but that's where the similarity ends. Envoy Yu insists on keeping her head up and her eyes defiant while Rushi tucks her chin down and doesn't dare a glance at anybody. She looks so young and terrified that I'd feel sorry for her if I didn't know what she was capable of.

Peter pats my hand, and I realize how tightly I've been gripping the armrest. I give his fingers a squeeze, grateful that he's here.

As the hearing officially begins, I try to keep up with the legal jargon. The prosecutor speaks first, stating the charges that they're leveling against Zhu Rushi and her accomplice Envoy Yu before introducing the physical evidence—namely the video caught on Sam's camera—to persuade the judge that there's enough of a case to proceed to a trial. The whole time a translator quietly translates for Rushi and Envoy Yu, and when the prosecutor is finished, it's time for the defense to poke holes in the case, but, oddly enough, they don't have an attorney on their side.

"We have no need for a lawyer," Envoy Yu explains in English after the judge questions her through the translator about the whereabouts of her representation. "We wish to plead guilty."

Whispers erupt throughout the room. Both the judge and prosecutor look taken back.

"This is a hearing, Envoy Yu, not an arraignment where you may enter your plea," says the judge.

But she barrels on. "Rushi and I confess to poisoning Lukas Sauer, Zoya Federova, and Josephine Linden. We also confess to tampering with the Soviet's float and causing the electrical fire."

My back goes straight at the mention of my name, and I swear the whole room is taking turns staring between Envoy Yu and me. What is her game plan? Why is she so eager to confess to everything?

"This is very unconventional," the judge says, looking a bit flustered and staring at Envoy Yu like she's begging to be hauled off to prison, which she kind of is. "Let me ask you again. Do you want to consult an attorney? You're entitled to representation."

Envoy Yu shakes her head vehemently. "No. I waive my rights."

The judge motions at Rushi. "Are you in agreement?"

I can see a slice of Rushi's face in profile, and it's plain as day that she hesitates as the translator speaks softly to her. But then Envoy Yu gives her a sharp glance, and Rushi looks at the floor again.

"Yes, Your Honor," Rushi says quietly.

The judge seems to go speechless for a few seconds before gathering his wits. "You can repeat your pleas at the arraignment, which we will schedule shortly. Until then, might I remind you one more time that you have the option to speak to a court-appointed lawyer. Our rules here are different than back in China."

Envoy Yu presses her lips together at the slight and hits one right back at him. "We have no desire to work with your capitalist dogs."

Some of the attendees gasp while the reporters scramble to write down their notes, but they better keep up the pace because Envoy Yu isn't finished talking.

"The Pax Games are a sham. They uphold the dominance of countries that only know how to start wars and take resources that were never theirs. This might fill their own stomachs, but the rest of us go hungry. Only the Chairman understands the true path forward. He alone carries the legacy of Lenin," she says, her voice pitching louder. Then she pivots to search through the audience, and her gaze lands on me.

No, wait a second. She's looking at Minister Tran.

"We won't forget those who sided with the imperialist aggressors, who gave in to their own greed," Envoy Yu says before the judge starts banging his gavel and yelling, "Order!"

The bailiff grabs her by the waist to remove her, but she plants her feet into the carpet and motions at Rushi, prompting her to do something. Or say something. I'm not sure what exactly is happening.

Rushi looks shell-shocked, standing there by herself. She hesitates again before she looks up at the judge and says, "Envoy Yu and I acted alone. We take full responsibility for what we did." She utters these two sentences without emotion, like she has been practicing lines for a play.

Soon, the two of them are whisked out of the room. The judge looks relieved and sets a date for the arraignment before dismissing everyone in record time, probably so that he can get a drink for himself. The reporters lurch out of their seats to speak to the prosecutors, who seem both surprised and elated about the turn of events. They've just been handed a win, and all they had to do was sit back and let Envoy Yu dig her own grave.

"This is great news," Peter says, amazed at what has transpired. "Envoy Yu and Rushi will have to go to prison if they confessed, right?"

"I guess so," I say. But after witnessing this debacle, I've got more questions than before.

Dad and Peter are ready to leave, but I tell them to go on ahead of me and I'll catch up in a minute. I turn to Minister Tran, who appears a little shaken, and ask, "Are you all right?"

He gives a little sigh. "I'm afraid Envoy Yu speaks for many Chinese officials who feel betrayed that my country has aligned with yours."

I'm not sure that I understand. "But South Vietnam will be a democracy. It's the North that's communist."

"And they are allied with the Soviets, not with Mao," he points out. He sighs again, longer this time. "The Chinese are leaving empty-handed."

Something clicks in my head.

I should've seen this sooner. It's beginning to all make sense.

"The Chinese wanted to trade for your esterium," I say, more of a statement than a question. Come to think of it, Senator Appleby mentioned this to me yesterday, how China was gunning for a trade deal to get access to South Vietnam's mines. They needed that esterium. And they were desperate enough to work with a democratic country to get it. I saw with my own eyes how Rushi had to pilfer extra batteries at the training center, squirreling them away like she had to save up for the winter.

I'm betting that China had tried to sweet-talk South Vietnam into expanding their current trade agreement to include esterium, but they realized that they had competition for it—the Americans. But the US had its hands full as the Vietnam War simmered to a rolling boil. Kennedy had no time to explore a trade deal when he was busy sending advisers to Hanoi and mapping out a war strategy.

But what if that war came to an abrupt halt? A newly independent South Vietnam would want to ally itself with the most powerful and richest country in the world, and the Chinese could kiss that esterium goodbye.

So China set out to stop the Washington-Moscow Accord.

They had to break up that treaty before it got signed.

As long as the war kept the US and the USSR locked in a

fistfight, the Chinese had a chance at cutting themselves a decent slice of that esterium pie. I remember how Envoy Yu had tried to talk to Minister Tran throughout our time here at the Games—maybe to get him to change his mind?

Minister Tran looks concerned. "Are you unwell? Your face is very pale. Perhaps you should sit and I'll get you some water."

I nod absently as my thoughts spin faster and faster. The Chinese had to stop the Accord, but they had no clout to bring to the table or to even get a seat. So they had to do something underhanded.

Something like poisoning the fighters at the Pax Games.

It's no wonder then why Team China made a sudden return to international competition after decades away from the limelight. As soon as they arrived in Washington, they tried to drive a wedge between the Americans and the Soviets. They targeted their fellow Communist fighters and pinned the crimes on me—the fire on the float, the poisonings ahead of the matches—all with the goal of enraging Khrushchev so much that he'd yank his team out of the Games and perhaps out of the treaty too.

Khrushchev, however, didn't buckle. Not when his own fighter was poisoned. And not when the Chinese poisoned their own in a desperate bid to push the Soviets over the edge. Because how could they ignore the fact that *three* Commie fighters had been targeted? Even if Mao and Khrushchev no longer saw eye to eye, they still had their communism in common.

But the Chinese underestimated how much Khrushchev wanted the Accord signed, so much so that he was willing to overlook

Lukas's death and Zoya's and Rushi's poisonings, all to secure a few gold and uranium mines.

That had left the Chinese with a big problem on their hands. They had to switch tactics. If Khrushchev wouldn't budge, then maybe Kennedy would.

That's why Rushi poisoned me next.

The thing is, the gamble almost worked. If Sam and I hadn't caught Rushi on his camera bot, who knows where we'd be right now? Certainly not here.

I can't forgive or forget what Rushi did to me, but now I have to wonder how much of it was really her idea. Did her own government force her into poisoning me and the others? I can see Envoy Yu carrying out Mao's orders with a salute and no questions asked, but Rushi seems to have a conscience. What was being held over her head to make her follow in lockstep?

Minister Tran returns with a glass of water for me, but I don't take a drink from it. I'm too worked up.

"I don't think Rushi and Envoy Yu were acting on their own. I think they were told to poison the fighters and set fire to the float," I say quickly. As soon as the words fly out of my mouth, I hear how far-fetched they sound, but I can't take them back and I don't really want to. I finally feel like I'm seeing the bigger picture.

Minister Tran eyes me carefully. "Who do you think gave them the orders?"

"Somebody in their government. Most likely someone high up." I know this probably sounds like a conspiracy theory, but Rushi doesn't come across as a criminal mastermind. Neither does Envoy Yu, who seems more naive and brainwashed than ruthless.

To his credit, Minister Tran doesn't start looking for my dad and telling him to take me to the nearest sanatorium. He surprises me instead. "I've suspected the same," he says quietly.

I blink. "You have?"

"I've lived and worked in China. I've seen how the Maoist government runs," he says by way of explanation but doesn't delve into it further, ever the diplomat. "But what proof do we have?"

None whatsoever actually. "Then their whole government should be on trial!"

"I'm afraid that won't happen. Envoy Yu and Rushi have already confessed, and the world is moving on," he says gently before gesturing at the reporters, who are peeling off to write their stories and start on new ones. After tomorrow's headlines are printed and tossed out, Rushi and Envoy Yu will be blips in the history books.

I grind my teeth together. "We could talk to Rushi and Envoy Yu. Get them to confess what really happened."

"And risk hurting their families?" He looks at me sadly. "Rushi wouldn't do that."

Our gazes lock, and I realize that he's talking about Rushi's sister. If Rushi came clean, no doubt the Chinese government would toss her sister in a reeducation camp for a decade or two. Or worse. Minister Tran is right. She'd go to jail before jeopardizing that. She'd give away her fighting career for it too.

But wouldn't I do the same for Peter?

"I will see what I can do. Set up a few meetings," Minister Tran says before clasping his hands together. "I'm headed to the Capitol to see Senator Appleby, but I hope our paths will cross again soon. There's something I'd like to go over with you."

I'm not sure what he means by that, but I don't ask him to elaborate. My head is buzzing with everything we've discussed—about Rushi, about her crimes, about the Games—and I wander out of the room to find Dad and Peter. As soon as he sees my face, Peter asks me what's wrong, but I only tell him that I've got a lot on my mind. Rushi's and Envoy Yu's confession might seem like a victory to most people who attended the hearing, but it doesn't feel like much of a win to me. The two of them are merely the scapegoats for their government, and what do they get for that? Mao is leaving them high and dry. Rushi might have blood on her hands, but whose crime is this really?

It makes me feel sick to my stomach and, even worse, completely helpless.

"Why don't we walk back to the Pavilion? The weather isn't too swampy," Dad offers, and I grunt in agreement because I could use the fresh air.

We exit onto K Street and make our way south, eventually walking through the National Mall and toward the Smithsonian Castle, which is a museum but resembles more of a church. Peter asks if we can go inside because there's an exhibit on the history of worker bots in the nation's capital.

"You go on ahead. How does thirty minutes sound?" Dad says. "Jo and I will wait here in the garden."

I toss Dad a glance, but he tilts his head toward a wooden bench surrounded by butterfly bushes. He waits for me to sit down before he gets down to business.

"Might as well come out with it. Something has been chewing you up since the hearing," he says.

"You could say that again," I mutter. "I don't want to talk about it."

Dad shrugs like he often does. It's his little way of telling me, *Suit yourself,* but soon enough the simmering pot of emotions inside me bubbles over and I tell him everything, starting with how the Chinese desperately need esterium to how they used Rushi to try to secure it. When I'm finished, I feel out of breath. Dad takes a minute to follow my train of thought, but he seems to understand.

"Those Commies are never up to any good huh? Although I can't say that I'm shocked," he says. "What do you want to do about this? How about you talk to Senator Appleby?"

"I don't know what she could do. I swear Envoy Yu would jump into a shark-infested swimming pool if that's what the Chairman wanted, and Rushi—" I swallow a lump in my throat. "She wouldn't risk her family taking the fall."

"It sure sounds like a mess, but you'll figure it out." My father stares off at the Mall's grassy expanse of lawn before letting his eyes roam back over to me. "You always do."

"I don't know about this time." I'm not only talking about Rushi, but everything else—how my life has imploded in the span of two weeks. People worldwide know my name now, but not for the reasons I necessarily wanted. And who knows what we'll be going home to? "Have you talked to the landlady—"

"We've got two extra months to pay up our back rent. I don't think she wants the publicity of evicting America's newest heroine," Dad says wryly.

It takes me a second to realize who he's talking about. "America's heroine? Me?"

"Sure thing. You should've seen some of the headlines when you were in the hospital. People were spitting mad that you were poisoned and on our own turf to boot."

I have to believe that Malcolm worked some publicity magic behind the scenes to get that reaction because a few days earlier those same papers were hinting that I might be a secret Maoist.

"The *Chronicle* even called you San Francisco's hometown sweetheart," Dad adds.

Hmm, maybe I won't swear off that newspaper forever, although that nickname needs work.

Dad chuckles when he sees the look on my face. "You might not be the sweetest, but you sure got a lot of heart. Peter and I couldn't be prouder at how you played the Games." With his voice soft, he adds, "And your mom would be too."

I draw in a sharp breath. He rarely brings her up, but my mother has always lingered between us, and pretending that she isn't there hasn't helped us much. I guess we're both realizing that now.

"I wish you could've known the girl she used to be," Dad says, his voice thick with emotion. "So smart. So stubborn. She was a real force to be reckoned with."

"And then she had me," I say flatly.

Dad is quick to shake his head. "Nah, she adored you. She really did. Maybe you came as a surprise, but once you were here, she toted you everywhere she went."

I try to picture this version of my mother. Doting. Caring. Loving. I never would've thought that possible a month ago, but Dad's account squares with what Old Wen told me too (before he sold me out to the press).

"So what happened? The mom that I remember"—the one who shouted and neglected us—"wasn't like that at all."

Dad rubs his face, looking tired, looking older. "All I know is that something changed after your brother was born." He says this quietly, almost a whisper, even though Peter is in the museum and well out of earshot. "The docs said that she had a nervous condition, but that it would work itself out. After a couple months, she did seem to be getting better."

"But?" Then I answer my own question. "That's when you went to Korea."

Dad looks grim, his mouth tightening at the corners. "Yep."

That's all he says and he doesn't explain further, but judging by the pained look on his face, I start to connect the dots of what happened. After he left, Mom's "nervous condition" must've come back. She stopped getting out of bed. She cried a lot and slept even more. Our little apartment seemed to divide us into halves—her against

Peter and me. I couldn't count on her anymore to feed us or take care of us. To love us.

"After you came home, I heard you and Mom fighting one night," I say slowly, choosing my words with care because I don't want to hurt him but I need to ask. "She said that you broke a promise to her. What did she mean?"

Dad's face screws up tighter. "That was so long ago. Do we really need to bring this up?"

"Please?"

He crosses his arms and starts talking, albeit reluctantly. "Your mom wanted to fly more than anything else. After you were born, she put those plans on hold, but she told me over and over that she wanted to get her pilot's license one day, so I promised that she could after I got back from Korea and we had more savings." He sounds more defeated as he goes on. "But life gets pricey, Joey. We had Peter by then too, so it made more sense to me to put our savings toward buying my own shop." He flinches and won't look at me. "I told your mom that the flying lessons wouldn't be in the cards."

My mouth goes dry as burlap. So *that's* what happened all those years ago. My dad had to support the family and he sacrificed my mother's dreams to do it. She must've been devastated.

But there's a rock in my heart that won't budge.

"She didn't have to leave us," I say fiercely. "She still made that choice in the end."

"That she did," Dad says plainly.

"Then why aren't you mad about it?"

"I'm too tired for that, Jo. And your mom's gone. Nothing will bring her back, and I can't change the choices I made that led to her leaving."

"You were trying to look out for Peter and me."

"Sure, but I wasn't looking out for her. Not at that moment." A long pause stretches between us, and when he speaks again, his voice sounds like gravel. "But she lives on in the two of you. You got your mom's spirit, and Peter got her smarts. She gave you two the best parts of her." Dad sniffs and I wonder if he's crying, but he stands up and turns away from me. Gruffly, he says, "Let's find that brother of yours and get something to eat. I'm half starved."

I get to my feet, with my heart feeling heavier and lighter at the same time. I know now why my mother left us, and while I'll never forgive her for it, maybe I can understand her better too. Maybe I don't have to be so angry anymore.

Maybe I ought to focus on what Mom left me with—Peter and Dad.

My father is already a couple steps ahead of me, but I catch up to him and thread my arm around his like I did when I was little. He startles a bit at the unexpected touch, but he doesn't pull away. In fact, he leans in.

We'll never be the type of family that hugs or cries together or says *I love you* every day, but walking together like this?

It's enough.

27

It's time to book it out of Washington. The Games have ended, and the ink on the Washington-Moscow Accord has officially dried. The Cold War has cooled by a few degrees, and we don't have to worry about a battalion of Vostoks attacking our shores any time soon.

Well, at least until the next crisis hits.

I zip up my bag, shut the door to my room, and head down to the dormitory's lobby to turn in my badge and key. The Pavilion has almost emptied by now, and all that I have to do is catch my flight home. The '63 Pax Games are truly over, and aside from a few new bruises, I'll be leaving empty-handed. No title. No prize money. Not a single endorsement either.

But there's some decent news to come out of this.

The IC has decided to hold a vote as to whether they should nullify the results of the Games or not—not only the championship match between Lidiya and me, but the entire '63 cycle. They're under pressure from the public at large as well as numerous national sporting federations, with Senator Appleby leading that charge. If everything shakes out the way that I'd like, the 1963 Games will be a wash, a dark mark on the record books, but at least it'll be fair. Isn't that what the fighters deserve?

Plus, it'll make Lidiya furious.

Slinging my bag over my shoulder, I make my way across the quad to wait for my ride. The sun beats down on me, and I plop onto a bench where someone has left a copy of the *Washington Post*. My eyes drift over the headlines. The Kennedys and Khrushchevs had a private dinner after the Accord was signed. Esterium from South Vietnam will make its way to the America market in the coming months. And there, toward the bottom of the page, I notice a short article on Rushi. Due to her age, the US has agreed to extradite her to Hong Kong, a city under British rule, not Chinese. She'll serve her sentence there, and I'm glad to hear that. Maybe her sister will be allowed a visit or two since Rushi will be much closer to home.

I set the paper aside because I might have enough time to grab a Coke from the dining hall when I hear someone calling my name.

"Where are your dad and brother?" Malcolm says, walking up to me.

"Peter wanted to visit another museum before we left, so they'll head to the airport straight from there," I explain. "You here to see me off?"

I haven't seen Malcolm much since the final match. He did visit me at the hospital before I got discharged, but he didn't stay long since he had "pressing matters" that required his attention, whatever that had meant. He skipped out on Senator Appleby's brunch too.

"More like see you soon," he says, squinting in the bright sun. "There's the North American Invitational at the end of the summer down in Mexico City that you ought to start training for."

I lift a brow. "You actually want me on the team? Even with my mother's 'background'?"

"You certainly have areas for improvement, but you've made a name for yourself at the Games. In any case, the cat is already out of the bag when it comes to your mother and it hasn't made much of a difference with the general public. Most of them are still riled up that you were poisoned on American soil. So the fighting slot is yours if you want it."

I give myself a minute to think this over, but the decision is an easy one. Another go-around on Team USA? In Mexico City? I'm ready to sign up now, but I decide to play my cards a little closer to the chest.

"What I really want is a rematch against Lidiya at the World Championships next summer," I say. If I can't have the Games, then I want the next best thing.

"That's a bold statement," Malcolm replies dryly.

"You know full well that I can take her on."

"Don't get cocky now, Linden. She's still ranked number one." But he isn't saying no to me either. "Let's see how you perform at the Invitational and a few other tournaments, and we'll talk more about this."

"You'll be coaching for the World Championships then?"

He nods. "The Association has hired me on for another four

years. The '63 Games might as well be a DQ in their book, so I'll be keeping my eye on '67."

I round my shoulders. As much as I want to stay on Team USA, we've got a few things to clear up.

"If you're going to be my coach again, we've got to get some things straight. I can overlook the fact that you underestimated me, but I can't ignore that you flat-out didn't believe me when I said that I didn't poison anyone."

Malcolm's jaw works. "In my defense, I did find the evidence in your own room."

"And that *evidence* wasn't mine, now was it? You never even apologized."

Color flushes over his throat and up into his cheeks. "You sure you want to go down this route?"

"If we're going to work together, you have to trust me. And, yeah, I want an apology."

I think he's going to turn around and walk away, especially since his face is getting pinker and pinker by the second, but in the end, he says grumpily, "I apologize for not believing you."

I'm tempted to gloat. To be smug. To say, *Now that wasn't so hard, was it?* But since we'll be spending a lot of time together over the course of the next year, I opt for a nod and a handshake.

"Looks like we have a championship title to win," I say.

"It won't be easy. Chances are that Lidiya and Zoya will both be there."

I grin. "Good."

In the distance, I see a car pull up to the entrance gate and realize that my ride is here. But Malcolm isn't quite finished yet.

"One more thing. You've got yourself a sponsorship offer."

"I do? *Who?*" I say, utterly shocked. I'd figured that every endorsement deal had dried up like the Sahara days ago.

"It's an esterium refinery in South Vietnam. Minister Tran reached out to me and made the introductions."

I almost laugh. So that's why the minister mentioned that he had something to discuss with me back at the hearing. "What do they want me to sell? Batteries?" I imagine myself with a made-up face and a pasted-on grin while holding a heavy esterium battery under each arm.

"My take is that they want to snap a few photos of you in front of their logo and cash in on your newfound fame to raise their profile over in the Orient," Malcolm says.

This time I do laugh, mostly out of bewilderment. The only company that wants me as a spokesperson is a refinery halfway across the world that happens to appreciate the fact that I'm half Chinese. It feels a little too scripted, a little too Hollywood, but I'm not complaining because this means that I won't leave Washington with empty pockets.

"Take a few days to think it over," Malcolm says.

"Nah, I don't need that much time. How's the compensation?"

"It won't make you a millionaire, but it's fair."

That's all I needed to hear. "Then when can I sign on the dotted line?"

Malcolm clucks his tongue at me. "I'll drop the contract in the mail for you to look over. Read the fine print before you agree to anything, rookie."

I smirk as I shoulder my bag, "Don't flip your wig, but you shouldn't say *Orient* anymore unless you want to sound like a dipstick. Later, Coach."

I jog away with a new pep in my step, not only because I got in one last dig against Malcolm but because this sponsorship money will go a long way back home. For the first time in a long while, I feel a tension ease inside my chest, and I start breathing a little easier.

I open the car's trunk and shove my things inside.

"Thanks for picking me up," I say to Sam, who's in the driver's seat of his Thunderbird.

"Don't mention it. You all set?" he says as he leans over to open the front passenger door for me.

I slide right into those soft leather seats. "You have no idea."

Sam presses on the gas, and we drive straight past Malcolm, who slowly vanishes as we coast through the Pavilion. I can't say that I'm going to miss my coach very much.

"Did Malcolm invite you to the Invitational? He mentioned that he would," Sam says.

"I start training for it next month."

He takes a hand off the wheel and gives me a high five. "Attagirl. Looks like I've found a replacement on Team USA."

"Don't worry. Your slot will be in good hands," I say teasingly. "If all goes well, I'll be heading to the World Championships next summer."

"Getting cocky already, huh?" Sam chuckles before sliding a glance my way. "Promise me you won't let Lidiya take that title again?"

"She'll have to pry it out of my Goliath's cold dead hands." I let myself relish that thought, of beating Lidiya on the world stage and hoisting that medal above my head. I swear that image is going to fuel me through the end of this year and into the next. "How about you? Have you decided to go pro?"

"My first match will be in September. It'll be in Macau against Pyotr Karelin."

I whistle. "Karelin the Cretin. Watch out for his uppercut, although he must be pushing forty by now. You'll beat him."

"I better. I do have a reputation to maintain, you know," Sam says in his breezy way.

I look out the window. Even though the Games are over, a fair number of tourists bustle about the city, heading to the memorials and posing in front of the Reflecting Pool and waiting at a monorail stop.

"You know, I kept meaning to take a ride on that thing," Sam says as we drive parallel to the monorail tracks.

"Same here," I reply. We both could've stayed longer in Washington if we really wanted to—played tourist and all that—but I get the feeling that Sam wants to put the '63 Games behind him just as much as I do. We'd rather focus on what's ahead. "Any big plans for the summer?"

"You're looking at it. I'm driving cross-country and aiming for San Diego this time. Never been before, so why not? I have a cousin there who'll probably let me crash with him for a while."

"Probably? As in he doesn't know you're coming?"

"Nope, but how can he turn away this handsome mug?" He bats his eyes at me, and I swat at him like old times. "I plan on heading up the coast after that. Maybe I could stop by Frisco on the way up."

"Oh God. Nobody calls it Frisco." This makes me crack a smile. "But yes, you better stop by. I can show you around town and take you out to the best seafood you've ever had."

"Your treat?"

"My treat, you cheapskate."

"Then pencil me in for sometime in July."

"You sure it won't be August? You know, in case you decide to bum around the beaches of San Diego for a while." I can't resist ribbing him. "I bet your fan club would take turns rubbing tanning oil on your shoulders."

"As tempting as that sounds, I've got other plans around then." His easy smile fades and his face turns somber. "I'm finally going to do it. I'm heading to Iwo Jima."

"Wow," I breathe out. "That's really something, Sam."

"It's the closest I'll ever get to meeting him. The wreckage is too deep, but being out there, smelling the air, touching the water, I think it'll be enough."

"Your father would be proud."

"Yeah, well . . ." Sam shrugs. He's still staring through the windshield, but I can tell his eyes are focused on something else. On the open ocean, maybe. Or on his dad. "What about you? Ever thought about visiting where your mom died?"

"No, not really," I say swiftly, but it's the truth. I've never been curious at seeing where she passed. It hasn't held any appeal to me—because it wouldn't change the fact that she left us.

But I am starting to think more about where she came from. Not only the little farm town where she grew up, but where her family called home long before that, way back in China. Long ago, one of our ancestors decided to sail across the Pacific and make a new home in a place they'd never seen. They're the reason why I was born in California and why I'm an American today.

And even though they couldn't become citizens or cast a vote, they were Americans too. No matter what anyone else believed.

If it weren't for them, could I have ended up like Rushi?

Or Envoy Yu?

The thoughts make me shiver.

"You look like you're plotting to kill someone," Sam says, breaking the silence. "Hope it isn't me, kiddo."

"It will be if you call me kiddo again," I say, thinking quickly.

His grin returns. "I only call you that because I can never remember your name, youngster."

We share a laugh and he punches me on the arm but I don't mind it one bit, and I get a strange feeling that I'm going to miss him. Just a few weeks ago, I would've spit on the ground he walked on if given the chance. I guess it only took an international crisis to get us to this point.

When we reach Washington National Airport, Sam and I say our official goodbyes. He deposits me on the curb, gives me a great big hug, and sees me off.

"See you soon, Jo," he calls out, one arm waving at me lazily before climbing back into the car.

The airport isn't huge, so it isn't too difficult to locate Peter and Dad. I chuckle when I spot them because it looks like my brother has dragged our father to one of those tacky souvenir shops that hawks magnets and beer mugs. Peter is sporting a new red-white-and-blue baseball cap while Dad is clutching on to a couple of gift bags and looking none too pleased about it.

When Peter sees me coming, he's already on his feet and pulling me toward his chair because he wants to show me something.

"Look!" he says, riffling through one of the bags to lift up a white T-shirt that looks perfectly ordinary until he unfolds it to reveal a print of Sam's face and mine right next to it, under the words *Team USA!*

It scares me a little because my face has been printed in a garish orange hue, giving me the look of a jack-o'-lantern. "What *is* that, Peter?"

"I had to get something for Mrs. Watters! And wait until you see this." He proceeds to hold up the newspaper article he has been reading that includes a picture taken during my official photo shoot where I look like a spiffed-up cream puff. I feel myself blush, so I turn the page.

"You didn't even read the thing!" Peter says. "It said that the mayor of San Francisco wants to rename a street after you. What do you think about Josephine Linden Way?"

"Can they even cram all those letters onto a single street sign?"

"Or they could shorten it to Linden Street," he offers.

"And let you claim some of the credit? No thank you," I tease.

"Hey, I did save your butt on the National Mall."

"You're going to keep reminding me about that, aren't you?"

"Sure will. I'm not too bad working a Goliath from the inside. Maybe I'll join you in the pit more."

I turn to look at him, *really* look at him. My little brother who isn't so little anymore, and I smile because I can't think of anything I'd like more than having a sparring partner. "Sounds like I'll have some competition."

Over the loudspeakers, we hear that our plane is now boarding first-class passengers. It doesn't quite register that she's talking about us until Dad gets to his feet and motions for us to do the same.

"Let's get moving. Don't you two want to go home?" he says. "Peter, help your sister with her things."

It's more of the other way around in that I have to help Peter gather all the magazines he has bought from the newsstand to keep him company on the plane—there's a copy of *Popular Mechanics* and another of *Bot Daily* and another of *Mechas of*

Tomorrow. And while I'm doing that, I hear a gasp behind me.

It's a young white boy, probably eight or nine years old. He's staring at me with big eyes. "You're . . . you're her!"

I can't help but chuckle. "I am her. What's your name, buddy?"

"G-G-George." He starts rooting through his backpack and quickly produces a notepad and a pen. "Say, could you sign this for me?"

I'm smiling as I uncap the pen. Who would've thought that I'd be doing this last month? Heck, just a couple days ago, I'd figured that my whole reputation would be stained for the rest of my life and now here I am signing an autograph. And no one's throwing rotten rice at me this time.

"I want to be a fighter like you when I grow up. So does my sister," George says.

That's when I glance behind him to see a little girl, maybe six years old, hiding behind their father's legs. She's clutching on to a camera and her dad is trying to push her toward me, but she's shaking her head.

"Hi there," I say, my voice going soft as I kneel down. "You want a picture?"

She nods.

"Let's take one together, okay?"

Shyly, she gives her dad the camera and shuffles toward me, her eyes flitting between mine and the floor until we're side by side. Her father tells us to say "Cheese" and the flash goes off.

"I heard you want to be a fighter," I say to her. "Is that right?"

"Yes," she practically squeaks. "Just like you."

"Well, you can and you should. We need more girls in this game."

"I watched all your matches on TV." She gets this twinkle in her eye. "I shouted so loud that my mommy told me to be quiet."

I let out a deep laugh and give her ponytail a playful tug. "I think I might've heard you all the way in the stadium." Then I crouch down again so that I can talk to her eye to eye. "And I'm going to need you cheering for me next summer. You think you can do that?"

"You'll be on TV again?"

"You bet I will, and you know what?" I make sure to lean in close so that only she can hear me. "I'm going to win the World Championships, just you wait."

Acknowledgments

For my editor, Jody Corbett, especially for your endless patience and generosity while I tried (and tried some more) to get this book right. Thank you for never giving up on me! *The Great Destroyers* simply wouldn't exist without you.

For my literary agent, Jim McCarthy, who has stuck with me through thick and thin for over a decade. I'm so lucky to have you on my side.

For all the folks at Scholastic who worked on this book and got it in your hands: Stephanie Yang, Josh Berlowitz, Jael Fogle, Janell Harris, Erin Berger, Rachel Feld, Shannon Pender, Elisabeth Ferrari, Lizette Serrano, Emily Heddleson, the entire sales force, and the Clubs and Fairs.

For my two children, who make me smile every day, even when you've been very naughty. This book is dedicated to you.

For my sister, Kristy, who has listened to me gripe and groan whenever I struggled with writer's block and who sent me funny memes to cheer me up. I'm forever grateful for you, little sis.

For Allie and Amanda, who are the best friends I ever could've asked for. Thank you for always cheering me on, even when I was extra surly in high school.

For the childcare providers and teachers who watched over my two precious overlords so that I could draft and revise in blessed quiet. You're the real heroes.

For all the writers who are struggling with their manuscripts. I feel you. I *am* you! And I'm here to say that you can get through this. Take a breath, take a break, scream into a pillow if you need to—and come back to your book when you're ready. We writers can be a solitary bunch, typing away in our little darkened corners, but I hope you know that you aren't alone. I raise my cold mug of coffee to you in salute.

And finally, for the readers: thank you!

About the Author

Caroline Tung Richmond is the author of the alternative history novels *The Only Thing to Fear* and *Live in Infamy*, as well as the historical fiction novel *The Darkest Hour*. She also works for We Need Diverse Books, a nonprofit that seeks to create a world where all children can find themselves on the pages of a book.

A self-proclaimed history nerd and cookie connoisseur, Caroline lives in Maryland with her family and her dog, Otto von Bismarck—named for the German chancellor (naturally). You can find out more about at her at carolinetrichmond.com.